STREETS
∾*of*∾
SHADOW

REBECCA BISCHOFF

IMMORTAL WORKS
SALT LAKE CITY

Immortal Works LLC
1505 Glenrose Drive
Salt Lake City, Utah 84104
Tel: (385) 202-0116

© 2023 Rebecca Bischoff
www.rebeccabischoffbooks.com

Cover Art by Ashley Literski
http://strangedevotion.wixsite.com/strangedesigns

ISBN 978-1-953491-51-0 (Paperback)
ASIN B0BV641D2D (Kindle)

To my husband, David

CHAPTER 1

Estate of Lord Ramsay, Earl of Chessington
East Lothian, Scotland
November 1665

Ladies do not scramble up the outer walls of their homes with their skirts hitched high. They do not cling to trellises filled with shriveled roses, prick their fingers on thorns, and bite back oaths they are not supposed to know. And ladies never creep through the windows of forbidden chambers.

But at times, there are more important things than being a lady.

The leaded casements defy my cold fingers at first, but I finally work my nails into a narrow crack and pull. The hinges give way grudgingly and the window swings toward me with a low groan. When last granted permission to see my sister, two days ago, I purposefully left the casements unlatched. Smiling at my success, I ease inside the darkened chamber, my body trembling from the effort.

As my feet stretch toward the floor, my knotted skirts catch on a corner of the casement. A harsh tearing sound reaches my ears.

"God's beard!" I mutter under my breath, frozen in stark realization that I likely damaged my new winter gown.

I thump down on the carpets in Cinaed's chamber to inspect my heavy overskirts. The green silk, shot through with silver thread, is split in front to show the lighter skirts beneath. A jagged rip, as long as my hand, mars my lovely clothing. To my horror, 'tis not a mere separation of the threads at the seam but a conspicuous tear through the fine cloth. I frown at the ugly sight. There will be no hiding this.

My sister, Cinaed, moans and stirs in her bed but does not open her eyes. With a sigh, I straighten my shoulders. Were my sister in possession of her health, she would gently scold me. Grandfather will simply chide me with the ever-present spark of amusement in his eye. But Oliver, Cinaed's husband, will freeze me with his stern gaze, chide me for an interminable length of time for my unseemly behavior, and banish me to my chamber. Or forbid sweets for a fortnight. I prefer banishment.

The thick air within this stifling chamber is tinged with a sourness like the smell of curdled milk. Wrinkling my nose, I fling the curtains wide and leave the casements open in defiance of the brisk wind. The gray autumn mist that haunts our shores swirls about Grandfather's home, dimming the afternoon sun. Footsteps crunch over the fallen leaves below, signaling the passage of a household servant who was fortuitously absent when I made my ascent moments ago.

The tang of brine fills my nose while a distant rumble speaks of an approaching tempest. Closing my eyes, I breathe deeply, welcoming the ocean breeze that flows over my skin like gentle fingers soothing a fevered brow.

When I turn back to my sister, her slight, fragile form on the bed steals my breath. Thoughts of my ruined raiment and any upcoming punishments flee. Hurrying to Cinaed's side, I am truly thankful the terrible English plague has not come here. Yet, she suffers while we stand by helpless. Would that the sea air could soothe and heal her of this strange distemper that defies any cure the apothecaries and physicians have applied!

Leaning over her, I place a hand on my sister's cheek and study the rise and fall of her chest. I fancy that her breathing eases as the cool air fills her chamber. But the wan light reveals a visage so wasted and lined with pain, my eyes sting with tears.

My sister's damp hair clings to her glistening forehead, and her pale cheeks sink into her face, giving her the look of a crone rather than a woman not yet thirty. Another tooth lies in a tray on the carved table beside the bed. The chip of bone tinged with red holds my gaze for a moment, and my stomach folds at the sight. I am glad Cinaed does not appear to be aware of her surroundings.

"*Och*, does Oliver not see what is happening to you?" I whisper the words aloud as I touch my sister's pale skin. "Does he not have eyes, that mutton-head?" For a moment, I picture my brother-in-law's face as if he were to hear me. Each time I speak without thought, without guarding against any "un-ladylike" words, a deep line appears between his eyebrows.

No matter. Oliver is not here to scold me for destroying my overskirts or for my rash words. I came to draw Cinaed's portrait. I pull a stool close to the bed, sit down and pluck a scrap of parchment and a bit of charcoal from my pocket. With care, I also remove my bundled handkerchief and unfold it to reveal the tiny bouquet plucked from the surrounding fields. The golden-hued blossoms are like drops of sunshine fallen to earth to give life to our gray autumn days. 'Tis such a wonder to me they bloom even now when all other flowers have long since withered away. Hissing as my poor fingers touch the sharp spines, I place the blooms near Cinaed's head and commence my drawing.

Forced to squint thanks to the wan light in the chamber, I add lines to the parchment. While my drawing takes form, Cinaed's breathing sounds more strained, like the scraping of rough stones. A heavy sensation fills my chest. My sister is the only mother I've known since our parent's death. They died so long ago, their faces no longer come to mind. I cannot bear the thought that one day I may no longer recall my sister's image.

I bow my head as though in prayer. Why do I create a memento of my sister? She will recover. She must. I close my eyes and fill my lungs with great gulps of the biting air that now fills the bedchamber.

I only draw Cinaed's portrait because she so oft asked me to, I tell myself. My heart eventually slows to a walk. I raise my head and return to my drawing.

After a few minutes, I regard my work and frown. I made the mistake of recreating in exactness what was before me, drawing the sharp angle of my sister's cheek, shrunken with illness. Scrubbing with my fingers, I redraw her as she was before, with round cheeks and clear eyes that dart here and there, quick like a robin's.

My sister's eyes, like mine, are the color of storm clouds, but this does not speak to her nature. Hers is a disposition like a day of bright sunshine—not a brooding sky filled with the promise of icy rain. Tears threaten to spill again, and I squeeze my eyes closed. I miss Cinaed's smile. Biting my lip and blinking rapidly, I trace the lines of my drawing with a smudged finger and sigh. Why can I never create a drawing that matches what I envision?

"Miss?" Our maid, Lorna, speaks from the corner of the room. Yelping in surprise, I dart to my feet. The lass had escaped my notice, sitting silently in the shadows with her knitting on her lap.

"I am only here to draw her portrait," I whisper. "I'll not take long."

"I've already waited to speak as long as I dare, miss." Lorna's forehead crinkles and indecision is clear in her amber-hued eyes. She understands. She is my age, having not yet reached her sixteenth year, and we have always been particularly fond of each other. We used to play together in the kitchen when we were but wee lasses. But the maid faces a cruel choice. She must never disobey the master of the house, or she will lose her place. And her mother will no longer have her daughter's wages to help feed the many wee ones at home.

"I must see my sister! Surely, you understand."

As we gaze at one another, both pleading silently, Cinaed moans once more. Lorna's shoulders droop.

"Please, be quick." The lass seats herself again and takes up her knitting. I flash her a grateful smile and promise myself I'll thank her with a gift. Perhaps she'd like a new length of scarlet ribbon or a bit of lace for her bodice.

As I hold my drawing up to catch the window's meager light, Lorna whispers once more: "'Tis nearly twelve o'clock and the surgeon is to come. Ye must hurry."

I only manage to add a few lines when footsteps approach. Lorna gasps and I dart to my feet while my drawing flutters to the floor.

"You were asleep," I whisper to the maid. "You did not hear me enter." She obligingly leans her head against the wall and closes her eyes.

The moment the final word falls from my lips, the door bursts open and my brother-in-law marches inside.

"Kenna?" He scowls at me. The line between his brows carves deeper than ever. "Why are you here?" His accusing eyes sweep to the corner where Lorna feigns a yawn and rises to her feet, bobbing a curtsy.

"I am sorry," she says in a faltering voice. Her eyes fill with tears.

"She was sleeping." I march to stand before Oliver with my arms crossed. "Of course, she was. You make her stay here at all hours. Why do you not sit with your wife for a while and let the others rest?" I tap my foot, waiting for my brother-in-law to answer. "Let Lorna go to her room. She can return later."

Oliver's face darkens and his lips thin to a mere line. This is also something that happens often when we cross paths. But thankfully, he bobs his head in a nod to Lorna, who curtsies again and scurries from the room.

When Oliver turns his stern eyes to me once more, I settle myself on the stool again and arrange my skirts. "I'll not leave until I finish my drawing."

But my brother-in-law sweeps me off the stool as our cook might shoo a kitten away from her favorite chair. "You shall leave now. The surgeon has arrived."

"Please, Oliver, let me stay with Cinaed! You've kept me away for two days."

Ignoring my pleadings, he jerks me to the door of my sister's chamber, gripping my arm stronger than necessary and closes me without.

Dismissed in such a way, I bite my tongue against the sharp words I wish to hurl at my guardian. Some call him my father, since he married my sister when I was a wee one, having only seen five winters. My brow crinkles. Oliver was meant to take on that role when he married Cinaed, but from the time of the wedding until now, ten years later, I've yet to see a single sign of fatherly affection.

I call the man my keeper. My jailer.

The thick carpets beneath my feet are a mockery to me. They are Oliver's folly, unrolled in the corridors only yesterday so the sound of passing footsteps would not disturb my sister. I wrap my arms around my middle and shiver. My sister is not dead. Why does Oliver insist we creep on silent feet as though we tiptoe down the aisles of the kirk with prayer books in hand? And why did I forget my drawing? I raise my hand to knock on Cinaed's door. I must have it back. Oliver will tread on it with his great, booted feet or throw it into the fire.

"Ah, Kenna," Grandfather's deep voice speaks from nearby and his tall form approaches from the direction of the stairs. The thick carpets have muffled his heavy, measured tread. I fly to his side, and he holds me so close I feel his steady heartbeat. I lean my weight against his solid form, and my breathing slows.

"Do not fret, child. Take courage, your sister may yet recover." Grandfather strokes my hair as he speaks. His words are even and measured, still heavily accented in the manner of our English kin. He was born and educated in Canterbury, though he has lived in our northern kingdom of Scotland for many of my lifetimes.

"Oh, Grandfather," I murmur into his coat. He smells of apples and mulled wine. Our paths cross often when we sneak into the larder searching for a bite of something sweet or a sip of claret. We are comrades in household thievery, causing no end of grief to Mrs. Harris, who rules over her gleaming pots and strings of onions like a grand duchess. I swipe at my tears. Aside from our clandestine meetings over midnight feasts, Grandfather expects me to behave like the lady I am to become.

"Grandfather, what can be done?" My voice trembles.

The man smiles at me, though I read his weariness in the dark smudges beneath his great blue eyes. He places a hand on my shoulder, and I cover his fingers with my own.

"Do not weep, lass." His lips curve downward in a slight frown as he pats his doublet. "I am sorry, but I seem to have misplaced my handkerchief." He straightens his clothing. "No matter. My good friend and surgeon, Sir Robert Ogilvie, is here, Kenna, come especially from town. He shall help Cinaed. I am certain of it."

As the words leave my grandfather's lips, the surgeon himself approaches from the staircase. He pants with the effort of heaving his portly form up the stairs. Swallowing the lump in my throat, I remember my manners in time to sink into an ungainly curtsy. The air touches my bare ankles and I remember my unshod feet. Cheeks stinging, I turn to the side, hoping Grandfather will not see the ragged gash torn into the rich fabric of my skirts.

I lift my gaze in time to spy the clear look of disapproval the esteemed physician wears on his round, unpleasant face. His egg-shaped head is wider at the bottom than the top, and his chin dissolves into the folded flesh of his neck. Despite his mussed coat, his pursed lips and upturned nose lend him an air of self-importance. His demeanor turns my stomach.

"I shall do all within my power to help your sister," the man says in a smooth voice. "Though I must say I've not heard of such a case before."

"Please, sir!" My throat closes.

Grandfather pats my shoulder again, while he motions with sharp, impatient gestures to old Tom, his valet, who has appeared in his noiseless way. The wizened servant receives his master's curt orders and escorts Sir Robert to my sister's bed chamber with haste.

"Come. My friend shall attend to your sister while you follow me to the kitchen. A cup of ale will do you good."

He holds out his arm, and I link mine in his. We descend to the ground floor, passing the portrait of Grandfather as a child. The small painting sits in a half-hidden alcove at the head of the stairs. The lad in the portrait poses stiffly in his old-fashioned jacket, his wan features and spindly limbs giving no indication he shall one day grow to become a tall and broad-shouldered man. I never once questioned why the painting resides in this out-of-the-way place. The painted child's face is so sour he looks as though his fur collar makes his neck itch dreadfully. I used to giggle each time I passed it, but today, nothing brings a smile.

At the ground floor, Master Williams, my tall and pale tutor, greets us in silence. He nods in deference to Grandfather but only peers down his sharp nose at me, taking in my bare feet and ankles. The man's thin lips twist into a sardonic smile. I straighten my shoulders and hold my head high, despite my flushed face. Years ago, Grandfather hired the English-bred tutor to instruct me. The haughty man chides me when I forget my lessons in diction. I must not say *"I dinnae ken"* when I do not know the answer to my lessons. I must not tell one of the maids, the petulant Kate, *"Do that again and I'll give ye a skelpin!"* when she takes the sugared almonds I hide in my chambers.

The man slips silently into the library and my embarrassment dissolves back into dread. The servants glide through the front hall like silent, tiptoeing ghosts who never lift their gaze as we pass. They, too, feel the heavy sadness of my sister's plight. Do they also fear she is dying?

"Kenna, there ye are," Mrs. Harris says as we enter the kitchen. Tempting smells of cooking meat fill the air. Lorna chops vegetables while another girl stirs the steaming pots. A suckling pig turns on a spit in the great fireplace, its skin just starting to brown and sizzle. Grandfather orders ale without words, his imperious gestures known by all in his house. After a curtsy to her master, Mrs. Harris fills a tankard with spiced ale, which she warms by plunging the glowing end of the fire iron into the liquid. She hands me the steaming drink and I nearly drop it. 'Tis not too hot, but my clumsy hands are shaking.

I draw closer to the crackling fire, seeking to warm myself from the chill of fear that seeps into my bones. Grandfather pats my shoulder and turns to leave. "I've business to attend to." His face is grave, yet his eyes are gentle when he looks at me. "Take courage, Kenna. Your sister will be well again."

Will she? I dare not speak such thoughts aloud. Grandfather strides from the room while the maids scatter out of his way like a flock of frightened geese. I take to pacing in the warm room, noting again how the servants, even Lorna, keep their heads down. Only Mrs. Harris regards me directly. Her eyes fall upon my skirts and she gasps.

"Why must ye traipse about those thorny fields, Kenna? Ye catch your skirts on the gorse, and I shall no' keep mending them! Why can ye never stay on the pathways in the garden?"

Gazing down into my drink, I sigh. 'Tis no surprise the woman assumes I've damaged my skirts outdoors. I've never quite dared tell her why I often flee to the open fields. The graveled pathways that circle Grandfather's house do not take me away from the sight of its many, many windows and ever-watchful eyes. But when I wander far from the trimmed hedgerows and flowers arranged with exactness in solemn ranks, I am free. Each time I drink in the honeyed scent of the gorse blossoms blooming in the fields, I know I am alone. Blessedly so.

"I am sorry."

"*Och,* 'tis no great matter. Now, then." She smiles at me and speaks with a false cheer that irritates me, like a pebble in my slipper.

"We'll have guests this evening. Of course, there's the surgeon from town, and I hear he has a sweet tooth! I'll make the cakes ye like, Kenna, with currents. And, er..." The woman turns to the fire and pokes absently at the roasting pig, as though she is at a loss for words. "And someone else is joining us."

"Who?" I hold my breath, fearing I already know.

"Remember last month, lassie, when ye broke the..." Her voice trails off, and she continues to jab at the piglet sizzling over the fire.

My body freezes in place. *When I broke the harpsichord.* The recollection makes me grimace, scrunching my nose in a childish fashion. *In front of Grandfather's most distinguished guest.*

The esteemed man who visited, the piggish and self-important Sir I-Forget-His-Name, had quaked with amusement, and so had his haughty, horrid daughter. I still hear her laughter as she watched me struggle to my feet with splintered wood tangled in my skirts. That was the night Cinaed first began to feel the effects of her strange malady.

Before I can answer, Mrs. Harris turns to me, clutching the salt box to her ample bosom as though it is her greatest treasure. "Oh, lassie?" She clears her throat. "Sir Oliver says ye must go to your chambers. He ordered a new gown. The dressmaker waits for ye."

A new gown? My spine stiffens. I slam my tankard onto the table and clench my fists as rage surges through my body, burning like the fire beneath the bubbling pots. Does Oliver think that all shall be made well for me simply by ordering a gown? He once said, females care only for their finery. Never mind that my sister, his *wife,* lay so ill!

Can he truly believe that is all I care for?

Pivoting on my heel, I flee the kitchens, ignoring Mrs. Harris's startled spluttering at my sudden exit. Lifting my skirts high, I leap up the stairs two at a time in a most unladylike fashion.

Oliver will see what I think of my new gown. Aye, that he will.

CHAPTER 2

The elderly maid, Mrs. Hale, gasps and clutches her sunken chest when I burst into my bedchamber.

"Kenna," she gasps. "What is it, my lass?"

"Go!" I shout, pointing at the swarthy, dark-eyed man who waits with her. His mouth gapes wide and he stares, which gives him the appearance of a scaly herring lying in a market stall.

"Leave NOW!"

My dear old maid flees the room with her handkerchief over her face. The dressmaker follows. My entire body trembles. I should be ashamed for treating the kindly woman in this manner, but I only feel anger surging through my veins. I am tipsy with the flood of feeling, unsteady on my feet as one who has taken too much wine.

The gown lies on my bed. Full skirts and matching bodice, all of silk the color of soot. Though 'tis rather plain, the gown is sewn with the finest of stitches, nearly invisible. And a hooded cloak of black-dyed wool lies beside the gown.

Mourning garb. The sudden realization causes a lump to rise in my throat. Oliver does not think to distract me with pretty things. He is sending me a message. My lips tremble at the sight of the clothing. Cinaed yet draws breath, but her husband obviously thinks she will not do so much longer.

The man who created this drab garb left his satchel on the table. I rifle through it and locate his scissors. Stifling sobs, I use the sharp blades to slice through the fine fabric with ease. Within moments, the remains of my gown slither to the floor, slain by my own hands. I toss the scissors onto the pile of severed silk and admire the inky pool of ruined skirts at my feet.

Shaking, I stumble to the window and gaze out. A gust of autumn wind tosses withered leaves against the glass. They tap and hiss like spirits seeking shelter. Were any lost spirits to entreat me for welcome, I should warn them they seek to enter a place that holds as much joy as a graveyard.

My sister's lute catches my eye where it lies on my dressing table. I had taken it from her chambers after she fell ill. The hint of a song whispers in the air as my fingers brush against the strings. Sorrow presses upon me with a heavy hand. I bow my head while my eyes spill over. A teardrop splashes against the polished wood.

Snuffling, I place the gleaming lute back onto the table. My sister loves music and voices raised in song. She loves the sound of the larks in the branches outside her window; even the crows as they cark and caw in the fields come autumn. She dearly loves to laugh. Why do we shut her away in silence? Though she lies weak and mute, perhaps she still hears what transpires around her. Would she not wish to hear the voices of those who are most beloved? Would that not cheer her and help her grow strong once more?

I nearly trip upon my skirts as I pivot on my heel and fly to my door. Peering around the frame, I spy the heads of Grandfather and his surgeon as they exit Cinaed's chamber and descend the stairs at the end of the corridor, their voices indistinct. Oliver's low baritone voice murmurs from somewhere below. Good. There is no one to chase me away. I creep on the new carpets; now glad they are here to muffle the sound of my footsteps. But before I arrive at Cinaed's chamber, more voices float from below, and the high-pitched giggle that assails my ears makes me curl my hands into fists.

It's *her*. That awful daughter of Grandfather's pompous guest, Lord So-and-So! How *dare* she come now for a visit, when a member of the family is gravely ill! How could Oliver allow it? With a start, I spy my visage in the smoky looking glass on the wall in the corridor. My lowered brow and snarling lips do not flatter my already plain face. My square jaw and pointed nose have long been a disappointment to me.

I plant my fists on my hips and march to the head of the stairs to wait, making no attempt to compose my features. My anger grows as the young woman floats into view. Her ebony hair gleams, coiled into tiny ringlets that frame her face, which she has artfully colored with powders and potions, for her cheeks and full lips cannot be so red. Her eyes are the color of a night without stars. Her peacock-hued dress is such as one might expect to see on a lady of the court. Such fancy clothing, and for a visit to the country?

Behind her, a maid who is a mere child with flaxen hair in ragged braids huffs under the weight of heavy boxes she carries for her mistress. An older maid, as well-dressed as her Lady, regards me with a curl of her lip and slanted eyes that gaze at me as though I am merely an obstacle in her path.

"You are not welcome here," I say, minding my cadence and tone, hoping to sound as learned and as ladylike as my tutor would wish. "There is illness in this house."

The young maid yelps and drops one of her boxes. The other arches one brow, while her black-haired mistress gazes frankly into my face with a tilt of her head. She pauses on the stair, regarding me coolly with her black witch's eyes.

"You refer to your sister, I believe?" As she speaks, she removes a pair of embroidered fawn gloves casually, as though our conversation is of no import. A waft of her jasmine perfume engulfs me.

"Of course," I snap. "She's gravely ill and suffers. She does not need the trouble of unwelcome guests. She needs to rest."

What happens next will forever remain burned into my mind. 'Tis an ugly blight like a scar that mars once-smooth flesh.

The girl laughs. She laughs! Her giggling fills the air, while a blinding rage fills me.

"Oh, my dear, girl. Katherine, is it? Or Kirstin?" she says, waving her hand dismissively. Her blood-red lips curve into a smile while she inclines her head in my direction, lowering her voice as though she is sharing a secret. "It is of no importance to me that your sister is ill. I have not come to see *her*."

I gasp as though a solid fist has struck me in the stomach. How *dare* she? Without conscious thought, my hand raises in the air. I will strike that smirk from her painted face! But before I can act, a sharp voice jabs the air.

"Kenna!" Oliver marches to us. The severe line is once more carved between his lowered brows. "What are you doing? You are not properly dressed! Where are your shoes and stockings?"

In unison, three pairs of eyes dart to the floor and gaze upon my unshod toes. The girl's lips curve into a wide grin while her maids snort and titter at the sight of my bare ankles and feet. My cheeks flame with anger and humiliation.

"Oh, Viscount Ramsay," the girl croons, looking at my brother-in-law, "how is your dear wife? I have *yearned* to see her." Her soulless eyes dart to my flushed face with a clear challenge writ across her features. "I was just telling your young ward how truly sorry I am to hear the lady is unwell."

Oliver inclines his head in acknowledgment of her words and offers her his arm. "Thank you, Cecelia. Allow me to show you to your chambers."

They sweep by me, but not before Oliver shoots me a warning look, motioning with a jerk of his chin for me to return to my own bedchamber. The dark witch-girl does not spare me another glance. Neither do her maids.

Cecelia. While I flee back up the corridor, my fingers itch to yank every crimped hair from that pig of a lass's scalp. Panting more from the effort to keep from screaming out curses than from exertion, I duck into my room, wait until the corridor is empty, and then sneak back down the hall to Cinaed's chamber. Neither Oliver nor that horrid beast will keep me from her.

The room is stifling. The fire roars in the grate and Oliver has closed the windows once more. Beneath the coverlet, my sister's body is so terribly slight. I touch her hand and am startled by how cold it is.

"Cinaed." My voice shakes. "'Tis Kenna, come to see you."

My sister breathes in and out again, her lips quiver. Her eyelids flutter open.

"Kenna," she whispers.

Tears spill out, and I do not try to stop them. "I miss you. Please, you must get better."

"Shhh," she breathes out, trying to comfort me as she did for so long, as though I am merely a wee one with a scraped knee. "No tears." With effort, she manages to free one arm from beneath the coverlet and seeks to stroke my face, but she cannot lift her trembling hand.

"Oh, Cinaed." I sob as I take her hand in my own and press it to my lips. Her skin is so cold! My sister smiles, though her eyes have closed once more. She whispers something inaudible. I lean my head close, dismayed at the thinness of her lips, once rosy and full.

"Courage, poppet." Cinaed's voice is weak, and her words are ill-formed. "All will be well."

I squeeze my eyes closed. "Poppet" was Cinaed's pet name for me, one she used when I cowered under the bedsheets during a thunderstorm. That was years ago. And I am no longer a child.

"Sing to me, Kenna," Cinaed murmurs. "I've missed your voice."

Shaking, I straighten, gulp, and blink away tears. This is perhaps the only thing I can do for her. My voice is hardly above a whisper when I begin. The lullaby is one my sister used to sing to me when I feared the night's shadows.

"The swallows are gone." My warbling is off-key. Wretched voice!

"The summer has flown. Wee child of mine, come with me."

My voice trembles and I must pause once more to draw breath. Cinaed's cracked lips part and I lean closer, but she does not speak again. I brush her hair from her face and stroke her cheek, continuing my song.

"The world shall await, 'ere long you are grown, but for now you shall sleep..."

My sister gasps and cries out: "Oliver!" Her eyes open and she thrashes, bucking and kicking like a young colt.

I leap to my feet and turn to call for aid, but before I utter a sound, Oliver flings the door wide and hurtles inside.

"Why are you here again, Kenna?" he growls. "Leave her be!"

Oliver flies to Cinaed's bed and kneels beside her. My sister seizes her husband's doublet with one flailing fist, and with the other hand, scratches at his eyes; though I cannot believe she is aware of what she does. In vain, Oliver struggles to detach her hands and to hold his wife's slight form still. The velvet of his doublet tears and he shrugs it off and flings the damaged clothing to the floor. His tawny hair escapes the ribbon that tied it back and falls past his shoulders.

"Go, Kenna!" When he turns to me, his face is contorted with pain. A livid streak of red crosses one cheek. "Find Doctor Ogilvie!"

I could vow my feet are woven into the stuff of the carpet beneath them. I cannot do what Oliver says, for at last, I must fully admit what everyone else sought to tell me. It is too late to call for aid.

My sister is dying.

The pain of my realization causes me to sink to the floor. I clamp a hand over my mouth to keep from crying out. At that moment, a hint of jasmine touches the air around me. It is Cecelia's perfume. How dare she enter here? Bolting to my feet, I whirl toward the door, but no one else is with us. My eyes search the room, darting from the thick red draperies to the bright portraits on the walls, but I can find no source for the flowery smell.

Wrapped in her husband's tight grip, Cinaed convulses once, twice. Her eyes lose their wild look, and for a moment, light shines within them. She is herself once more. Oliver bends his head until their foreheads touch.

I do not breathe. It is as though I am gazing at a tableau of tender intimacy, something I should not witness.

My sister gazes into the eyes of her husband, so near at hand. He murmurs words too faint for me to hear. Cinaed listens. Her ebony hair spills across her pillow; her face is pale as chalk. Her body is nothing but skin stretched tight across sharp bone. Her eyes, far too large, gaze at her husband with an intense longing. The love she possesses for this man is written in every single pain-caused line on her wasted face.

My foot touches something on the floor. 'Tis Oliver's torn doublet. As I move my leg to shove it aside, my toes brush against something smooth and cold. Beside the fallen coat lies a tiny bottle resting against the wall. I bend down and close my hand around it.

Oliver continues to murmur low words to his wife. His eyes are fixed upon her, so he does not see what has transpired. I recognize the bottle at once. It holds the poisonous liquid we use to kill rats and mice in the barns. Raising my wondering eyes, I spy the reason for the smell of jasmine that fouls the air in here. In one hand, Oliver holds one of Cecelia's fine gloves, soaked with her costly perfume.

Cinaed gasps for air. The sound pierces me. My sister breathes out once more, a long, slow sigh. And then she remains still, her eyes fixed on her husband, a heartbeat away.

As the moments lengthen, I stand frozen, clutching the bottle, staring at my sister's wasted face, willing her to breathe again. But she does not.

Oliver turns in my direction. His face is a mask of utter stillness until his eyes fall on what I hold in my hand.

"Kenna." His voice is strangled. His eyes dart from the bottle to my face and back again. "Where did you get that?"

I stumble backwards, clutching the bottle to my chest, one thought alone tearing through my entire being.

He killed her. Oliver killed his wife, my beloved and only sister. *Why?*

Darkness clouds my vision while my wild thoughts taunt me.

The bottle. The witch with black hair. The scent of jasmine I will forevermore despise. The glove Oliver grips in his hand. Did he kill his wife for *her?* So that he would be free to marry Cecelia? It cannot be!

My throat closes, and I choke out a sob. When Oliver rises to his feet, I scream and turn to run.

CHAPTER 3

"Grandfather!" I fling the door open. "Grandfather, help me!" Oliver's rasping shouts, like the roar of an enraged beast, pursue me as I burst from my dead sister's chamber.

"Help me!" My screams echo as I stumble down the stairs. Doors slam and running footfalls sound all around me. Someone pushes past me, ascending to the upper floors. Blinded by tears, I barrel into something solid and arms encircle me.

"Kenna!" 'Tis Grandfather's voice. "What is the meaning of this, child?"

"He has killed her!" My voice is so ragged with tears, grief, and rage, my words are barely intelligible. I hold out the bottle. "Oliver killed Cinaed!"

He takes the phial from my fingers while I collapse on the floor and bury my face in my hands. Grandfather heaves me to my feet and settles me into a chair. My sobs turn to wails, which turn to screams. The man seizes my shoulders and shakes me until my head snaps back and forth, but I cannot stop the harsh sounds that pour from within. My own voice is strange to my ears. It is the cry of a wild creature caught in a trap.

Grandfather's strong hands press a goblet to my lips. I choke on burning liquid as the odor of whiskey fills my nose.

"No more." I cough and push the drink away while tears pour down my cheeks.

"You must control yourself." Grandfather flings the spirits aside and dark liquid splashes against the wall. "Can you walk now, child?"

I nod, and Grandfather helps me to my feet and puts an arm around me. He guides me to his study, near to dragging me most of the time, since my feet wobble beneath me as though I trod upon skittering pebbles. Around us, servants scramble in a harried manner.

Grandfather hustles me inside his study and closes the heavy oak door. He turns the key in the lock.

"Tell me how you came to possess this." He places the bottle of poison onto a table. His face is a thundercloud. His eyes spark with lightning.

My knees hardly hold my weight. Wrapping my arms around myself, I draw in a deep, shuddering breath.

"I found it on the carpets in my sister's chamber." My voice is ragged. "Cinaed seized Oliver's doublet, and it tore, so he threw it to the floor. This bottle lay beside the doublet. It must have fallen from his pocket." I gasp for breath. "He killed her, Grandfather. Oliver has killed my sister!" Hot tears pour once more from my eyes. "He is a treacherous, vile scoundrel! He gave her poison as one does to a rat..." My voice rises into a sobbing wail. Once more, a scream rises from my throat.

Crack!

My head spins, and the sharp pain in my cheek silences me. I raise my hand to my stinging face. Grandfather hit me! I hardly dare believe it.

"I am sorry, Kenna." Grandfather's breathing is labored. He holds me against his chest and strokes my hair. "Dear lass, you must cease that wailing at once!" He places gentle hands on my shoulders and gazes earnestly into my shocked face. "The others will hear." He releases me and turns his back, rubbing his jaw as he is wont to do when deep in thought.

"That is a grave accusation." Grandfather's words carry a note of disbelief. "It is a grave thing, indeed, to accuse my son of murder."

"I know what I saw." My voice shakes. "The bottle was on the floor beside his doublet. How else would it have gotten there; save he had carried it with him?"

Grandfather turns to face me. His eyes are wild, and when he speaks, his voice is rough. "How can you think to accuse my son of murdering his wife? Why *would* he, Kenna? What would make him do such a thing?" His mouth continues to move as though his lips seek to form more words but cannot.

I lower my head. "He did it for *her*," I whisper. "For Cecelia. He wished to be free to marry again." Once more, rage curls my hands into fists and tremors shake me. I wrap my arms around my shivering body while more tears flow.

"Foolish child!" Grandfather speaks sharply. "Oliver has always been a devoted husband to your sister as well as a father to you, has he not?"

No, he has not. But I only say the words inside my head. And I nod, wishing to spare Grandfather any more pain. Oliver is his son, after all, but certainly he can see the truth. He must have been aware of the strain we all felt last year, after Oliver and Cinaed's loss. He must have seen the quiet despair of my sister, who grieved for the babe she no longer held in her arms, while Oliver withdrew into silence. Devoted husband, indeed, who would not even comfort his own wife!

Though it may break Grandfather's heart, his beloved son is cold as the snows that fall upon our fields in winter, selfish and unfeeling. And a murderer.

My grandfather strides to the door. I open my mouth to speak, but he places a warning finger to his lips to silence me. "Wait here a moment and remain calm, lassie. I'll return straightaway."

Grandfather hurries from his study, closes and locks the door behind him. I pace the floor, my thoughts a jumble of images and my heart twisted like a tangle of thorns within my chest. My jaw aches as I press my lips together to keep from sobbing. I must control myself. Oliver must not discern my whereabouts. Nor will my wails bring my sister back to me. After a brief time, the sound of a key in the lock makes my heart leap within. The door creaks open, but 'tis only old Tom, who approaches me with a pained expression. In his arms, he holds Grandfather's plum-colored coat.

"He said ye might be cold." Tom thrusts the raiment in my direction. Gratefully, I wrap myself in its velvety warmth, inhaling the musky and comforting scent that comes with it.

"This way, miss," Tom says. Blinking in surprise, I follow the man as he shuffles to the far wall of the study. He sweeps aside a woven tapestry curtain, revealing a door that until now was unknown to me.

"Where does this lead?" But Tom shushes me with a finger to his lips.

"Lord Ramsay is sending ye away. 'Tis no' safe to remain in this house."

My heart leaps, and a warmth spreads through me. Grandfather believes me. He will make certain that Oliver will not harm me the way he harmed my sister. More tears spill from my eyes.

Silently, we hurry through the door and Tom rushes us along a narrow corridor of damp sandstone that leads upward on a slight incline. It must let out far beyond the house because many minutes pass while we hasten, our footsteps echoing. My bare feet ache with cold. My abandoned slippers yet lie hidden in the hedge beneath Cinaed's window.

At the end of the passageway, we stop before a door darkened with age and silvered with cobwebs. The old man wrestles with the squealing latch until the door inches open, and we emerge onto the grassy side of a small hill, south of the house. A chill wind rustles my skirts and makes me shiver.

"Where are we going?"

"Wait over there." Tom points to a dirt road a few paces away, only just wider than a footpath. "Lord Ramsay called a driver. He'll take ye somewhere safe."

"But where?" I pull the coat more tightly about myself. "When will I hear from Grandfather?"

The old man does not answer. Instead, he regards me for a

moment. His rheumy eyes are wide with confusion and his mouth trembles.

"Tom?" But the man turns away from me and disappears behind the hillside door. The hinges squeal as the door shuts. There is no latch on this side.

My quiet sobs join the murmuring of the wind as it rushes among the long grass, now shriveled and brown. My sister is dead. If only I could kiss her one last time! But Oliver is there, in Grandfather's house, fully aware that I have discovered his secret.

How could he do it?

"How could you?" I scream into the wind. As though in reply, the blowing air increases in intensity and tears at my hair, my clothing. Clouds scud across the sky, swollen with moisture. The air is thick with the scent of the coming storm.

I grit my teeth and aim a kick at the door in the hill but think better of it. My bare toes would not profit from my fit of rage.

Instead, I head to the dusty path before me. I want time to think, and blessedly, Grandfather has given me that. No more than a minute passes, though, before my conveyance announces its approach with the rattling and jostling of its wheels and the snorts of the stately white mare, Bridie. She pulls Grandfather's small chaise, and the driver is Johnny, a dark-haired lad of twelve. He raises his hand in greeting. His face is solemn, his eyes are round with fear.

Without speaking, I settle myself onto the firm leather seat. Johnny shuts the door, returns to the driver's perch, and we are off. A wail bursts from me and I cover my face with my hands and sob. Cinaed, my sister, the only mother I've ever known, is gone. Taken from me.

My sobs turn to shudders, and I gulp air to compose myself. Grandfather must be confronting Oliver by now. This thought alone brings me some small measure of comfort. Sniffling, I glance around. Where is Johnny taking me? Nothing is familiar.

Spent and exhausted, I huddle on the seat, snuggling into the thick folds of Grandfather's plum-colored coat, and drift off to sleep.

I'll allow myself to rest for a few minutes. When I awake, I shall knock on the roof of the chaise to alert Johnny that I wish to speak to him. He will know where we are going.

Shouts awaken me. Befuddled with sleep, I try to rise but roll onto the floor, tangled in Grandfather's coat. Someone wrenches open the door of the chaise and seizes me, holding fast to both arms and pinning them to my sides.

"Out ye go, lassie," a gruff voice says. Without ceremony, a man lifts me out of the chaise and settles me on the hard-packed earth, cold beneath my feet. We are on a narrow lane lined with tall oaks, their bare branches undulating in the wind. The place is unknown to me.

"Who are you?" I demand. The short man before me grins but does not respond. His face is reddened as though he has worked in the sun for years. His hair hangs in lank strings over his shining forehead and falls into eyes that look like scuttling black beetles.

"In ye go," he announces, seizing me once more and carrying me to a great black coach that waits behind Grandfather's chaise. A cloaked driver sits up high, but his face is covered by a thick scarf and he wears a hat pulled low over his eyes.

"No!" I struggle in vain against the man's grip. "Johnny, help me!"

"Do that and ye'll earn a knife in your gullet, lad!" my captor shouts. "Go on back home and keep your mouth shut tight or ye'll no' live to another sunrise!"

"Lord Ramsay will hear of this!" I scream as the greasy man slams the door of the coach in my face. "He is my grandfather! Do you hear me?"

The man laughs, throwing his head back as though he is greatly amused.

The coach jerks and bustles away. I press my face to the glass in the window. Johnny takes up his reins, flicks them at Bridie, and she lumbers off. As the lad passes, driving in the direction we came from, he turns his face away but cannot hide the blood that drips from his swollen nose.

Without warning, my imprisoning coach shudders to a stop. I peer through the glass to see what has happened, praying that someone has come to my aid. The door flies open.

"I'll take that coat," the man says, shoving his head and shoulders inside. He seizes my sleeve.

"No!" I scratch and pull away from him in vain.

"Aye," he says with that same detestable grin. He nearly wrenches one arm from its socket as he tears the coat from me. ""Tis a fine coat, lassie, and I've taken a liking to it." He winks one of his beetle eyes at me. "That I have."

The villainous man folds the plum velvet in his arms. "Be glad I'm no' taking your gown, to boot. I've a lass who'd like that pretty thing. 'Twould suit her far better. She's round and soft, and you're all corners and bone."

With that, he slams the door, and the coach jostles away. I scream again, though I hardly have any voice left. I try the door handle and find it unlocked. As though the driver senses my plans, the coach gains speed. I dare not leap, not yet. The horses must first lessen their pace.

Rain first patters, and then pounds on the roof of the coach. I squint in vain through the window. My eyes behold nothing but the water that runs in fast rivulets down the tiny square of glass.

The sky weeps for my sister, pouring its sorrow on the earth. I would do the same had I any tears left to shed. Sadness spreads through me as though some viscous liquid has seeped into my veins and fills me with its heaviness. But something else stirs within me as well. 'Tis a jagged, most-unladylike feeling that grows as the rain pounds harder and the coach jostles and bounces, the wheels now bumping over an uneven surface.

Oliver has done this. Somehow, he learned where Grandfather was sending me, and he sent that leering man to intercept the chaise. I can scarcely breathe. My pulse throbs with rage. He will not succeed! He will not be rid of me as he rid himself of his wife! Were Oliver with me at this moment, he would die at my hands.

I gasp at the thought, but with the passing of one breath and a single heartbeat, I am certain.

How and when elude me, but I vow before Heaven and Hell that I will do it.

The coach slows. Trembling with fatigue and fear and anger, wearing leaden chains of grief, my shaking fingers search for the coach's door handle. When the driver stops, I shall fling the door wide and flee.

And then I shall find Oliver.

CHAPTER
4

The coach makes several turns. The rain has stopped, but the window is fogged. My efforts to wipe away the moisture are in vain, for our passage through the rain spattered mud onto the conveyance as we drove, and the muck-encrusted glass blocks my view. However, there are noises all about: occasional shouts, the clopping of hooves, the snorts of horses, and the passage of other conveyances. We are in the city.

With the meager gray light that filters through the coach window, I study my hands with disdain. My bony wrists and long fingers have no strength to them. How could I, such a slight lass, overpower anyone? Mrs. Harris used to fret and fuss and add more honey to my wine, but 'twas no use. After all, I was as powerless as a newly hatched gosling when I attempted to fight the greasy man who seized Grandfather's coat.

Clenching my fists, I scowl at the memory. No, I shall not be able to win my freedom by force. I must use my cunning. Lord Ramsay's name is known everywhere. *Someone* will come to my aid.

The driver bellows: "Whoa!" and we shudder to a stop.

I straighten my shoulders and take a single breath, gathering my courage about me as I might wrap a shawl around myself for warmth. I fling the door open and burst forth from the coach, falling directly into the arms of a square, black-headed man, who seizes me with a laugh.

"Eager to see me, are ye now?" Murmurs and a few snorts of

laughter erupt nearby. I blink in recognition. The dark-haired man's name is unknown to me, but his weak-jawed face with its great double chin and the mop of unruly black hair are familiar. I have seen him before but cannot recall where.I struggle in vain against his forceful grip. We are at the edge of a crowded street. Tall houses surround us, and the stench of horse and human waste rises from the cobbles below our feet. Passersby stop mid-step and gape at us.

To my side a narrow opening, no wider than a doorway, leads away from the thoroughfare. An iron gate with posts set into the stone blocks the passageway. Several poorly dressed and ill-favored men are standing before the tall barrier.

"Who are you? What is the meaning of this?" Renewed struggles only cause pain as the black-haired man tightens his hold on my arms.

"Unlock that gate," my captor orders the men who stand before it. One does so and then pulls on the bars until the barrier swings open with a grating squeal.

"Good. Now spread the word, lads." Nodding, all of the men save one, a tall man with bowed shoulders, dart through the gate and disappear. Then my captor drags me across slippery cobbles, and with a fist in my back, shoves me through the gate and closes it with a loud *clang*.

Mute with disbelief, I whirl to face him and freeze at his expression of contempt. His brow is furrowed and his lips draw back from darkened teeth, giving him the look of a guard dog baring its fangs at an intruder. He turns the key in an iron lock. The grating sound causes a lightning bolt of fear to shoot through me.

"What are you doing?" I scream, but growing cries of alarm from the gathering crowd drown my voice. I seize the bars of the gate and shake them to no avail.

The black-haired man raises his hand and voices die away as people see his grave severity. "Silence! Plague has struck Stewart's Close." His voice rings out in the chilly air. "By order of the Town Council, all must remain within until I give leave to unlock this gate. And all who are outside shall no' enter until I lift the quarantine." As he speaks, the tall man takes a white cloth from his jacket and fixes it to the bars. The cloth ruffles and flutters in the chilly breeze, and alarmed murmurs rise once again.

"But my family!" A woman with bowed shoulders and a face crinkled with age hurries forward, trembling with sobs. "Our house is on the close. Please, Bailey, allow me through the gate."

The bailey? I gape at the man as the woman continues to sob and plead. This solid man with a familiar face is the local man of law, charged with keeping the peace in the city. And he shut *me* in here? Me, the granddaughter of an earl?

With a placid expression, as though nothing of great importance has occurred, the bailey brushes away the feeble woman. She covers her face with a dirty apron and wails. Then the man bellows out another announcement, while jabbing a thick, stubby finger in my direction.

"This lass fled from the very house afflicted with plague."

A brief silence ensues, broken only by gasps of shock. The eyes of all those without the gate turn to me. I release the bars and back away from the barrier.

"What? No! 'Tis not true!" My screamed protests gain me nothing.

The bailey squares his shoulders and withdraws a parchment from his doublet. With an unhurried and self-important air, he unrolls the parchment and intones his next words as though he is a priest speaking to his parishioners. "Kenna Somerled: I hereby charge ye with willfully attempting to spread pestilence and contagion on this, the 22nd of November 1665. Ye shall remain within Stewart's Close until I lift the quarantine."

He holds out his hand once more to quell the rising protests and shouts from the surrounding crowd.

"'Tis no' right, Bailey! The lass will spread plague to our families. She'll have us all dead in a week!"

"We've never seen this lass before, Bailey! She does no' live on our close! I say off with her, ye cannae leave her here!"

"Please, let me inside. I care not about the plague. I must get home!"

Silencing all with a scowl and a wave, the bailey continues. "If ye survive, ye'll stand trial at the assizes for your crimes. May God have mercy on ye." He whirls and marches away, brushing aside the few who follow, their desperate pleas ringing up and down the street.

"I am innocent! I swear it!" None spare me another glance. The tall man who had remained standing beside the gate sits without a word upon an overturned barrel and takes a short knife from his pocket.

"Please!" I reach a hand through the cold bars. "My Grandfather is Lord Ramsay. He will tell you the truth. He'll not allow you to do this to me!"

The man raises one eyebrow but continues to studiously ignore me.

"Didn't you hear me? Lord Ramsay will not stand for this! I am his granddaughter!"

He keeps his head bent and polishes the knife with a bit of cloth.

"Look at me!" I scream. "Listen to what I say, you great oaf! I can have you thrown into prison!"

Without warning, the man leaps to his feet and slams his knife against the iron railings of the gate, inches away from my clutching fingers.

"Silence!" he roars into my face. "Off with ye, lass, or ye'll feel the sting of *this*." He waves his blade before my nose and growls, looking like a dog ready to attack.

I release my grip on the gate.

"Aye." The man sneers. "That's right. I'll slice off that wretched lying tongue of yours if ye dinnae hold your peace."

"Please, sir?" My voice shakes, and my breath comes out in puffs of white fog in the cold air. "I am not lying. 'Tis true. I am Lord Ramsay's granddaughter. I do not live here in the city."

"Stay away from the gate." The man waves his knife in a

menacing way. "Seek shelter within the close if ye can." His face twists in contempt. "Though I dinnae ken who'd want to help."

I collapse on the solid surface beneath me, gasping and trembling with cold and shock. Sparing me a final glare, the guard turns his back.

"Why?" The man does not respond.

I rise on shaking limbs. Behind me, roughhewn steps descend from the gate. I take one step, then another. If that man will not listen to me, there must be someone here, in this strange place, who will. Few could have heard the bailey's words. And there must be another way out of this enclosed city lane.

At the foot of a short flight of stairs, I pause to get my bearings. I am in Stewart's Close, so the bailey said. Our city of Edinburgh has many closes. They are narrow passageways formed by the cramped gaps between houses and buildings that lead away from the main thoroughfares. To each side of me are towering houses, at my feet a hard paved lane only just wide enough for two people to pass one another. It stretches away and angles steeply downward. The lane has the look of a narrow tunnel, buried deep as it is between walls that stretch to the sky.

Shivering, I realize for the first time how my bare toes are blue with cold. Why did I not have the foresight to stuff my slippers into the leather purse, I carry tucked inside my skirts, such as I did with my stockings?

With a gasp, I tug my stockings from within the purse and hurry to a dark doorway to put them on. They might help my poor feet, if only a little. Once my legs and feet are covered, the cold surface beneath my toes is not quite such a shock. I straighten my shoulders and pat my hair, which is a ruin.

An old woman hobbles past. I dart from the doorway and clutch at her sleeve. "Madam?"

"Eh?" She peers at me with bulbous, watery eyes. Her gaze travels over my dress and back to my face.

"Please, you must help me. I am the granddaughter of Lord Ramsay."

"Who?"

"Please, help me! They've locked me in here and I must get out."

"What d'ye think I can do?" Her brows lower. "The gate's locked each night. Keeps out the thieves. They'll unlock it in the morning."

With that, the woman yanks her arm from my grasp and hurries into an alcove out of sight. And before I can find someone else to speak to, the voice of a young lad rings out in the twilit air.

"By order of the bailey, the gate is locked. Plague has struck!" I whirl and spy the lad atop a barrel, cupping his hands around his mouth to shout.

With one voice, the crowd gasps in alarm and a woman screams. And another. People fly by me, running to and fro. A lass nearly knocks me down as she bolts past, weeping with a hand over her mouth.

"Plague has struck! Beware any strangers ye meet. Allow no one into your houses!"

Strangers. A flash of anger ignites within me. Strangers like *me*. I hurry down the lane, trying to put distance between myself and the shouting lad. Soon every soul within Stewart's Close will hear the bailey's lies!

When the lad's voice fades behind me, I approach the stall of a fishmonger as he hurriedly packs away his stinking wares in a large barrel. He shoos me away without a glance and closes his door in my face. A gaunt woman with a dirty-faced child in her arms regards me with narrowed eyes and turns her back. A ginger-haired lad with a split lip that bleeds onto his chin sees me and calls out to his friends, who all swivel in my direction and stare with gaping mouths.

With a curse, I hurry along the emptying lane. I try again and again, but no one will speak to me. Admitting failure, I sink down within a doorway. The bailey has done his duty. He has closed me in here and warned everyone to shun strangers. The sun is going down and all the shops, taverns, and houses on Stewart's Close are shut to me.

My stomach growls and I rub my empty middle. How long since my meager breakfast of oatmeal porridge this morning? I hadn't eaten much. I was too eager to sneak into my sister's chamber.

Oh, Cinaed! My eyes sting and I drop my head into my arms. With a pang, I envision a solemn service in the kirk of the village near Grandfather's home. Oliver will feign to mourn, gravely accepting the condolences of all who knew us. Dear God, it cannot be! And what of my poor drawing? 'Twas likely crushed beneath passing feet. 'Tis truly all I had left to remember my sister. Why did I have to drop it?

"Not long 'til sundown," a gruff voice says. Before me is a white-haired man who carries a squiggling piglet under one arm. "'Twill be a cold night, to be sure. Best get indoors, lassie."

I peer at the man's face. No crinkled brow. No air of disgust. This man must not have heard about the quarantine.

"Please help me, sir. I have nowhere to go." I cease breathing, praying that aid has come to me at last.

"Well, now." The man squints at me and works his jaw as though chewing the remains of a recent meal. "I could use a hand with me cows. If ye dinnae mind a bit of work, ye may bed down for the night in an empty stall in the sheds. Clean straw, mind ye."

I shake my head, unable to comprehend the man's words. Cows? In the city? Inside one of its narrow closes? I glance behind me at the gate, now barely visible at the top of the stairs. The tall man is still watching, and my spine crawls.

"I can work. And I'm acquainted with animals, sir."

"Good." The man grunts and walks away. I scurry after him and he rewards me for my eagerness by promptly handing me the wee piglet.

"There."

Words escape me. The tiny pig struggles in my arms and the smell of the creature assails my nose. I hold it away from my person while hurrying to follow my benefactor, sliding about on my stocking-clad feet. One foot lands upon something cold that oozes and gushes beneath my toes. My poor stockings. I dare not look down.

"Here we are," the man says, after we pass several more houses. We stop at a wide, battered door. It opens with a squeal and a warm and stinking rush of air hits my face.

We enter and find ourselves in a space not much greater than that of my bedchamber at home. The walls and floor are of rough stone. Wooden stalls separate a variety of animals: cows, pigs, a few sheep, and from the noise that floats from the far corner, chickens. Tools hang from rusted hooks on the walls.

After no more than a hurried glance, the man gives me my orders, and I obey. I muck out the stalls of two rather scrawny cows, trying to ignore the feel of dirt and sharp bits of hay that stick to my shredded stockings, blinking hard and fast to stop fresh tears from coursing down my cheeks. What is to become of me?

"What's your name, lass?" the old man asks while he mends a splintered gate that keeps several grunting pigs, including the wee one I'd carried, penned into one corner of this strange stone barn in the city.

"Kenna." I close my eyes in dismay. I should not have used my true name. He will hear what the bailey said soon enough. And once he does, he'll toss me out into the cold.

"And where d'ye belong, Kenna?" The man's mild features betray no guile, but I must choose my words with greater care from now on.

"Far from here." I gulp as more wretched tears well. "I've nowhere to go."

"So ye've said." The man regards me for a moment while I squirm. My dress is of fine stuff and richly embroidered; not the type of clothing one sees on a milkmaid or a servant. What if he doesn't believe me?

"Shall we see if ye spoke truthful, now?" He smiles, removes a tattered cap and scratches at sparse wisps of white hair on his reddened scalp. "The cows need a firm hand. Shift old Doss over there from that stall to this one." He bobs his head to one side. "And I'll fix that latch."

With the man staring, I scratch Doss's ears and murmur low words. From the time I could barely totter about, I've been friends with animals, be they the scolding geese on the grounds, the wee kittens Cinaed adored, or even the lumbering cows in the fields. But I never had to actually care for them. Nor did I ever learn to make them mind me. Holding my breath, I slap the cow's side and tell her to move. She does not. Cursed beast.

The cow ignores me until I offer a shriveled apple core that my toes discovered by trodding upon it. When I tempt her with the rotted bit of fruit, she follows, lowing and gazing at me with her liquid eyes. When we are both within the new stall, I with my back to the wall, old Doss near to filling the narrow space and blocking my way, she takes the core from me and crunches. I edge around her. My feet strike something squashy and yielding, and I yelp.

A small creature pops out from beneath a pile of soiled straw and darts from the stall before I can blink twice. A wee head of matted hair disappears from sight. The old man shouts in surprise. The shed door squeals open and thuds closed once more. Closing Doss's gate behind me, I gaze after the escapee. Was that a child? 'Twas so small!

"Do ye ken what that was, lass?" the old man asks me. He scrunches his face and squints until his eyes are mere slits. "My own eyes dinnae work so well any longer. All I can see of ye over there is a bit o'green. Like a summer leaf."

I breathe out in relief. That at least explains why he did not question me when he learned I had nowhere to go. His eyes are blind to the wealth I wear on my back.

"I did not see what, or *who* that was, sir."

The man grunts and shrugs in response. "Now, then." He slings a coil of rope about his shoulder. "Ye've earned your keep. Here." He hands me a cup filled with fresh, warm milk. I gulp it down and only remember to speak my thanks when the cup is empty.

"Take old Dossie's empty stall," the man says. "Ye'll wish to muck it out and add fresh straw, but 'twill be a nice warm place to sleep." He spits and scratches his head. "Perhaps we can talk of more work for ye tomorrow."

"Thank you." The words nearly stick in my throat. My benefactor leaves me the stub of a candle flickering in a battered tin that he sets upon the floor. The door squeals closed behind him, and I collapse onto a milking stool.

My sister is dead. I am now a prisoner in a strange place, friendless and frightened, accused of willfully spreading the plague. Somehow, Oliver has done this. He found me out and used his influence, and likely a fat purse filled with coins, to get the bailey to declare a quarantine and trap me inside Stewart's Close. But for the moment, I am safe.

With bones that ache with weariness, I rise and sweep out my sleeping space. I pile fresh straw high within the stall to form a makeshift bed that's as clean as possible in this stinking animal shed. As I work, something catches my eye upon the wall of the stall. Someone has scratched out a shape onto the wood. I hold the candle high to study the symbol. There is something familiar about the curving lines that form three intersecting triangles, and a tiny smile plays upon my lips as I remember. Cinaed used to tell me this symbol called forth good spirits or faeries and helped chase away the bad. She'd once shown me where our own mother had carved similar lines into the wood of one of the beams of our old cottage.

I blow out the candle and settle myself gingerly upon the prickly pile of hay. Grief holds me in a tight grip, but I make myself a promise. Tonight, I will strive to rest. Though it seems impossible, I am somehow comforted by the familiar carved image, now invisible above my head. Tomorrow, I will escape the close and return to Grandfather. He will make things right.

But for tonight, Lord Ramsay's granddaughter shall sleep with the cows and pigs.

CHAPTER
5

The crowing of the rooster does not wake me. I have already been up for a good while, picking straw from my hair, bodice, and skirts, struggling to ignore the gnawing hunger clawing at my stomach. My face grows hot at the thought of what I'd been forced to do when I needed to relieve myself. Finding nothing like a privy or a chamber pot, I resorted to desperate measures. Hopefully, no one will be the wiser, as so much animal waste covers the floor of this stinking place.

Attempting to pick straw from my hair, I gaze into the tranquil water of a trough. My watery reflection stares back with tired eyes. I shall ask the old man for a bit of bread in exchange for more work. Then I must leave my shelter and seek to escape Stewart's Close.

I yawn aloud, stretching my mouth wide and not bothering to cover my face as a lady should. Gathering my confidence, I square my shoulders. After a bit of rest, my mind is clearer than it was last night. Oliver's lies may have caused the bailey to lock me in here, but I am not the only one imprisoned upon the narrow lane. All those who live and work here are trapped along with me, thanks to the sudden quarantine. To be sure, those who heard the lad's shouted warnings were frightened last night. But this morning, will they not listen to reason?

A small smile appears on the face reflected in the trough. Though scrawny, my visage shows no signs of sickness. No fever. No betraying flush to my cheeks. Satisfied, I rise and shake out my skirts one more time. Once others realize there is no outbreak of plague and that I am here by some trickery, they will be sure to break the lock and open the gate. The horrid man who stands watch there will be no match for a great number of us.

The barn door bursts open with a screech as though in protest of its harsh treatment, and a stout woman with a dirty apron tied over dark skirts rushes inside.

"Out! Get out! Ye're no' welcome here. Ye'll have us all dead in a week's time!"

My startled limbs knock over a wooden bucket filled with grain. Chickens scurry to my feet, pecking at the unexpected meal.

"Look what ye've done! Away with ye!" The woman's howling mouth gapes wide to reveal a few dark stumps of teeth.

"I'm sorry." I take the bucket and sweep handfuls of spilled grain back inside it, but the woman seizes a rake and lands a rough smack on my backside.

"Go now or I'll knock your head off!"

I obey. The white-haired man is at the door. His eyes remain downcast as I pass. "There is no plague!" He turns his back and slams the door in my face.

So much for my new plan.

Outside, the lane is already coming alive. Women scuttle by with loads in their arms. They carry laundry, paper-wrapped parcels, and baskets of bread. My stomach twists at the sight. Several people glance in my direction with wary faces, but no one flees from me. My spirits lift a wee bit.

I head uphill, retracing my steps. The yeasty scent coming from the open doorway of a bakery makes my knees grow weak. A man whose hard face is pitted with scars dumps bread into a box by the door. One small seed loaf falls from the box onto the cobbles. Without thinking, I leap forward and snatch it.

"Three pence," the man says without a glance at me.

"Three!" A woman shoulders past me and marches to the scarred baker. "'Twas two yesterday!"

"Aye." He scowls at her. "And until they open that gate, no new supplies can come to us. Flour's almost gone. Three pence."

They argue. The bread is warm in my hands. My mouth waters. Without thought, I back away, and both the baker and the harried woman cease their bickering. The woman's eyes widen. She whirls and hurries off.

"Three pence," the baker repeats. His gaze travels up and down my person. He closes the distance between us and reaches for the loaf. I hold it to me, and back away.

"No coin, no bread, lassie."

"Please, sir, I can work. There must be some task you have for me. I can read and write and could help with your ledgers." I hold my breath.

The baker studies my face with a gleam in his eyes. With languid steps, he draws near and brushes a finger down my cheek.

"There might indeed be something ye can do for me, lassie." He shows all his yellowed teeth in a leer.

"How dare you!" I bat his hand away.

The baker's lips curve downward and an expression of malice paints itself on his ugly visage.

"Thief! Call the bailey!" he roars.

I gasp and turn to flee.

"Stop that lass!" The baker's cries follow me, seeming to bounce off the tall houses surrounding us. "She stole bread!"

I knock over a small cart laden with apples as I fly away. After losing my footing on the rolling fruit, I right myself and continue to flee. More angry shouts pursue me. Where to go? Before me is naught but the cobbled path that stretches ahead. My chest aches and my lungs burn with fire by the time I spy a gap between two houses. With no other options, I take my chances and duck into the small alcove, no more than a narrow space filled with boxes and barrels piled high.

Doubled over and gasping for air, I squeeze myself behind a rotting barrel and curl up as small as I can, struggling to gasp without a sound. The pounding of running feet and more shouts draw closer and then pass me by. No one discovers me.

Finally able to breathe, calmer and certain no one is in pursuit, I glance down at the wee loaf, still warm, still gripped in one hand. And in the other hand, I hold tight to something small and round. I laugh at the sight of the russet apple. I must have seized one as it bounced from the cart. Bread and an apple. Breakfast is served.

Two bites later, I pause as a low whimper, like that of a small pup, comes from somewhere nearby. Munching, I ease my head up and peek over the barrel. Across from me, a mere few paces away, is a bundle of rags. From that bundle comes a faint sob. I worm from my hiding place and inch forward, poking the bundle with a wary toe. It unfolds itself and I gasp.

The bundle of rags is a child, small and filthy. Eyes like pools of cool water gaze at me, round with fear, and the hair is matted and so dirty the color is impossible to tell. The tangled strands are entwined with straw and bits of twig. Could this be the tiny creature I'd stumbled upon in the cowshed last night?

Poor child! I crouch down and offer my apple. My hand shakes a bit, I admit. Not with fear but with the difficulty of giving away my food when my own stomach is so empty. The child seizes it and devours the fruit, growling like a wee kit. Sighing, I lick a bit of remaining juice from my fingers and then break the loaf of bread in half. The wee creature snatches the proffered food and downs it in a trice.

After finishing my meal, meager as it was, I rise and brush off my skirts. I must be off to seek aid. If I do not find something more to eat, I shall faint on the cold cobbles. And I cannot give up my original quest. There must be *someone* who will listen to me!

The child tugs at my skirts as I try to pass and exit the alcove. I pull them away from her, but the filthy creature seizes the cloth again.

"Come, now." I place my hands on my hips. "There is no more food. I am hungry myself. Let go."

The child does not. Instead, the creature crawls closer and wraps tiny arms around my legs. The babe appears to be a lass, a wee one no older than three years. But how is it that no one seeks for her? Her mother must be frantic. That's it! Smiling at my luck, I kneel and take the child's hands.

"Come on, then." I rise, keeping hold of the wee one's chilled fingers, so small they are like frostbitten twigs in my hands.

"We'll find your mother, shall we?" With the child's wide eyes fixed on me, I lead her out of the alcove. I must keep a sharp lookout for that ugly baker, but now I have purpose and a plan; for when I return this child to her family, they will be sure to help me! I will find food, and perhaps even shelter for a brief time, but most importantly, I will find my way back home.

I knock at the nearest house. The door opens and an elderly woman gazes at me with eyes that peep through folds of ancient skin.

"Do you know where this child belongs?"

"Naw." The woman does not even glance at the child at my skirts. She shuts the door in my face.

Such gall! Squaring my shoulders, I lead the child to the next doorway. And the next, and the next after that. After an hour, my feet ache from walking back and forth on the cobbles, and my knuckles burn from rapping against so many doors. The man in the tanner's shop, the woman boiling laundry in a great steaming pot in her home, the countless faces that squint at me in open suspicion, all claim ignorance. No eyes light with recognition and relief. As far as I can ascertain, the child has no home.

With a weary sigh, I sink down to rest on the steps that rise to yet another barred doorway. My stockings are mere shreds by now, but the chill in my feet is no greater than the icy feeling that has overtaken my heart. My search has revealed yet another alarming fact.

The houses and shops on Stewart's Close are so tightly squeezed together that most have no space in between them. The few gaps I find, such as the alcove where the child and I hid ourselves, lead nowhere. One promising alley ends at a towering wall. Another wee space brings one into a courtyard, but the child and I were met there with wide-eyed alarm as a woman with two bedraggled children backed away from us. A man with shifty eyes blocked the entrance to the house and ordered us to retreat, which we did with haste.

Some buildings have no entrances at all, which must mean their facades face away from the close. And all entrances that do face the lane are barred to me, thanks to that bailey's announcement. This close is a prison, indeed.

"Come, lass." I rise and shake away the hopelessness that threatens to consume me. I cannot give up, yet.

Voices babble ahead and we come upon a stout woman beside a large barrel. She lowers a great dipper into her barrel to fill the buckets and containers others bring to her. I wait for a few moments but see no sign of money exchanging hands. Holding the wee hand of my newfound companion, I lick dry lips and we join the queue, my heartbeat quickening at the thought of a drink.

The voices cease at once. The sudden silence draws more than one eye. A man who was passing by, leading a mud-covered mutt with a tattered rope about its neck stops short, and the dog whines and strains at its tether. A white-haired woman leans out an upper window and points in my direction.

"Off with ye, lass!" The water woman glares at me and brandishes her dipper. Two of the women leave the queue and scurry off, whispering and glancing back with wide eyes.

My shoulders sag. I will not be getting a drink after all. At least they might offer one to the child.

"Please. I only want a drink. For her." I bend my head, indicating my newfound friend.

The woman fingers a few scraggly, white whiskers that poke from her small chin, studying me with eyes narrowed to slits. "For the bairn."

She fills a small wooden cup and hands it to me. Swallowing hard, I must force myself to abstain as I kneel and offer the water to the wee one who gulps it noisily. She takes in each drop and with trembling fingers I hand the cup back to the woman, who snatches it and waves us off. The child and I back away while narrowed eyes follow every step.

Someone shouts out in surprise. A few paces ahead, a woman has dumped her chamber pot onto the street below, narrowly missing an unlucky man who was passing beneath her window. They exchange insults, and those who were regarding me with interest moments before now turn their attention to the pair, laughing and adding mocking commentary.

One woman who stops to enjoy the entertainment sets a basket at her feet and a potato spills out and rolls away. She does not notice. Nor does anyone else.

"Stay here," I whisper to the child.

Feigning interest in the shouting match, I surreptitiously kick the brown lump with my foot, sending it in the child's direction. As though she can read my thoughts, she snatches it and hides it in the folds of her crumpled, shapeless clothing. We flee, partners in crime, and find refuge behind the barrel in the alcove where we first met.

Luncheon is served. We share our meager meal, which disappears in seconds. Fortified by the few bites of potato, I should persist in my search for this lass's family, but at the thought of rising to my feet, a great and heavy feeling overwhelms me. My grief for my sister is fresh and sharp, ripping at my chest with its claws, and the tears I have been trying to suppress flow anew. I put my head in my arms and sob.

When my tears are spent, I swipe at my swollen eyes and lift my head. The lass is still beside me. She gazes at me with solemn eyes that are far too large for her tiny face. Suddenly, she darts onto my lap and snuggles into my arms, and I hold her close.

Weary from weeping, I lay my cheek upon her tiny head and we both fall asleep, while the residents of Stewart's Close go about their business, ignoring the refuse heap they pass each day. Ignoring the two lasses others have tossed aside, like the piles of rags and bits of broken crockery that hide them. As I give in to exhaustion, I remind myself of my promise.

My sister's murderer may believe he has won, but he has not. Not yet. I am still here.

He will not rid himself of me that easily.

CHAPTER
6

S houts of laughter jerk us from our slumber. I blink several times before I make sense of my surroundings. I rise upon feet that ache with the cold and peer around the barrel. 'Tis only a knot of lads who speak with merriment and jest as they pass by, unseeing. The child's eyes meet mine when I turn back.

"Shall we go, then?"

Her hands reach for me and a pang strikes my heart. How did such a wee child come to be here?

We leave our alcove when no one is looking, and I shiver the moment we are in the open lane. The windy afternoon sky is filled with scudding clouds and a biting chill wraps itself around me. I glance at my poor toes. *Och*, but why did I have to forget my shoes?

Rustling sounds make me jump. A rat darts from beneath a pile of rags and streaks away from the alcove. My stomach churns. I was sharing my space with vermin! But the sight of the rags gives me an idea. After rummaging through them and selecting the least filthy ones, I get to work. Within a few minutes, I inspect the dirty cloths I've tied about my feet. Though ugly, my new foot coverings provide relief from the cold and unyielding surface of the lane. A few more bits of cloth suffice for the child. And thus, with our feet shod in rags, we leave once more. The thought of what Cecelia would do were she to spy my cloth-bound feet brings a sharp pang of anger. To be sure, a mocking expression would fill her laughing eyes and curve her ruby lips with disdain.

Lifting my chin, I turn in a downhill direction and focus on finding this child's family. First, I shall discover the full length of Stewart's Close and then begin my search from the far end, gradually ascending the hill to the black iron gate. That way I shall avoid the baker, whose shop lies close to the imprisoning bars. We plunge lower and lower as we descend the lane. We pass more tall houses, a tailor's shop, and come to a narrow kirk with a bell tower. My heart leaps. The priest will offer me aid, will he not? He will wish to fulfill his duty to perform acts of Christian charity.

But when I open the battered door, I groan. The kirk is empty. Marks upon the cracked tiles show where wooden pews once stood. The kirk has the solemn, forlorn air of a building that has far outlived its usefulness. We return to the lane.

After another ten minutes of walking, the lane before us suddenly ends. A solid house looms directly in front of us, mere paces away. I have reached the edge of my prison. The door of this house is sealed with boards affixed across it, while a limp white cloth hangs in the window of the second story. I gulp and back away. Then there *is* plague here? Did Oliver lock me inside this close knowing I would sicken and die?

I square my shoulders and turn my back to the empty house, and ascend the lane, once again knocking upon door after door. After another hour of fruitless wandering, speaking to men whose eyes are like shuttered windows and to hard-faced women who turn away, I blink back tears that threaten to spill and admit defeat. Perhaps there is nothing for us but to return to our garbage-filled alcove.

After trudging upward until my legs ache, we draw near the bakery not far from the gate at the head of Stewart's Close. I slow my steps. That vile man must not see me again. But when I would turn back, the child whimpers and tugs at my hand.

"No," I whisper. "We cannot go that far. That horrid baker will see me."

She persists and her whimpers grow louder as she tugs at my

skirts with a ferocity surprising for one so small. The tear in my skirt grows longer.

"Stop it!" I cast a fearful glance at the bakery door. "Stop this at once!" The child must be far hungrier than I, but I cannot allow the scarred beast of a man to see my face!

In response, the child bursts into tears, releases her grip on my skirts and turns to run toward the bakery, wailing all the while. A striped cat darts from a nearby doorway and streaks past us, hissing. Heads turn in our direction.

Gritting my teeth, I sprint after the child who evades me by ducking and weaving between the legs of passersby, who exclaim in surprise. After I narrowly avoid knocking over an elderly woman hobbling by with her cane, I just manage to get hold of the child's ragged clothing. Thanks to her sudden flight, we are now close enough to the bakery to hear the worried voices of the women who form a ragged queue by the door.

Breathing hard, I pick up the child and turn to retreat. Her wails increase in volume and echo off the walls around us.

My frantic shushing has no effect. Faces appear in windows and the women waiting for bread turn our way. A lass with hair like a wind-tossed haystack passes us on the lane and stares with frank curiosity.

"I've a bit of cake here, wee one." The child gulps back her tears and the messy-haired lass rewards her with a smile, displaying a gap between two large front teeth.

"Here." She holds out a dried tidbit of something that may indeed have once been a cake. With a whining growl, the child seizes it and stuffs it into her mouth. Now that she is silent, save for chewing and smacking sounds, others turn their gaze elsewhere and my shoulders droop in relief.

"Thank you." I manage a weak smile. "She was so hungry." At that moment my stomach growls loudly.

With a knowing sigh, the lass tosses a ragged braid over one shoulder and reaches into the bag she carries. When she proffers me an oat cake, hesitation only stays my hand for a moment until I snatch it in a most unladylike fashion. My cheeks flush. The lass's sharp eyes, green as a cat's, travel up and down my person as I stuff food into my mouth. Perhaps she wonders why one dressed in silks must wear rags on her feet, but the lass does not speak until I have devoured the final crumb of my oatcake.

"Many here will soon starve if that bailey will no' open the gate." Her face grows solemn. "Old McGraw was turned away at sunrise with his cart loaded high with cabbages. He went away cursing the bailey, but he'll sell elsewhere, while some of us with houses on the close will have nothin' to eat."

I wipe crumbs from my bodice. Does this lass know the reason for the locked gate? "Surely he won't wish to enter the lane when there is sickness here."

The lass purses her lips again and taps her chin while her sharp eyes travel over my clothes once more. "Most of us dinnae think plague has struck. None we know are sick."

"But I saw the house at the end of the close, near the kirk. There's a white cloth in the window and the door is sealed."

The lass waves away my words with a languid hand and her eyes dance with mirth. "Old Flannery's house? He hung that cloth because he wanted no visitors. No pestilence there. He's dead these last five years. His son sealed the door after the roof caved in."

I blink and open my mouth to speak, but no words come. Before I can gather my scattered wits, the lass grins at me. "I'm Una. Who are you?"

"Cinaed." My face grows hot at the ease I now seem to possess for speaking lies. Lord above, forgive me.

"I bid ye good day, Cinaed." The lass gives me an encouraging smile as she retrieves a cloth-bound bundle and turns to go. "Get inside before sundown. There's a curfew. The bailey sent a man to walk the lane last night to keep us in our beds." She whistles, skips lightly over a pile of dung and disappears inside a house.

I shiver and rub my arms, though 'tis not the cold that makes me tremble. What will I do if I cannot find shelter tonight and that man finds me?

The child whimpers again as several more women pass us and join the small group waiting for bread.

"Hush." I pat the wee lassie's matted hair, but she commences her wailing once more. "Not *again*." I groan and back into a doorway to avoid more curious stares.

The bakery door opens and a bell jangles, drawing my gaze. A woman with a hard-lined face and lank, yellow hair dumps an armful of misshapen loaves into the box outside the door, and the women hurry forward. They haggle over the price, gone up another penny since only this morning. The child resumes her crying.

"Wait here." I set her down beside a pitted wall and crouch so we are nose to nose. "I shall get you some bread, but you must hush!"

The wee one gulps and her howls cease. She gazes at me with wet eyes. I breathe out a sigh.

"Just stay here. Please." The child quiets and puts her fingers into her mouth.

The women continue to haggle. Without a conscious plan, I inch forward and ease my way into their midst. Passing behind a crone with a shrill voice who shakes her fist, I wait until the shop woman turns her back. For a moment, my resolve fails. Lord Ramsay's granddaughter reduced to stealing bread? 'Tis not becoming of my station! I glance back at the child. *Och*, but her face is so thin! The child starves. What else is there to do?

My hand is outstretched the very moment the baker bursts from his shop with a basket of small loaves under his arm. His eyes meet mine. His face grows florid and contorts into a hellish mask.

"Thief!" he hollers. He shoves his basket at the lank-haired woman and turns in my direction but cannot move for the tight cluster of the women who crowd about the richly priced bread.

My fingers clutch a loaf and I whirl to run. Startled babblings and harsh shouts ring in my ears. And when I have only gotten a few paces away, something hard strikes me in the back with a stinging blow and falls to the ground with a clatter. Gasping, I stumble and glance down at the cobbles where a short-handled blade lies at my feet. He threw a knife at me?

I swoop to seize it and continue to run, sobbing aloud, slamming into more than one person, as my tear-filled eyes blind me. Oaths and curses follow me but running footsteps do not. With a gasp of relief, I spy my small alcove and dive inside, worming my way between boxes and behind my wretched barrel, until I am hidden.

My back does not bleed. I ascertain as much with trembling fingers. The place where the knife struck me aches and I cannot calm the tremor in my limbs. I stole a loaf of bread, indeed, but does one deserve a blade in the back for that? Grandfather will punish that horrid man! I shall make certain to tell this tale when I return to him. A pang strikes me. Grandfather must be so worried. No, he must be frantic by now!

Only then do I remember the child, and I groan. I should go back and retrieve her, but how can I return to the bakery? The boxes that hide me shift, and I freeze. Bits of twine and wood shavings fall on my head, and above me, the wee child's bright eyes peer down from a precarious perch on a broken cart. The dirt on her face is smeared with tears.

Relief and a touch of annoyance war inside as the lass crawls closer and curls up beside me on my little spot of cold and hard-packed earth. Glad I am indeed for her safety, but I would never have attempted to steal that bread were it not for her.

"You have brought me naught but trouble." She doesn't answer, but merely holds out her tiny hand. With a sigh, my building frustration melts. This wee lassie and I have something in common. Right now, we have only each other. I take the bread from my lap and break the loaf in two.

"You've never told me your name." I offer the lass her share of stolen bread.

She seizes it and stuffs the food into her mouth. "Annie," she mumbles.

After I eat my own few mouthfuls, I lean back against the wall behind me. Annie leaves my side and rustles about in the refuse that hides us. Within moments she returns to me and drops a piece of wood, roughly shaped like a loaf of bread, or perhaps a small babe, into my lap.

"Would you like a doll?" For the first time, the child's tiny lips curl into a smile. I search for something I can use and find a torn scrap of filthy wool within the broken cart. I wrap it about the piece of wood and give it to the child.

"For you."

Annie takes the makeshift doll and cradles it to her chest and the tiny smile remains on her smudged face. And from somewhere close at hand, a lad shouts out words that stop my heart.

"Sun sets! All abed! The watchman comes! All abed! The watchman comes!" I must not have heard those cries last night, closed as I was inside the warm animal shed.

Doors slam. From somewhere far above, a woman laughs, and a child's voice squeals, but soon, all is quiet. Slumped behind the pile of garbage, I admit defeat for the day. The child's head bobs and bends low over her ragged doll. I settle against the wall and try to make myself as comfortable as possible.

Last night my bed was a cow's stall. Tonight, 'tis the street, huddled and hidden in a trash heap. But tomorrow offers a fresh start. And thanks to the day's misadventures, I have a warm, wee body to snuggle against. And a weapon.

CHAPTER
7

The night is a cruel one. Though I've tucked my cloth-bound feet inside my skirts and wee Annie is a warm lump on my lap, my toes ache with the cold. And as I drowse away the endless stretch of darkness, my thoughts center on one person.

Oliver. His face comes unbidden to mind, and I cannot chase it away. His clear hazel eyes used to gaze upon my sister with such warmth. When did that end?

A fitful sleep overtakes me, but some time later, sounds awake me. The clattering of a rock. A faint intake of breath. Heavy boots clomping along the solid surface of the lane. I hold Annie closer, shivering with the cold of the merciless autumn night and the sudden fear that jabs at me. The steady beat of one foot placed before the other draws closer and closer. Someone is heading toward my hiding spot, like a beast crouched low as it closes in on its kill.

I shiver so much that Annie stirs and murmurs. The footsteps stop. I hold my breath while my wide eyes peer uselessly into the black and my heart thuds against my ribs. I count the beats. Nine. Ten. Eleven. And a single footstep falls once more. And then another. He is creeping closer! We shall be discovered.

But a sudden sound pierces the air. 'Tis a jaunty tune some brave soul whistles from a place beyond this alcove, behind the approaching watchman. The man gasps and his cloak rustles as he turns. Rapid footfalls fade as he pursues the whistler.

I remain awake the rest of the night. Twice more, footsteps draw near and fade away, but do not stop near the alcove again. After an interminable wait, dawn approaches. I can tell by the feel in the air. Thanks to the towering houses around me, early morning light cannot truly penetrate here. There is only a gradual lessening of the darkness, as though someone has swept aside a curtain that covers a filthy window and allowed a few weak rays to filter in.

The light gradually grows brighter, and the inhabitants of Stewart's Close come to life around me. A babe cries from somewhere in the house above our heads. A dog commences a shrill barking, and a man shouts to silence the creature. My heart sinks within. I am surrounded by walls of dark stone, brimming with the men and women who live and work in this place, but their doors remain barred to me.

Oliver chose my prison well.

The wee lass sleeps on, and I have no heart to rouse her. God knows I am weary enough myself, after dozing on and off in the cold, straining to hear the dreaded footsteps of the bailey's watchman. I settle myself more comfortably and breathe a sigh of relief, now that the man will have abandoned his vigil with the arrival of the sun.

As the child is still asleep, I remove the baker's knife from my leather purse and study it. The handle is carved of well-worn wood with a blade the length of my hand. I finger the edge of the steel and draw a prick of blood. Good! 'Tis sharp. I have not forgotten the promise I made to myself. Though I know it is rash and childish, my oath to kill my sister's murdering husband remains with me. My vow remains wound around my heart like a thorny vine.

The day is long begun when Annie fidgets and stirs. I place a hand on her matted hair, and she quiets but opens her eyes. She blinks and at once seizes her oddly fashioned doll from where it fell from her arms. She shifts herself from my lap and gazes at me, waiting.

I sigh. Why did the child choose to cling thus to me? If I cannot get beyond that gate, it is not likely that I will survive this place much longer. I may have become a thief out of necessity, but not a particularly good one.

Shaking my head, I rise, stretch aching limbs, take a deep breath, and then wrinkle my nose at the stench that invades my being. Our latrine at home never smelled this bad. Mrs. Harris kept it clean by pouring lime into it each week. Our home was fragrant with the scents of beeswax polish and the herbs hung in the kitchen. Baking bread and cakes. Freshly picked roses. My shoulders droop at the memory of such sweet scents. I fear the reek of this place will forever be with me.

Annie whimpers. "Hush." I kneel beside her. "I'm here. Do you remember where your home is?" She told me her name; perhaps now she will tell me how to find her family.

"Hungry."

I close my eyes. "Now, then." I pat her shoulder and the feel of her thin frame, skin over bone, calls to mind a starving kit I once found. It also calls to mind my dear sister. I swallow. "When we find your family, I'm sure we'll have something to eat." *If* we find them.

Her eyes regard me for a moment. Then she hugs her doll to her chest and smiles at me. Tears prick my eyes at the trust shining from her dust-smudged face. I clear my throat.

"Come." I adjust my skirts, tighten the laces of my bodice, and scratch at my dirty skin. My hair must look much like Annie's. I make a halfhearted attempt to plait my fallen locks and keep the strands away from my face but soon give up the fruitless task and sigh. I was never good at dressing my own hair. Lorna did that for me.

We ease past boxes and refuse heaps and creep onto the lane when no one is looking our way. I pick up the child so we may travel faster. Striding with purpose, I head back in the direction of the abandoned house at the end of the close.

"We've not yet knocked on all doors, wee Annie." Of a truth, the words are for my benefit, not the child's. The tall houses around us have many floors. Many rooms filled with numberless occupants.

Somehow, I must get inside the houses to ask within. Annie *must* have a family!

After only a few paces, we pass a thin lass emptying a bucket of slops onto the cobbles. As she looks up from her distasteful task and our eyes meet, she yelps and flees inside the nearest shop. I stumble, dismayed at her reaction. Meeting Una yesterday had taught me to hope there were others like her. Others who understand I do not carry the pestilence with me. But it seems that I am to remain an object of fear.

With a sigh, I continue on my way. Soon we pass a surly shopkeeper arranging two wilted cabbages in a box. He scowls as we pass.

"Stay away, lass." He brandishes a broom as though he aims to beat us with it.

I duck my head and hurry on, slowly shaking my head. The fear which grips the residents of Stewart's Close is even greater, somehow. More intense. Did that baker spread word of my theft?

As we hurry onward, most of those who pass by avoid my gaze, but the eyes of the few who do either narrow with disgust or widen with fear. How will I be able to find the child's family if no one will speak to me?

From somewhere ahead, a man's rough voice sings a song whose words bring a flush to my face. The voice is familiar, and I peer through a small knot of people heading my way until a hard-eyed, scarred face comes into view. *Och*, 'tis the baker! I hold Annie to me and duck into a doorway. Unfortunately, someone else was there before us.

"Move on, lass," a rough voice grunts, and a fist made of rock punches me in the side. Gasping for air, I back away, trying to apologize but unable to form words. Annie whimpers as we stumble on the uneven pavement. I back into the next doorway, one that is fortuitously uninhabited. The child and I huddle there until the baker passes by, too busy balancing a large bundle to take note of us.

Once his voice fades away, I step from the doorway when fingers seize my ankle. I cry out and struggle but am unable to break free. Thickly muscled arms extend from between the bars of a low window, and two large hands keep their tight grip.

"Dinnae be alarmed, bonny lass. Fancy coming down here to give me a bit of company? I'll share my ale."

"Let me be!" I tug in vain against the ever-tightening grip. Annie wails.

"Use your blade, lass." This rough voice belongs to the person who struck me. Why should he wish to assist us? Yet, with a gasp of relief, I yank my knife from its hiding place.

The clutching fingers release me the moment I slash at them. Howls and curses follow us as I hurry Annie away from the spot.

"Best to stay on the other side from now on when ye pass by here," my former doorway companion says. "And keep that knife at the ready."

"Thank you." I turn my attention to the man who assisted us. He is far shorter than I and thin as a bundle of sticks, and though the light is weak in the shadows of the lane, 'tis enough to betray the evidence of long years etched into his skin. I clutch my knife, wary of one who struck me only a few moments before.

The man peers at us through narrowed eyes. He studies my face with his head cocked to one side and pursed lips. Then he motions for us to follow.

"That child is like to blow away in a gust of wind. Come."

For a moment I hang back, but Annie tugs at my skirts. Taking a deep breath, I follow the old man with wary steps. We may have a chance to eat.

We enter the building at our backs by climbing a short and creaking flight of steps. A key scrapes in a lock and the man opens a door that gives way with a loud screech. Inside, a flickering cruise lamp set on a low wooden table lends its dim light to the chamber we enter. A spicy scent fills the room. I breathe it in, gratified and bewildered. How can a poor man afford sweet-smelling oil for his lamp? Mrs. Harris spoke of the horrid smoking lamps her mother used, filled with fish oil or a bit of mutton grease.

The old man shuffles to another room and I study my surroundings, keeping one hand on the knife and another on the child's shoulder, ready to flee at any moment.

The room is bare but for the lamp on the table and a low bench against one wall. The tiny chamber somehow appears as ancient as its occupant. The walls weep with moisture. There is no fire in the grate, though I am certain the man must feel the chill, for his beak-like nose is red with cold.

"Eat." The man returns carrying a trencher of bread and cheese and plunks it upon the table. My mouth waters at the sight. With a cry, Annie darts over and seizes a bit of bread, stuffing it into her mouth.

"Easy, wee mouse." The man chuckles. "Go slow or it'll come back out. I know that kind of hunger."

"Do you, sir?" I edge closer to the trencher. God knows my hunger is great by now, but something gives me pause. What does this strange man want from me?

"The name's Donny." The man gestures toward the trencher. "Eat."

The smell of fresh bread is my undoing. I snatch a piece and cram it into my mouth and then gobble a bit of cheese in a manner that would have shocked my genteel sister. Brushing away the memory of Cinaed's face, I grab another piece.

Donny takes his own bit of bread and sits on the bench. Short-cropped white hair caps his skull like a sprinkling of ashy snow. He stares at me as he munches, and his pale eyes, squinting from between folds of papery skin, regard me with calculation.

I shrink away from his gaze but do not stop eating. Annie makes whimpering noises as she stuffs more food into her mouth, taking bites that are far too large. I shush her, though one can hardly blame the child for eating like an animal.

My shoulders sag as a memory assails me. I used to come to a place near here to give charity. Cinaed and I would come to the city and hand out food from baskets Mrs. Harris prepared each Sunday. I was proud to say I fed the poor, yet shrank from the grabbing, grubby fingers that reached for the pitiful offerings proffered with disdain. Now, my own filthy hands are grateful for any bit of food they can find. What a change to my life within only two days!

The old man holds up a wooden cup and raises one bushy white eyebrow in an unspoken question. A drink! I seize the full cup, gulping the watery ale in a trice. With a wheezing chuckle, the man refills my cup and offers one to Annie as well.

Once the lassie has had her fill, the man takes her cup and returns it to the trencher. He turns toward us.

"Ye dinnae belong here." Donny squints at me. "Now that I see ye in the light, I know who ye are."

"How do you know who I am?" My fingers seek for the reassuring feel of the knife within my leather purse.

The man's thin lips curve into a grin. "You're that lass whose house was struck with plague. The one who fled, taking her pestilence with her. The reason we're all locked in our lane like rats in a trap, waiting to die."

"That is not true! I swear it!" My fingers curl tightly around the handle of the knife.

"Perhaps." The man's eyes glitter as they hold mine in his gaze. "But 'tis no' such a great thing when ye think on the new tale that reached us this morn. Ye've done more than spread pestilence, I hear."

My mouth falls open. "What do you mean, sir?"

"Word is you're the granddaughter of Lord Ramsay. And ye poisoned your own sister."

CHAPTER
8

My throat closes. The air in the tiny room seems hot and thick, hard to draw into my lungs. My chest heaves and my eyes burn with unshed tears.

"That's a lie." The words nearly choke me. "I loved my sister! Never would I have done anything to hurt her!"

The old man's bushy eyebrows fly upward. "That so?"

"I swear it!"

Forcing my tears away, I unthinkingly raise my knife. In one swift motion, Donny rises to his feet and knocks the knife from my grasp with a single sharp blow.

"Do that again and I'll no' be so kind as I am now, lass."

Rubbing my stinging wrist, I back away, motioning for Annie to follow. She darts to my side and gazes at me with eyes round as a kit's.

Heaving out a great sigh, the man stoops to retrieve my knife. I jump back, but he merely holds the weapon in his open palm and proffers it to me, handle first.

"Ye'll be needing this." His voice is gruff, and his words are clipped short. "Everyone knows who ye are. The bailey passed a letter through the gate. Told us all to spread the word."

I take the knife and return it to my pouch. My mind is nearly overcome. Murdered my sister? Me? The food in my stomach weighs me down as though I have eaten a stone.

"I presume that's why I cannot find food. Or a place to sleep."

My voice trembles. "As if telling everyone I am stricken with the plague wasn't enough."

Donny purses his lips. "Aye. Who wants to shelter a lass taken with the plague, let alone a murderer?"

"But I'm not sick and I am not a murderer. I would never have killed my own sister!"

"Perhaps ye did nothing." The man returns to his seat on the bench. "But them outside this door dinnae care. They have themselves to worry over. Now that we're shut off from the rest of the city, food dwindles. Most don't have enough for themselves and their own families, let alone for any stray locked inside our gate."

I place a hand on Annie's head and stroke her rough hair. It calms me, as does the sight of her wee face gazing at me. Despite the initial shock of learning the bailey's new accusation, I am more determined than ever to find at least one ally. And the fact that this strange wee man has allowed me inside his home gives me at least a drop of courage.

"Please, sir. You can see I am not ill and I killed no one! I can work if you only give me a spot where I may sleep and a bit of bread each day. As well as the child," I hurry to add. "'Twill only be until I get past that gate."

The man studies me, letting his gaze travel over my person, much as the baker's did. My strange host's eyes, however, do not gleam with a predatory hunger. The wee man cocks his head to one side.

"My Sheona is an herbwife. Acquainted, she is, with that plague. Twenty years ago, this city lost near to half the souls who lived here. Sheona nursed many who died. Many who lived as well."

"Sir, I vow I do not have—"

He silences me with a curt wave. Moving swiftly for such an old man, he rises and comes closer, squinting at my face. He lays a withered hand upon my cheek and touches my neck, drawing a gasp from me.

"I know the signs, lass. I dinnae see a single one upon ye." He backs away. "Plague has no' struck in the close. Wait here." He hurries from the room.

I take in a deep breath and must release my too-tight grip on Annie's hand. Shaking with relief, I pick up the lass and she wraps her arms around my neck.

The man returns with a heavy sheet of cream-colored paper, covered over with black letters crammed together. 'Tis one of the newspapers Grandfather likes to peruse. The old man hands it to me.

"Read."

I blink at him. Why this sudden, strange request? Then I remember. Not everyone in the city has the means for tutoring. Many can neither read nor write. I clear my throat.

"Edinburgh, the 19th day of July 1665." I glance at the man. "This is several months old." He motions for me to continue.

"A proclamation emitted by his majesties' Privie Council of this Kingdom, prohibiting and discharging all trade and commerce betwixt this Kingdom, and the merchants and inhabitants of the city of London, its suburbs, and all other towns, villages, and places of the Kingdom of England, which are infected or suspected to be infected with the Sicknesse or Plague of Pestilence."

My voice trails off. "If the plague has returned to London, it may indeed have come here." A stab of fear tears at me like a beast sinking its claws into my flesh.

"Read on, lass. Be there no more?"

My trembling fingers make the paper flutter in my hand. "The receiving of any trade goods from England is prohibited by the Council until the first day of November next to come."

I drop the paper and it rustles to the floor.

"The proclamation is no longer in effect." I measure my words. "Not for these three weeks past. The Council only barred trade with England until the first day of November. So, the season of the plague has passed?"

"Ye have a good mind, for all that hot-headed blethering of yours. Use your wits and ye'll find this place is no' so bad as ye think it is."

My audible scoff makes Donny's face crinkle with mirth. Setting Annie down, I retrieve the paper from the floor and hand it to him.

"Do others know this? They must see by now that there's no outbreak. Why do they not force the gate open?"

The man laughs and folds the paper to tuck it inside his threadbare doublet. "And find themselves locked in jail by the bailey?"

Scowling, I pick Annie up once again. This man only felt pity for the far-too-thin child with me. He has no desire to help me. "Thank you for the food, but the time to leave has come."

"Dinnae be such a fool, lass. I have more to say."

"Do you, now?" I pause while Annie plays with a stray lock of my hair that long ago escaped from my ribbons and pins.

The old man rises and smooths his worn doublet. "I wish to be certain of something. I believe that child with ye is one who used to live with the Lindsay's. Their house is near the bottom of the close by the old kirk. I'll take her to them."

A jolt of hope strikes me and my shoulders sag in relief. At last, a bit of luck! Perhaps my meeting with this odd man was not in vain. If I have found Annie's family, they may offer me shelter for work.

"Thank you." But before I can utter more, a fierce pounding commences on the door.

"Sheona! Open the door, please! We need the herbwife!"

The man mutters under his breath as he hurries to the door. Annie buries her head in my neck. The lass who rushes in wears an apron covered with great reddish-brown blots and smears. Her face is a mask of fear. I recoil from her.

"'Tis our ma." She gasps for breath. "The bleeding will not stop! The babe was born at sunset, but our mother..." Choking off her words, her face crumples and she sobs.

"Bide ye here. I'll call the woman." Donny disappears again, hurrying back through an inner archway into the depths of his house, leaving me with the slip of a child who clings to me, and the distraught lass covered in gore.

She pays us no mind, but continues to wail, her thin shoulders shaking. I place a hand on her arm and guide her to the only seat in sight. As I do not wish to sit beside the bloodied lass, I remain on foot and wander about the chamber as we wait.

After what seems an interminable amount of time, dragging steps and rustling skirts announce the approach of an old woman who shuffles into the room. Her hair is hidden beneath a smudged cap that droops over her face. She is wrapped in a ragged gray shawl, and her black skirts are torn at the hem. She carries a wicker basket on one thin arm. The woman is curiously bent at the waist, bowed so low she seems to be posed in some sort of perpetual curtsy.

"I am here." She speaks in a quivering voice. With a cry of relief, the lass darts to the door and flies outside.

I stare for a moment. "Sheona?"

"Aye." The woman lifts her head but ducks it before I can see her face. "Come along. Ye cannae remain here alone."

Annie and I follow the crone down the stairs, across the lane and into the ground floor of the opposite house. Within, the dark corridor reeks of damp and rot. The lass leads us into a tiny chamber. On entering, I choke back an exclamation of disgust at the overwhelming odors—the coppery scent of blood, mixed with other mightily unpleasant smells. A fire crackles within the small hearth, and a cruise lamp filled with fish oil sputters on a table near the bed where a dark-haired woman lies. A squalling babe is bundled in a basket beside the fire. The woman's face is pale as bone, her skin glistens with a sheen of sweat. She does not open her eyes when we approach.

Sheona sits on the bedside with a groan and rifles through her basket. She mutters orders to the lass, who flies from the room to do her bidding. I place Annie upon the floor and approach the crying babe. Its head is larger than I'd expect, rather like a good-sized cabbage. No wonder the woman lies bleeding. The babe's wee mouth is stretched wide in a wail. I pick up the wailing bairn and memories filled with sadness flood through me. Cinaed and Oliver once had a child. A babe that did not reach her second year.

With Annie in her usual place at my skirts, I pace in a circle about the room, whispering softly. Its cries soon quiet and the wee one sleeps, its round face content. I return the babe to its bed beside the fire.

"Well done," the woman Sheona says, peering at me from beneath her drooping cap. At my glance, she turns back to her patient. A pile of blood-soaked rags lies at her feet. The woman stirs and moans.

"Drink this." Sheona lifts the woman's head and holds a cup to the pale lips.

"I found more." The lass rushes back into the room with a bundle in her arms. She places a new pile of rags on the soiled linens of the bed. "We have nothing to pay, ma'am" she adds in a halting voice, while the old woman tends to her mother. "Give us a day or two and we'll find something."

"Of course." Sheona holds out a scattering of black seeds in her palm. "Here. Give no more than two or three to your Ma again when she wakes. Ergot will help stop the bleeding."

"Yes, ma'am." The lass takes the seeds and enfolds them into a cloth while the herbwife swiftly explains how to prepare and administer the remedy.

"Mind ye dinnae let Jamie there get his hand on those." Sheona rises from the bed while pointing at what I'd taken to be another pile of rags in the far corner. The rags stir and reveal a small lad with a filthy face and a darting gaze.

"I'll return with some broth." Sheona groans as she rises to her feet.

Babbling her thanks, the lass follows us. She studies me with interest as she picks up the blood-soaked rags from the floor, taking in my dirt-smeared silk skirts and embroidered sleeves. Something dawns in her face.

"Sheona, who is she?" Her voice quivers.

"Never ye mind." The crone motions to me. "Come."

The lass follows as we leave. She swiftly closes the door the moment my feet pass the threshold.

Once we are back outside, I draw in a deep breath, expecting to breathe clean air. I am wrong. The city's stench is ever-present, as are the baleful stares that greet me. I drop my gaze to my rag-bound feet.

Sheona holds up her hand when we reach her house. "I'll fetch my husband. Wait here." Her bowed form disappears inside the house.

Annie clings to my hand and we hover in the doorway. I duck my head as people wander past, willing the shadows to hide my face. Before long Sheona's wee husband returns. He brushes past us.

"Sheona tells me you're no' so useless as I thought ye were." He ignores my gasp of outrage and motions for us to follow with an impatient gesture. "Come. Let us see if this child belongs to the Lindsay's."

"Dear God, I hope so," I mutter to myself as we hurry after the man.

CHAPTER 9

Annie's hands remain tangled in my hair as we hurry along, following the strange, wee man. I stick close, not wishing to lose sight of him. My skin crawls as we pass the bakery and descend lower into the close. The place is silent and dark, and 'tis only mid-morning. The man must have already run out of flour. I sigh in relief when we are far away from the scarred baker's shop.

"God's gown, Donny, where are ye going with that fancy lass?" a woman screeches from an upper window. "That the one who gave her sister a bit of a drink? *Och*, I'd no' take what she offers ye!"

She cackles at her foul joke while her words bore into my soul. I have only learned of this accusation against me within the hour, and it twists inside like a living thing trying to choke my life away.

Something splashes onto the cobbles, and Annie squeals. The woman's dumped chamber pot splattered onto the child's already filthy garment.

"Gardy loo!" the woman shouts. "Oh, bless me, I didnae warn ye soon enough!" With a laugh that sounds like the braying of a donkey, she gives her chamber pot a final shake and slams her shutters.

"Dinnae do that again, old sow!" Donny shouts. He keeps moving, motioning for us to follow. But the old man's heart is not entirely formed of stone, for he ducks inside a tanner's shop and emerges with a cracked pitcher filled with water.

"Here." He thrusts the water into my hands. I nod my thanks and give Annie a drink. When she is done, I use my handkerchief to wash her tear-stained face and daub at the recently soiled spots on her clothing. Under my breath, I invent new curses to hurl at the horrid woman who caused the spots, should our paths ever cross again. Donny sits on a crate and glares at anyone whose head turns in our direction, though he does not allow us to linger.

"Enough of this idleness." The man gets to his feet. "Come."

I barely have time to leave the pitcher at the tanner's door before I must seize Annie's hand and scramble after the man. We pass a small knot of women haggling over a scrawny chicken in a woven basket and continue ever downward.

As we trudge along, I peer into the slice of gray sky that shows from between the towering houses that line our way on each side. A light, drizzling rain begins to fall. The rain cannot continue into the night. It must not. If by chance we do not find Annie's family, we will yet have no place to sleep. Our little alcove will be damper and chillier than ever.

Something catches my eye that makes me pause mid-step. High above me at the top of a tall house, a man leans out and stares down. I had not thought of how tall the houses are here, and how close they stand, cram-jammed together like a jumble of child's blocks. Could one perhaps leap from the roof of a house on Stewart's Close to the roof of one outside this lane, thus bypassing that locked gate? My heart hops inside, filled with a sudden sense of hope.

Slowing my pace, I gape openly at the man, blinking rain out of my eyes and straining to see beyond him. The man's head lowers as though he is gazing back at me, and with a jolt, I resume my walk. The stranger wears a cloak pulled low over his face, and a single backward glance reveals that his head swivels to follow my progress along the narrow lane. I duck my head and hasten along. Perhaps a rooftop escape is not a possibility unless no other soul is about.

My mind races as quickly as my cold, hurrying feet. Was that the watchman hired by the bailey? The bailey who lines his pockets with Oliver's money? My legs turn to jelly and my mind opens as though a key is twisting in a lock. Oliver wanted to be rid of me, so I was first shut within Stewart's Close and accused of trying to flee a quarantined house. My brother-in-law must have thought no one would give shelter to one who carried the plague. But that first night I found safety in the cowshed. I smile and breathe out a short, mirthless laugh. My breath comes out in white puffs under the chill drizzle.

Annie whimpers, so I pick her up, recalling my second night in the close, huddled with the wee child in our rubbish-filled alcove. Oliver's plan to be easily rid of me didn't work as he wished. That is why the bailey forthwith accused me of murder.

My insides turn to lead. Oliver is waiting for me to starve or sicken and die of a chill. And once I am gone, as I stand accused as Cinaed's killer, she shall be avenged in the eyes of those who enforce the law. And Oliver will be free to court Cecilia. *Cecelia!* My face contorts with disgust and helpless rage.

Annie is suddenly taken with a fit of coughing. The air is grown hazy and stinks of burnt wood. I settle the child upon a cart and squint through the foul smoke, seeking its source. It comes from higher up the lane, in the direction from which we have come. Smoke pours from the open door of a shop not quite out of sight. I freeze. 'Tis the bakery.

"That's no burning bread." Donny takes Annie and seizes my arm. We retrace our steps, and within moments, join the gathering crowd. "Quick! Find buckets!" The old man returns the child to me and hurries to give aid to the others.

"Keep her away! I'll wager that lassie set the fire herself!" My mouth gapes wide as my accuser, a gaunt woman with a shining red face jabs a finger in my direction.

"I did no such thing!"

"Likely story, lassie." A man saunters from behind me and slings an arm across my shoulders. "We all know what ye've been up to."

"Leave me be!" I twist from his grasp and shove him as hard as I can. He falls onto his backside with a loud 'oof.' Seeking to escape, I slip, lose my balance, and fall to my knees. Something strikes me on one shoulder, and I cry out as the loud voices rise in mocking laughter. I am surrounded, unable to rise, unable to see anything beyond the tangle of bodies that edge closer.

"Murderess! That bailey foisted her on us and now we all suffer for it," a woman cries. A cacophony of shouting voices rises and echoes, bouncing off the high walls that close us in.

"Keep the head, all of ye," Donny shouts. "Put out the fire! D'ye want it to spread?" He punches one man in the side and aims a kick at a woman who's brandishing her broom. Glaring, the small crowd that surrounded me dissolves and a few of them head back to the bakery, where sweat-soaked men and women have formed a clumsy bucket-brigade and are trying to douse the flames.

Donny takes Annie with one hand and offers the other to me.

"Forgot your blade again, eh?" He glares while he helps me to my feet.

I swat at the dirt that smudges my skirts and scowl at the man.

"How could I use it against so many? What defense do I have when they all come at me at once?"

"Use the knife first chance ye get, and ye'll make the others think twice. That may be what saves ye."

I clench my teeth as I shift Annie onto my hip and follow Donny, who has apparently decided the others have enough assistance in their efforts to douse the fire. The old man jerks his head, motioning for me to quicken my pace. We descend the lane once more and my thoughts bubble and boil like one of Mrs. Harris's thick stews. How could I have forgotten my knife? I purse my lips. Perhaps as I move about the lane I should openly flaunt my blade. Let all who pass worry that I'll jab at them if they so much as look at me!

After a tense and silent walk, we draw near the end of the close and stop at a house not far from the abandoned one with the white cloth at the window. Winded from carrying the child, I set Annie down and take a deep breath, then crinkle my nose at the ever-present miasma that fills the air. Scowling, I pinch my nose closed.

Donny knocks on the tall door of the solid house in front of us with the side of his fist. The thuds echo around us.

"Kenna?" Annie says in an urgent voice. She speaks so seldom I blink at her in surprise.

"What is it?"

Instead of answering, Annie yanks on my hand, trying to pull me away from the door.

"What are you doing?" At that moment, the door creaks open. Annie screams and buries her head in my skirts.

CHAPTER 10

"What's all this, now?" A round woman frowns at us from the doorway. When her eyes fall upon Annie, they widen. She says something and Donny answers, but I only hear the child's piteous cries. She continues to wail, sobbing and shivering as though she'll never be calm again.

"There now, Annie." I kneel and wrap my arms about her. "You're safe. I'll not let anything happen to you."

My heart twists. Cinaed used to say such words to me. Her gentle hands would stroke my hair and her whispers would ease away my childish nightmares. But why is Annie so frightened? The moon-faced woman regards us with a deep line carved between her brows. She pulls the door open wider and holds a taper aloft to light our way.

"Come in." Her voice trembles.

Murmuring words of comfort to Annie, I take her in my arms and follow Donny inside the house. A chandelier glows above, filled with flickering beeswax candles that lend their sweet scent to the chamber we enter. Fine wood floors gleam beneath my feet. A fire in the grate crackles and emits a cheerful glow. On one paneled wall hangs the portrait of a man with a cloud of white hair on his head and an expression of thunder.

"Where is Mrs. Lindsay?" Donny approaches the fire and stretches his hands to the flames. The woman grimaces and edges away from him. Her eyes flick repeatedly to the child in my arms.

"My mistress is out." She holds the edge of her apron in her hands, twisting and ringing the fabric.

"She's gone to the butcher." The timid voice of a young lass comes from the shadows in the far corner of the room. She rises from a spot of wet floor beside a wooden bucket and sweeps strands of fiery hair off her eyes to reveal a thin, freckled face. At once, Annie ceases crying and holds out her arms. With a tremulous smile, the lass hurries to take Annie from my arms.

"This is her home?" The red-headed lass smiles at me. Her eyes are wet. I return the smile, surprised at how reluctant I am to let my wee friend go. But it must be so.

"Catriona!" The round woman scowls at her. "Leave the child be, ye lazy house cat. Back to work, lass."

Catriona plants a swift kiss upon Annie's cheek and settles the child back on the floor. Annie whimpers as the lass takes her scrubbing brush in hand and resumes her task. I take the child's wee hand in my own. She squeezes my fingers. Donny regards us all with narrowed eyes.

"When will Mrs. Lindsay return? Is Annie her daughter?" I ask.

Catriona emits what sounds like a laugh she turns into a cough. The woman glares at the lass but says nothing.

I fumble for words. Why won't these people simply answer me? "I found her shivering in a pile of rubbish yesterday. I can see this is her home. Has no one sought for her? She's but a—"

"I know it." The older woman cuts me off with a curt wave before turning to the child.

"Now, wee one, don't be afraid of old Mrs. Wallace." Her face softens a mite. "I always saved a ginger cake for ye, or a bit of honeycomb. Don't ye remember good Mrs. Wallace?"

Annie peeks out from behind the folds of my skirt. The woman sighs and rubs her hands together. She glances over at Donny, who regards all with glittering eyes and a face as set and still as a mask.

"Now, then, Annie," Wallace says with a tremble in her voice. "Why'd ye run off last week? We were so worried."

"Were ye, now?" Donny asks.

Mrs. Wallace's rotund face darkens to the color of wine. "Annie?"

"She's hardly spoken a word since I found her. That's one reason I've had no luck finding her home." I squeeze Annie's hand.

At my words, Mrs. Wallace's shoulders sag, and she breathes out an audible sigh. She whirls toward Catriona. "Bring us some food! Our wee Annie is home." The lass hurries from the room, giving me a fleeting smile as she passes.

Soon, she returns with a trencher laden with food and sets it upon a scrubbed wooden table in the center of the room. Mrs. Wallace curtly waves us to a bench beside it. My mouth waters as I settle myself with Annie upon my lap. Donny says nothing as we eat. Neither do I. I'm too busy stuffing my mouth with salted pork, baked apples, dried figs, and gulping a sharp wine.

Annie eats as heartily as I do, but her gaze often darts to the corner where Catriona endlessly scours the floor. That corner must be particularly dirty. The lass does not move an inch from that spot all the while we eat. The bristles of her scrubbing brush scrape across the wood in a rhythmic cadence that accompanies us through the entire meal.

"Now, then." Donny wipes his mouth with his sleeve and leans back in his chair. "Kenna, here, took Annie and cared for the child until she found her home. She needs a bed and a roof as well. I trust your mistress has a place for her."

"N-no." Mrs. Wallace stammers and returns to her habit of twisting her apron in her hands. "We've no room for that, that…"

"Poisoner?" My hands tremble as I pick up my cup. "Is that what you were about to say?" Food is now dust in my mouth. I'd felt a spark of hope at Donny's words. I could have a bed, a fire, and a full belly until I managed to get past that locked gate. But now my hopes are dashed.

Mrs. Wallace blinks twice and glares at me with narrowed eyes but says nothing.

On my lap, Annie smooths her doll's threadbare blanket. The flame-haired Catriona scrubs at the interminable spot on the floor. The fire crackles in the grate. Donny clears his throat. He regards me for a moment.

"I dinnae ken what this lass may have done, but she's trapped inside the close, same as us. Anyhow, what can your mistress say about sheltering a murderer in her home? That floor come clean yet, lass?" Donny calls over his shoulder to Catriona, who yelps and jumps, causing darkened water to slosh from her bucket.

Mrs. Wallace plants her fists upon her ample hips. She wears the expression of a woman who's just found a bit of sheep's dung floating in her ale.

"What do you mean by that?" I ask Donny.

The door opens and a tall, stately woman sweeps inside. "Wallace? Come here. Oh." She stops short at the sight of us. Her voice trails off and her face pales to the color of goat's cheese. She clutches a jeweled crucifix at her neck. "Who is this?"

"Any luck at the butcher's, Mrs. Lindsay?" Donny asks. "Oh, and we found your ward, Annie."

Mrs. Lindsay gapes at her. She remains rooted to the spot, leaving the door to the lane open behind her. The smell of smoke mixed with rain floats inside. The woman blinks several times. Then her lips curve into a false smile and she holds out a slim hand in our direction. "Oh, Annie, my sweet. Thank the Lord we've found ye! Won't ye come here and give me a kiss? I've worried so."

Annie buries her face in my neck.

"Hmph." Donny grunts out the sound while Mrs. Lindsay drops her hand to her side and a flush of pink dots each cheek.

"Oh, we *are* so relieved to have found her," Mrs. Wallace says, moving surprisingly fast for a woman of her girth. She rushes to close the door and takes Mrs. Lindsay's cloak from her hunched shoulders. "She's a mite worn from her troubles and has no' said a word. No' a sound since she came in."

With a chuckle, Donny rises to his feet and plants himself in front of Mrs. Lindsay. He folds his arms as he gazes up at her and the much taller woman visibly shrinks from him.

"This is Kenna." Donny waves a hand in my direction. "She needs a place to stay as well, but your housekeeper says there's no room for them in this grand place. I'm sure ye'll put her to rights."

Mrs. Lindsay straightens her shoulders and compresses her lips into a thin line while folding her own arms, mimicking Donny's stance.

"We have no place for guests. Of course, our Annie will stay. She's my ward; an orphan I've cared for since she was a wee babe in arms. But that lass must leave."

Annie wails and wraps her arms more tightly about my neck.

"I thought as much." Donny chuckles again, though 'tis a sound without mirth. "But no matter. Annie has no wish to stay." The man's wizened face crinkles even more as he regards the child. "Cannae say I blame her. I wager something here, or some*one*, has frightened the wee bairn near out of her mind."

Mrs. Lindsay's eyes dart to the floor, and Donny's face grows hard. "The wee lassie can stay with old Sheona and me, but we'll be needing an extra coin or two to buy food."

I scowl. Annie is welcome to stay with Donny and his wife, but *I* am not? Am I to be cast out in the cold again? On impulse born of my desperation, I rise from the bench and hurry to the door so I may plant myself between the outside world and Donny's exit. If this wee man has decided to take Annie into his home, he'll not do so without taking me as well! Annie clings to me and whimpers. I whisper in her ear.

"Hush. I'll not leave you." She stills in my arms.

"Well?" Donny glares at Mrs. Lindsay.

"Please. I must care for her. We gave our word. If he finds out, there'll be trouble." Mrs. Lindsay and her housekeeper exchange anguished glances.

"If *who* finds out?"

Mrs. Lindsay's eyes plead, but she makes no sound.

"He pays ye?" The old man's voice is low but threaded through with filaments of steel.

The woman nods.

"Then pay me what he gives ye for the child's keep. If ye do that, I'll keep my lips closed."

Mrs. Lindsay's lips thin once again into a tight line, but she mutters curt orders to Mrs. Wallace, who bustles from the room. The housekeeper returns in a moment and shoves a small purse into Donny's hands. "Here."

The man tucks the purse inside his jacket. "Send me word when 'tis time for the next payment. I'll come."

Mrs. Lindsay's face becomes pinched and sour, and her black brows meet above her sharp nose, giving her the appearance of a rather cross crow. "We all suffer want. Until the Town Council lifts the quarantine, goods and coin will dwindle. I found no meat at the butchers."

Donny's face crinkles with mirth. He joins me in the doorway. "*Och*, 'tis certain ye weren't hoping to buy a nice, salted ham from the butcher. Did ye find what ye truly wanted?"

With that, Donny sweeps past me and I follow, carrying the child in my arms and the sight of Mrs. Lindsay's outraged face in my mind. She slams the door behind us.

Donny descends to the lane and stretches his arms out to us. "I'll take the child."

"No." I tighten my grip on Annie. Donny's white eyebrows raise high. "You know I need shelter as much as she does. You'll not keep her unless you also give me leave to stay with you."

The man drops his arms and studies me again with his icy gaze until a sly smile creeps onto his face. "I wondered what ye'd do. That I did. And now I know." He fishes a pipe from within the folds of his doublet and places the stem into his mouth. "Come along, then."

With that, he whirls and marches up the lane. I hurry to follow, my feet sliding on the rain-slick stones. 'Twas that easy? My heart leaps with a tiny flicker of hope.

"I must warn ye, I'll no' go easy on ye. Ye'll work for your keep." Donny pauses and glances back at me with laughter glinting in his pale blue eyes. "Beware, Poisoner. Ye'll no' be living in a grand house with servants to do your bidding. Ye'll *be* the servant. Mine and Sheona's."

"I know that." I lift my chin. "And don't call me 'Poisoner.' Please," I add after the man throws me a steely, backward glance. After a moment, his eyes soften and a gleam shoots through the icy blue orbs.

"I'll call ye what I wish, Poisoner." He chuckles and picks up speed.

"Of course, you will," I mutter under my breath. And I quicken my steps so the old man will not leave me behind. I have found shelter and food. Soon, I will escape this vile city.

CHAPTER
11

I breathe out a great sigh when we return to Donny's small home. His house is a two-story box that squats beneath a taller house like a chick beneath a hen's wing. 'Tis not even half so grand as the home of Mrs. Lindsay. Yet a smile touches my lips. Let Oliver send his watchman after me now. He'll not find me.

Once inside, Donny leads us from the small chamber facing the lane, into a warm kitchen. A long wood table sits against the far wall, and an iron pot hangs from a heavy chain, suspended over the winking coals in the wide fireplace. A lovely, finely carved chair of black walnut is beside the fire, out of place in the humble room. A wood shelf extends the length of the wall above the table and is covered with neatly stacked bowls and plates.

I wrap Annie in the shawl the man offers and settle her onto the floor beside the fire, in front of a low screen that will protect her from sparks. I expect to find Sheona waiting, but the house is silent. Perhaps she is off curing someone else, or prefers to remain in her chamber, tucked in a nice, soft bed.

Annie's weary wee head nods over the doll lying in her lap. Poor sweet one! I pat one of her thin shoulders. What did she see that frightened her so?

Rising to my feet, I clear my throat. "Donny? What happened in Mrs. Lindsay's home?"

Donny's shrewd eyes glitter at me. "Mrs. Lindsay has a sharp tongue and a sharper temper. Many's the time I heard she gave her husband a great skelping with one of her cooking pots or the iron for the fire. Likely she gave him a final blow he could no' recover from."

I gasp. "Surely not!"

The man shrugs. "A bloated thing he was, who liked his wine. And his women. Neighbors heard the most awful screeching and wailing last Saturday night. And none of us has laid eyes on Master Lindsay since that time."

"You cannot mean that the stain Catriona was scrubbing—"

"Aye."

My stomach sours and I kneel to place a gentle hand upon Annie's head. What she must have seen! Glad as I was to have found her home, I am now doubly glad she is no longer there, but will abide here, with me.

I rise and brush at my filthy skirts, wrinkling my nose. Will I ever be clean again? *Och,* but my black-rimmed fingernails are a sight! Donny leans against the wall and chews on the stem of his unlit pipe. His eyes seem to peer afar off, but his gaze snaps to me so suddenly I jump.

"Tell me about your sister," he says.

"What do you mean?"

"I mean what happened to her, ninny. Ye vowed your innocence. Who killed her, then?"

My legs tremble so much I must sit upon a nearby stool. "She was poisoned."

"We heard as much. Who did it?"

"Her husband." A tear spills down my cheek. "The man who pledged before God to love her all his life."

Donny continues to gaze at some far land only he can see, chewing on the stem of the wooden pipe.

"And how do ye know this?"

"I saw it." My voice grows stronger as I recount my tale. It rushes back with such clarity: Cinaed's labored breathing, her wasted face, the bottle. The smell of Cecelia's perfume and the glove; that wretched, damning glove on Oliver's person! I clench my fists and my voice trembles with emotion.

Donny's face remains impassive. When my tale is done, he says nothing for a while. Annie breathes softly beside the glowing embers of the fire, and I take to pacing the small space, unable to keep still. Several minutes pass, and my impatience mounts.

"Well?" I plant my feet directly in front of the old man. "Do you believe me?"

"This may be the truth," he concedes. "I see no treachery in your eyes."

"Thank you." The sudden sting of tears surprises me. I had not realized quite how much I wanted someone, *anyone*, to believe me. 'Tis such a great relief!

Donny's face softens a mite. "I am sorry for your sister."

I attempt a watery smile to show my thanks. "My sister had hardly lived. She was not yet thirty years old. And she loved Oliver." I take to pacing again and clench my fists at my sides. "But he began to fancy someone else. A lass with money and an important title. And there you see his reason for murder."

The sharp glance Donny gives me is startling. But as soon as the storm cloud appears on his weathered face, it dissipates, and his usual impassive expression returns. He shoves himself away from the wall and heads toward a narrow staircase in the corner of the room.

"Seeing as how you're no' a murderess waiting to kill me in my sleep, I'm going to rest. Sheona will come down soon. We'll give ye an evening meal and ye'll begin your work tomorrow."

My heart sinks at the drudgery awaiting me, but I straighten my spine and square my shoulders. Lorna is my age, and she is capable of work. Hard work. She rises before the first rays of the sun glint on the nearby sea and often does not rest until long after all the others are abed. She's a servant, after all. *My* servant. I strive to ignore the prick of guilt that stings somewhere inside my chest. 'Twas not my fault she was born the servant and I the lady! But 'tis no matter. Lorna knows how to work for her keep, and so do I. I'm certain of it.

"Up, now! We've shared our food and fire and there's work to be done, lass."

Blinking, I stare up at old Sheona. The bent crone is swathed in a thick woolen shawl that is the deep blue of a summer twilight sky. The shawl mostly covers her head and face, but the beaky tip of her nose sticks out, making the woman look like a great oversized bird pecking at its food.

"Oh. Of course."

Rubbing my eyes, I rise and fold the woolen blanket the woman had given me last night. The fire is out in the grate and I stretch my chilled, stiff limbs, unaccustomed to sleeping upon the floor. I am grateful, though, to have slept beside a warm fire and not outside on cold ground, hiding behind a pile of stinking trash. Annie dozes at my feet, wrapped in the ragged but thick shawl Donny gave her last night. I touch the child's shoulder to wake her, but Sheona waves a gnarled hand at me.

"Leave her. 'Tis no' the child who must work. She may sleep." And the woman forthwith hands me a chamber pot. I stare in horror at the foul contents inside. Never have I done such a task as this. 'Tis servants' work! My shoulders slump as I remind myself that I am now a servant.

"Well?" Sheona demands.

"But where do I..."

"In the lane, lazy lass! Off with ye, now!"

The air of the early autumn morning is chilly and my toes, though bound in cloth, do not like the feel of the freezing cobbles beneath them. The lane stretches to my right and left, and the tall houses tower over my head and block the sky. Though 'tis barely dawn, a few hardy souls are already about. Heads swivel in my direction as I, Kenna, granddaughter of Lord Ramsay, the Earl of Chessington, dump the stinking contents of the chamber pot into the trickling river of filth that flows down the middle of the lane. I make haste to return inside.

When I arrive back in the kitchen, Sheona sets me to my next task: to scrub away burnt-on bits of food that cling to the insides of a stack of copper cooking pots. She gives me a bit of brick for the scouring, and I sit with a sigh at the worn table set against the wall, resigned to my fate of working to keep that treasured spot of floor beside the fire.

After an hour, my fingernails are near to worn off and I have only cleaned half of the pots. My temper rises. Is there to be no morning meal for me? How much work earns me my food?

I glance at Annie, who has awakened and sits quietly beside the fire. Sheona smiles and murmurs to her, but the child merely clutches her doll more tightly and gazes back with wide eyes. Soon, Sheona waddles in her bent and goose-like way across the floor to a tall wood cabinet leaning against one wall. The old woman removes a key from within the folds of her shawl. Once she has released the latch, she reaches inside and withdraws a small seed cake. She closes and locks the cabinet swiftly before offering the cake to the child.

I swallow as Annie stuffs bites into her mouth.

"May I have some?"

"Aye." Sheona grunts. "When you're done with your task."

My stomach rumbles. "But that will take me all morning! These pots are filthy."

"*Och, aye.* That they are, lass. That they are." With a wheezing chuckle, the old woman leaves the room.

I clamp my lips tightly closed to keep unladylike words from spilling out. Bending my head, I scrub at a blackened kettle until my fingers bleed as the fire crackles and pops upon the hearth.

Unbidden, my sister's face comes to me. Her pale cheeks, her colorless lips. Beads of perspiration dripping from her forehead. And the roaring fire, kept hot day and night, though she obviously suffered from the heat. Sniffing, I sit up straight. I will not weep. Not here.

Not in the home of the strangers who have taken me in. Mourning must wait.

With a scowl, I scrub harder and try to ignore not only my empty stomach but my itching, filthy skin. When but a wee lass, Cinaed made me bathe once a week in our tin tub despite my many protestations. She scrubbed me while I wriggled and protested. Later, when we lived in the grand house in the country, I grew accustomed to washing daily. Such a luxury! I sigh and chide myself for longing for something so impossible. There's work to be done.

Once I scrape the last bits from Sheona's copper pots, the crone gives me my own seed cake and some ale. I gulp my food greedily, and the moment I'm done, Sheona has more work for me. So much more work! I empty another chamber pot. After that, I spend the remainder of the morning dusting, sweeping, and rubbing grease into a pair of old and battered boots. After a brief midday meal of tasteless mush, Sheona gives me a bit of beeswax with which to polish the carved chair beside the fire. Thrice that afternoon, I am set to sorting herbs into piles. I tie them inside cloth bundles and Sheona locks them away in her tall cabinet.

As I work, Annie sits and plays with her doll or eats bits of cake or apple the old woman gives her. When not doting on the child, Sheona smokes or dozes in her chair before the fire. Donny never appears, and the old woman says he's out. By nightfall, my back aches with a fierce pain, and I am weary. Oh, so weary! My heavy lids close and I yawn.

"You're a hard-working lass. I'm pleased." Sheona nods at me.

"Thank you." If only that meant tomorrow would not bring yet another day of ceaseless drudgery! I wipe the sweat from my forehead.

"Well done." Sheona limps to her cupboard and unlocks it. I am gratified when she withdraws a few small potatoes. At least I have earned another meal. "I am truly pleased. Certain it is my Donny will also be pleased. I'll speak of this when he comes back."

Sheona allows me to sit beside the fire as she cooks a thin potato soup. Annie sits in my lap and amuses herself by picking threads from the embroidered leaves on my overskirt. I pay it no mind; the gown is ruined anyway. When she's done, the old woman pours soup into two bowls and hands them to me and Annie. She takes none for herself but seats herself once more by the fire. And she does not offer us a spoon.

I can barely keep my eyes open during the meager meal. Am I to spend each day thus working? How will I ever get away from this city? Sitting with bowed shoulders, I sip my soup straight from the wooden bowl while darkness seeps into every thought. I'm trapped here. I'll be a servant forever, doomed to work my fingers to the bone. Never to see Grandfather again. And Cinaed will never be avenged.

No! Shaking myself fully awake, I sit tall and clear my throat.

"I cannot stay here forever."

"No?" Sheona bends her head, hidden within the folds of her shawl, in my direction.

I rise and place my empty bowl upon the table. "I must find a way out of the city."

"And return to your grandfather's home?"

"Of course! He must be frantic by now!"

Sheona shakes her head back and forth and taps one finger upon the armrest.

"Ye've been charged with murder, lass."

"But I did not do it!"

"Others dinnae believe ye as I do."

I blink. "So, what, then? I am to stay here the rest of my life?" The food curdles in my stomach.

Sheona rises to her feet and shuffles in her bent-over way toward the corridor. "Naw. But ye must take care, lass, and wait for a bit. We need to see what comes of all this. The quarantine, and this accusation of murder."

"For how long? When will I be able to leave this house?"

"Soon enough, lassie."

"When?" I glare at her retreating form.

"Soon enough."

Tremors of rage seize me as I curl beside the fire. If I did not know better, I'd vow the old woman aims to keep me here forever to scrub her pots and empty her slops. Perhaps she likes the idea of having the close kin of an earl as her servant.

I must think. And I do so for many hours, unable to stop the confusion of thoughts that fly through my mind like a flock of unruly geese honking and hissing at one another.

Grandfather does not know my whereabouts. I am trapped in the city, accused of murder. I will starve if I do not spend all day working the skin off my fingers to earn my food and a floor to sleep upon. And thus, I have no chance to find a way out of this place. What am I to do? I lay awake beside wee Annie, whose cheeks are flushed in slumber. But rest does not come to me until long after the fire has died down and the night has crept far too close to another sunrise.

CHAPTER
12

Five days have passed since Oliver's brutish men brought me to the city.

I bite my lip in concentration as I chop a strange and slippery brown root for the herbwife, Sheona, to use in one of her cures. The pungent smell of the root makes me sneeze, and my knife pierces the already torn skin of one finger. A crimson drop oozes from the cut and I wipe it away and continue my task.

Five days have passed since they locked me inside the gate that guards Stewart's Close.

My lips curve into a grim and angry smile. Oliver must be certain I am dead of hunger and cold by now. I cannot wait to show him how wrong he is.

Five days have passed since my sister died.

Tears smart my eyes and the knife clatters from my fingers. I clear my throat and clench my teeth together to prevent any more tears. I sniff and curl my lips in disgust at the wholly unpleasant smell coming from my person.

Five days have passed since I was clean.

A great *clang* startles me from my miserable reverie. Donny has set a tin washtub upon the floor. A chance to bathe!

"Sheona tells me the wee lassie needs a good scrubbing. Heat water." He gestures toward the bucket in the corner. "I'll fetch more." He turns on his heels and marches out.

Leaving the wretched root, I lug the bucket to the great kettle which hangs from a chain over the fire and empty the water into it. Stoking the coals, I scratch at my skin. My benefactor made no mention of whether his newly acquired kitchen help might bathe. He and his wife cannot wish to have a servant who smells like something one would find rotting in the middle of the lane. Or do they not care?

Donny returns with several more buckets to add to the kettle. Soon, the man decides the water is heated enough and has me fill the tin tub. "I'll fetch the woman to help. Put the child in the water." And he leaves.

My throat tightens at the sight of the lass's ribs that stick out so from her tiny frame. Mrs. Lindsay was indeed a harsh mistress. Who would begrudge this wee child a bit of bread? I sigh as I settle the child in the water. Were I at home, Mrs. Harris would like as not take these filthy garments and burn them. As it is, Annie will likely end up donning her shapeless shift again after she bathes, for Donny and Sheona will not have anything a child could wear.

Annie splashes and smiles at me, and I smile back despite my growing desperation and my rancor. Sheona shuffles back inside the kitchen and hands me some clean rags and a dish filled with a slimy brown clump I recognize as soap, the kind my sister used to make long ago. The herbs Sheona must have added to her soap lend it a pleasant perfume of rosemary mixed with the sweetness of lavender, and I breathe in the scent with pleasure.

Without a word, I bathe the child as gently as possible as she splashes me and squeals in delight. Sheona chuckles and even I cannot help enjoying myself. Annie's simple joy spreads through me and into the chamber around us like some lovely magic has floated in from a land filled with faeries.

The child's matted hair, tangled as a starling's nest, takes time to clean. Only after bits of twig and twine and specks of mysterious substances float in the bath water do I begin to perceive the color of Annie's hair. The tawny locks likely shine like a pale gold sunrise when dry. Brushing aside a curl from Annie's forehead, I spy for the first time a wee scar that resides there, just beneath the hairline. My breath catches in my throat.

Time whirls backward and I see myself, two years before. I am a fretful girl of thirteen, part child myself, jealous of the babe who demands so much of my sister's attention. Alone with her in the nursery, I amuse myself reading a book pilfered from the library and do not keep watch on the infant who crawls about. And Isla, Cinaed and Oliver's daughter, had struck her head against the sharp leg of the upturned chair I'd placed across the doorway. 'Twas only meant to serve as a harmless barrier, keeping the babe inside with me while I read at my leisure and she crawled amongst her toys. She'd screamed as the blood dripped.

Cinaed had understood, but I'd never forgiven myself. How the memory stings, now! Only weeks later, the child was taken from us by the croup.

"Mind ye dinnae drop that." Sheona's sharp voice jolts me from my painful memories. I'd nearly let go of the dish filled with soap and allowed it to fall into the water.

"Sorry." I finish washing the wee one. Once Annie's hair is finally clean, Sheona hands me a bottle filled with a pungent, dark liquid. The spicy smell is much like that of the box of special herbs she and Donny keep on the mantle. Every so often she takes a pinch from the box and smokes it in her pipe.

"'Twill kill the vermin, if there be any," the herb wife tells me. "Rub this onto her scalp."

Vermin? The thought had not crossed my mind until now, and my scalp itches terribly as I anoint the child's wee head with the liquid. My own head earns a vicious scratch once I finish helping Annie.

"You're next, Poisoner." Sheona's face remains hidden behind the folds of her shawl. "Heat more water if ye need it."

"Thank you." I smile at her, so relieved at the offer of a bath that I decide to forget the horrid nickname she and her husband continue to call me. "My head itches so dreadfully I can hardly bear it!"

Sheona smiles while she wraps Annie in a blanket. She settles the child by the fire with orders not to leave until she's warm and dry. Humming to herself, she leaves the kitchen.

"Donny in't here," she calls from the corridor. "He's taken himself off. Be gone 'til nightfall, he will. Take as long as ye like."

At last! The feel of the water on my skin is heaven. Annie dips her wee hands into the tub to splash me, giggling and squealing. I splash her back. When I am clean, scrubbed until my skin is raw, and my own scalp anointed with the vermin-killing liquid, I turn my attention to washing my linen shift with the sweet-smelling soap. My bodice and skirts I dare not touch. The embroidered silks would be ruined by my clumsy attentions. Well, ruined even more than they already are.

Wrapped in my thin sleeping blanket, I wring out my shift and place it on a chair beside the fire to dry. Then I sit beside Annie and gaze at the dancing flames. With a relieved sigh, I squeeze the water from my hair and fling droplets onto the coals, where they hiss and steam away. My reddened fingers smart as I attempt to plait my sodden hair. My lank brown locks have never obeyed my fumbling fingers; therefore, I rarely paid attention to them before. But Lorna had a gift for finding a way to make my hair presentable.

Lorna. My fingers pause upon my half-twined tresses, and a pang strikes my chest. Does she wonder where I am? Does *she* believe I am the one responsible for Cinaed's death? No, it cannot be! Grandfather will have told everyone the truth.

With a sigh, I recommence twisting my hair into clumsy braids and wince at the pain in my injured fingers. Every single fingernail is jagged and torn. My shoulders slump at the sight of the roots I have yet to chop and the new stack of dirty pans on the table. I press my lips together and sweep my pitifully thin braid over my shoulder.

Waiting for my shift to dry so I may return to my labors, I attempt to brush away a few smudges here and there from the hem of my skirts. Annie giggles as she touches the green silk. I smile at her. The presence of this sweet one lightens the darkness of my current existence. My brief stay here has shown me that Sheona and Donny both have a tenderness for Annie. I am glad. Fond as I have already grown of the child, I cannot take her with me when I leave. For leave, I will, despite Sheona's warning to "wait a bit."

Glad for the brief respite from my labors, I lie down as I wait for my hair and shift to dry, and Annie settles her warm body against mine. Sleep takes me swiftly. When I awake, Sheona is sitting in the carved chair near the fire and drawing deeply from her pipe. The blue shawl swaths much of her person, and a drooping lace cap hides most of her face. The pale smoke that she puffs out forms a light fog about her bent head. Annie sits upon her lap. Wrapped in a blanket, the child is eating something. My stomach growls.

"Dress yourself." Sheona waves her hand toward the front of the house. "Go to the other chamber." I rise to my feet. My shift, skirts, and bodice are all neatly folded and waiting upon a three-legged stool.

I take them with me and don my clothing with pleasure. What a good feeling it is to be clean! My skirts appear to have been brushed, for some of the stains are lighter. Smoothing the fabric in place, I gasp aloud. The jagged tear in the silk has been mended in neat and even stitches, though with a dark thread that does not match. The old herbwife's doings, certainly. I purse my lips. Though grateful, I'd prefer to earn bread for my labor, not mending. I fasten my leather pouch around my waist and tuck it within my skirts, after first peeking inside to make certain the knife is yet within.

Returning to the kitchen, I open my mouth to speak my thanks but fall mute at the sight greeting me. Dressed once again in her shapeless, though now clean garment, Annie wears a golden coronet of woven braids on her head. Her hair gleams in the flickering glow from the cruise lamp.

"Why, Annie, you look the grand lady. Sheona, how did you plait her hair like that?"

"Had a lassie of my own, once," Sheona says. My spirits rise, despite my stinging hands and aching heart. I was right. The old woman does indeed like Annie. Very much.

"There, now." Sheona puts down her comb and gives Annie a pat on the shoulder. "Go and play." And the woman's beaky nose turns to me.

"Ye might at least thank me for mending that skirt of yours. 'Tis no longer easy for me to do such a task. My sight in't what it used to be."

"Oh, I do thank you." My cheeks sting while my chest tightens. She might have at least given me the chance to speak.

But Sheona is satisfied with my delayed gratitude. She nods her head, and her smudged cap droops ever lower over her face. "Good. Eat." She waves me to the table, where a tiny loaf and a steaming bowl await. The woman rises heavily to her feet and shuffles toward the food. I do not stand on ceremony and fly to the table to seat myself, no longer able to wait when there's a chance to eat.

I mumble my thanks around my first mouthful of bread while Sheona places Annie in my lap. Only a few days ago, I would have scoffed at the thought of eating boiled cabbage. Not today. I drain a wooden cup filled with ale and Sheona fills it again.

The woman takes her own meal seated in her carved chair. When she finishes, she leans closer to the hot ashes to poke at them with a fire iron until the coals glow red and orange. Then she sits back and removes something from the folds of her shawl.

"This be yours, lass?"

I gasp at the sight of the object that lies on her palm. 'Tis my knife! Well, the knife I stole from the baker. Only minutes before it was nestled safely inside my leather purse!

"How is this possible?"

Sheona cackles and motions for me to take the object from her hand. I do so and fumble with my skirts so I may tuck the blade back inside its pouch. Did I drop it? I must have, though I never heard it clatter to the floor!

"I'm pleased with all ye've done here. I didnae believe Lord

Ramsay's granddaughter would be willing to work as hard. Lost my wager with Donny, I did."

Grinning, I rinse out my bowl in the washbasin.

"Well, then. Now 'tis time for ye to learn another sort of work," Sheona says.

I whirl. "What other sort of work?"

The woman cackles. "We need a set of sturdy legs and nimble fingers. And someone who can run if need be."

My heart flutters. What does this strange woman mean?

"Why?"

"I'll tell ye why." Sheona chuckles once more. The lace of her cap trembles. "You're living in a den of thieves, lassie. And thieves can always use an extra pair of hands."

I freeze as an unbidden memory comes to me. Grandfather warned us to be on guard for cut-purses when Cinaed and I came to the city with our charity. With a start, I pat the purse once more tucked inside my clothing. I did not drop my knife after all! Sheona somehow managed to take the knife from me, hidden as it was within my skirts! How could that have escaped my notice?

Clenching my fists, I stretch to my full height and face the old woman who trembles with mirth. "You and Donny are thieves?"

The old woman cackles out loud. "We are."

I fold my arms. "You jest. What here in this part of the city is worth taking?"

Sheona cackles again and rocks back and forth in her chair. "Ye might be surprised, Poisoner. Ye saw the Lindsay's home. Surely ye cannae think that all who live here have no' a penny to their names, now?"

I shrug. The Lindsay's home *was* grander than any I'd expected to find here on this tiny, winding city lane, but compared to my home with Grandfather, well, Mrs. Lindsay's house is nothing but a quaint cottage. The home Donny and Sheona share is a mere hut.

Sheona trails a crooked and knobbly finger along the carved arm of her chair. The polished wood gleams in the glow of embers from the grate. "There's more than enough here to tempt us. We pocket what we can, lass. But fear not. We've no wish to train ye as a cutpurse. 'Twould take far too long. I only took your knife for fun. Your face was a sight, it was!"

Despite my indignation, my lips curve into a small smile. "I cannot understand how you managed to take it without my knowledge." I clear my throat. "But Sheona, I am the granddaughter of an earl! I cannot sink so low as to become a thief!"

Sheona's laugh grates upon my ears. Why is every blessed thing so amusing to this woman?

"Sure, ye can, lassie. Ye dinnae wish to be back out on the street on your fancy fanny, now, do ye?"

I clench my fists. "No."

The woman pokes the fire again. "Fear not." Her voice trembles with mirth. "We only take what no one will miss."

"How can anyone not miss what you steal from them?"

Sheona ceases her rocking. Her voice grows pensive. "Do the dead need fine clothing, or larders filled with food? Do they need silver salvers or gleaming candlesticks?"

My mouth falls open. "What?"

"Many there be who die each winter." The old woman's weak voice barely reaches me. "'Tis the way of things. Many bairns, and the oldest among us, leave this life when the chill comes and brings the ague and the croup. And, of course, there's that dreaded pestilence. It struck when I was young, and then again not twenty years ago."

I nod.

"The plague is a hellish demon. Most of the time, all within the household die."

I twist my skirts in my fists, much as Mrs. Lindsay's nervous housekeeper did a few days before.

"Whenever the pestilence kills, the men come to cart away the dead. The 'foul clengers,' they call 'em; those who carry off the bodies and burn all the possessions left within their homes, be it a humble or a fine dwelling. Long ago, when I was yet a young woman, my husband and I passed a house with the dead piled high in the carts like God's kindling. Donny says to me, 'now then, woman, what of their goods? Why burn 'em all?' And that very night, we went back. And we took what we wanted. No one was the wiser. And taking those goods put food on our table, lass. We found others to help us, and we formed a guild."

"A guild?" I choke back a sudden laugh. "A group of thieves calling themselves a guild?"

"Aye." For once, Sheona does not laugh. "Mock us as ye please. We do no' call ourselves thieves. We only enter houses to take goods from those who no longer have need of them. That's all. God may judge us as He will, but I dinnae call that stealing."

I shake my head in disbelief. "I *do* call it that. Anyway, if you and others in your guild dare to steal from those who died of plague, are you not afraid illness will befall you?"

"Naw." Sheona puffs placidly on her pipe. "I wash what we take and we dinnae grow ill ourselves. Besides that, I learned herbs and cures from my own ma. Taught me how to keep hale and hearty, she did. Dinnae fear, lass. We'll keep ye safe with my special cure." The woman takes her small box of herbs from the shelf. "Here, smell this."

I sniff, then inhale deeply. The scent is marvelous, with the sweet tang of orange peel. Only once in my life have I tasted an orange, a Michaelmas gift from Grandfather. There are also strong notes of cinnamon and rosemary, among other pleasing scents within the box of herbs. Such rare and costly things! The pile of dried leaves and bark inside the box is pungent and lovely.

I hand the box back to Sheona. "But how do spices cure one who is ill? Or keep one from falling ill?"

"I dinnae ken that for certain." Sheona draws deeply once more from her pipe. "But my Ma swore by it, and I swear by it myself. I have a nice pipe before I head out to treat my ill. When my Donny goes to his work, most of all if it be to a house where there was sickness, I put a pinch or two from this box into a cloth what's rubbed with some grease, so it'll stick. The old man keeps that tied over his mouth and nose. And he in't been ill for many a year."

"But you should not be stealing." The severe note in my voice calls to mind old Mrs. Harris, each time she derides me for eating too much or speaking ill of my tutor.

"Passing judgment, are ye?" Sheona chuckles. "I suppose 'tis no matter that ye stole from Shaw when ye scarpered away from his shop? I'll no' soon forget the look on his face when ye nicked his knife from the ground and run off with both blade and bread in your hands."

"You saw that?" I gulp. "But that's different." I lift my chin. "The bread was for Annie, you know."

"Never ye mind, Poisoner. Call it thievery if ye will, but 'tis another kind of work we have for ye. Donny is growing tired and I'm too old to do it, and now that I've seen ye toil this hard for me, silk skirts and all, I know ye've got the spine and muscle for it."

At that moment, I yelp as someone pounds on the door. Annie hugs her doll to her scrawny chest with a startled cry. Her eyes fill with tears.

"Open up!" a muffled voice bellows to us. "I know you're hiding that lass!"

My body grows weak. The baker!

"Speak o' the devil and he comes," Sheona creaks out in her ancient voice. "Do ye think he fancies a drink?" Puffing placidly on her pipe, she rises from her chair. Bent low, she shuffles into the front chamber as the pounding increases in intensity.

"Hold your wheesht!" Sheona screeches. "I'm coming." The thunderous blows continue to rain upon the door until it groans open.

"Off with ye!" Sheona shouts. "Ye'll break down my door with those ugly fists!"

"I'll not leave without that lass. I know she's here. Bring her out! We all want that murderess brought to justice. We've had naught but bad luck from the moment she was forced on us!"

"No!" Sheona barks. And the next moment the baker emits a

sharp, pained cry. After that, the door bangs closed, and I hear the distinct sound of a key scraping in a lock.

"Open up, ye foul witch!" Shaw bellows and pounds anew on the door.

"Off and bile your head!" Sheona shouts. "I'm calling Donny, I am. He'll stick ye with a knife like he did before if ye dinnae stop that howling."

The pounding ceases as my jaw drops. Donny stuck the baker with a knife? I am still gaping when Sheona returns.

"Close that mouth, lass, or bees will fly down to your gullet."

I close my mouth with a snap. Before I regain the power to speak, the old woman and I both whirl toward the door as Shaw pounds a final time and shouts, "Ye cannae guard her forever. I'll be watching."

CHAPTER
13

In the morning, I am nudged awake again by a rough foot poking my ribs. I rub sleep from my eyes and smile when Sheona gestures to an apple and a cup of ale upon the table. After thanking my thieving benefactress, I fall upon my food, which disappears in an instant. Chewing, I drain my cup and place it in the pan of warm water to wash it. And as I wipe it dry and replace it on the shelf, I call up my courage to speak.

"Sheona?"

"Eh?"

"Do you and Donny truly plan to train me in thievery?"

She cackles and I grit my teeth. That cursed laugh of hers!

"Keen to learn, are ye, lassie?"

I scowl at her. I've no wish to become a thief, but what choice do I have? With a wide smile, Sheona points to more dirty pots on the table, and with a sigh, I grab one and commence scrubbing.

"How many more dirty pots do you have, Sheona? 'Tis as though you feed all within the great household of a lord, not merely four people, and one no older than a babe!" I swipe away a bead of sweat from my forehead. "And less than a week ago, you were feeding but two."

The old woman cackles. "'Tis true, lass. You're cleaning the neighbors' pots as well."

My jaw drops. "Why?"

"Why not? Donny and I wished to test your mettle. We wanted as much work as we could find for ye."

My shoulders slump. "This was a test of sorts?"

Sheona smiles. "Aye. Fear not. After today there'll be no more extra pots." She studies me for a moment with keen eyes. "Leave that scrubbing for now. 'Tis time for a lesson. We'll have ye out that door soon enough."

My hands cease their endless scouring. "A lesson?" I close my eyes for a moment. Our good Lord only knows what such a lesson might entail.

Sheona smiles and rises from her chair, accompanied by a chorus of creaking and popping sounds as she stretches stiff joints. She shuffles toward the corridor that leads to the staircase and the remaining chambers of this mysterious house.

"I'll call my husband. Donny!" She screeches. "Donny! Come!" The house is silent.

Shaking her head in disgust, the woman begins her achingly slow climb to the upper floor. "Deaf as an adder. I'll get the man."

"Sheona, wait. I can't do this. I cannot become a thief. 'Tis not right."

"Hush!" The old woman pauses on the stairs. "The guild needs a young one with a strong back. Not a crone like me or an old man like Donny. If ye dinnae help us, we'll send ye back outside."

She resumes her ascent, and I bite back a retort, glaring at the cursed pots. Unless I wish to take my chances outdoors, I must do as my benefactors say.

But then my head snaps up. Thievery will get me out of this house! Sheona said as much. I will be in the company of others who, hopefully, are not all bent on turning me in. And these thieves know their way around the close. Perhaps they also know a way to get past the iron gate that keeps us trapped inside Stewart's Close. Or of another way one might leave this narrow lane. Then I huff at my foolishness.

"Anyone who knew how to leave the close would have done so by now." I mutter to myself.

Before long, Donny marches down the stairs, holding the cane his wife uses to get around. He taps it smartly on each tread as he descends.

"Come." His wizened face calls to mind a contented cat. "I'll leave the child some bread," he adds, noting how I glance at the slumbering Annie. "Like as no' the lassie will still be sleeping when we've done. Follow me. 'Tis time for a bit of training."

"What training? Sheona said you'd have a lesson for me." I dry my hands and happily leave my drudgery behind.

Donny spares me not a single glance. "Call it what ye will. Come." Tapping the cane, he leads me to the chamber that faces the lane outside.

"Nothing here to get in our way." He faces me. "Ready yourself."

"For what?" The way the man handles the cane, moving it from one hand to the other, fills me with unease.

"Your task is to avoid this." And, without so much as a 'by your leave,' or a 'mind I do not knock your teeth from your head,' the old man lunges at me with the cane.

Shrieking, I leap back, lose my footing, and fall upon my backside. "What are you doing?" I scrabble away from the man until my back strikes against the rough wall and I utter a rather loud and decidedly unladylike "*oof.*"

Donny stops with the end of the cane uncomfortably close to my face. He straightens and sighs. "I thought as much." His lips bend in disgust as he glares at me. "Ye've been cosseted and coddled in that great house until ye turned into a useless, mewling kit. Ye heard Shaw, lass. He's waiting for ye out there." He jerks his head in the direction of the door. "If ye wish to join the guild, learn to fend for yourself. We dinnae have time to tend a wee, twitching rabbit. We need a strong, brave lass who's quick on her feet and won't slow us down."

With a huff, I rise to my feet and dust off my skirts. "What exactly do you expect of me? How is beating me with your wife's cane going to teach me anything?" I fold my arms across my chest and lift my chin.

"Daft as a broomstick, she is." Donny shakes his head as he mutters to himself. "Did I no' tell ye we need a strong lass what's quick on her feet?" And once again, he crouches low and holds out the cane as though he is a soldier wielding the blade at the end of his musket. "Do what ye can to keep clear of this." He lunges again and promptly strikes me in the shoulder. And he lunges yet again before I have found my footing.

"That's not fair!" I squeal and duck, barely avoiding the cane as it swishes over my head. My attempt to flee to the kitchen earns me a sharp smack on my backside.

"Stop!" I whirl and glare at Donny, whose eyes gleam with laughter.

"Ye think Shaw will stop if ye ask?" He waits for my response, holding the cane with both hands at the ready to strike again.

My aching shoulders slump. "No."

"Do ye no' remember those fools outside the bakery?" He shifts the cane once more from hand to hand. "They had ye on the ground in a trice."

He leaps forward to strike again, but this time, I dart to the side and his cane smacks against the wall. And as I back away, keeping my eye on that damnable walking stick, Donny's words come to me. *My knife.*

I yank the blade from its hiding place but manage to hold onto it for a mere moment before Donny rewards me with a sharp rap on the knuckles and the knife clatters to the floor.

"Good!"

I blink at the man. He praises me? But I dropped the weapon meant for my defense! The man grins, retrieves the knife, and holds it out to me.

"Again."

For the following quarter of an hour, I duck, dodge, and

otherwise seek to avoid having my head bashed in, my stomach struck, or my face battered, all while striving to keep my grip on my knife. Before long, I'm sweating, panting, fuming, and bruised. The old man means to kill me!

But as suddenly as the attack had begun, it ends. Donny leaves the cane upon the low bench and motions me to follow. I tuck my knife inside its hidden pouch, and we return to the kitchen; I with limping, halting footsteps, rubbing a sore shoulder, and Donny with the spryness of a man far younger. Annie sits up as we enter. Her cheeks are flushed with sleep and her limpid eyes regard us with alarm. She scoots aside as Donny pokes at the fire and adds more coal. I hurry to pick her up, realizing too late that she has soiled herself and is soaked.

Without a word, Donny drags the tin tub near the fire and fetches water to heat. Soon 'tis warm enough and I bathe the child. My host leaves the room and returns with a pretty, wee beribboned night dress he has magically produced from the off-limits upper floor of his house.

"Did that belong to your own child?" I work the dress over Annie's head and tie the strings in the back. The garment is yellowed with age, but lovely.

"Aye." Donny takes a cracked pitcher from the cupboard, warms the liquid inside by plunging the glowing end of the fire iron into it, and pours me some warm ale. I sip gratefully while the man coaxes Annie to his side with the offer of bread spread with honey. He removes a wee wooden cup from the cupboard and gives Annie her own portion of watered-down ale.

I finish my drink and ask for more, which I am promptly given.

"Well done, lass." The old man slurps his own drink while his icy blue eyes regard me over the rim of his cup. "That is, ye did well enough for now, though ye must learn to move faster. Ye must be wary the moment ye set foot outside."

The ale nearly chokes me. If I am in danger of such violence, how will I make it out of Stewart's Close?

Donny plunks his cup on the table and wipes his mouth with his arm.

"Come. Time to get back to work."

I groan but do as I'm told. Annie picks up her doll and her light footfalls pit pat along after us into the front chamber. Donny helps the lass hop onto the bench.

"Take out your knife and be quick about it," he orders me.

When I remove the blade from its pouch, Donny takes it from me.

"Hold it thus." And he shows me how to wield my knife properly. He places his gnarled hands over mine and moves my fingers into position. After that, he demonstrates different places where I might strike an opponent to have the greatest effect: the softness of the body below the ribs, the neck, the face, the eyes. I gulp.

"This is only if ye find yourself in a bind as ye did the other day at the bakery." Donny steps back and regards me with a wide grin. "I say keep your distance from anyone ye might encounter outside. Now, try again. Show me how ye'd strike someone in the pudding-house."

At my confused expression Donny laughs and pats his middle. "Stomach, ye silly lass."

For the first time this day, my lips curve into a smile and tremble with a laugh I can barely suppress as I feign the act of plunging a knife into someone's innards. The proper Mrs. Harris would never recover from the shock of seeing me learn how to slash at someone with a knife, as though I truly am a cut-purse looking to rob a gentleman of his money. Nor would she approve of such familiar, coarse speech. Grandfather would roar out such a great laugh. At that thought, my amusement withers. Where *is* the man? He must be searching for me by now. I'd spoken his name often enough. Has word not spread?

"Hold the blade as though ye mean to use it." Donny's voice wrenches my attention back to the room where we train. "'Tis no matter if ye have great skill or no. Just keep your blade sharpened with the stone I keep on the mantel, and when ye go out, keep that knife at the ready. For now, more practice. Try to stop me from knocking it from your hand."

I cannot. My wrists and forearms ache from the blows Donny rains upon them and my fingers are numb from clenching too tightly to the handle of my blade.

At last, Donny decides I've had enough. I slump with relief onto the bench beside Annie.

"Fine soldier ye'd make, lass." He laughs. "But 'twas your first day, after all."

Sighing, I swipe at my damp forehead. *Och,* but my bones ache.

"Do I train for a post in the King's regiment?" I struggle to catch my breath. "Women are not soldiers, Donny!"

"A woman should learn to fight, same as a man." Donny says. His eyes narrow. "Women here in town understand that. Even my old Sheona could teach a thing or two to that fool what guards our gate, if given half a chance."

I surprise myself by giggling. "I believe that. She got the better of Shaw when he came here. Even though she is so bent she's like a bit of parchment folded in two."

Donny's gummy smile gapes wide and he joins in the laughter. At that moment, a bell chimes a single time. My eyebrows raise. I had not noticed bells ringing before this.

"I hear a bell, but where is the kirk?" I pour myself another cup of ale from the pitcher Donny had placed beside Annie on the bench. "That small chapel down the lane is long empty."

"Not so empty as ye might believe." Donny nods toward the door. "That bell's our signal. I've one more task for ye this day, Poisoner. Think of it as another bit of training."

"Can I not first have something to eat?" I clutch my middle. Will I never lose this feeling of gnawing emptiness?

Donny ignores my query. "Go to the old kirk. The south door will be open. The one who sounded the bell is waiting."

"Whatever for?" My insides grow cold. After my so-called

"training," my confidence in my ability to fend for myself has plunged to the ground. I dig into my purse and wrap my fingers around the handle of my knife. "What about Shaw, or the others who said they'd be watching?"

"They been doing that since ye got here." Donny leans forward and lights a taper in the flame of the oil lamp upon the table. He touches the glowing taper to the bowl of his pipe and smoke drifts up in lazy spirals toward the ceiling.

"Then why make me leave on my own?" I rise to my feet. "First you beat me, then you send me out there to be accosted by ruffians who want to lock me up, or worse?"

"My friends were to sound the bell when Shaw wasn't about. No sign of a watchman, neither. Them's the ones to worry over. No one else'll bother with ye. They're too busy scrounging for scraps to pay ye any mind, but ye'd best hurry. Go and do whatever task you're given." He motions toward the door.

Annie leaps to her feet and clings to my legs.

With gentle hands, Donny detaches Annie's thin arms from about me. "There, now, child, don't fret. Your Kenna will be back in a wink. Come, Sheona has left a cake for ye."

At those words, Annie's face lights with delight and she allows Donny to lead her to the kitchen. I stare at her tiny, retreating form. How easily she abandons me for a sweet!

"Off with ye!" Donny calls.

I stomp my feet and slam the door behind me. It is childish of me, of course. My knife is in my hand before I leave the shadowed doorway.

Outside, the afternoon sun paints all with a falsely cheerful hue. I must blink and allow my eyes time to adjust from the dim light of Donny and Sheona's home. Harried women visit shops in the hope of wrangling some of the fast-dwindling supplies, and here and there small knots of people mutter in hushed tones. Servants sweep steps or lug heavy buckets filled with water, and a few weary souls are emptying chamber pots from windows, gazing about with a dejected, listless air.

Most turn their heads away as I draw near. At least no one seeks to accost me. Then a man hurries across the lane, heading in my direction. My hands fumble, and I drop my knife. Fool! Yet as I kneel and scrabble to find it, the man passes by with nary a look.

Once I've retrieved my weapon, I rise and struggle to ease my breathing. A stifled cry comes from nearby. I peer into a dark space between a shuttered tavern and a neighboring tall house. The man who'd passed me by has his arms wrapped around a young woman. Close to my stature, she cannot be all that much older than my own fifteen years.

I stare for a moment. Does she require my assistance? The man is broad of shoulder with thick muscles. I am a young lass who has just received "training" that so far taught her no more than how to receive stinging blows and darkening bruises. He will kick me aside like a stray pup, yet I wish to help. I creep nearer, grateful that my rag-bound feet make no sound on the cobbles. A small lad darts out from the shadows beyond the couple, and instead of shooing him away, the man scoops the child into his arms.

What is the meaning of this? The woman murmurs something I cannot hear, and the man responds, his face grave, his shoulders bowed with care. He shakes his head. The woman's face crumples, and she weeps.

I hurry away, relieved that the woman does not require aid but grieved at the same time. I know too well I am not the only person trapped on this cursed narrow lane. Like as not, the man was out searching for food, and found none. Or perhaps learned that what goods remain are now at a price well beyond what he can offer.

My head whirls as I pick my way through refuse and head for the kirk. What will happen to this family, to all of us, if the town council does not soon open Stewart's Close once again to the outside world? A heaviness settles inside me. Oliver's cruelty knows no limits.

The wee kirk waits ahead at a bend in the lane, silent and dark. I quicken my pace with a new determination to complete whatever task is set for me. 'Tis a bit of luck Donny and Sheona have elected to send me outside, for I've already wasted too much time slaving for them simply to earn a bit of bread.

Pressing my lips together, I cross the lane and dart into the shadows of the forlorn kirk. Switching my knife from hand to hand, I keep a wary eye upon any soul who passes me. Whatever thievery I must do, I shall do it, but only until I find my way out of the city.

CHAPTER
14

The south door of the silent place is unlocked, as Donny promised. It groans as I swing it open with my shoulder.

A bird flaps its way across the transept. Light filters in through the oval window above the altar, its beams weakened by layers of filth that cover the once colorful glass. My footsteps echo as I cross the broken flagstones.

"About time ye got here!"

A man nearly as wide as he is tall limps toward me from behind the altar. He carries a lit taper aloft, and in its flickering light, he aims a gap-toothed smile at me. His face is round like the rest of his body. Like me, he wears no shoes, but his feet are torn and bloody. The man leaves a trail of dark smears on the floor as he approaches. I edge back.

"Pay ye no mind to my feet." The man spits upon the floor and continues toward me. "Had to leave my boots behind. *Och*, what a job that was! Left a watch, they did. Had to flee with what I could carry in my hands, running on my bare feet. Rotten business! I cut my poor toes on a sharp stone in the courtyard. But old Sheona'll fix my feet up right quick, and I've sent my lad back for my boots."

"Oh." No other words come to me.

"You're her, ain't ye?" The man lurches from side to side as he shuffles forward, lifting his taper high and squinting at me. When he moves into the patch of light from the window, it makes his thick thatch of white hair glow. He's a fallen, portly angel with a ghostly halo.

"Ain't ye that murderess what took up with old Donny? He told me ye'd be here to help, and I'm short-handed."

"No."

At my word, the man's eyebrows meet in the middle, and I realize my mistake. I square my shoulders and draw closer.

"I mean, yes, sir, I'm here to help." I strive to keep my voice steady. "But I am no murderess."

The annoyance clears from the man's face. "Good. Follow me."

Do his words mean he is glad I'm no killer, or that he's pleased to have my assistance? It does not matter, but nonetheless, I clench my hands into fists and grit my teeth as I follow him, taking care to step around the dark footprints he leaves on the tiles. Hardly a week ago, I would have responded to such an accusation with a great many sharp words. But now, an all-too-familiar tightness in my chest renders it difficult to draw breath. I have ceased to be surprised that all who live on the close know the accusations against me. What cuts me deeply is that they so easily believe I murdered my own sister.

My guide opens a narrow door, hidden by planks placed carelessly against the wall. We descend winding stairs to a crypt below the kirk, guided only by the tiny glow of the man's taper. The rotund man before me barely fits inside the confining stairwell. He breathes heavily as he shoves his body through the cramped space.

What on earth are we doing here? I am half mad to go along with this! My breath catches in my throat as we emerge into a wide and empty space well-lit by iron lanterns that hang from rings affixed to the walls. The stone floor is covered with a layer of dust and speckled with many footprints. The walls are damp and lined with deep niches. A handful are sealed with names carved into the stone. Others gape open. I take in a breath and utter a silent, mirthless laugh. One must expect to find tombs below a kirk.

A muted scratching comes from within an unsealed niche that yawns open at my back. I edge away from it while every childish nightmare I've ever had floods my mind. What could make noise inside a tomb?

"Rats."

I yelp and whirl, gaping blankly at the man.

He grins as he drips wax onto a spot inside one of the open tombs and fixes his taper in place. "Rats down here. We need a cat."

"Oh." My heart still hammers while my face grows hot. Of course. Vermin made that sound.

"Come on." My guide beckons me to follow.

We leave the wide, echoing chamber and head down a passageway lit by more hanging lanterns with flickering candles inside. The long corridor is lined with tiny rooms on either side. The rooms at first appear empty, but after we've passed several, my eyes adjust. Bulky shadows tell of objects piled high within.

"Here we are." The man points to one of the chambers and my jaw drops in amazement. The tiny space is crammed with barrels. In the chill air hangs the faint, earthy odor of potatoes. Potatoes, here? But everyone complains about the dwindling supply of food within the close!

"I was pleased when Donny said he'd send someone to help me load these. They're too heavy for one man." He slaps one of the barrels. "*Och*, my manners! I'm Munro."

"Kenna." I help the man turn a barrel on its side and roll it out of the storage room.

"So that's your name." The man grunts as he shoves the heavy barrel before him. "Well, lass, I ken ye'll understand that I aim to keep a close eye on ye."

I bite my lip to keep from muttering an oath. Such nerve! While I seethe and curse under my breath, Munro and I roll the barrel along the passageway and onto a strange contraption: a wooden platform one can raise by employing a system of thick ropes and pulleys. I squint into the blackness of the area above the platform.

"Where does this lead, sir?"

"To the lane above."

"Outside the close?" My heart does a jig.

"Naw."

My shoulders droop and Munro laughs at my expression. "To be sure, if it led outside, we'd no' still be locked this side of our gate, now would we? Dinnae look at me like that, like ye be at your granny's funeral." He heaves another barrel to the floor.

This time, I mutter aloud a few phrases that would have raised Grandfather's eyebrows, earning me a laugh from my round companion. I help him until the platform is loaded with three large barrels and several heavy bags.

"What is all of this?" I collapse with a sigh against one wall.

"Oh, potatoes, meal, some turnips, and other such truck. And some ale."

My eyes grow wide.

Munro pries the lid from one of the barrels and fishes out a fist-sized onion. "Ah, this is a fine one! Take it to Sheona and tell 'er to add a bit of flavor to her soup. Last time she fed me, I swore I was eating naught but boiled water with a few bits of cabbage floating in it." He offers me the onion, and I cradle it in my hands with near-reverence, marveling at its pearly paper-like surface.

"So much food!"

I approach the barrels as though drawn by an invisible thread. They're full of bounty, with so many living above who grow hungrier by the day.

"Where is this going? Who gets it?" I tuck the onion inside my leather pouch.

"This order be for Lochlan, the owner of the shop near the top of the lane." Munro spits on the floor. "Now help me with this wheel. My feet are like to fall off if I dinnae get myself to the herbwife soon."

"Wherever did this all come from?" I help Munro rotate the handle of a large wooden wheel to the side of the platform. With an alarming creak, the platform rises from the floor.

"From the larders of them what left their houses. There were a few families, mind ye, who fled right after the bailey declared the quarantine." The man squints at me in the flickering light, and I catch a gleam of humor in their dark depths. "That bailey set a guard and sent in a watch, that he did, but some with enough coin bought their way out."

My mouth gapes wide. "That means I may leave if I can pay the man who guards the gate?"

"He'll take ye by the hair and drag ye before the bailey." Munro cuts my words off with a sharp wave. "You're the reason that gate is shut. Keep turning that handle, lass."

A bolt of anger pierces me. "I thought your guild only stole from the dead. What will those people say when they come back?"

Munro's voice is matter-of-fact. "Took their chances, they did, when they left us here to rot. Let them call the bailey when they creep back and find their larders empty." He chuckles. "Donny's in the right, I admit to it. We mainly take goods from the dead, like that old fellow living above the fishmonger's shop. Introduced himself to St. Peter yesterday morn. Clothing he left, and a fine sideboard, and who knows what else. To be sure, I'm going back there, watchman or no."

I remain silent for a while, my thoughts churning, all dark. My arms burn from turning the crank that moves the blasted wheel and the rope creaks and strains as the platform inches its way upward. When I am certain my aching arms will fall off, Munro grunts at me, which is apparently his signal to stop, for he manipulates the ropes in some way so that the platform remains where it is.

"How much food is down here?" I rub my sore arms.

"Not all that much." Munro squints at me. "But there's enough, I wager, to keep our little guild fed and clothed for the winter." He clears his throat and spits again.

"All winter?" My voice is faint. "Yet you say 'tis not that much."

"Aye," Munro replies. He shoots me a glance. "This may be the last order we'll fill, lest the bailey ends the quarantine, and his vermin scurry off and leave our gate open. We cannae feed everyone else and ourselves. Else we'd starve along with the rest of 'em."

I rub my temples to fight a growing headache.

"Does everyone living on Stewart's Close know they may buy food from your guild?"

Munro pauses and leans his large bulk against the weeping wall. "Not all, no. We do fine business with those who have the means to pay us. Course, not all have coin to pay, but we accept many forms of payment, like a trade in goods or services. Got a fine pig a few months back for a lovely carved bedstead."

I snort and cross my arms. Of what import is carved furniture or swine? There is food available, a wealth of it in these vaults, and yet my sister and I, and many others, brought bread each week to feed those who were hungry! With this pile of food beneath their feet?

"Sir, many people here have great need of food and do not know where to find it. 'Tis not right!" My voice is loud, echoing in the dark tunnel.

Munro's placid expression does not alter at my words. "We must make a living, now, eh? Only those who can pay a fair price learn o' what we have in these vaults, though they must no' know exactly where we keep our truck. And we make certain they can be trusted before we let them in on our secret."

"But—"

"Silence." Munro holds a finger to his lips. "I must listen for the signal."

At that moment, a whistle sounds from somewhere far above.

"There, now." Munro's lips curve into a placid grin. "Done. Off we go."

"Sir, I—"

"Come." The man leads the way to the stairs, moving faster than I would have expected given his injured feet. As we ascend the narrow, winding steps, Munro slows enough that I catch up and speak again. I cannot let the matter drop, for the image of the young weeping woman haunts me.

"Mothers have no food for their children. Is it not right to share with them?" I puff from the exertion of climbing. "The guild has more than enough below."

Munro stops and laboriously turns himself around until he faces me. 'Tis no easy task in the narrow stairwell, and his filthy shirt scrapes and snags against the walls. He leans down until his sweaty, red face is inches from mine. His moon of a face, ghastly in the wan light of his taper, is no longer kind in any way.

"I'll warn ye, lass, only once." He speaks through gritted teeth. "Tell no one o' this place, or ye'll find yourself with nary a friend among us. We'll call the bailey or his watchman to come take ye. That we will."

The man twists his body once more, heaves himself up the remaining stairs and squeezes out the narrow door. His footsteps shuffle away across the transept. My knees buckle and I collapse on the steps, burning with rage and unable to stop the hot tears from coursing down my cheeks.

What a cruel trap this is! I am at the mercy of thieves whose hearts are locked tighter than the unyielding gate at the head of the close. How will I ever escape this place? And why has Grandfather not come for me?

The darkness wraps itself about me and my sobs die away to shuddering breaths. Finally spent, I feel my way through the thick blackness of the stairwell and return to the storerooms. There, I fill the stained apron Sheona lent me with potatoes, turnips, and onions. I'm careful to take only one or two from each barrel so that a thief who might glance within will notice nothing missing. Then I climb to the kirk above and ease my way out into the street.

I shrink away from each man who passes. Shaw might be about, or perhaps the bailey's watchman is already making his rounds, even before night falls. I knock at the first door I find in the narrow space between the tavern and tall house. The door creaks open until the dark eyes of the young wife I'd seen earlier peer out, wide with fear.

"Here." I hold out a few potatoes. "For your child."

She slams the door in my face. Startled, I jump, and the potatoes fall from my hands.

"Starve, then, you cow!" With a weary sigh, I sink to my knees to gather the scattered vegetables, and an onion spills from my apron.

"God's nightgown! These people…" I mutter and curse as I scrabble for the fallen onion. My fingers have just curled around it when the door creeks open and pale hands snatch it from my grasp, then seize the potatoes as well. The woman slams the door once more.

"Do not believe what you hear," I tell the scarred wood before my face. My cheeks burn and my chest is tight. 'Tis such a jest that I, a mere lass of fifteen, with scrawny knees and mouse-brown hair that never obeys the comb, am a fearsome being so shunned and avoided.

I hurry back to my temporary lodgings with the remaining vegetables tucked inside my apron, my knife in my fist and my thoughts a dark swirl. I square my shoulders and meet all who pass me by with a fierce gaze. People edge away from me at the sight of my blade. It makes me smile. Donny and Sheona have given me shelter and food, but they are part of a group of unlawful thieves who only serve themselves. Well, I shall do the same. I shall only do that which serves me in some way.

Rain patters upon my head as I pick my way across the filthy track and climb the doorstep. Tucking my knife inside my pouch, I make a vow. I'll obey the thieving guild's orders out of necessity for now. But my obedience *and* my silence will only last until I find a means of escape. Donny, his wife, and their precious "guild" can stay here and rot.

That is, until I tell Grandfather all about them. With a sour smile, I open the door and duck inside.

CHAPTER
15

I suffer a momentary panic once inside Donny and Sheona's home, in the tiny front chamber that faces the lane. How can I appear with an apronful of stolen vegetables? The thieves will toss me onto the lane on my backside.

Donny calls from somewhere in the house and I jump.

"Back, are ye?"

Searching in desperation, my eyes fall upon the cold ashes of the unused grate. This chilly chamber never seems to benefit from a lovely fire. 'Tis just what I require. As swiftly and silently as possible, I tuck the vegetables inside and cover them with ashes. I wipe my sooty hands on the apron before I answer the man's rather obvious statement.

"Yes, I'm back, Donny."

Annie darts to me and clings to my skirts the moment I enter the kitchen. I pick her up and plant a kiss upon her plaited hair and she giggles.

"Eat." Donny sits in the corner, smoking his pipe. He motions to the table, and I sit down to an evening meal of dried fish cooked into a barely palatable stew.

Annie plays in the corner with her doll, which now has a new, clean bit of woolen cloth for its blanket. I smile at her and a bit of the tension in my neck and shoulders eases away. Warmth, a full belly, and a gentle hand have cleared the haunted wariness from the child's eyes. Thieves or no, Donny and Sheona have done a great kindness in taking Annie into their home.

Donny rises the moment I take my last mouthful and leave my wooden bowl and spoon in the wash pan at the end of the table.

"Training." After that curt announcement, he marches to the front chamber. With a sigh, I follow, and Annie toddles behind me. She plays upon the floor beneath the bench while I am once more made to suffer another bout of this so-called training. I am wont to glance repeatedly at the ashes in the grate until I fear Donny will inquire as to the reason for my interest in the cold fireplace.

"Where is Sheona?" I asked. Donny swings his cane at my head, causing me to squeal and duck.

"Gone to treat a child grown ill." He strikes me in the shoulder.

"That hurt!" I back away, rubbing the already sore shoulder.

"Move faster."

After a bit, I am better able to dodge the blows Donny aims at me, yet still unable to avoid dropping the knife if he strikes my knuckles with his cane or lands a good, sharp rap on my wrist.

"Ye cannae lose that blade, or the battle is lost. That knife is your best protection." He pauses for a moment while his crinkled brow crumples even more and he seems lost in thought. Then his face flushes with pleasure and he grins widely.

"Ye must learn to throw the knife. Come."

"I...*what*?"

Donny does not answer. He takes Annie's hand and leads us to the end of the "forbidden" corridor. We enter a narrow doorway and clomp down to a cramped storeroom below. There, slabs of wood nailed together in a sloppy fashion lean against one wall. This room, not surprisingly, houses a few barrels and fat cloth bags. A cloth-wrapped ham even hangs from a hook in the ceiling.

A smile hovers upon my lips as I sniff appreciatively and my mouth waters at the meaty, salty scent. Wooden shelves cover one wall, laden with crocks and jars of assorted sizes. One pitted container oozes fat, clear droplets from cracks that mar its surface.

The smell of vinegar tickles my nose. I've never enjoyed the scent of pickles until now. I must tiptoe back here for a secret repast when my hosts are abed.

Donny settles Annie against the opposite wall. He fishes bits of dried apple from one of the sacks upon a low shelf and proffers them to the child. She snatches the food with her usual swiftness, cramming the apple pieces into her mouth until her thin cheeks puff out like a squirrel's.

The man whisks the knife from my hand and throws the blade. It sticks squarely in the center of the ham dangling from its hook. I gape as the haunch swings back and forth.

"Here." Donny yanks the knife from the ham. "Hold this by the handle." He points me toward the boards nailed together. "Aim for the wood. Now, throw."

My eyes travel from the man to the boards and back to the man once more. "How?"

"Just throw it, lass."

Biting my lip, I raise my arm and throw the knife. It flies in a low arc, strikes flat against the boards and clatters to the floor. Annie giggles. Donny raises one eyebrow.

"I thought as much. Have ye never thrown a stone at a stray dog?" he asks.

"No."

"Or at a fox creeping in to steal the chickens?"

"Of course, not." I straighten my shoulders. "I was raised to be a lady. I did not spend my time with the servants who cared for our animals."

Donny snorts as he bends to retrieve the knife and hands it to me. "Do it again. This time dinnae grip that handle so tight. Move your arm with a quick swish and release the handle. Like this." He demonstrates the action with his arm a few times before releasing his hold on the knife. It flies and lands, embedded in the scarred wood.

I throw the blade over and over, doing my best to mimic Donny's movements. Alas, my efforts earn me nothing but a giggle from Annie each time I miss, which occurs at every single attempt. I scowl and grunt in an unladylike manner as I try again and again. Such a foolish endeavor! I would never throw my knife at anyone. I dab at the sweat on my forehead and a sour grin curves my lips. No, 'tis not true. I'd dearly love to throw this blade in Oliver's direction, if only to make him flinch in fear.

A sudden pang fills my heart. What would Cinaed say to all this? I gaze in disbelief at the sharpened metal in my hand. What a wicked lass I have become. I live with thieves and receive training in weaponry! What would Grandfather say? And how will he ever find me if I do not escape?

With a scowl, I throw the knife with all the energy I can muster. It misses the boards by a wide margin and clatters to the floor. I would utter my favorite oath but have not the heart. Donny reads the chagrin painted on my face.

"Time for the child to be abed," he announces. 'Tis true, for her eyelids droop. I pick her up and trudge back up the stairs.

For the first time, as I arrange a pallet for her on the floor near the glowing embers of the kitchen fire, I notice Annie wears a different gown. Of plain design, 'tis a lovely, becoming shade of dark blue. The fabric is thick, woven with a pattern of embroidered leaves. Grandfather's dressmaker himself might have used such fabric to stitch gowns for Cinaed or me. Dismay strikes me and I snort. 'Twas stolen, no doubt.

I help Annie remove the clothing and place it over a chair. Beneath her shift she is clad in a cloth nappy pinned about her waist. Glad I am of it, for I have no wish to wake again and find the child has soaked herself once more. I wrap her tight in the rough, yet warm blankets Donny has provided.

"Where did this gown come from?" I whisper as Donny enters the kitchen.

"Vaults."

'Tis as I'd feared. A small sigh escapes me.

"Made that myself, I did." Donny gestures to the wee gown upon the chair.

"You?" I squint at the man. "Truly?"

"Aye. Apprenticed to a tailor, I was." Pride gleams from his eyes, though he feigns disinterest by casually studying his pipe. "Found a bolt of that fine stuff after old Kerr, the tailor on Cockburn Street, died. Sheona and I thought we'd use some of it now, as the wee one is come to stay here." He glances at Annie, curled like a pup on her pallet with a tiny smile on her sleeping face.

Donny is a cipher that I cannot work out, but I find myself warming to this odd man. During my brief stay here, he has more than once revealed a gentler nature beneath his gruff exterior. He and Sheona will give Annie a permanent home. How could they not? When I leave, as leave I must, the child won't starve, and she'll have someone to care for her.

I shake my head as I wrap myself in my blanket. Annie will also have someone who will teach her to steal for a living. *Och,* but 'tis a strange thought. Can I leave her to that fate?

"Did you truly stitch that lovely dress yourself?"

"Ye dinnae believe me?" Donny chuckles. "My Ma made certain all her lads learned how to use a needle; that she did. 'Twas why I first apprenticed to a tailor. Thought it a right fine way to earn my keep in the world until I set my heart on soldiering. Served me well when I joined the regiment. Many of our lads needed my assistance, whether to mend torn breeches or stitch up torn flesh."

"Well, 'tis a fine gown indeed, Donny. And truly kind of you."

Donny nods at my words, a pleased expression crinkling his face. His leathery skin glows in the firelight. "Now, get some rest. A few hours at least. I shall call ye when it's time."

"For what?" I snuggle next to Annie's warm body.

"For work. Munro wants to return to his job. I'm sending ye to help the man and his son, Rob."

I sit upright.

"Munro?" My mouth is dry. I am not anxious to meet with him again so soon. Or ever, to be truthful.

"Sheona bandaged his feet this afternoon before ye came back." Donny leans against one wall, ever smoking his pungent pipe. "I promised him your assistance." He regards me with a steady gaze, his eyes gleaming from beneath the heavy, papery lids.

I stare back. Did Munro tell Donny what I'd said? A moment passes. Two. I swallow. Donny's eyes spark at me.

"To bed." The old man rises and heads upstairs.

Rest evades me, so I make plans while Annie breathes steadily beside me and the embers crackle. The kitchen still smells of fish stew and it makes me crinkle my nose. Gazing into the darkness, my thoughts race. I am keen to know where the "job" is tonight. Will the man's home perhaps consist of rooms on the upper floor of a tall house? Would I be able to find my way to the roof? I've not forgotten the idea of a rooftop leap that came to me at the sight of the hooded man peering at me from high above. God willing, the tall houses on Stewart's Close may provide my means of escape. And after today's doings, I am more than ready to leave this wretched city behind.

CHAPTER
16

I doze on and off, wakeful with dread of what lies ahead, and mindful of the need to arise all too soon. At some uncanny hour in the depths of the night, someone stirs upstairs. I rise and dress hurriedly, as the time to leave must be near.

"Good," Donny whispers when he creeps into the kitchen. "You're up."

He hands me a cloth to tie over my face. It smells of spices and I recoil. "Do we go to a house where there is sickness?"

"Naw." Donny grins at me. "Only to a house where a man died of living far too many years. His carcass is gone, too. There was no carting him away thanks to that locked gate. His neighbors buried him in his wee back garden." The man chuckles. "The cloth is to hide your face. Sheona added the herbs to make certain ye'll no' catch ill in the night air."

"Sheona?" I tie the kerchief about my face. "I did not hear her come in."

Donny shrugs. "She's an uncommon woman, that one. She can move silent as a cat creeping after a mouse."

"Oh." I must have been asleep when the woman came in. I glance with regret at my warm spot beside Annie, who sleeps blissfully on.

Munro taps at the front entrance only moments after I settle myself onto the bench in the front chamber. Donny motions me away, so I sigh, open the door, and creep out into the night.

The wide man greets me curtly and we creep up the lane. We

carry no lantern, and my bumbling feet earn me a hissing "hush." We pass the house where a man had caught my ankle from a low window. Instinctively, I move towards the center of the cobbled lane.

"Get back here, lass," Munro hisses. "Cling to the walls."

Down we hurry, squeezing through a shoulder-wide space between buildings, crossing a tiny courtyard, and ascending rough steps. I stumble more than once. How can anyone see aught? 'Tis black as the Earl of Hell's waistcoat!

Munro stops short. I run into his solid body, uttering a loud yelp.

"Quiet, fool!" he whispers. "The watchman is about."

My wide eyes scan the surrounding blackness, but of course, I find nothing. And no other sound besides Munro's wheezing breath reaches my ears.

We stop before a high house that reaches into the night sky. A tiny, flickering light glows from a paper-covered window, blessedly lighting our surroundings enough that I can see Murnro's face. Of a sudden, a hand grabs my waist and pulls me into a strange, stumbling jig for a moment or two. Too late, I scrabble for my blade. Where is it? Did I drop it?

"Stop!" I splutter. "Stop or I'll stick you with my knife!" But where is it? My fumbling hands cannot find it within the folds of my skirts.

"Ye dinnae wish to dance with me, milady?" a laughing voice whispers in my ear. The hands release me, and I stumble back, my fingers finally closing on the handle of my weapon.

"Rob, leave her be." Munro makes a horrible snorting noise and spits onto the ground.

"*Och*, and now the lass has learned my name." My dance partner laughs. "And what do I call her?"

I glare at the lad, obviously Munro's son. He is much taller than his father. Dark hair hangs in his eyes and the rest of his face remains hidden, for he, too, has covered his mouth and nose with a cloth.

"My name is Kenna." Though I strive to speak with grave dignity, my trembling voice betrays me. I am gasping for air after the sudden, twirling jig and the jolt of fright at thinking myself in danger. I must admit that my breath catches for yet another reason. Heat rises to my cheeks, and I am glad of the veiling darkness and the cloth covering my features.

I turn aside to tuck my knife back inside its pouch. I was not in peril. I had simply experienced my first dance with a lad. Never before have I felt a man's arm about my waist. My heart flutters as I study the lad's tall form. Cinaed wanted me to visit neighbors and perhaps even attend a ball or a party, but Oliver did not think his awkward and wayward "burden" was ready for presentation to the world outside the walls of her home. After tonight, I must allow that he was probably right.

"Come." Munro jerks his head. "This way."

I follow the sound of Rob's light tread as he hurries to the side of the house. Together, we crouch behind a pile of rubble and wait until Munro gives the signal.

After the sound of a low whistle, Rob touches my shoulder and whispers: "All clear. Follow me, Poisoner."

My jaw drops. He called me Poisoner? How dare he? My gallant dance partner is a ruffian and a thief, and a member of a scheming guild that does not share with its own neighbors!

"Do not ever call me that again or you shall regret it," I hiss as we enter the house through a narrow door with a broken lock.

Before Rob can answer, a bright light appears. Startled and momentarily blinded, I back away until I strike against the wall.

"Steady on, lass." Munro waves a lantern this way and that, revealing a richly furnished chamber. "'Tis only my light. Rob, you and the lass go to the man's bedchamber and find his clothing." He lights a taper from the flame of the lantern's candle and hands it to Rob. "Be quick."

Mutely, I follow Rob, who throws me a single narrowed glance before we enter a short corridor. His brows meet in the middle. I straighten my shoulders. If he is angry, it does not matter to me. The lad should learn his manners.

The dead man's chamber reeks. Even with the scented cloth tied over my mouth and nose, the fetid odor reaches me. How long had his body lain here? My stomach complains and grows sick and my legs grow weak.

"*Och*, 'tis a wretched place, to be sure." Rob presses his kerchief tightly over his nose. "Search that chest over there, Kenna."

Even as I make my way to the wooden chest in the corner, my spirits lift a mite. He called me by my name. Though the lad has not apologized, I am a trifle mollified. 'Tis far more pleasant to hear my Christian name than that cursed nickname.

I wrench the brass handles, and the chest creaks open. Inside lies an assortment of clothing: a thick cloak, leather boots, breeches, and two linen shirts. I enfold all within the cloak. At the bottom of the chest is a tiny pistol. It fits into the palm of my hand. I study it by the light of the small taper Rob placed on a table. 'Tis no firearm, 'tis a tiny glass jar shaped like one. A cork plugs the end, and an inch of liquid remains inside.

"What'd ye find?" Rob steps closer. I try to ignore the jolt I feel in my stomach as he brushes against my shoulder.

"I'm not sure."

"Ah, now that's a prize." Rob takes the glass pistol from my palm. "A prize fit for a lass who knows her potions. Isn't that right, Kenna?" He gazes frankly at me as he speaks. Above the concealing cloth on his face, his dark eyes glitter in the light of the taper. He waits for my response. What does he expect me to say? Does he wish me to admit that I know my "potions?" My *poisons?*

"How dare you say such a thing? You are all alike." My voice trembles again, this time with rage. "You and your father and Donny and all the cursed thieves of the guild." I snatch the glass pistol from Rob's hand and throw it against the wall. It does not shatter, but it falls to the floor with a pathetic clink.

With a scoff, Rob bends to retrieve the phial and pockets it. "Keep the head, Ladyship! Not too good to join our business, but we cannae mention your past life. Is that it?"

Without thought, I fly to stand before Rob, eye to eye, our noses nearly touching.

"I. Did. Not. Kill. My. Sister." I hiss out the words from between clenched teeth. The cloth against my face muffles my words somewhat, but my meaning cannot be misread. I am breathless, shaking, glaring. Rob's eyes widen for a moment before they narrow to slivers. Then his brow lifts, and he laughs and pulls the kerchief away from his face.

Blinking, I step back. His face, thin and sharp-angled, is pleasing. His teeth are even and white, his skin unmarred by pockmarks, like some of the lads who work in Grandfather's stables.

"To be sure, most of us didnae believe the story of such a young lass being a murderess. 'Twas only word spread by the bailey and his watchman."

I force my fingers to uncurl from the handle and drag my gaze away from the lad's face. Cinaed always told me not to stare. To keep my hands otherwise occupied, I retrieve the bundle of clothing and hold it in my arms.

"Then why do you all call me 'Poisoner?'"

Rob ties the kerchief around his face and shrugs. "'Tis what everyone calls ye. I'd no' heard your real name until now." He lifts a pair of silver candlesticks from a side table, takes the taper in his hand, and motions for me to follow. "I meant no harm. I'll no' call ye that again."

Flushed, I follow him through the house. I am pleased, but no words will come to me. We find Munro waiting near the door with a pile of pilfered goods on the floor at his feet.

"Good bottle of whiskey, here." He surveys his treasures with a wide grin of satisfaction. "I'll see if all's clear. Pack our things." The man exits through the narrow doorway, no easy task given his girth.

With weary movements, I help Rob tie everything into two large bundles. Then he clears his throat, and I glance at him. His eyes are unreadable in the dim light of the lantern Munro left us, as its soft glow is close to snuffing out.

"The bailey's sent a watchman to keep us safe at night. Ye've heard of that, I'll wager."

Shards of ice seem to shoot through my veins. I jerk my head in a nod. "Of course. I heard his footsteps myself as he walked up and down the lane while I hid and tried to sleep. I understand he's here to keep everyone in their beds."

Rob regards me with open curiosity in his dark eyes.

"Aye." He rifles through one of the bundles, removes a bottle of wine, uncorks it, and takes a swig. With eyebrows raised, he holds the bottle out to me. I shake my head.

With a shrug, Rob takes another drink and recorks the bottle. "We're no' even allowed to step onto our own lane after nightfall. I've never heard of folk forced to remain inside their houses, nor of locals locked behind the gate of their own close. That gate was to keep us safe at night. Not keep us from leaving Stewart's Close."

"How does the gate keep you safe?"

Rob laughs. I like the way his eyes curve as he does so and how they crinkle at the corners. I drop my gaze for fear he will somehow read my thoughts.

"Keeps out the robbers," he says with a laugh.

Even though I am trapped in the city, accused of murdering someone most dear to me, and happen to be in the act of robbing a house in the middle of the night, I cannot help laughing myself. But my humor dies within a moment.

"That watchman is here to protect everyone from me." I blink away sudden tears and clear my throat.

Rob nods. "Aye. And I was most keen on seeing ye. Wanted to know for myself if ye seemed the sort of person what would kill her sister."

"And do I?" I am suddenly seized by a strong desire that this young thief thinks no ill of me. "You said yourself most people here do not believe the stories."

Rob grins and picks up the wine bottle once more. "From what

I've seen, you're more likely the sort of lass who twitches at a wee mouse or frets if her fine slippers get wet."

My face flushes and I cannot help sinking lower so my skirts may hide my cold, rag-bound and decidedly slipper-less toes.

"I am not afraid of mice," I mutter.

Rob laughs and offers me the bottle again. Once more, I refuse. A lady does not do such things. Even a lady with ragged skirts and no shoes who is engaged in thievery.

Cocking his head to one side, Rob regards me with amused interest. "The white cloth is still at the gate. I hear quite a few folks from the city all around our wee close fled to the country to escape the sickness."

"But there is no plague!" I throw my hands into the air. "Surely by now all who see me must realize I am not ill. And how can anyone flee if they're locked behind that gate?"

"I was speaking of folks *outside* the gate, Kenna. An outbreak so severe the bailey quarantined an entire city lane will no' remain a secret. But there are some from our own close who left. Those who could buy their way out."

"I've heard as much." This time, when Rob offers me the wine bottle, a sudden daring seizes me and I take it, earning an admiring grin from the lad when I take a drink. "I cannot understand why anyone would choose to stay here if they could simply hand over a few coins to leave Stewart's Close until the 'quarantine' is over, and the 'Poisoner' is gone." I hand the bottle back with a sigh.

"Are ye daft, Kenna?" Rob's eyes widen in disbelief. "It takes more than a few coins to buy your way past the bailey's guards. Most of us here dinnae have the means to leave."

"Even the members of the guild?" I huff. "Certainly, *they* have more than enough to buy their way out of anything."

Rob huffs. "Perhaps. But Da says this quarantine will no' last more than a week, or maybe two. Besides, we have more than enough work to do, even in our own wee close."

My heart springs to life inside me. "Then, after the quarantine ends, the bailey will unlock the gate."

"And nip ye the minute he claps his eyes on ye." Rob shakes his head at me as though I am a particularly thick-skulled pupil, and he the all-knowing tutor. "*Och,* Kenna, Donny said ye had sense in your head, but I can hardly see it."

I have no time for a retort, for Munro returns and gruffly orders us to take up our stolen treasures. As we tiptoe from the silent house into the cold, quiet night, Rob nudges my arm and leans down to whisper, "Ye found yourself here for a reason, Kenna. Someone powerful wanted ye gone and gone ye are now. Ye'll never leave this close again. No' unless you're wrapped in a shroud."

My boiling blood steals away my power of speech until we have left the pillaged house and taken a good many steps.

"We shall see about that, *thief.*"

Rob laughs.

CHAPTER
17

Three more days of drudgery pass with no chance to leave Donny and Sheona's house. My toil lasts from sunrise to late in the evening. I vow in my heart to do something about the long hours our servants must work when I return to Grandfather's house. How weary Lorna must be each night!

There is also no word of any more work with the guild. I tell myself this is of no importance while sweeping, making a poultice of comfrey leaves, or crushing fern leaves and adding them to melted beeswax to make a healing salve, with the herbwife hovering over my shoulder. I strive to feign disinterest in anything to do with the guild and feign great interest in learning weaponry, as I throw the cursed knife that simply will not stick to the wood. Yet my impatience grows with each passing day. If the thieves do not call for me to assist in their thievery, when will I have another chance to leave this house?

My mind often wanders as I work. I would like to see Rob's face in the sunlight. Are his eyes as dark as they appeared in the dead man's home? And are they black like the pieces of coal Sheona burns for baking in the hot fire, or do they glow warm with hints of gold, like the lovely eyes of the lad who used to mind Grandfather's sheep?

After my third long day of labor, I dream of my early years. In this vision of things past, my sister and I are content, laughing and jesting as we spread our laundered blankets and shawls to dry on the gorse bushes surrounding our home. Soaking in the warm sun, they fill with the wonderful scent of the golden flowers. Each night, the cocooning blankets surround me with the clean smells of earth and sun, wind and blossom.

When I awake, the tears on my face are still warm. For a moment, a ghostly scent of gorse lingers and fills me with longing. I stretch and arise quietly so as not to wake Annie. Though fragments of my lovely dream float before my eyes, I push the memories away. This is no time to mourn. Not yet.

After washing my face and hands and making a futile attempt to do something with my hair, I creep to the front chamber and dare to peer out into the graying darkness that comes before dawn. The chill air holds the promise of a cold winter. Pinching my nose, I turn away from the trickle of filth that flows down the lane mere paces away. The stench of waste and dung and rotting refuse is somewhat dampened, thanks to the cool air, but my eyes still water, and I nearly gag.

Bolting the door behind me, I return to Donny's kitchen, grateful to inhale the scents of rosemary, thyme, and sweet marjoram that hang in bunches above the table. The lovely smell of the lavender buds Sheona had me crush earlier lingers about me. This perfumed air reminds me of the old physick garden that lies abandoned behind Grandfather's house. His wife, Lady Ramsay, had tended the garden until she died, soon after her son was born. The wildly overgrown place had become one of my playgrounds, until my time was taken up with lessons in diction, French, and history.

Sheona's large carved chair beckons, and after a furtive glance to make certain no herbwife or old soldier is about, I settle myself upon it. My bones ache with a deep fatigue that makes me yearn for my soft bed at home. The memories of Grandfather's house and all its comforts bring an ache to my heart. Then the memory of my sister, which floods into me each time I think of home, sears pain to my very soul.

Blinking back tears and shaking away the darkness of grief, I rise to my feet. Mourning must wait, and I must use my wits or remain trapped here forever! My thoughts turn to my growling belly, and I kneel before the ashes of the fire. I may not be able to remedy my sadness, for soon my taskmasters will awaken. But I can at least alleviate some of my hunger.

When I lift the lid on the pot, my nose wrinkles at the leftover pong of last night's rather scorched mutton stew. I'll not eat this when I know where the cellar storage room is! And besides, Donny and his wife are abed.

Once in the cellar, I use my knife to carve myself a bite or two, or twenty, of ham that dangles from the ceiling. A handful of dried apples rounds out my meal and thus fortified, I return upstairs, only to sigh at the sight of dirty cups and cutlery on the scarred wood table. My labors await.

I shuffle toward the dreaded tasks but then pause. All is silent. My hosts do not yet stir. Annie breathes deeply and evenly, swathed in her blanket beside the coals. I could flee this house and search for a way beyond the gate! My heart skips within. Whatever chance I have, I must take it now.

Returning to the wee chamber facing the lane, I ease open Donny's front door. Holding my breath, I slip noiselessly outside and close the door with only a faint *click*. To my left, the lane stretches upward; to my right, ever downward. There is no sign of anyone about; no tradesman heading to his labor, no housewife sweeping her steps.

Pausing to decide which direction to take, a thought strikes me, and I laugh. What a ridiculous situation this is! Oliver has imprisoned me within a single lane. Me, and a good number of others unlucky enough to live here. 'Tis something I never would have thought possible.

Yet here I am. How can one find herself trapped in such an absurd way?

Shaking my head, I tuck my cold hands inside the sleeves of my gown. Now that I have been sufficiently fed and warmed and my head is clear, I should be able to find my way out of here. Taking a deep breath of the cold and smelly air, I begin my exploration.

I hum softly to myself for company. Choosing to descend the close, I hurry on, gazing into the spaces between buildings and peering within the shops. The miasma seems to thicken as I go, for the smell intensifies and makes me cough.

A door bursts open a few feet away without warning, and I yelp. The foul odor of animal slops assails my nose. I've arrived at the cowshed, the place where I found shelter my first dreadful night locked inside Stewart's Close.

I cling to the walls as a handful of pigs rush out onto the cobbles, driven by a squat, bald man. A cow and two chickens follow, driven by the tall man I'd know anywhere. He is the man set to guard the gate! Bleating, lowing, and squealing, the creatures pass the spot where I cling to the wall. Thankfully, the weakness of the dawn light does not reveal my presence.

"That's my cow!" a man cries out in a plaintive voice. "And my pigs!" He follows the two men driving away the stolen animals. I do not need to see clearly to recognize the voice of the kindly old man who'd given me milk and shelter my first night here. "Please, ye cannae take them!"

He cries out in pain. Scuffling and grunting sounds emanate from the cluster of dark shapes farther down the lane, while the animals squeal and wail. I reach for my knife but pause. What could I do? I wait too long in my indecision, and momentarily, the dispute ends. The old man moans and limps away while the thieves drive the animals toward the gate.

"They were selling 'em," one of the men says in a loud voice. "Butchering 'em for food. Bailey says we can have what we take."

"I want the biggest cow," the other says.

"I spoke first, ye greedy sot!"

And on they argue until they disappear with their noisy captives.

Tears of rage well in my eyes. Everyone here suffers because Oliver wants me dead. God in heaven, what am I to do? The quarantine wasn't enough, nor was the accusation of murder. Now the bailey takes away dwindling sources of food by confiscating the animals that belong to the residents here. He cannot do that! Such an act is against the law. Wearily, I tuck my knife away. The bailey *is* the law.

A sound cuts through my befuddled thoughts. 'Tis the tread of slow, steady footsteps approaching from somewhere to my right. The air leaves my chest. The watchman. How foolish was I to forget to be wary of him!

The dawning day grows ever lighter. By now, if I leave the doorway, the watchman may see me. I fear my knees will give way under me, but I cannot cower in doorways, a "twitching rabbit" as Donny says, waiting for someone to save me. I am alone. I must act now, but where can I run?

Leaping away from my hiding place, I sprint toward a narrow gap and squeeze through. The watchman shouts and his footsteps quicken in pursuit.

With barely any room on either side, I forge ahead. The dirt beneath my feet rises ever so slightly with each running step. My chest heaves. My pursuer shouts again; the sound echoes and bounces off the weeping masonry that surrounds me.

And then I stop short before a crumbling brick wall. I have run directly into a trap. Ragged, harsh breathing draws closer, and my fear seizes me.

"Dear God, help me escape!" I pray.

"Got ye now, has he?" a high-pitched voice giggles. I follow the sound and spy the flickering light of a wee cruise lamp. A ground level window gapes open at my feet, and a woman smirks at me from within.

"Help me, I beg you!" I drop to my knees. The spectral figure of the watchman is now within sight, closing in on me. He holds a lantern aloft as he swoops toward me like a giant, monstrous creature from the underworld. His face is in shadow beneath the low-drawn hood of his cloak.

"Please." I beg. "I'll pay you to let me inside!"

"Shove off." The woman says.

I seize her hand through the window. She cries out and drops her light.

"I've changed my mind. I'm not paying you now." I force my way through the window and the woman squeals and wrenches her bony wrist from my grasp. I fall into the room and collapse onto the earthen floor. The woman curses me and rushes away. A door slams from somewhere within the house.

There is barely time to leap to my feet and seize the shutters, but I close them just as the watchman reaches the window.

"Open in the name of the King!" he shouts in a deep, grating voice. The voice of a monster. The shutters rattle, but I hold tight to the interior handles. A bolt! Where is the bolt?

"Leave me be!" I shout back. "I'm off the street, now. 'Tis nearly dawn. You cannot arrest me for breaking curfew!"

"Kenna Somerled, open this window!"

He knows who I am? My insides grow cold, my hands are slick with sweat, nearly causing me to lose my grip. While my mind races and I frantically seek a solution, raised voices and swift footfalls draw ever closer. The woman must have given the alarm and the people of this house are on their way to aid the watchman.

'Tis a good thing I have my knife. A good thing, indeed. I gulp air and try to force my voice to sound timid and terrified. It takes no real effort.

"I'll come out. Please don't hurt me."

The shutters stop rattling. I dart my hand into my leather pouch and seize my knife. Then I take one more breath, steel my spine, fling open the shutters, and plunge my blade directly into the space before me. It strikes a solid but yielding surface.

The man howls. I whirl and run. Someone stands in the doorway, but I double my speed and forge ahead. The woman leaps aside with a scream, clinging to the wall of the passageway.

"Get out of my house," she howls.

"I'm trying." I pant for breath. "Which way?"

The woman raises a trembling finger and points down the

passageway. I fly in that direction and burst into a room where a man waits, holding a bottle in one hand and a wooden club in the other. His eyes glint in the light of the guttering candle on a table.

"I only want to get out. Please!"

"Stop!" the man roars, taking a few lumbering steps toward me. His movements are clumsy, his breathing labored, and 'tis easy to duck beneath his swinging club. I reach a stairwell and pound upward. At the top of the flight, no one lies in wait to stop me. I make a split-second decision that I pray will not haunt me forever.

Instead of fleeing outside to make my escape, I continue to ascend. I do not stop to consider the logic of my rash decision but continue to hurl myself upwards, climbing five flights. When my legs are ready to give out, ahead is a roughhewn ladder that leads into a dark space a few paces above my head. The square door at the top yields with a groan, and I clamber out onto the roof. I slam the trapdoor and stand on it, though no one has pursued me yet.

The sun has just risen, bathing the city in a shower of golden light. The castle upon the hill shines like a beacon that calls me to it. And when I raise my face to the sky, tears threaten to fall. The late autumn sky is clear. It seems a century has passed since my eyes have beheld this much blue. The air up here is far purer than on the city streets below. I inhale the crisp, clean November air again and again. Would that I could tarry here, in this moment of peace and freedom. From six stories above the street, I am a bird viewing everything from the heavens and must use this to my advantage. I was nearly caught and barely escaped. I must now find a way out of the close.

Blinking away my foolish tears, I search for something with which to block the trapdoor. There is nothing but the wood slats beneath my feet, black with soot. A few coils of smoke drift from a nearby chimney. I turn in a slow circle. The buildings are so near one another, my heart leaps with hope for a moment. May I not jump from one building to the next? The timing is perfect, for wee Annie has a good home. I hurry closer to the edge of the building, trying to ignore the sinking feeling that befalls me at the thought of never seeing the child again. She is such a sweet thing. But when I take a closer look at my surroundings, all thoughts vanish as my hope of escape dies inside me.

The rooftops that encircle me are all crowded together like a jumble of blocks cast without thought onto the earth by a divine hand. Luck was apparently with me when I chose to run up here, for while my fleeing feet found a flat surface, the roofs of the other dwellings within sight are steeply pitched. They are great and sharp triangles that would defy anyone who sought to stand on them. My heart sinks. Where shall I go now?

I sniff and swipe at my face with my sleeve, remembering with a pang how Cinaed would have scolded me for such unladylike actions. Even if I escape this hell, Cinaed is no longer part of the world I return to.

And tears threaten me once more. I will not give in to them. Instead, I raise my head to the ever-lightening sky and howl. I scream out the anguish I've felt all those past weeks as my beloved sister wasted away. I scream at the squalor below my feet and the cruelty of many. I cry out until my voice is hoarse.

I feel empty and cold for a moment, until something else pours into me, as though borne on the wintry morning wind, filling my entire soul. Rage. I will not give up. Though Cinaed now lies cold beneath the earth, Oliver is alive and free with blood on his hands, sure as if he'd slit my sister's throat. And I will not allow him to get away with it. He thought he could throw me away, sending me to a friendless, pitiless place where he believed I'd simply give up and die.

He was wrong.

With new clarity, I scan the city once more, trembling with fatigue and cold. A stone's throw away is a familiar place. 'Tis the wee kirk, the chapel with the empty transept above and full vaults below. And its narrow bell tower is so near one just might be able to leap into its window. Yet will there be a solid floor to land on?

I must try. From below, muffled shouts and thumping noises grow close. They are coming. Of course, they are. I was howling like an injured cat.

Hurrying to the edge of the roof, I teeter on a little raised wall, balancing there for a moment. Below my feet, people are awake and now scurry along the lane, like a swarm of ants squabbling over crumbs and scraps, not knowing of the abundance below.

Behind me, the trapdoor bangs open. Mustering my courage, I leap.

CHAPTER
18

I land on my stomach with my head and arms inside the bell tower and my legs dangling outside. The air whooshes from my lungs, leaving me stunned and in too much pain to do little else but hang there for a moment, likely looking as foolish as I ever have in my life. Shouts and screams come from below. Perhaps those on the street think I aim to jump to my death.

When I catch my breath, I haul my wounded body inside the crumbling tower and fall onto the warped, wooden floor of a tiny room. In the center is a square hole above which hangs the bell. Ropes dangle through the dark hole to somewhere below, and rays of early sunshine illuminate the top of a splintered wooden ladder, to my great relief.

My stomach and sides protest, yet what else can I do? With trembling limbs, I ease myself onto the ladder, which shakes alarmingly. But it holds my weight, and I clumsily inch my way to another cramped space below to find a door and stairs that wind down to ground level. At the bottom step, I drop to my knees for a moment, for my shaky legs are no longer able to hold my weight. No sound comes from the main transept, yet I cannot remain here long; my pursuers will soon arrive.

I exit the tower and hurry along the former aisle between pews, evidenced by markings on the floor where the legs of the benches once rested. The moment I sigh in relief, certain of escape, someone opens a door to my right.

"Kenna!"

As I whirl my fingers seek for my knife. The blade is no longer inside the leather pouch. Of course! I left it stuck inside the watchman's innards.

"Steady on," the familiar voice says. "'Tis only me."

I slump with relief as Rob hurries to my side. "Kenna, ye must hide! I heard ye stabbed the watchman." I detect a hint of laughter that paints his words in lighter tones than befits the somber situation. "He wailed like a babe as he fled. We left our houses to learn the reason for all that blubbering. Do ye no' hear the commotion outside? The bailey's come into the close and is even searching inside the houses. He's declared a price on your head."

"I had no choice." Rob guides me to the hidden door that leads to the vaults. "Wait!" I stumble to a stop as a dreadful realization hits me. How badly did I hurt that watchman? Am I a true murderess, now? What will Grandfather say? Rob seizes my hand and half-drags me down the narrow stairs.

"Did I kill the watchman?"

The lad's laughter echoes about us and fills the vaults into which we emerge.

"Course ye didnae kill the man." He motions for me to follow him farther down the corridor. "Else there'd be a celebration, now, wouldn't there?"

Though Oliver must have sent the watchman to find me, my shoulders slump in relief when I learn I am not a killer. Then a hot prickle of anger rushes in. I must stiffen my spine! I cannot worry so about hurting someone, especially that monstrous man who wished me harm! What will I do when a chance to kill Oliver and avenge Cinaed presents itself? Grow faint and fail at my task?

"Where are we going?"

Rob is strolling along these dim underground corridors at a peaceful pace, with his hands clasped behind his back, rather like a young gentleman taking a leisurely outing on the grounds of his estate. I close my eyes. Rob, a gentleman? His rough hands and ragged clothing tell a different story. He's a stable hand, not a lord. Still, my spirits rise. Rob came to help me! And what color are his eyes? Despite my discomfort, I quicken my steps and smile when the lad waits for me to catch up, standing directly beneath a glowing lantern.

"There's another way out, but we must wait for the rumpus to die down before we go up to the lane. Come, Lady Kenna. We'll find something to eat." His grin is wide and a mite mocking. A real lady should feel affronted by such a familiar, teasing manner, but I am not. He used my Christian name, after all, not the detestable nickname Donny gave me. And his teasing eyes are a warm brown, with flecks of gold.

We arrive at a packed storeroom. I sit on a wooden box and munch the apple Rob tosses me. He works the tap of an ale barrel until a thin stream of liquid flows into a cup he's procured from a shelf. He offers the cup to me, and I nod my thanks. As I drink, Rob chatters, laughingly wondering whether the watchman will survive the damage I've inflicted.

The cool vaults echo and throw his words back to us. The sound is eerie, like ghosts whispering their secrets to each other. I study Rob when he is not looking at me. I like the angle of his cheek, his thick, dark brows, and the tuft of hair that falls into those melting brown eyes. He is not what Cinaed would have called handsome, but his face is as pleasing to me now as it was the night I'd caught a brief glimpse of his features.

"Well, now." Rob wipes his mouth. "Tell me what happened."

"I want to hear this myself." A short, scraggly haired figure pops into the storeroom and plops down at my feet. I yelp and drop my half-eaten apple.

"I'll eat that if you're no' wanting it." She grabs the fruit and takes a large bite. "I'm Una." She speaks with her mouth full and gazes at me through the tangle of matted blond hair that hangs in her face.

Her nose is smudged with dirt and her wide eyes are greenish yellow, like a cat's. "Remember me?"

"I do. You're the one who gave Annie a bit of cake."

Una gazes at me in frank admiration. "I thought the lass in green silks must be the poisoner our wretched bailey warned us about. Fine work that was when ye took the blade old Shaw threw at ye. And clever work today." She swallows and smiles, revealing the gap-toothed grin I remember. "That watchman will be wary of ye now. Unless the bailey hires a new one. Well done."

Meekly, I take the hand she offers. Her clasp is firm and her fingers rough and calloused, like Rob's.

"Well done, yourself, Una," Rob says. "We didnae hear ye coming. Ye used to be so loud clomping down those stairs, I hear your da warned ye he'd cut off your big feet if ye didnae quit stamping about like a great cart horse."

Una laughs and takes another large bite of her apple, spraying juice onto my skirt. And at her insistence, I tell the two of my morning's misadventures.

"Donny will be surprised," Una says, once she stops laughing. "I am glad the watchman met with ye. He knows he cannae trifle with ye, now."

"Aye, yet now there's a price on her head." Rob's voice is serious. "Kenna must take care. 'Twill be near to impossible for her to show her face outside during the day."

I raise my eyes to the low ceiling. "I could hardly move about this cursed lane, anyway! Shaw already threatened to turn me over to the bailey. How can the price on my head make a great difference? Then again..." My voice trails off. "Rob, how much is it?"

Rob's mouth twitches. "Not all that much, to be sure. A lame cow would earn me far more than I'd get for ye."

Una shouts with laughter.

I stare at Rob for a moment. He tries not to smile. "You're teasing me," I say. He winks, but forthwith his face grows serious. He draws near and leans close to my ear. My breath catches in my throat.

"A purse full of gold is what they offer. Ye must take care," he whispers. "Many would gladly hand ye over to the watchman for far less."

"A lame cow." Una wipes her damp eyes. She leaps to her feet and places her hands on her hips. "Fancies himself a great wit, our Rob." She cuffs him on the head. He grins and punches her on the arm, though not hard.

I duck my head and take a sip of ale as strange feelings war inside me. On one hand, the news of the price on my head is alarming. More than ever, I cannot allow anyone to find me wandering on the lane. Yet, despite my fears, a prickle of jealousy taunts me. I long for the camaraderie that exists between Rob and Una. The two are old friends, that much is sure, and are so at ease with one another. Likely, they've grown up together from the time they were babes in arms. But are they as brother and sister, or...?

I shake my head. It does not matter! Rob is a lowborn lad of the city and a thief. I am a lady, the granddaughter of an Earl. I blush.

"Enough blether." Una folds her arms. "The others will be here any minute."

"Others?" I sit up straight as shadows glide over to us and hover in the opening of our storeroom. Two, three, four. I leap to my feet.

"Steenie, Edan," Rob says. He waves at a couple of the figures. They are two lads, a scrawny one no more than eleven or twelve and the other a ginger-haired stout fellow tall as Rob. Both grin at us. The young one, Steenie, scratches his bum and spits on the floor before he bows low.

"Greetings, milady." His voice cracks. The other lad cackles. My hunched shoulders relax, and I smile until I catch a glimpse of the two older men who hang back a few paces. One holds a flickering lamp aloft. His face is forged of iron.

"That there's my father, Callum." Una dips her head at the man, who stares at me, his square face expressionless. "The other one's Duncan." Duncan gazes into the distance as though we are of no import whatsoever. I am glad of it, for the now brighter light reveals wide scars that mar his face, giving him a feral look.

"Hello." My voice echoes through the vaults.

Callum draws closer. He stares at me for a moment and the others grow silent.

"We keep a close eye on our vaults." His voice is low and toneless. It brings a nervous flutter to my insides. "One of us stands guard at all times."

I nod my head, for the man expects a response, but I do not trust my voice. The silence grows, broken only by the sound of faint breathing and the scritching of a rat somewhere on the earthen floor. No one moves.

After several heartbeats, the man speaks again. "I give ye one day to return the food ye took from us when Marcus Munro brought ye to these vaults." Callum's voice is a mere whisper. His eyes bore into mine. "If ye don't, we'll turn ye over to the bailey."

"I didn't know." My voice trembles. "I thought I could take a little since I did work for the guild." Despite my fear, my hands clench into fists. What an unfair accusation for these thieves to cast up to me! After all, Munro and his son both took food without thought. "If someone was here and saw me take an apronful of potatoes, why did they not stop me right then? And why are you not angry that Rob has taken some food just now? You'll have seen him do that very thing if you guard the vaults all the time."

At my words, Callum shoots a narrowed glance at Rob, who clears his throat and squares his shoulders. "That is true. I was on watch this morning. I left to find Kenna when Una brought me word of what happened. Lucky for her, she made it to the kirk, and we came here. I shared food with her."

"Members of the guild can take what they need as they work down here," Callum says. "And they may take a bit here and there to share with others if they choose."

"That's simply what I did." My fingernails dig into my sweating palms. "I took a bit of food to share with someone."

"To share with members of the *guild*," Callum clarifies in a taut voice. He glares at me. "This time tomorrow, return here with your payment. Bring us the food ye took or pay us in coin."

I glance at Rob and Una. Rob's face is rueful. Una gives me a tiny smile but says nothing. No one else speaks. I am defeated and outnumbered.

"Very well. Let me go now, as I must find some way to repay you." Ah, the words have a bitter taste! I wait, keeping my head held high and not shrinking from Callum's hard gaze.

"One day," he repeats.

Una clears her throat. "All clear up there, Da?"

"Aye." After shooting me a final glare, Callum turns his back. He and the others shuffle away and blend into the blackness of the corridor.

Filthy thieves. How dare they! I am near to speechless with outrage, but I refuse to remain silent.

"Steal from thieves? What nonsense! They behave as though taking a handful of potatoes is a high crime, punishable by death!" I gasp as the pain in my ribs twinges anew.

"We must go." Rob does not meet my eye. He takes my elbow and I wrench my arm from his grasp. "I can walk on my own." Una whistles a jolly tune. I cannot bear to look at the lass or Rob as they lead me on. My mind seethes as I follow.

"Why do we go deeper into the vaults?" I ask after a moment. Our footsteps echo about us as neither of the two answers my inquiry. "I need to go back to Donny's house, Rob. We must turn around."

"The bailey and others are searching for ye in the kirk, ye dolt," he says. "Do ye wish to walk straight into their hands?"

"What does that matter?" My voice grows louder and bounces off the solid rock that surrounds us. "The guild is ready to hand me over to the bailey all because I took a few rotting potatoes!"

Rob whirls and seizes my shoulders. "We must no' steal from each other." His eyes are wide with dismay. "We're a family." He drops his arms to his sides. "Ye must learn to play by the rules, Kenna.

Ye didnae know them, I give ye that. I'd hoped Callum would show mercy, but he's a hard man, and for good reason. What would happen to us if everyone up there knew about this place?"

"If people knew about this place, perhaps fewer 'up there,' would starve, Rob! For that's what's going to happen, don't you understand that?" My words echo. "Before the watchman spied me, I saw men stealing animals from the cowshed. They beat a poor old man when he tried to stop them."

Rob remains silent, but his widened eyes betray him. My words have gotten under his skin. After a moment, he walks on.

"We cannae feed all the world, Kenna," Una says. She rushes to me and links her arm in mine. "We must care for our own."

We resume our walk. Sighing, I set aside my anger at the wretched, greedy guild and its blasted code of honor, and turn my mind to a more pressing matter.

"Una, how exactly am I to pay for that food?" *Och,* the thieves give me one impossible task after another in this hellish place!

"Donny will help. Tell him what happened. He'll know what to do."

We come to the wooden delivery platform sitting in its place on the tunnel floor and Rob bows low and motions us forward.

"My ladies, your carriage."

Una giggles and hops onto the platform. I clamber beside her, feeling the fool.

"Where will this take us?" The platform creaks and sways, and I drop to my knees, wishing for something to hold on to.

"Back of the tanner's shop." Rob grins at me. "It's best to hurry outside once ye get there. When old Smith hasn't wet his whistle lately, he's in a fine mood, he is."

As I settle myself onto the platform and arrange my skirts, Rob leans toward me, fiddling with the ropes. His lips brush against my cheek and his breath tickles my ear.

"We're not all so cruel as ye think, Kenna," he murmurs. "Have faith in the guild."

He backs away and turns the handle of the pulley. With a squealing groan, the platform inches higher and higher.

What did he mean? I do not understand anything in this strange place, but his words and his momentary nearness warm me. I can somehow tell that Una is smiling at me in the darkness.

The platform sways and dips if either Una or I so much as twitch, so we remain as still as possible. We are inside a rough-hewn shaft, black as pitch and stuffy. Mercifully, the ride is short, and we soon emerge into a tiny room that reeks of spilled wine. I scrabble from the platform and am grateful that we are indeed alone for now. The room opens into the back of a shop, where tools lay scattered on tables, and a layer of dust lies thick over everything. I sneeze.

"Who's there?" a man shouts from upstairs.

"Only me! Una!" the lass shouts.

Mumbled grumbles emit from the upper floor, but the man is apparently satisfied and does not approach us.

"This way!" Una seizes my arm and leads me back onto the lane. "Follow me and stay in the shadows."

We scuttle along like two large rats, hiding behind barrels and piles of refuse, darting from one house to another. Soon I recognize the pitted cobbles ahead and spy Donny and Sheona's scarred doorway.

"Thank you." I pant and hold my aching sides.

The girl turns to go but pauses and glances back over her shoulder. "I'm keen to have ye join the guild. So is Rob." A wide grin splits her round face.

My face grows hot. "Is he?"

Una nods. Her cat eyes gleam as she vanishes around a corner.

My lips curve into a smile. Rob wants me to join the guild? The thought is both alarming and pleasing in equal measure. With a sudden lilt in my step, despite my fatigue and my aching ribs, I climb the stairs to the entrance. As I reach for the handle, the door is flung open and Sheona yanks me inside. The old woman opens her mouth.

Before she utters a sound, Annie hurtles toward me and wraps her thin arms around my knees.

"Mamma!" she says with a sob.

CHAPTER
19

I t requires many long minutes to calm Annie. The child's wails fill the house to the rafters. She only falls asleep after Sheona gives her a warm drink.

"What was in that?" I wince at the ache in my sides as I carry the child to her pallet on the floor. The herbwife shuffles after us into the kitchen.

"Honey and a good jigger of whiskey."

The old woman motions for me to clear off the remains of a meal from the table after I stoke the fire. My exhausted limbs tremble and my ribs ache fiercely from the early morning leap into the tower. Would that I might simply lie beside the child and sink into the kind oblivion of sleep, but 'tis not to be. I must complete the many new tasks an angry Sheona and Donny are certain to assign me, and find out how to pay the guild.

"Chop this," the old herbwife orders. She hands me another slippery brown root and a knife. Blowing stray hair out of my eyes, I bend to my task. Sheona stokes the fire until it burns bright and hot. The room grows stifling and *och*, my ribs ache!

"Why must the fire be so hot?" Without a reply to my peevish words, the old woman gives me a new task of crushing tiny black peppercorns with a mortar, such as Mrs. Harris was wont to use for crushing the bitter herbs of her ague remedy. One tiny seed flies from beneath my fingers and rolls to the floor.

"Mind ye dinnae lose that." Sheona speaks in a sharp voice as I crawl beneath the table to collect the errant seed. "That spice is worth as much as our Poisoner is with that price on her head. Perhaps even more."

I rise so fast I strike my skull on the underside of the table and the lost peppercorn pings away once more.

"How did you know about that?" I rub my aching head.

"Words fly faster than birds fleeing winter skies, lass." The woman chuckles as she settles herself into her chair beside the fire. As she laughs, I notice for the first time her even, white teeth. It strikes me as odd that the ancient woman's teeth are so fine while her husband has hardly a single tooth left in his head. They must be false, like the ones Grandfather has.

"Donny was mighty pleased. He says ye've done better than he ever thought ye might."

"Thank you." I'm almost ashamed by the swelling of pride I feel at the woman's words. With a tiny smile, I locate the peppercorn and return to my spot at the table. "But now I've lost my knife."

Sheona lights the ever-present pipe that she and her husband so favor. The old woman draws in a deep breath and puffs out lazy clouds into the air.

"That ye have. 'Tis a true loss. You're such a weak thing ye cannae defend yourself without it." Her bent head swivels to the side and she studies me from behind the lace of her cap as I work at my task, grinding the peppercorns into a powder while I summon the courage to ask if she knows about the payment I owe. When I open my mouth to speak, the peppery scent in the air tickles my nose and I sneeze.

"I'll no' have ye sneezing all over my herbs, lass."

"I'm sorry." I sniff and suppress another sneeze.

"And we'll no' have ye going about stealing from our guild."

I lift my head and gaze with wide eyes at the woman. She studies the fire with a decided air of complacency. With a snort, I return to grinding the dried spice with a renewed vigor; anger lending greater strength to my hands as I crush the tiny grains. Word does fly upon the wind. Sheona laughs at my scowling face.

"They are in the right. Ye must pay for what ye took."

I slam the mortar onto the scarred wood of the table so hard that the tiny mounds of leaves, twigs, dried berries, rinds, and other strange stuff I cannot identify tremble and collapse. More peppercorns roll from the table and ping on the floor.

"And how exactly am I to pay?" I whirl and face Sheona with my hands planted on my hips. Ah, this wretched guild! If God willed it and were I able, I'd empty their vaults of all within and scatter it to the four winds, let it fall where it may. "You know I have no money. If I did, I'd have bought my way out of here long before this."

Sheona's cap trembles. It takes me a moment to realize she is laughing.

"*I'll* help ye, ninny." Cackling, she takes another deep draw from her pipe and blows out several smoke rings while I gape at her. "I'm the one what took ye in and talked the guild into letting ye join. It's my duty to pay for your mistake. One that ye'll no' make again, I vow."

This time, her crinkled face turns my way, and her keen blue eyes peep out at me from behind the lace of her cap.

My eyes fly open wide at her response. "You'll help me?"

"Aye. Now, back to work, lass."

I retrieve the fallen spices and return to the table, where I bend my head to my task once more, preparing the various herbs, spices, and unidentifiable substances on the table. Pleasant, pungent scents fill the air. Annie slumbers away on her pallet. The fire burns ever hotter. A bead of sweat that rolls down my face. I must not complain. What blessed luck this woman is willing to help me!

Once Sheona is satisfied with my work, she limps off and returns with the strangest contraption I've ever seen. 'Tis a great three-legged pot, not dark as the iron one that hangs on a hook in the grate, but a bright copper.

"In it all goes." We sweep the stuff off the table and into the gleaming pot. To that, Sheona adds a goodly amount of whiskey. She stoppers the bottle after taking a gulp and places her pot over the fire. The flames have died down, though the heat remains and makes my shift stick uncomfortably to my itchy skin. The old woman settles the pot's legs deep into coals that gleam like demon's eyes and attaches a lid that fits tight with a thin tube that extends outside the grate. She settles a smaller three-legged pot under the opening of the great tube. And from that second small pot another tiny tube extends. The herbwife places a tin cup beneath its opening.

"There." She places her hands on her hips. Her voice bears a note of pride.

"All that work will only give us a cup's worth of whatever it is you are making?" I swipe at my sweaty face.

"Aye. Takes a fair bit of toil to make my tincture, it does."

My shoulders slump. "I should say it does."

Sheona chuckles while she fidgets with the dreadful cap that covers her face. "My tincture sells well. I may not earn any coin, but many are willing to make a trade. I wager ye'll earn what ye need to pay back the guild."

"How shall I sell this tincture if I cannot go outside?"

"Our Poisoner must keep out of sight during the day, so I shall do the task for her. When the medicine is ready, I'll go out to sell it. It must be me, at any rate," she adds with a toothy grin, "for who'd wish to buy potions from a poisoner?"

I scowl but bite my lips to keep from speaking. Sitting cross-legged on the floor near Annie, I cock my head to the side and study the old woman while she removes her stained apron and hangs it on a peg. She and her husband steal from the dead. Such wickedness! The Bible clearly condemns thieves. But my ire soon drains away. Thieves they may be, but this wee, white-haired couple helped me when no one else would. My mouth stretches wide in another yawn and my eyes droop.

"Now then," Sheona settles herself on the great carved chair beside the fire. "Before ye take your ease, I've something to say to ye."

I glance up. "What?"

"We'll have no more of your dashing off, Donny and I." Her mouth is set into a frown as she glares at me, leaning down and placing her gnarled hands on her knees.

"Ye heard what that child called ye! Ye must be here when she wakes. Donny and I took ye both in, but we'll no' care for the bairn ourselves. Dinnae think for a moment ye can run off when the notion seizes ye and leave her with us, Poisoner. She's yours, now."

"Annie is mine? That makes no sense." I glower at the crone. "She was confused. You know I am not her mother."

The old woman flies from her chair like a great black vulture swooping on me. The cuff I receive to the side of the head is not hard, yet it brings tears to my eyes.

"Enough!" she barks. "Ye'll only leave if we say so. And if ye try to take yourself off again without telling me or Donny, ye'll find yourself out in the cold, hiding from the bailey and his watchman and begging for bread!"

She shuffles toward her chair. Annie murmurs in her sleep.

"Fine, you old cow!" I leap to my feet. "I'd rather starve than be your servant any longer."

I whirl and march toward the front chamber, but do not make it that far. Sheona seizes me from behind in a grip of iron, pinning my arms behind my back, and squashes my face painfully against the weeping stone wall. My ribs are on fire and my arms lose feeling.

"That child needs a family," she hisses in my ear. "I'll not allow ye to abandon her. She has no one else."

"That hurts!" I gasp. "Please, Sheona, let me go!"

"I want your word." The woman gives my numb arms a shake. I fear she'll wrench my limbs from their sockets.

"I'll stay! You have my word."

She releases her grip, and I sink to my knees. Blinking away tears, I gape at the old woman. She stands with her back straight as a fire iron. In the scuffle, her cap has fallen from her head. Her white hair is cropped short, nearly to her skull, and her eyes are chips of blue ice.

For a heartbeat, I do not understand. Then a confused, wild thought strikes me.

"Donny?" My voice trembles.

"Aye." The man seizes my wrist and jerks me to the bench beside the table. I touch my cheek where it was mashed against the wall. The scraped and raw skin stings.

"I do not understand." I rub feeling back into my arms as I speak. "You don the skirts of a woman?"

Donny snorts like a draft horse. "I *am* a woman, ninny."

CHAPTER 20

My head pounds and I rub aching temples.

The more I ponder these past days, the more I feel the fool. Not once did Donny and Sheona appear in the same room at the same time. They never dined together, and if Donny was present, old "Sheona" was to be found napping in her bedchamber, unless someone called for the herbwife. How blind I was to not see this!

"Donalda was the name my ma gave me." He, well, *she* fishes her pipe from within the folds of her skirt.

"And Sheona?"

Donny chews her pipe and paces the kitchen. "Sheona was the old herbwife who lived in my village. My ma learned all she knew from her. And Ma taught it to me."

"Oh." I nod as though I understand. "Why must you feign to be two different people, Donny? It is not, er, well, it is not a usual thing." I bite my lip. What I'd nearly said was *'tis not proper for a woman to dress as a man*. No indeed, it is not, but my raw face and aching arms and head caution me against further angering this odd, wee woman with the strength of a man.

Donny sits in her carved chair with a satisfied sigh. "'Tis simple, Poisoner. An old herbwife like me must have a man to provide protection. 'Tis far safer."

"Why? Protect you from what?" I cannot quite understand the drama that plays before me. Sheona is of a truth merely Donny, a woman who wears breeches? By the heavens!

Squinting at me, Donny stokes the fire and lights her pipe. She does not speak until she has taken a great draught, inhaling with such pleasure she closes her eyes.

"I shall tell ye a tale, Poisoner." Smoke trails from her mouth as she speaks. "Though I learned the uses of medicinal plants and how to set broken bones, I had no wish to become the next herbwife of the village, so I ran off to join the regiment when I was fifteen."

My mouth gapes. Donny became a soldier. And at *my* tender age? I scoff.

"Surely not! A woman cannot be a soldier!"

"Course not." Donny snorts. She rises to pace, her face alight with mirth and bends to tuck the blanket more tightly about the sleeping Annie. The child's doll is in her arms, and for the first time I notice that eyes, a tiny nose, and curving lips have been carved into the rough wood.

"They all said so." Donny straightens, unties her skirts and allows them to fall to the floor. She wears her breeches underneath. Grinning wickedly at my wide-eyed expression, Donny gathers her fallen clothing and tosses it over her chair. "My five brothers told me I'd never join the regiment, so I decided to prove them wrong. I joined and served for seven years."

"How?"

Donny barks out a loud laugh. "Told my ma I was heading to the city to work. Brought a pair of my brother Jamie's breeches with me and a knife. I ducked into the neighbor's barn and sheared off my hair while the horses stomped. Kept my bonny braid, though."

She hurries to open her locked chest and retrieves a coil of bright, gleaming copper hair. "See?" She hands the braid to me.

"Your hair was beautiful." I run a finger over the smoothly entwined locks. "Had I such lovely hair, I'd never cut it."

"Grows back, hair does." Donny smiles. "Least for the young." Pursing her lips, she rubs a hand across the cap of white fluff that barely covers her scalp.

"When did you become an herbwife? And you have not yet

answered my question about why you now need the protection of a man."

"I'll get to that, snippet. I was a soldier for many years, as I told ye. I married after returning to my village. I was done with soldiering." She barks out a laugh at my expression. "I see ye dinnae believe that a man would wish to wed an old creature like me." She squints in my direction. "I was still a young woman then. Think what ye will, Poisoner, but I was comely enough to draw a man's eye as well as any other lass."

"I do not doubt that, Donny." But I cannot meet the woman's gaze and duck my head to study the severed braid in my hand. Her hair *was* comely. However, no trace of beauty remains in the old woman's face, so like a shriveled apple or an over-baked oat cake that has fallen in on itself. *I shall never look like that.* I gulp. *Dear God in heaven, I hope not!*

Donny gurgles out a laugh and continues. "After Ma died, those of the village who came to her for cures came to me instead. I became the herbwife after all. I didnae mind it so much by then." As she speaks, her eyes gaze far into the past. "I'd done my adventuring and had a daughter and a wee son to care for. My work earned us extra coin. So, I sold cures and set broken bones and helped birth many a child into the world."

The woman whom "Old Sheona" kept from bleeding to death comes to mind. Donny saved a life that evening, and to be sure, she has saved countless others throughout her many years. I study the old herbwife's face. A gleam of pride shines from her eyes and she sits tall as she speaks of her past. Well should she take satisfaction in all she has accomplished!

Something inside me envies Donny that pride. What pleasure it must be to know that one has done such important things. Part of me rankles at the thought that even if, no, even *when* I escape the city, I will not accomplish half as much as this strange elderly woman, for I am a gentlewoman. A lady. I will have no occupation save that of becoming someone's wife. For the first time, the idea does not please me. Why can I not learn something useful, something that will let me prove my worth? My intelligence? *Och*, 'tis not right! Why can women not do as they wish?

Donny sighs. "When the year of the plague came on us, much changed. My daughter died first. Then my husband."

My throat grows tight. "I am sorry."

"My son and I lived, thanks be to God, when so many others in the village died. But after that summer, all those who were still alive stopped coming to me."

"Why?"

Donny pauses a good while before she answers. "There are those who fear women like me, Poisoner." She pierces me with her azure gaze. "Woman who are wise in the ways of healing are often feared. Some take us to be witches."

"Surely not!" I rise to my feet. "They must have known that you could not save everyone, especially from that great sickness! And your own husband and daughter died." My voice trails off.

Donny shrugs. "'Twas long ago. No matter. We found a new life." Her face falls and an expression of deep sadness paints her features. The old woman stoops to check on the steaming pots nestled within the coals. "I came to the city after the plague. I missed making my cures and knew the good I could do here as an herbwife. But I needed to live under the protection of a man, remember. Either a husband, an official, or a man of the cloth, who would provide proof that I was a respectable woman. Not a witch."

Understanding blossoms. "I see. You *must* be two different people. The man, Donny, and the herbwife, Sheona."

"Aye." Donny rises and takes a small crock from the shelf to the table. She motions for me to help her, and we prepare a simple meal. We do not talk; words do not come to me, and Donny's face is blank.

When we sit to eat, my mood grows more placid while my belly fills. As I drink my ale, a thought strikes me. Mere days ago, I would have turned my nose up at the plain fare set before me. Now, after being imprisoned within this strange corner of the city, and finding myself close to mad with hunger, I relish the mashed turnips and coarse bread I am given. Indeed, I am far more grateful for this food than I used to be for the rich viands I'd grown accustomed to. The roasted meats, hot bread, the sweet desserts, the fine wines. Would Cinaed be disappointed in me? My tastes are now those of a servant rather than a fine lady.

I slurp my ale and shrug to myself. 'Tis what hunger will do. An empty belly makes us happily settle for dust when we'd had diamonds before.

Annie sleeps on, her breathing even and slow. A coil of bright hair has escaped from her braided coronet and lies across her cheek, gleaming in the golden glow of the embers. Again, the tiny scar is visible high on her forehead. The memory of Cinaed and Oliver's babe pricks at me with needle-like teeth. I thrust the thought away and force my mind to this new situation. The child is now my full responsibility. The thought warms and chills me at the same time. 'Tis a burden that will make my escape from here much more difficult.

"Tell me something, Poisoner." I glance at Donny in surprise, wrenched from my thoughts. "Out there," she waves in the direction of the lane, "they call ye a murderess. What makes ye so determined to leave? There is naught but the noose that awaits ye beyond our close."

My throat closes as though the rope is already there, knotted tight. "I mean to clear my name and seek justice."

Donny places her spoon on the table, her eyes fixed on me. She rises to her feet. "Justice or revenge? 'Tis a strange business, that of vengeance." Her voice is soft. "Take care, Kenna. Oft times it be the one seeking revenge who is destroyed."

There is nothing to say to this. Donny does not understand. She did not witness her beloved sister wasting away day after day! She did not stand by, helpless and powerless as her sister took her last breath. The old woman places a steaming washbasin before me and turns to inspect her copper pot nestled in the coals. We speak no more. I am grateful for the silence, broken only by muffled voices from outside. The sound grates upon my nerves in comparison to the whisper of the sea, close as it is to Grandfather's home.

Grandfather. Sadness weaves through my heart. Where is he? Oliver must have him fooled, or he would have found me by now! I squeeze a dishcloth so tightly in my fists that water sprays onto my gown. The scent of mulled wine and apples comes to mind. I can almost feel Grandfather's strong arms around me. I felt so safe in his presence. A lump forms in my throat when I picture Grandfather's face; his great blue eyes troubled, his brow lined with sorrow as Oliver makes his claim that I am the one who murdered my sister.

When the last bowl is washed, dried, and placed in its proper spot upon the shelf, I drop to my knees beside Annie. The child stirs and opens her eyes, then holds her arms out to me. I lift her onto my lap, and she snuggles into my embrace.

Stroking her head, my thoughts turn to the child's family. She lived with the Lindsay's for a time. Before that, had she any mother? She must have!

Finding the lass's gaze upon me, I smile down at her. In the firelight, the color of her eyes strikes me with an unexpected feeling of familiarity. They are not the stone blue hue I had first believed them to be. Rather, Annie's eyes are almost green, with yellow and gray rings mixed in, like a polished agate I once found in a stream bed. Such eyes seem to change shades depending on the color of a person's garments. Who else do I know with eyes such as this? No person comes to mind. Why are they familiar?

Sighing, I push my wondering thoughts aside. Perhaps I shall remember who Annie reminds me of. Poor, wee thing. I kiss the top of her head. What happened to her? How did she come to be the ward of the Lindsay family? If the opportunity comes to me, I must ask Catriona, the young lass with red locks who works for Mrs. Lindsay. The servants always know.

"Well, ye'll have your payment by tonight," Donny says.

I examine the woman's pot and strange contraptions that sit in the grate. The brew simmers over the coals and fills the kitchen with its spicy scent. A tiny droplet of dark liquid oozes from the spout of the smallest pot and falls into the cup with a muted *plink*.

"Do you know how much money I'll need?" The child clings to my skirts when I attempt to rise to my feet, making it difficult for me to move. "Please, Annie." I groan with weariness and discomfort and clutch my aching ribs. Pain lends a sharp edge to my voice. "Go play with your doll."

She remains at my side, her eyes wide and fearful.

"There, poppet." Donny hands Annie her doll. "Sit here beside me." She settles Annie onto a low stool and hands her a bit of bread. When she glances at me her mouth is twisted into a frown. A prickle of shame runs through me. I smile at Annie to reassure her, and she beams at me with shining eyes.

"How much did ye take from the vaults?" Donny asks.

"Some potatoes, a few turnips, and some onions." I am unable to meet her gaze and focus on my torn nails instead. "Though Munro gave one onion to me.."

"Hang me! That's all?" Donny caws like an old crow. "'Tis naught but a mite." She wipes her eyes and squints at me, and her face grows serious. "But I must say Callum and the others are in the right, Poisoner. Mind ye dinnae forget that. We keep a close watch on our vaults."

Donny does not require anything of me for the rest of the afternoon. She sings quietly and holds Annie on her lap, rocking beside the crackling fire. Desperate to rest, I wrap myself in my blanket and fall into the deep slumber of exhaustion, imagining the feel of Grandfather's arms encircling me and hearing the rush of the sea.

And I strive to ignore the haunting, nagging dread that I will never again feel the embrace of those strong arms, nor hear the ocean's voice as it sings me to sleep.

CHAPTER
21

Several hours later, Donny shakes me awake. 'Tis early evening and the kitchen is lit by the glow of the fire and a lamp that burns steadily, filling the room with a soft glow. The spicy, sweet smell of Donny's tincture fills the house.

With a grin, the woman shows me the tin cup, now full to the brim with her magical remedy. I stifle a yawn as I regard the pitiful fruits of all my labor, a mere cup's full of liquid. I still cannot fathom why we do not have more tincture than this, for all the chopping and grinding and mincing I did! But the proud gleam in her eye and the pink flush of her withered cheeks tell me that Donny is highly pleased.

Annie, clad only in her shift, is under the kitchen table, happily eating bites of apple after first proffering them to her doll. The old woman places her cup of liquid on the table and points to the washbasin that sits in the corner with tendrils of steam floating from it.

"Bathe the child. She's soiled herself again. I must fill my bottles."

When I try to lift Annie into the tub, I cry out at the pain in my ribs.

"What's this, now?" Donny hurries to me. She places Annie in the tub and the child laughs and splashes happily. Donny makes me sit in a chair and pokes and prods my ribs, which is not at all to my liking.

"That hurts!"

"I can see that." She regards me with pursed lips and a furrowed brow. "What'd ye do?"

I sink down beside Annie's tub. She splashes me with water. While I bathe the wee one, I tell Donny the details of my early morning adventure, sharing the reason for my aching ribs. More than once, she cackles out loud in delight and heartily congratulates me when the tale is done.

"Well done, lassie! Well done." She takes out her pipe and lights it. "Wish I could've seen ye flying in the air like a great, green bird."

"My sides ache when I move or take a deep breath. Did I break any bones?" I grunt with the discomfort of lifting Annie from the tub and dry her with the rags Donny hands me.

"Cracked the bones, I think." She studies me while fingering the bristles upon her chin and feels my ribs once again. "I'll give ye cloths to wrap around your ribs. 'Twill ease ye a bit, and I've a liniment to help with the pain."

Within the quarter hour, Annie is clad in clean clothing and plays upon the floor, banging together a pewter plate and cup Donny gave her. And I shiver beside the fire, hidden behind a faded screen so I may slather my ribs with the sticky liniment Donny gives to me. I gape at the sight of the great purple bruises covering my abdomen.

"I'm covered with marks." I scowl. "I can hardly believe I did not break all my bones."

Donny chuckles from the other side of the screen. "That'll pain ye for a good while." Her liniment smells strongly of the mint leaves she keeps in a crockery jar with a tight lid, safely away from the other herbs so they will not also smell of mint as well. The scent is pleasant, and the sticky stuff warms my skin. My pain does ease a mite. I wrap my aching ribs with some cloths Donny gave me, don my clothing, and relace my bodice with a sense of relief.

"Now, to your payment." Donny takes me to her locked cabinet and opens it. 'Tis jammed full of bottles like an apothecary's shop. My old benefactress hands me several tiny bottles and we return to the kitchen to fill them. Donny's special "concoction" is in fact five parts whiskey to one part herbal infusion. The old woman laughs at my expression.

"The whiskey itself does a body a world of good." She stoppers the final bottle with a bit of wax and arranges all within a basket. Then Donny assumes her skirts and cap, and old "Sheona" goes out to sell her wares.

Annie and I play a game of sorts. With a pang of sadness, it brings the recollection of long autumn nights before the fire with my sister, when we'd play Fox and Geese and eat apples. I try to teach Annie using bits of firewood as the geese and a chip of stone as the fox, but she only wants to arrange the geese in rows and count them. So, we do.

The child does not stray far from me. It is somewhat trying, especially when I must leave the room to relieve myself or wish to stretch my stiff legs.

"What shall we do, then?" I whisper, more to myself than to Annie, as she once more cradles her doll and I stoke the fire. How can one seek vengeance when a wee child will not leave her side? 'Twould be impossible! Though I care for the sweet lassie, she must stay here.

A timid knock sounds at the door. This cannot be Donny, nor another member of the guild. I hold my breath, prepared to wait until the caller leaves. The knocking only grows louder. With a gulp, I rise and inch toward the door, with the child as usual clinging to my skirts. I keenly feel the lack of the blade stolen from Shaw. Where did Donny put the knife I'd used earlier to chop roots? I was a fool not to take it.

"Who's there?"

"Mrs. Lindsay. Please, I beg you, let me in!"

After a long moment of hesitation, I unlatch the bolt and open the door. Perhaps it is because so many doors were closed to me on my arrival here that I cannot bear to shut anyone out. Even one who is likely a murderess. The irony of what I call the woman, though only in my own mind, is not unknown to me.

Yet, this being who creeps inside is no longer the haughty woman I'd first met. Her shoulders bow as though she is of great age, and her eyes bear black smudges beneath them. She keeps her cloak of fine wool pulled tightly about her.

Annie emits a frightened squeal and flees to the kitchen. I am grateful for the reprieve from the constant vigilance required of me when the child is at my knees, but my heart is pained at the sound of her muffled sobs. 'Tis no longer a mystery why Annie fears this woman.

"Why are you here?" I'm glad I'd placed a taper on a shelf to light the dim front room. Though Donny's house has two small windows made of real glass that face the street, not much light filters through the grime-coated squares.

Mrs. Lindsay ignores my words, and her eyes dart about. "Where is Donny?"

"Not here. State your business and leave. I'll pass the word on to him. And to the herbwife," I add in a rush. A tiny prickle of enjoyment brings a smirk to my lips, when I would feign a fierce, menacing mien. 'Tis rather amusing to play a part in Donny's deception.

Mrs. Lindsay's face crumples, and she bows her head. Silent sobs shake her frame, and the woman sinks to the floor, burying her face in her hands.

I hold up my hands, feeling suddenly as if I've done something wrong. "Please don't do that. What is wrong?"

"I did no' mean to hurt him." Mrs. Lindsay sobs.

My breath catches in my throat.

"He made me so angry." She raises her tear-streaked face to me. "Gone at all hours, only coming home when he could hardly walk for the wine he'd drunk, spending time with that, that…"

"Trollop?" The word is one a lady must not use, but 'tis one familiar to me. Mrs. Harris used it sometimes when she believed only the other servants were nearby.

Mrs. Lindsay covers her face with a lace handkerchief. "I had no mind to kill him. I only meant to hurt him as much as he had hurt me."

"Hello there." Sheona shuffles through the open the door. "Thought I heard voices."

With a gasp of relief, I hurry to the kitchen. Annie runs to me. I do not pick her up for fear of the pain in my ribs, but I detach her hands from my skirts and draw her attention back to our counting game.

Low voices carry to us from the other chamber as the herbwife speaks to Mrs. Lindsay, who continues to sob. Though 'tis evening, the hour cannot yet be so late, but wee Annie yawns. I help her remove her dress and wrap her in Donny's old shawl. Then I comb her hair and attempt to re-braid it, though the results are not half so fine as when Donny had done the task. The child's wee face is still pinched and fearful. I cannot bear it.

"Hush, now." I hold her close. "Do not be afraid, Annie. Donny and I will not let that old Mrs. Lindsay harm you."

I sing softly, wishing my voice was half so fine as my sister's. Or Oliver's, for that matter. The moment the first words spill from my trembling lips, a vision of my sister's shallow breathing springs to my mind. I have begun to sing the very song I sang as Cinaed lay dying. Tears well; the memory fills me with pain and my voice breaks.

> *The swallows are gone, the summer has flown,*
> *Wee child of mine, come with me.*
> *The world shall await, 'ere long you are grown,*
> *but for now, you shall sleep, and in dreams fancy free*
> *you shall fly like the swallows, float with the wind,*
> *and awake bright as day with the golden dawn.*
> *Come, dearest one,*
> *Come with me.*

I stroke the child's wee face until she falls into a fitful sleep. At last, I rise and stretch as much as my aching bones allow. My adventures of the previous night have near done me in.

Yawning, I gaze at the small child with more than a bit of envy. As soon as Donny gives me her earnings, I shall steal to the kirk, for Callum wanted his payment within a day. I prefer to resolve my debt as soon as possible. At least I no longer fear the darkness as much as before. 'Tis almost like a benevolent friend, covering and protecting me from the bailey's watchman. The man's injured now, at any rate. Wincing, I rub my sides. So am I.

Donny's front door closes with a thud and after a moment my hostess enters her kitchen. She says nothing of her whispered talk with Mrs. Lindsay as she places her basket upon the table. I do not ask her to tell me what words passed between her and the other woman. 'Tis not my affair, and besides, I already know what Mrs. Lindsay has done.

The herbwife places her wares on the table. It does not look to me as though she sold many bottles. However, a pair of battered boots lies nestled within the woven basket, along with a linen-wrapped parcel. Without preamble, Donny proffers the boots to me.

"'Tis too cold for ye to go about with only rags on your feet."

I snatch the well-worn shoes from her hands, spluttering my thanks. A rush of excitement fills me. Without ceremony, I hurry to a chair and shove the boots onto my aching feet. They are a mite large but will fit well enough if I leave the cloths bound around my toes. Swiftly, I fasten the buckles and arise, testing my new footwear. They are battered, brown, mud-spattered and a world away from the dainty shoes I'd slipped off my feet before climbing into my sister's chamber on the dreadful day she died. But they are mine; my poor, cold, and bruised toes seem to sigh in relief.

The old woman laughs as I arise and attempt a few recently learned dance steps. Rather than glide, I clomp across the kitchen floor. I pause to gaze in dismay at the sight of the substantial footwear beneath my silk skirts and emit an unladylike snort. Fine dancing slippers, these! I smooth my skirts and raise my head. Fine slippers do not belong in this part of the city: this frigid, stinking lane filled with so many who have so little and thieves who steal from those who do.

Donny counts out a handful of pennies and extends her arm, offering me the coins.

"Here. 'Twill be enough for Callum."

My breath catches in my throat. "Thank you." I take the coins from her and pocket my payment with a relieved smile. "I am truly grateful, Donny. For the boots, the liniment, and this payment. You have been exceedingly kind." Straightening my shoulders, I head for the door.

"Keep a sharp eye out for that watchman. If ye did no' kill the man, he'll be fairly burning with wrath."

My stomach drops. Indeed, I must be more wary than ever. How could I believe that venturing outside would now be any less dangerous than before? Donny follows me to her front chamber, where she busies herself unlocking her cabinet and placing items inside.

"After ye pay Callum, hurry to the Lindsay's home. The woman needs assistance and offers payment for the work." She places her hands on her hips, regarding me with her sharp eyes. "'Tis work I cannae do or I'd do it myself. Though ye be covered in bruises, ye'll fare well enough. And I've plenty more liniment and a draught for pain if ye be needing it when ye return."

"What work does that woman have for me, Donny?" The heaviness of dread creeps into my chest and my heart, already quickened at the thought of the watchman, now taps an even faster beat.

Donny removes her cap and runs a hand over her shorn head with a great sigh. "Go to the Lindsay's house and help dig a hole for a grave. Munro will be there to help as well. The master lies there in the cellar, wrapped in a mort cloth to await burial."

The silence that chokes the room is thick, like the darkness that covers the city streets on a moonless night. I find it impossible to breathe and so must remain mute for a moment. First, this woman forces me to help her thieves steal from the dead, and now, she sends me to *bury* the dead?

"You cannot mean this! That woman killed her husband, Donny! You must call for the bailey!"

The old woman barks out laughter while I digest the implications and the impossibility of my hastily spoken words. With flaming cheeks, I draw a deep breath and attempt to compose myself.

"Ye ken well enough, lass, why we must no' call the bailey, I'll wager." Donny places a gentle hand on my shoulder and turns me to face her. Her blue eyes glitter in the light of her lamp upon a low table. Lit from below, her face somehow seems another thousand years older.

"She didnae mean to do it, Kenna," the old woman whispers. "She'll live knowing her soul's covered in blood all the remaining days of her life. 'Tis that no' punishment enough?"

"But—"

Donny shushes me as one might silence a naughty child. "She hardly eats and finds no rest. All she sees is her husband's face when she closes her eyes. Besides, do ye truly wish to see that woman condemned to death?" The herbwife drops her hand from my shoulder and glares. "Now, if it had been, say, Master Lindsay who struck his wife in a fit of passion, such a man with a fat purse and an important name might indeed be granted mercy at his trial. Especially if a purse filled with gold changes hands. But Master Lindsay didnae do the killing now, did he? 'Tis a hard truth but a truth, nonetheless. A wealthy man has a far better chance of escaping the noose than a woman, especially a shrew and a sharp-tongued one at that."

I gulp and struggle to form words. "I do not wish to see Mrs. Lindsay condemned to die. I know what it's like to be accused of murder. But why must we bury him in the cellar of his own house?"

Donny shakes her head in disbelief. "Where else are ye going to bury him, lass? We're locked in our close with no' a graveyard in sight. Bless me, child! Use the head. Now go. And take this."

The woman hands me a small knife and I take it in silence. Though relieved to have a blade once more, I cannot open my mouth to speak my thanks. My dinner of stale bread spread with goose drippings sits like a stone in my stomach as I silently take leave and close the door behind me. Once outside, I square my shoulders. I've no desire for the grim task ahead of me, but as there's no choice in the matter, I'm off to visit the Lindsay's fine home once more. I'll complete this dreaded work first since I have until tomorrow to settle my debt with the guild.

The air is chill, and a fine drizzling mist falls on the cobbles, making them slippery. I yelp and sidestep to avoid treading upon a dead rat floating in a greasy pool. The sliver of sky high above is a sheet of iron and the sun will soon set. A sinking feeling weighs me down inside. I've been stuck here for more than a week. So long already, and with no sign that Grandfather is seeking me. 'Tis as though I've stumbled into some gruesome, terrifying faery story.

Before long, my destination is before me. I've made good time and have yet to be accosted by anyone. I sigh in relief and smile to myself. Luck is on my side, for once. A moment later, something strikes me hard in the belly. I drop to my knees, gasping in pain.

Luck? I should have known better. I hug my aching middle. My luck ran out the moment the bailey locked the gate behind me.

CHAPTER 22

Rough hands seize my shoulders and drag me into a doorway. I grope for my knife, but my trembling hands cannot obey. I am bruised and weakened.

"Kenna?" someone whispers. A tall, wiry form looms over me and my heart stutters before I return to reason and recognize Munro's son.

"Rob?"

"Hush!" He places a finger to his lips. "Shaw is near at hand."

Down the lane, voices murmur and laugh. In the faint light that glows from within a blackened shop front, shadowy figures flit. I hold my hand over my mouth to cover the sound of my breathing until the light disappears and the voices die away.

"Why did you accost me?" I rub my aching ribs and scowl as we emerge from our hiding place.

"Sorry 'bout that. I didnae mean to strike ye so hard. I was certain they'd spy ye at any moment, and Shaw is no friend of yours."

"That I know." I wince at the pain of my many bruises. "Why are you out on the lane after dark? More thievery?"

"Not tonight." Rob chuckles softly. "Da's foot is swollen, so he sent me to help you dig the grave." He takes his kerchief from his threadbare doublet and ties it over his face.

"Oh." Despite my aching bones, and the dreadful task awaiting us, the thought of spending time with Rob brings a smile to my lips. We hurry to the Lindsay's home, which looms silent and dark ahead.

I raise my fist to knock, but Rob seizes my hand in his. My face floods with heat.

"Are ye off in the head? We cannae risk any noise!" My comrade in mischief takes my arm and leads me to the side of the house, where a short flight of narrow steps leads to a kitchen.

The red-haired lass, Catriona, lets us in. She eases the door closed and motions for us to wait, but she vanishes like mist at sunrise before I can ask her about Annie.

We warm ourselves at the fire. This kitchen is three times as large as Donny's, and as fine as that of my home in the country. The scent of baked bread lingers in the air.

Catriona returns carrying a flickering cruise lamp and a shovel. Her eyes are enormous.

"This way." She motions with her head in the direction of a box of tapers on the mantel. "Bring light."

We do so, igniting the tapers by touching them to the embers of the fire. Then we follow the lass along a passageway and through a narrow door that leads to a staircase. In silence, we creep downward, the wooden treads creaking beneath our feet until we emerge into a storage room where a trapdoor yawns open in the center of the floor.

"He's down there," Catriona whispers. She holds out her shovel to Rob.

The knowledge of what awaits beyond the black maw of that trapdoor strikes me with the force of a winter storm. I drop my light; it fizzles out when it strikes the floor.

Swearing an oath, Rob retrieves it and lights it once more with his own taper.

"I've no wish to end up in the dark down here," he says.

Catriona flees back up the stairs, taking her lamp with her. Rob gazes after her with a rueful expression.

"Could've used another pair of hands." He shrugs and motions for me to go first. My dinner roils within my stomach.

"I cannot do it. You go."

Rob swiftly descends the ladder and backs away from the

opening. "He's good and dead. He'll no' harm ye, Kenna. Come down." I tremble from head to foot. After several false tries, I make my way onto the ladder, holding my taper with one hand and fumbling to keep from tripping over my skirts. The ladder creaks and shakes as I descend. I make it to the solid dirt floor and force myself to turn around.

We are in a small, square root cellar. Crumbling, empty shelves line one wall. A second shovel stands in the far corner. And Master Lindsay's body, wrapped head to foot in linen, lies a single pace away from my feet. I stifle a shriek.

"I dinnae have need of this now, do I?" Rob tugs the kerchief away from his mouth and nose. "Keeping the stiff here was a good idea. Nice and cold, so the smell in't so bad. 'Bout time to bury him, though."

I have nothing to say in response. Rob fixes his taper to a shelf with a glob of wax and I do the same. Then the lad hands me a shovel and we get to work.

Within minutes, my fear gives way to a heated anger. How dare Donny send me here to do this! The situation is horrifying, both because of the corpse lying at my feet and because I, the granddaughter of an Earl, am sent to dig a grave like a common servant. As if emptying chamber pots and scrubbing grubby cookware were not enough. What utter gall!

My hands are soon blistered and ache something fierce. My ribs pain me, and I pant from the effort of my work. The rocky soil beneath our feet has no equal. How can Donny and Mrs. Lindsay expect us to dig a trench deep enough to house a man's body?

"Let's rest a moment. *Och,* my poor back!" Rob winces as he stretches.

I cease my digging with no sense of relief. The hole is now merely big enough for a small dog, perhaps. We have much more work to do. I drop my shovel and plant my hands on my knees to catch my breath, but a timid voice from above calls me to the trapdoor.

"How goes it?" Catriona whispers.

"It goes well." Rob places his hand on my shoulder. "Kenna here has a strong back. Digs as well as any man, she does." He grins at me with a wicked gleam in his dark eyes.

My palms no longer sting, for I feel only the weight of Rob's hand on my shoulder. Is he teasing me, or were his words truly meant to compliment me? I cannot help smiling back at him, then duck my head in shame. I am a mere few paces away from a dead man. This is no time for levity!

"I've some ale. Shall I bring it to you?" Catriona's voice trembles.

"Here." I clamber part way up the ladder to take the two tankards from the grateful young lass. I whisper to her before she rises to her feet.

"Thank you for the ale. I must speak to you. Perhaps when we have finished?" Catriona nods and flees.

Our ale is freshly brewed and strong. At first, we speak little, but Rob soon heaves a sigh and places his tankard on the floor.

"Why are ye here, Kenna?" he asks of a sudden. His voice is soft.

"You know why I am here, Rob." My voice has a sharp edge of bitterness to it. Though a lady should keep her voice sweet and her demeanor calm, I can never keep my emotions from coloring my words.

"To be sure, we all know about the quarantine and the accusation of murder," Rob says. "But ye vow your innocence. What I mean is, what happened to your sister?"

I place my own tankard on the earthen floor and clear my throat, weary of forever having to fight back tears. Drawing a deep breath, I begin my tale, grateful for the faint light of the tapers that gutter nearby, which I pray will not reveal my wet eyes.

The words tumble out in a rush, telling of Cinaed, both mother and sister to me. I do not linger long on memories of Oliver but tell of how my sister caught his eye. I speak of the wedding, the grand ladies and gentlemen dressed in their finery, my sister's rich gown. Then I describe Grandfather. His booming laugh. How he loved to have me read to him while he drank his wine in the evenings. Our meetings in the larder as we laughed together and stole sweets.

Rob studies me while I speak. He blows out his breath in a stream when I pause to gather myself.

"I've heard of your grandfather. At least, I've heard talk of his grand house in the city." Rob's voice is soft.

"In the city?" I tilt my head to one side. "What do you mean? We live outside of town, in a house near the sea."

Blinking in surprise, Rob leans closer. "Have ye never seen his house on Leith Wynd?"

With a huff, I rise to my feet. "Grandfather does not have a house here, Rob. If he had, I would have heard of it. Surely you are thinking of someone else."

My fellow grave digger rises as well and offers me a shovel.

"I could be mistaken." He takes up his own tool and returns to our task at hand. "Ye've no' yet told me how ye came to the city."

I plunge my shovel into the hard-packed dirt and wince at the pain in my stinging palms and poor ribs.

"My sister was indeed poisoned, but not by me. By Oliver. Her husband." I attack my work with renewed vigor, envisioning that the swathed form lying nearby is the body of my brother-in-law, not the luckless Master Lindsay. If only I were here burying Oliver, not a stranger!

"Cinaed grew ill and weak." My voice trembles. "None of the apothecaries or physicians Grandfather sent for could understand why. She began to spit blood and lose teeth." I shut my eyes as though it will hide the images from me, but the memories are burnt into my soul. "She died in agony. I was there, watching as she breathed her last."

Rob places his shovel against the wall. "I am sorry." There is no hint of mockery in his voice. "Truly." He takes up his shovel again while I swipe my face with the back of my hand and clench my teeth together, determined to hold back the sobs that threaten to burst from me. I shan't wallow and weep here. There is a dead man to bury, and a living man to find, once I get to the other side of that devilish locked gate.

The hole grows wider and deeper as the night goes on. Rob glances at me every so often, and sometimes opens his mouth as though he means to say something. He does not, at least not until I drop my spade and lean against the cold wall to catch my breath. Rob quietly comes to stand beside me.

"Forgive me, Kenna. I must ask this. Are ye certain 'twas Oliver? Not someone else? Someone with a grudge against him. Or against the Earl?" His dark eyes are in shadow in the dim light of the tiny cellar, but the hesitant tone of his voice is plain.

I clench my fists. "At the very moment my sister lay dying, I found a bottle on the floor beside Oliver's doublet. It smelled exactly like a potion our servants concocted in the greenhouses. A draught to poison the rats and mice in the barns."

"The Devil fetch me! You're sure?" Rob leans closer and gazes into my face as I bob my head, not trusting my voice. "Why did he do it?"

An image of the smirking, simpering Cecelia, with her jet-black eyes and even blacker soul comes to mind, and my stomach twists inside me.

"I believe Oliver had his eye upon an English lady who often visited. And she had her eye on him." My nails dig into my raw palms. Despite my discomfort, I seize my shovel and stab it into the earth once again, as though I aim to dig my way into hell. To be sure, the place cannot be too far from this cellar inside the home of a dead man.

Rob joins me and repeats his former question. "How did ye come to the city?" He does not raise his head but attends to his own digging as though it is of great import.

"After I discovered Oliver's treachery, I fled from my sister's chamber and sought Grandfather's aid."

"Oh." Rob wipes sweat from his forehead and brushes his dark

STREETS OF SHADOW | 185

hair to the side. "Ye went to the Earl," he murmurs, as though to himself.

What does he mean by that? I cannot read Rob's expression for the dimness of the light. I rush to explain myself. "Grandfather was distraught. He knew I was in danger and had his man escort me away from the house through a hidden passage. He planned to send me to a place of safety." Swiftly, I describe the great black coach that overtook my cart.

Rob glances at my face. "And the black coach took ye here?"

"Yes. The horrible man who kidnapped me brought me to the head of Stewart's Close. The moment I leapt from the carriage, the bailey seized me and locked me behind the gate. He declared the close was under quarantine, set a man there as a guard, and left me here to rot!"

Rob pauses in his work and faces me. "Men with secrets come here to the city to disappear. There be many places to hide." He cocks his head to one side. His dark eyes glitter as they gaze into mine.

I drop my spade and wrap my arms around myself, trying to calm my trembling. "I did not flee here to hide myself! Oliver sent me here, believing I would not survive. Believing he could make me disappear."

Rob studies my face. "It does seem to be so."

Mollified by his agreement, I pick up my spade again. "'Tis a thing I can hardly bear, to find myself accused of my own sister's murder! What cruelty!" I grit my teeth. "When I escape this place, I shall find him!" I pause and take a deep breath. "I shall find him and then I shall kill him."

At those words, Rob drops his own spade. "I've no doubt ye mean it. Yet where will that leave ye, Kenna? It will not bring your sister back. Nor will the courts look any kindlier on ye than they do now." His dark eyes are wide with dismay.

I grip the handle of my spade until my torn palms bleed. "Of course, killing Oliver will not bring Cinaed back to me." My voice trembles with rage. "Yet it is justice, is it not? I watched my beloved sister die at the hands of the husband who vowed before God to love her! He does not deserve to draw breath, and while I am alive, I will seek his death." I return to my work. After a moment, so does Rob.

We toil for hours and no longer speak. Time creeps along. My back aches fiercely, along with my poor ribs and torn palms. Rob at last decides our hole is deep and long enough. The grave is shallow, to be sure. Any person of wits could see that, yet my bleeding hands can no longer heft my shovel.

Master Lindsay's body is heavy. I'd been dreading the time when I'd have to touch the linen-wrapped form, but by this point, I barely hesitate. We drag and shove the corpse over to the hole and roll him in; he lands with a dull thud. One of my bloody palms leaves a mark on the linen, a perfect crimson handprint. Something churns in my stomach at the sight. 'Tis as though I've left a mark of guilt on the man, naming myself his killer.

"Here." Rob hands me his kerchief. I take it gratefully and wrap my stinging palm tight.

At last, we cover the grave, shoveling dirt over the unmoving form below, where the clods land like the sound of rain tapping on a rooftop. After we tamp down the soil, our wretched task is done. We place our spades against the wall and climb the ladder, away from the secret burial site.

We find Catriona dozing by the fire. I am loathe to wake her but attempt to do so with a soft prod to her shoulder. Followed by a wee shake when she does not awaken. Then a rougher shaking.

Her eyes fly open. She bolts to her feet and wobbles, unsteady as a newborn lamb, blinking in the weak glow from the hearth.

"What is it?" she blurts. "Is anything wrong?"

"I only came to tell you we've finished. I am sorry to wake you, but I must ask something. Could Annie not return to live here? I must find her another home."

Catriona's eyes fill with tears. Rob's eyebrows raise and he sits at the table, where he slumps and rubs his shoulders, gazing at me all the while with open curiosity.

"No, miss! She must never come back." Sniffling, the lass plucks a tiny object from the mantle above the grate. A tiny smile curves her lips as she runs a gentle finger over the it.

I stand beside her and stretch my hands closer to the blessed warmth of the smoldering coals. "Surely now that Master Lindsay is gone, there shall be no more trouble such as she witnessed before." With a frown, I recall Annie's distress at the sight of Mrs. Lindsay but dismiss it. She is so small; she would soon forget what she beheld. Wouldn't she?

"If only she *could* come back," Catriona says in a voice thick with tears. "I miss her so. 'Twas like having a wee sister. But I pray she never crosses the Lindsay's threshold again."

"But—"

"If she stays with ye at the herbwife's house, she'll be a child with a home. A child who is loved. Here, she'll only be a servant, like me, who works night and day for her keep, and none to care for her one whit."

In one swift motion, Catriona seizes my hand and places the object she'd taken from the mantle, closing my fingers about it.

"This is Annie's." Her voice breaks. "Give it to her."

And with that, she flees the kitchen, holding a corner of her apron to her streaming eyes.

I hold the tiny thing closer to the firelight. Of blackened metal, 'tis a small round globe with a thin handle. A toy for an infant. I've seen such a thing before. The object makes a thin, rattling noise. Cinaed used to hold out a similar toy for her babe, who'd coo and reach for it. Pain strikes me inside. Both Cinaed and her babe are now gone. I tuck the toy inside my leather pouch.

"The lass is right." Rob rises from the table and wanders through the room, touching the fine painted ceramic dishes on a shelf. "Annie will have a good life with ye."

"I cannot remain here!" I whirl toward Rob. "This stinking city is a filth-ridden prison, not a place to live! 'Tis what I imagine hell to be, Rob. And I shall find a way out."

Rob's face stiffens. Without answering, he picks up a small cloth purse from the table.

"Our payment." He opens the bag, swiftly counts, and then hands me several heavy silver coins. "Your share." The metal gleams in the glow of the tapers and I take in a breath. The money will be more than enough to hire a coach to return me to Grandfather's home. My mood softens a bit, for now I feel a greater measure of hope than I've yet had occasion to experience in this place.

We creep from the Lindsay's home, and Rob accompanies me back to Donny's house. I am grateful for his presence, though my lips remain sealed. I am still angry at his words. He is likely angry at mine.

The freezing rain adds to my foul mood as we go, soaking into my already sodden clothing. As it's well past midnight, no other souls are about, and we arrive at Donny's door within minutes. I am determined to ignore Rob and sweep inside with my head held high, as any lady would do. But when I reach for the door, his hand closes upon my arm.

As I glance at him, startled, he leans down and my stomach dances within me. Rob murmurs in my ear.

"Though ye say for certain 'twas Oliver who killed your sister, the Earl has not sought for ye. I find this troubling, Kenna. Families care for their own. I cannot help wondering if Lord Ramsay has decided to forget about ye."

His breath is warm on my cheek, but his words stab me in the chest.

"Yet ye'll always have a place here, among us." Rob remains where he is for a moment. Then he steps back, and I shiver, more chilled than ever now his warmth is gone. "That is, if ye wish to stay. Ye have friends in this place ye call hell."

He turns his back, and his form fades into the misty darkness.

CHAPTER 23

The passageway before me is empty. My slippers make no sound on the thick carpets, but the rustling of my embroidered skirts is like the whisperings of invisible watchers who regard me with envy. Lush curls cascade about my face, forced reluctantly into the latest style by my maid. The scents of rosewater and lavender hover around me. My ruddy face is now pale with the thick makeup that Cinaed scorned, my cheeks rouged, my lips daubed in red. Though I've no scars to hide, I've placed a tiny patch of black silk on my cheek, near my mouth. The shape of a heart; quite coquettish, indeed! Cinaed would scold me fiercely if she could see me.

A footman awaits at the entrance to the grand hall. Grandfather is waiting for me inside with a special and most important guest. My hands tremble.

"A fine Scotsman, one of our own, returned to his rightful place," Grandfather loved to say. The Earl rejoiced when a Stuart returned once more to the throne of England. A small portrait of the King resides proudly above the fire in the grand drawing room. And now the man himself, our sovereign, King Charles the Second, is here in this very house!

Cinaed scorned to meet him, the profligate king who lives with his queen and his many mistresses, all in the same palace. I'd heard the whispered stories. Mrs. Harris was as fond of repeating the latest marketplace gossip of goings-on in London as she was of her spiced ale in the evenings.

"*A king should serve as a righteous example for his people,*" Cinaed often said.

"*A king can do whatever he wishes,*" Oliver would retort. Yet he spoke with a gleam of laughter in his eye, as he was wont to do whenever he contradicted his wife. And he did not insist that Cinaed present herself to the king.

Surprisingly, he gave me the opportunity, and I shall take it. I, Kenna, shall be a fine lady, one who has been in the presence of the king! Perhaps my sister and her husband will then allow my presentation to society. At last, my world will extend beyond the walls of Grandfather's house!

The footman opens the door, announces my name.

"Ah, yes, my granddaughter." Grandfather holds out his hand. His rings wink in the chandelier's light. "Come, child."

I step over the threshold. A man sits in a chair before the fire, a glass in his hand. My eyes fly to his legs. The king wears short breeches of black velvet, and white silk stockings encase his lower limbs, lending him the look of a strange, long-legged bird from one of Grandfather's zoology books.

With a sharp intake of breath, I raise my gaze. One must not stare so at the king's person!

Dark curls tumble past his shoulders and hide part of his face, yet I glimpse an angled cheek, a long nose, and a thin mustache. He raises his wine to dark-stained lips and takes a delicate sip before he addresses Grandfather.

"You have changed much, Lord Ramsay. I am hardly able to reconcile your visage with that of the young man I met so many years ago."

Grandfather does not move. His bearing remains erect, and I sense, rather than see, a tightness that stiffens his back and draws him to an imperceptibly greater height.

"You were a mere lad, your majesty. I admit the years have not dealt kindly with me. But allow me," he says, suddenly, his movements *now swift as he turns toward me. "Allow me to present to you, my granddaughter."*

I approach, holding my skirts, my palms slick with sweat. Will I be able to speak? If called on to speak, that is.

Grandfather clears his throat and gazes at me with sternness. He is an impatient man. It is taking me too long to make my way through the scattered chaises and little tables of this grand room. Trying to hurry, I stumble on my skirts. Righting myself, I continue, this time bumping into a footstool and losing my balance. I flail my arms as though I have become a living windmill and crash down on a painted harpsichord. Its spindly wooden legs collapse beneath my weight. I land with a loud crunch and end up sprawled across the unlucky instrument, my skirts above my knees. A discordant tinkling fills the air.

The man seated beside the fire laughs.

"I was never fond of that instrument, anyway," he says.

Grandfather barks for the footman, who helps me to my feet. I pray the thick, white paste smeared on my face hides the dark blush that must paint my skin by now.

The King has turned back to the fire. The red wine is like blood in his glass. I have yet to glimpse the whole of his face.

"Leave us." Grandfather's face wrinkles with distaste. The king laughs.

Female voices join the king's in merriment. Somehow, the room is now filled with many, many women dressed in fancy gowns like mine, with painted faces, crimson lips, and gleaming ebony tresses fashionably coiled and crimped; exotic birds perched on chaises and settees. They giggle and point at me with their fans.

The laughter grows until it echoes all around me as I flee back down the passageway, which grows longer and longer. Doors line the walls on either side, all closed and locked. How will I escape this wretched place?

Annie's giggling awakens me. I rise on one elbow, groggy and fogged with sleep, though my blood pounds with the terror of my dream. The child plays with my boots that lie where I'd tossed them on the floor. She has taken the bits of wood we'd used for our earlier game and placed them in a circle around the scuffed leather.

"Look." She gazes earnestly into my face.

"Well done." The child beams.

Blinking away the haze of slumber, I rise to draw on my skirts and lace my bodice over my linen shift. The dream was so real that for a moment I feel silk against my skin and smell the scent of my perfume. Strangely, I did not dream of the toil of digging into the rocky earth, nor of heaving a wrapped body into its hidden grave. I dreamed of something that did not happen. Not really.

But part of the dream was true. The memory squeezes my soul. I try to shove the thoughts away as I run fingers through my tangled hair. They will not leave me. Instead, they pester me like buzzing, biting flies.

The king never came to our house in the country. He was, of a truth, meant to visit Grandfather this past spring, yet he did not. The appointed day came and went with no visit. No one spoke of it in my presence, so I never knew why.

Though our sovereign never made an appearance, a man who was then a stranger to me did. He was Cecelia's father; a hawk-nosed man with a great belly and no hair. He came not long after the expected royal visit. He was a man with a title of import and wealth so great, even Grandfather behaved deferentially before such a grand being.

I was not richly gowned and painted when I glimpsed him, nor was I invited. I'd entered the drawing room unbidden, searching for a lost book. And finding myself so near to Grandfather and his guest, I'd overheard the words the man had murmured, while Oliver was pouring more sweet wine and Grandfather pointed out the view of the surrounding hills.

I can hardly reconcile your visage with that of the young man I met so many years ago.

Grandfather had dropped his goblet. His wine spattered the feet of his guest and soaked into the pale carpet.

Disconcerted to find myself in the company of these men, by the strange words uttered, and by Grandfather's lack of composure, I had backed away and tripped over my skirts, falling on the poor harpsichord.

I've never liked that instrument, anyway.

Grandfather had spoken those words. He had flown to my side, his laughter a bit too hearty, while the servants tended to the spilled wine. Grandfather had helped me to my feet, while his guest fussed and fretted over the dark stains on his fine new boots.

And the man's daughter, unseen until I arose, had laughed most prettily, with a note of mockery I could not miss. Cecelia, the haughty. The painted one. The ugly black-eyed cow.

Forthwith Oliver had escorted me out. *He* was the man mortified by my appearance that day. With drawn brows and an air of outrage, he'd scolded me and marched me off.

Grandfather had politely escorted his guests to the door only moments after I made my escape. From my favorite spot near the top of the grand staircase, I'd witnessed their exit.

How I had stared at Cecelia! Tossing her black curls, she behaved with the manner and bearing of one who was never disobeyed. She'd tapped on Oliver with her fan and asked him when they would see one another again. Her laughter, shrill and high, had floated to me in my perch on the stairs; I hated her in that moment.

Her painted face and her taunting words come to my mind unbidden in the moments when I miss my sister the most. Oliver killed for her, that laughing lass with the high title and mountain of wealth.

With heaviness of heart, I sit near Annie and help her rearrange the wood into different patterns. Remembering the object Catriona had given me, I retrieve it from my pocket; she smiles, seizes it, and gives it a shake. It produces its faint rattling sound. Once more, memories of the brief time of happiness when my sister and her husband doted on their own wee one weigh me down with sadness. Rising, I pace the room and focus instead on the dream that haunts me.

Why has Grandfather not sought for me? Because I embarrassed him in front of his important guests? Surely not for such a trifling thing as displaying a bit of clumsiness before company! I pause at the mantle and brush my fingers along the dark leaves of a bundle of herbs hung there to dry. A spicy smell tickles my nose while I hang my head at the memory of my embarrassing mishap.

That incident cannot be the reason Grandfather does not come for me! Sighing, I sit beside the hearth and shift the wee bits of wood yet again, this time arranging them in rows like soldiers. Annie giggles in delight and places her rattle among them. I attempt to play with her, but my mind wanders down ever-darkening paths.

Rob's whispered words cannot be true. He surmises Grandfather does not truly care for me.

He is wrong!

Donny joins us in the kitchen. She asks naught about the preceding night's activities. She does cast an appraising look at my bandaged hand and examines my wounds. After she coats my raw palms with a stinging salve of hers, bringing tears to my eyes, she re-wraps my bleeding hand in a clean strip of cloth. We are supping on our meager meal of oatmeal porridge when a knock sounds at the door.

Donny rises and goes to answer. I stay to comfort Annie, who now jumps and trembles each time we have a visitor.

"Callum." Donny strides back to the table.

I barely avoid spilling porridge on my lap. The payment! Strange that I'd forgotten. I close my eyes. I suppose burying the corpse of a man whose wife killed him in a fit of rage was rather distracting, to be sure.

Donny settles herself at the table again and slurps her porridge. "Well?" She raises her white eyebrows high. "Go."

I hurry to the door. "Here." I thrust the pennies into Callum's outstretched hand. The stone-faced man accepts the coins and counts them.

"Good." He stalks away, not even bothering to close the door behind him.

"You're most welcome, kind sir," I call out in a chirpy voice. The moment the words fall from my lips I regret them, remembering how Cinaed taught me that words spoken in haste can never be retracted. I let out a stifled breath, greatly relieved when Callum does not turn around.

At least now, I'm free from any obligation to the guild. My step is lighter as I duck back inside and help Donny wash our bowls and cups. I need not fear their retaliation, though I remain burdened by the bailey's price on my head.

After putting the room to rights, I decide to return to my pallet, hoping my host will take pity and allow me to catch up on the sleep that forever eludes me. I lie next to Annie, who already slumbers beside the fire. Wrapping my blanket about me until I am warm and snug, I sigh. I miss my comfortable bed, but the warmth is heavenly, nonetheless.

And at that moment, there is yet another knock on the wretched door.

"Answer it," Donny screeches from somewhere in the house.

"God's beard," I mutter as I rise, uttering one of the many oaths Cinaed used to forbid. What if I find Shaw, or some other angry being seeking for me? I take hold of my new knife and hold it at the ready when I cautiously open the door. Una is there before me with all her big teeth displayed in a wide grin. It calls to mind the poor harpsichord that I shattered.

"Ye'll no' be needing that, now, will ye?" she says, eyeing the blade in my hand. The girl enters and seizes me in a swift embrace. "Da says you're now one of us. Welcome to the guild."

"What?" I swiftly closed the door, lest some person outside spies my face and decides to exchange me for a purse full of gold.

"Ye heard me." Una's cat eyes twinkle. She sweeps into the

kitchen, gazes about for a moment, settles herself into Donny's chair and takes the pipe from the mantel, placing it between her teeth. I gasp at such bold effrontery. I consider telling her she is not allowed to do such things, but swiftly toss the thought aside. Donny can tell her if she wishes. 'Tis of no import to me.

Finally remembering my breeding, I draw some ale for my guest, which gives me a moment to take in this new information. I am a member of the guild now? A tremulous smile plays upon my lips. What would my old housekeeper say of this? Kenna is now a thief. A member of a great guild of thieves, no less. I rather wish I could see Mrs. Harris now, if only for the pleasure of witnessing the expression that would paint itself across her round moon of a face.

"My thanks, Poisoner." Una takes the proffered ale and slurps her drink. Over the rim of her wooden cup, she regards me with her gleaming green orbs. "And we've a job, now."

"A job?" I plop onto a low stool. Will they never leave me alone, these thieves? I've hardly slept a wink these past few nights! And after digging for hours, my torn hands throb. With bleary eyes, I glance wistfully at Annie, who sleeps peacefully before the hearth, her doll and rattle clutched in her tiny hands.

"Rob will be there." Una's sharp eyes study my face.

"Oh?" My wretched attempt to feign disinterest fails completely, for as I speak, I raise a hand to my rough hair to smooth it. The movement does not escape Una's shrewd, mirth-filled glance.

She giggles. "Come, we'll get to it, now. The bairn sleeps, and Sheona is here. And the day is a cold one. Few be outside their homes."

My protestations are weak. Even *I* hear the false notes in my voice. Donny emerges from wherever it is she hides in the depths of her dreary house, dressed in "Sheona's" skirts, and shoos us away, saying she'll watch over Annie while I'm gone. I do not miss the warning look she gives me.

Una and I steal outdoors, into a grayish-white day of misting fog.

My lips are dry and my heart flutters inside. I tell myself it is because I'm nervous about the task at hand, but that is a falsehood. Kenna, the would-be lady, finds pleasure in the thought of spending time with a young thief.

What would you make of that, Mrs. Harris?

CHAPTER
24

"Where do we go?" I am careful to speak in a whisper. We skirt round the back of Donny's house and emerge into a narrow space formed by a gathering of three tall houses that huddle together as if for warmth. The chill in the air seeps through me. At least the stench from the vile river that forever trickles down the middle of the lane is not so foul.

"Ye'll see soon enough." Una scratches her head and spits like a coarse stable hand. "We've a debt to settle."

I sigh. My own "debt" was repaid but an hour ago, and now I am sent to collect from others? Such a troublesome thing to do business with thieves. One must take care.

Shouts from somewhere overhead make my pulse race. I crane my neck and peer upwards, fearing that at any moment a servant or housewife will pour her slops on us.

"Come." Una pulls me through a narrow doorway. We emerge into a small animal shed, empty, though still thick with the smell of its former occupants.

"He'll meet us here." Una eyes me with the hint of a smile on her ruddy face.

This time, I keep from lifting my hand to smooth my hair. "Very well."

I walk about the stalls, studying them as though the reeking piles of moldering straw hold great interest, and remembering Rob's treacherous words. In short, he implied Grandfather does not care for me! Anger sharpens within. Then I recall the feel of Rob's breath in my ear as he whispered words of kindness. And I again pat my tangle of plaited hair. Una giggles. My face grows hot.

"I think he fancies ye." Una picks up a bit of straw and traces lines with it on the walls of the shed. Her eyes glance in my direction to gauge my reaction.

"Certainly not." Despite my words, my heart makes a rather pleasant skipping motion within. "He hardly knows me." I turn my back to hide the traitorous flush on my cheeks. "Besides, 'tis not becoming for me to..." I stop and freeze, dismayed at what I was about to say.

Not becoming for me to mingle with men beneath my station. Had I truly been about to say those words? Mrs. Harris's words. Oliver's words. My shoulders sag. Grandfather would have said the same. He would never even allow a lad such as Rob to be in my presence. Then a small tuft of stinking hay strikes me in the back of the head. I whirl with a shout of dismay.

Una faces me with another fistful of dirty straw, holding it at the ready. Her eyes gleam.

"Do ye mean to say, Lady Poisoner, that our Rob here is not fit even to speak with ye?" Her face hardens into a mask, betraying no trace of mirth.

My shoulders slump and I hold my hands up in surrender. "Please, don't throw any more of that. It's been hard enough to keep clean of late, and I've no wish to be further pelted with hay and dung."

I am too embarrassed and disheartened to say more and must force myself to stand my ground and meet Una's fierce gaze. She cannot possibly understand! I *am* a lady. Grandfather hired the best (though despised) tutors from England for my education. My lessons ranged from singing, to speaking French, and to drawing. Grandfather promised I would enter society when I was ready and mingle only with the best of gentlemen. And though Rob has a quick smile and is full of wit and humor, he is not of my station. He must labor for his keep. He is not a gentleman. My heart sinks at the thought.

Rob arrives at that moment, appearing as though blown in on a gust of wind. He shakes his dark hair from his eyes.

"Hail to thee, Lady Kenna, newest member of our guild." He bows low. "Keep your knife at the ready."

How dare he? My mouth gapes open. "Keep my knife at the ready? For what purpose?"

Una roars with laughter. "'Tis why we wanted ye to join us today, Poisoner. We need someone quick with the blade. And your knowledge of potions is fearsome, so we're told." Dropping the hay from her fist, she flings one arm over my shoulders and murmurs in my ear: "Though the Poisoner fancies herself high and mighty, she's here with *us* now, in't she?"

Una shoves me away. My hands clench into fists. "How dare you?"

The lass says nothing. Her lifted chin and the slant of her brow lend her the air of a cat that knows it's far superior to the lowly humans that regard it.

"Come, now." Rob places a hand on my shoulder. "Una means no harm, and I only meant ye must be wary. Do ye no' remember the ransom they've offered for ye? Keep the head, Kenna!"

Shaking away Rob's hand, I breathe out a stream of air and struggle to control the trembling of my limbs. "I did not murder my sister, and I will thank both of you to remember that. And if you cannot, then I'll have no more to do with either of you or with your guild!"

The following silence would be complete, save for the sounds of muffled shouts and voices that echo from the streets outside. Una's face grows even darker. Rob merely shrugs, his face a blank mask. "We know that. Come. We've work to do."

With a scowl, Una withdraws a dirt-stained, bedraggled cap from the bag she carries. She thrusts it into my hands. "Put this on. 'Twill help hide ye from unfriendly eyes."

With a sigh, I comply and take the ugly thing from her fingers. I tuck stray locks inside and allow the bedraggled lace to hang low over my eyes. Una shoves past me and plunges into the thickening fog, muttering more words meant for my ears only.

"We're all ye have, lass. No one else will have aught to do with ye, ye sow."

I grit my teeth and stomp after her. How is it I could have begun to see Una as my friend? And how could I have allowed myself to entertain romantic thoughts about Rob, the thief? These two are no more than lowborn thieves of the city. And I am the granddaughter of an Earl. I straighten my shoulders. Those two belong here. I do not.

Few of the close's residents have ventured outside, which suits our purposes, though we must keep our faces bent lest someone see us. I detest the frilly thing upon my head, but I am grateful I've something to help hide my identity. The poor state of my gown must help me blend in with the locals. I should be glad my skirts are torn and filthy, but I'm still aghast at the state of my clothing. I will not remain here forever.

We round a corner and Una, who had been hurrying ahead, drops back to my side.

"Nelly Morgan's place." She jabs me in the ribs as we pass a door. "Her husband died a few years back, so she takes in washing. Does a right fair job; she feeds her wee ones and herself with the money she earns. Now others, like old Maggie Gray, work for her."

Before I can respond, we pass a small house with lights in the upper windows. Una points, after another prod to my ribs.

"Mary Leslie owns that house and two of the shops in Stewart's Close. A shrewd businesswoman, to be sure. Ye'll no' want to cross her."

I rub my side. Though my anger simmers, I bite the retorts that lie sour on my tongue. I shall feign I do not hear Una, as Mrs. Harris taught me to do if addressed in an impertinent manner by one of the servants. But Una is hard to ignore. In a harsh undertone, she speaks of other women who live here within the city, always after a poke to my side.

Names and occupations fly from the lass's lips: Dorothea, who makes pastries and sweets; Hester and Joan, sisters who sell the finest wool thread in the city; Ada, Pennie, Susanna, all businesswomen according the wild-haired girl with her gap-toothed smile. All whose doings are apparently so fascinating she must regale me with their stories. My ribs ache. After another blow to my sore sides, I whirl to face Una and seize her by the arm.

"What is all this about?" I hiss. "Nellie, Maggie, Susanna? Why do I care what they do to pass their time?"

Una stops and folds her arms, regarding me with a satisfied grin.

"Our Poisoner is certain she'll find a grand gentleman who will keep her in ease all her life." She darts a glance at Rob, who has paused mid-step and regards us with frank curiosity. "And he'll keep her, he will. He'll keep her locked away like a spoiled house cat while she wears silks and eats dainty bits and begs all her life for every single rag she wears and every crumb he tosses her." Una draws closer until her nose nearly touches mine. "Lady Poisoner fancies living in a bonny wee cage like a bonny...wee...pet."

My mouth drops open; I swipe the tattered lace on my cap away from my eyes. "Whatever do you mean by that? A man should give his wife a home and hearth. 'Tis his duty and her right."

Una only laughs and turns her back to me. Rob shrugs and motions for me to follow, and I do so, seething.

"I do *not* wish to live in a cage." I dart around a scurrying rat as I hasten to reach Una's side. She pays no mind to my words.

"*I* shall beg no one for my keep." Una strides with her back straight as a washing board as we hurry through more shadows. "Ye turn your haughty nose up at all of us here, Poisoner, yet you're not half so grand as ye think."

"What?" I earn a shushing from Rob.

Una smirks at me. "We women of the city take care of ourselves. If I do marry, it will only be to a man who will no' try to keep me under his thumb." She chuckles. "And if he has no wish to work and earn his own way, he might find the need to beg *me* for a coin or two."

"Of that I've no doubt," Rob says with a teasing laugh. "And he'll be lucky if he ever squeezes a penny from your tight fist."

The two chuckle and forge ahead, both stealing glances at me from over their shoulders. Una's face fills with mocking glee, and even Rob wears a grin. His glinting eyes betray a message I do not wish to interpret. Does he, too, regard me as a silly and self-centered lass who wishes to be nothing but a spoiled pet?

My face stings with a rising blush. Una's words fly inside my head like birds caught in a small room, fluttering and striking against the windows as they try to escape. I've no wish to live in any cage, richly appointed as it may be. Grandfather's estate was not so confining! But to my dismay, memories of home prick and sting as we cross the narrow lane to approach yet another dark doorway. Grandfather's home *was* confining. I fled outdoors often to escape watchful servants and my sniveling tutors. And Oliver's stern gaze.

There, I had comfort, ease, and no friends, save the horses in the barns or the swallows in the eaves. Except for Lorna, with her quick laugh and freckled face. We used to run among the trees and play, making mud cakes and wee faeries from bits of twig and leaf. I smile at the memory. But of course, far too soon Mrs. Harris separated us, for 'twas not seemly for me to play with a servant.

"I do *not* want to live in a cage," I mutter to myself, hurrying after Rob and Una. I've had quite enough of one already, for this close is the worst sort of cage imaginable. I wrinkle my nose when we encounter a dead cat, lying bloated with its stiff legs extended to the side. Here in the city, there is only filth and want, illness and death. Una does not know of what she speaks. She scorns fine houses, decent food, and a life of comfort. Shouldn't *all* aspire to such things?

"I'll show you how wrong you are," I whisper as I gingerly step over the swollen carcass.

CHAPTER
25

"This is the house." Rob holds out his hand out to signal us to stop. "Inside, quick."

He eases open a door; we squeeze through and hurry up the stairs. After climbing to the third floor, we creep along a short passageway where Rob surprises me by crouching down without warning in a doorway. He speaks to a man sitting with his back to the wall, wrapped in a dark cloak. The man lifts his head and wheezes out a laugh, takes something Rob offers him and places a key into Rob's hand.

I follow wordlessly behind Rob and Una. At the end of the corridor, they pause before another door, unlock it, and we hurry inside.

"Come, Kenna, help us search." Rob eases the door closed behind us as Una lights a fragrant beeswax candle. The lad hurries to a tall cupboard and rifles through it while Una crouches in front of the empty, cold grate and peers up into the chimney, holding aloft her flickering light. At her harsh command, I join her and lift a box from the mantle.

"What are we looking for?" My insides quiver. Footsteps fall in the passageway outside, and the muffled voices echo all around us. Someone could discover us at any moment! Why did I go along with this madness?

Rob whispers. "'Twill be a wee purse or parcel with round black seeds inside."

"What?" I drop the box I was holding. "Are you serious? We search only for seeds?"

"They're worth even more than the Poisoner here with that price on her head." Una emerges from the grate, unknowingly repeating Donny's words to me when I'd helped her concoct her special tincture only yesterday. The lass dusts a scattering of ashes from her hair. "'Tis a handful of black peppercorns. Shaw promised it to Donny and took her payment. Then he said soldiers seized it from him when he returned from the port." She pauses to spit on the floor. "Liar. He kept her payment all the same. Donny knows it."

I shudder. We are in Shaw's home. What if the man returns when we are here? Gulping, I redouble my efforts and yank open the drawers of a small chest to search inside.

"Is Donny certain Shaw lied?"

"Aye." Rob continues to sift through the contents of a basket. "Donny knows a thief and a liar when she sees one."

I freeze. When *she* sees one. Not *he*.

"You know Donny is a woman?" My voice ends in a high squeak.

"Ye *finally* discovered it, did ye?" Una whirls to face me with a wide-eyed expression of delight on her face. We remain where we are for a moment, gaping at one another like two open-mouthed herrings in a market stall. Then Una's face collapses and she melts into laughter. I cannot help joining her merriment. I laugh until tears well.

"We'd begun to take wagers, Steenie and I." She gasps and shakes with laughter. "Wondered how long it'd take before ye figured it out."

"How many people know?" I giggle and swipe at my wet face.

"The guild members." Una smiles at me. "No one else. And Poisoner, I've only one thing to say to ye."

"You'll have my head if I tell anyone."

"True, that is." She links her arm in mine. I do not pull away.

Though Una's words about my desire to live in a cage continue to sting, my anger drains away, leaving a dull ache in my chest. Her words about the women here are true. They know how to care for themselves, whereas I, well, I would likely have perished without the help of a woman of the city. One of the hardiest women I have ever known, in fact.

Rob clears his throat.

"I'll search the bedchamber." He glances from me to Una and back again with a smirk on his face. "Ye'll want to keep up the search yourselves, if ye can find time when you're done with all this blethering."

This time, I respond before Una does. I seize a cloth from a nearby trestle and fling it at Rob's head. He ducks with a laugh.

Una soon finds our quarry. Shaw, the sly old baker, had folded the handful of black peppercorns inside a scrap of parchment and tucked it into a crevice in the wall beside the grate. We do not celebrate more than a moment.

After taking care to leave Shaw's rooms as we found them, we return to the man in the passageway. He snores and does not appear to awaken when Rob places the key into his hand. Then our mysterious assistant bolts to his feet and flies away before I've time to blink twice.

We make our way to Donny's home by a different route, and I am once more hopelessly lost, impossible as it must seem for one to become lost within a single, narrow lane. But we do not stick to the lane. We hurry through a short tunnel, creep through a wee courtyard, and fly through the corridor of one tall house only to enter another, keeping our heads bent.

We soon squeeze between houses through a space so narrow we must creep sideways. We finally emerge near the kirk. Una and Rob creep ahead. Before I can follow, a hand plucks at my sleeve. I turn with a startled gasp.

"Please, miss."

Before me is the young wife who'd grudgingly taken a few potatoes. She gazes at me with wide, frightened eyes and holds her hands up in a supplicating gesture.

"I mean ye no harm." She glances around to make certain no one is nearby. "We've no food. I have a wee son. I clean Mrs. King's house for pennies, but there's little left in the shops inside our close. Prices have gone up and my few pennies will not buy what we need." Her voice breaks.

"Where've ye got to, Bess?" an old woman calls from a nearby house. "These linens will no' wash themselves."

The young woman creeps away, ducking her head. Her hunched shoulders are thin. A chill creeps into my being. For all of Una's talk of their freedom, many women here, namely those without the money to buy their way beyond the gate or to purchase from the guild's hidden stores, are still in grave danger while the bailey maintains his so-called quarantine.

"Kenna?" Rob whispers as he returns to my side. "Follow me. We've one more duty before we can go home."

Taking my arm, he hurries me inside a nearby apothecary shop that smells of spices and ale. Una waits within. She speaks in muted tones to a shriveled woman who sits behind a large counter. The woman laughs, displaying pink gums inside her wide mouth.

Rob ducks his head in deference to the toothless crone. "Hello, Mrs. Kennison." He steps back and murmurs to me: "Who was that woman?"

"A mother who will starve soon, along with her son." I clench my fists at my sides. "While a great pile of food sits right beneath their feet."

Una flies to me and takes my arm in a painful grip. "We'll return soon, ma'am," she calls over her shoulder while dragging me back out to the street. She leads me toward the kirk and her grip tightens until I bite my lip to keep from crying out. Rob falls into step beside us, keeping a wary eye on the few souls who are about.

"Are ye off your head, Poisoner?" Una hisses to me once we duck inside the chapel.

"What do you mean by that?" I yank my arm away and rub the sore spots.

Una growls and mutters under her breath. She doesn't respond until we have crept to the hidden door leading to the stores of bounty below.

"I mean, Poisoner—" the lass grunts as she yanks aside the boards that hide the door, "keep your mouth shut tight about the vaults! We must no' speak of them above ground."

"And why not?" I tear off the dreadful cap. "People are hungry, Una. A woman just asked me for help. Me, the 'Poisoner,' the one they all fear!"

Una smacks her forehead with her hand. I refrain from asking her if it hurt though I am sorely tempted to do so. Rob motions for us to hurry, so we clatter down the stairs, skipping treads. Once we emerge into the corridor, Rob greets a tall shadow that materializes from one of the dark vaults. "Hello there, Callum."

My stomach tightens inside me. I do have the few potatoes and turnips that remain hidden in the ashes of Donny's grate, but 'twill not be enough for Bess and her child. And if Callum is on the watch, I cannot take more food from the vaults. Not when a man with a face of iron and a heart carved of rock will be there.

The man greets his daughter. He ignores me. Una shows her father a bit of parchment with some writing. "We didnae have time to get it read." She glances back at me with narrowed eyes.

"Let *her* read it." Callum tosses his head in my direction. "Let her make herself useful for something." Wordlessly, Una hands the parchment to me and I snatch it from her, seething at her father's insulting words.

"Beans, oatmeal. And tatties?" I raise my eyebrows.

"Potatoes." Una chuckles as a trace of her former humor returns.

"I know what tatties are," I mutter.

While I read, Rob and Callum load items onto the makeshift lift. The apothecary can afford to eat well, but what of his neighbors? Does the woman who sweeps out the neighboring house know about the vaults? Does *she* have the means to pay the thieves so she won't starve? 'Tis plain that Bess, the young wife, does not. I grit my teeth.

Once the men finish loading the platform, Callum barks

instructions to his daughter. She is to retrieve the goods from the raised platform and deliver them to the apothecary, making sure to receive payment. She'll then be free to return Donny's stolen spice to its rightful owner. Rob is to remain in the vaults, as it is his turn to stand watch. Then Callum, feet planted firmly, lamp held aloft in his hand, stares at me with hard eyes.

"And I shall accompany our Poisoner to her house."

"Of course." I nod coolly at the man as though bestowing a favor. Then, to stall for time, I offer to help Rob raise the platform. 'Tis no easy task, as Una has elected to take a ride. She grins at the two of us as she rises, her eyes traveling from one of us to the other and back again. Her thoughts are as clear on her face as though she has painted the words on her skin. The cow.

"How long must you remain at watch?" I whisper to Rob as we work together to turn the crank.

"Until midnight." Rob grimaces with the effort of operating the creaking platform. "'Tis no' so bad," he adds with a grin. "I've plenty of food, though I've always thought 'twould be pleasant with a lass to keep me company." He speaks so softly his words are for my ears alone.

I do not answer, for my tongue has frozen. The platform attains its destination and Rob ties off the rope, knotting it around an iron hook in the wall. Then he turns back to me and leans against the wall with one hand on his hip.

"Unless, of course, said lass dinnae wish to pass her time with a man who must work for his bread, and a thief at that," he whispers.

He allows the words to hang in the air as we face one another in the black recesses of the vaults, lit only by the sputtering lanterns. Rob studies my face as he awaits my response.

Callum clears his throat, clearly out of patience and eager to escort me away from this place. My time is nearly up. Hardly knowing how I dare, I lean forward to whisper in Rob's ear: "I'll be back later."

Before he can answer, I march to Callum's side. As we head

toward the winding stairs, I smile at the sound of Rob's cheerfully whistled tune. My heart sputters in a strange rhythm. I only set the rendezvous with him so that I might take more food to share with others. Still, my insides warm at the thought of spending time with the dark-haired lad.

We hurry through the stinking lane to Donny's house. Callum leaves without a word. I heave open the heavy door and return gratefully to the warmth inside. Leaning my back against the worn wooden planks, I sink to the floor and hug my knees, exhausted, chilled through, and filled with shame. I am wicked. For, no matter what I tell myself, I am a liar. I do not return to the vaults with only the thought of helping the helpless. I am no angel, and were Mrs. Harris to know my scandalous thoughts, she'd also know that I am no lady.

Truth be told, I cannot stop thinking about kissing a thief.

CHAPTER
26

I do not rest long, for only minutes after I remove my boots and settle myself by the fire, someone knocks at the door. Una and Callum are outside. The man does not greet me nor even ask to enter before he crosses the threshold, forcing me to back away with rapid steps. Why did he come back here? Only Una had the order to return the packet to Donny. She had no need to bring her father. With a sigh, I follow the two into the warm kitchen, where Donny grins and offers wine. Her crinkled cheeks glow at the sight of the packet Una proffers, and the old soldier takes it with a cry of delight.

Una and I sip wine while Annie lies on her pallet nearby, cuddling her doll. Though our earlier conversations were none too pleasant, Una is now friendly to me, and her eyes are alight with humor. She's tough, but her nature is also full of laughter and jest. 'Tis as though she cannot bear to be filled with anger for long. I relax and enjoy her teasing banter. The room fills with the fragrant scent of herbs and freshly baked oat cakes stacked upon a cloth to cool. The wine is sweet. Callum remains in the doorway, his face blank. He refuses a drink.

"I fear that was too easy a job." Una takes a sip from her cup.

"Naw." Donny shakes her head and noisily gulps her own wine. "He thought he tricked me is all. He didnae try to hide what he took. Shaw's a lying cur and a fool as well. He swore the soldiers confiscated my pepper, but I knew that was a cartload of pig dung!"

"Aye," Callum says. "Who'd have known he even had such a wee thing tucked in his pockets? Then we heard talk of Shaw's suddenly heavy purse, and how he took to buying oak barrels and bolls of malt."

"We all know why he burned his bakery." Donny chuckles and takes another sip of wine. "When I smelled the smoke, I knew he was making ready his distillery."

"Aye." Una giggles. "His wife didnae want him to stop selling bread, seeing as they made a good living, but Shaw is a sly one. He set that fire himself, so he'd have his way. I'd swear on my ma's grave he did."

"Aye." Donny's eyes narrow. "He was using that pepper to buy what he needed. and I swore to send my guild to search his house first chance I had."

"But surely he'll know that someone from the guild took it." My wine turns sour on my tongue as Shaw's florid face springs to my mind. By now, 'tis likely worded about that I am a member of the guild. Won't Shaw make that connection, and have an even greater desire for revenge?

"Ye must no' worry over it, Kenna." Una bumps my arm with her own. "Shaw's too busy making his drink to come haring after ye."

"Aye." Donny laughs. "'Twas my fault he kept my pepper in the first place. I was fool enough to caution him not to lose a single speck. The worth of that handful was enough to buy a house in the city." With that, she rises to her feet and takes a wooden salt box from the mantel. Swiftly removing a silver key from within, she unlocks the cupboard where she keeps her herbs and cures, deposits the tiny packet of precious seeds inside, and returns the key to its hiding place. I avert my eyes when she passes me.

"Surely that pepper would not be enough to buy a house, Donny" I say.

The old woman pins me with her pale stare. "More than enough, at any rate, for one to buy his way beyond the locked gate, if he spoke to the right man," she says in a low voice. "To be sure, Shaw knew that. 'Tis perhaps why he's been in and out of Stewart's Close more than a few times since the bailey locked the gate and set a watch."

I plop, none too gracefully, into a chair. "What if *I* were to bring such payment to the man who guards that gate?" I can hardly tear my gaze from the locked cupboard that now houses the tiny grains of the oddly valuable spice. "If I had that much wealth to offer, the man—"

"Fool." Una cuts my words off with a wave. "The man guards the gate to keep ye penned inside the city. He cannae take aught from the Poisoner or the bailey'd have him strung up."

My shoulders slump. Her words are true. Rob said as much the first time I met him. Annie stirs and I sit beside her, not wishing to gaze into the faces of the others in the room.

Una crouches beside me. "Dinnae forget that ye have friends here." She leans closer, her frizzled hair brushing against my face. "But dinnae go on blethering about the vaults when you're out there on the lane." Before I can respond, she rises to her feet and she and her father take their leave.

My head is as heavy as my heart. Ignoring all, I lie beside the slumbering child. Donny nudges me with her boot.

"What?" I groan, flinging my arm over my eyes.

"Come," she says. "And bring Annie."

Her clipped words brook no opposition. Yawning wide, I rise, lift the sleeping Annie and stumble after Donny.

She leads us from the kitchen and to the forbidden upper floor. I knew that Donny's bedchamber lay deeper within the house. Of course, I'd never searched for it. I'd feared to disobey and cause her to regret her hospitality. Besides, after sleeping in a barn and outdoors behind a pile of refuse, a pallet by the fire was more than enough.

Donny leads us to the end of the corridor, and we stop before a blue painted door.

"The two of ye may sleep in here." Donny opens the door, which squeals on its hinges. Without another word, she marches away and clomps back down the stairs. I gawk like a child staring at a pile of sweets, not quite comprehending what is before me. Then Annie stirs awake, so I carry her inside.

The room is small and square with a bed against the far wall. Warm blankets are piled on it, and there are two round pillows. Fat, stuffed pillows, white like summer clouds! I touch one of them. "Feathers!"

"Feathers!" Annie repeats the word with a giggle. I set the child on the bed, then lift a corner of the plain blue coverlet. Soft linens lie beneath. The scent of lavender wafts up to me. I breathe in deeply, and memories of home flood my being.

A small table beside the bed holds a washbasin and pitcher. A beeswax candle in a pewter candlestick lends a comforting scent to the room. Against the wall, a small chest holds extra linens, including a white shift, my size, and blue skirts, plain but clean. A clean though somewhat threadbare blue bodice lies folded next to it, and there are silk stockings.

What is the meaning of this?

Annie sits on the bed, rocking her doll. She hums a wordless tune while I take to pacing the room.

There is a small window in the wall, also made of real glass like the windows below stairs, not the oil-soaked linen that graces many of the windows of Stewart's Close. I open the casements and lean out. Below me is a view of the lane. Opposite is an empty house. Perhaps the occupants had the means to buy their way outside the close. To my right is the wall of another house, built against this one, as so many of the houses are in this beehive of a place.

A woman in the street below me glances up and darts away, clearly thinking I am about to empty my chamber pot on her head. I chuckle. I'd never do such a thing. Well, I might consider it if she were the woman who once attempted to empty her morning slops on my head. Or Cecelia.

"The room pleases ye?" I turn away from the window with a gasp at the sound of Donny's voice. I'd not been aware of the old woman's return.

Annie runs and embraces her. "Feathers!" she squeals.

"Our wee Annie is content. What of our Poisoner?" Donny eyes me with a strange expression on her old face. The late afternoon light that glows on her countenance from the window does her no favors but shows her for the crinkled crone she is. She appears to have passed a hundred years or more on God's great earth, with her aged face and her body so thin and worn with the cares of a long life.

I clear my throat. "This is lovely." Annie and I spent more than a week sleeping on the floor like common servants; now Donny has given us our own bedchamber? I should be pleased, yet I am not. The space around me grows somehow smaller, the air a mite too warm.

"Good." Donny turns to go.

"Wait." I study the wizened woman. "Why are you being so kind to us?" I fumble for the right words as a flush creeps over my cheeks. "You have already been so kind to shelter us when no one else would. What I mean to say, Donny, is why do we now merit our very own bedchamber? What has changed?"

"Nothing." Donny swivels on her heel and marches off.

Annie cavorts about the room, darting here and there like a tiny sparrow in the spring. Pausing in front of the chest, I open it again and brush my fingers against the supple stockings. Such a luxury to me now, whereas before I came here, they merited not a single thought. Despite the great kindness Donny has just shown me, I cannot feel the gratitude I should have. This bedchamber is comfortable. Annie and I are now the rightful occupants of this room. The problem is that this all feels final. 'Tis as if Donny is telling me, much as Rob did a few nights before, that this narrow lane within the city is now my home.

"No!" I blurt aloud. Annie trembles at my words and her eyes widen.

Trying to soften my stormy visage and form a smile, I shush her, though she has said naught. "I did not mean to startle you." She resumes her exploration, though her movements are now hesitant. I pat the fluffy pillows. Another luxury, yet I cannot forget that I am a prisoner in the city.

Outside, fewer and fewer venture out during the day. Faces grow ever more pinched. Angry. Frightened. They are desperate, like the soldier's wife who dared to approach me for help. We've been locked within the close for ten days now. The false flag of our "quarantine" still flutters upon the sealed gate, and the bailey's hulking guard keeps us penned inside these tiny, winding lanes. Tensions mount. I must escape! But how? My shoulders slump. Una insisted that the guard would not allow me to buy my way out of here. How can she be so certain?

Pacing the room, I ponder my options. I must carry through with my visit to Rob in the vaults tonight. I ignore the quickening of my silly heart when my wicked thoughts pester me. Such things are trifles when there are more important things at stake! Perhaps I can make Rob agree with my opinion, though Una did not. This might buy me some time to find a way out. If I share some of the food from the vaults with hungry residents, it could ease tensions a bit. Perhaps even make me a friend or two.

And then I gasp aloud. Donny's peppercorn! Those tiny seeds are worth so much! Una vowed the guard would never take payment from me and allow me to leave, but what if I were to explain that the valuable spice was worth the price of a house? Surely then, the man would allow me to leave, would he not? After all, his coat was ragged, worn, and faded. He'd welcome such wealth.

Every man can be bought if enough gold touches his palm. Grandfather had said that to Oliver once when discussing some business venture or another. My mind races at the idea of bribing the guard. And then my heart falls.

Donny would never give me leave to take the spice, even if I offered the repayment Grandfather will certainly proffer her. The old thief does not know Lord Ramsay as I do. She will not anticipate repayment, only great loss. Donny will not risk losing such a valuable commodity. Therefore, if I want to offer the spice to the guard, I must first steal it from the old woman. The one who took me from the cold streets, fed me, and gave me a home.

Licking dry lips, I sit upon the soft bed next to wee, chattering Annie. I ponder Donny's actions earlier this evening. Had she decided to trust me? She had no fear when she betrayed her hiding place for the key. Or had she forgotten who was in the room with her?

I shake my head, certain of only one thing. Donny will understand my actions. Taking the peppercorns will not be an act of stealing, but rather borrowing. The old woman shall have her payment.

With a yawn, I sink onto the yielding bed, and Annie snuggles against my side. Tonight, then, I shall steal from the thieves. Weariness settles inside me. Well, after I take a wee bit of a rest. I close my eyes and sink gratefully into slumber.

CHAPTER 27

Annie does not stir when I rise from bed close to midnight. I creep below, holding my breath and cursing to myself each time a footstep creaks on a stair. Devil take me, these stairs groan like an army of demons demanding fresh souls! My heart is hammering by the time I make it to the kitchen. Luckily for me, the house remains silent save for a muffled snore.

Using the wan light of a taper lit from the glowing coals in the grate, I retrieve the silver key from its wee box on the mantel.

The lock sticks at first but then releases after a brief wrestle and a few muttered curses. After Donny's cupboard door swings open, it only takes me a moment to remove half the peppercorns from their packet and enfold them inside a twist of parchment, which I tuck inside my leather purse. I shut and lock the cupboard and return the key to its spot.

But my heart will not cease its fluttering. My stomach drops as guilt settles in. I am stealing. I may call this "borrowing" all I wish, but it does not change the fact that I am taking something of great value without Donny's permission. I have already decided to take food from the thieves, but that is different. Many living here on the close are starving, and food is plentiful in the vaults. But I cannot trample on Donny's hospitality by stealing her possessions. The treasured spice is not mine to take. I simply must find another way to escape the close.

Trembling, swallowing hard, I turn around with the key in my hand. Once more, after another tussle with the stiff lock, I open the cupboard and return the peppercorns to their rightful place.

My heart is instantly lighter. I *will* find another way to escape the close. But I will do it without betraying the one woman who befriended me.

Returning to the stairs, my heart sinks. Why did I not first dress myself so that I could simply walk out the front door and run to the vaults? Rob is waiting, and I am clad only in my shift. I must return upstairs, don my clothing and face yet another descent of these groaning stairs.

My ascent is achingly slow. The warped wood of the uneven treads seems to create even more noise than before. Twice I pause and freeze when strange sounds emit from elsewhere in the house, terrified that Donny will emerge and demand to know why I am not abed. The old woman cannot catch me tiptoeing outside!

The final step emits a loud 'crack.'

"Who's there?" Donny calls.

Frozen in place, I do not breathe nor even blink. I do curse myself repeatedly within my head, counting the seconds that pass. Then the minutes. And finally, a loud snore tells me the old woman has gone back to sleep.

Once back inside my chamber, I throw on my new, though threadbare, clothing and ease the casements open. Not for anything would I risk descending those dreadful stairs again! Earlier, I'd noticed the pitted and worn outer wall of Donny's house, with its many missing bricks, and the narrow ledge that extends the length of the wall not far below my window. If I'm careful, I can climb to the cobbles below. After all, I often scrambled down the outer wall and then climbed back into my own window at home. Just as I entered Cinaed's room through her window.

That memory assails me as I gather my skirts and knot them at my knees, and a sudden pain, fresh and sharp, wounds me within. Barely more than one week ago, I climbed into my sister's bedchamber, not knowing 'twould be the last day I saw her. And my last day at home.

Closing my eyes, I picture her again in illness. Her unseeing eyes. The sheen of sweat on her feverish skin. Her matted hair plastered to her forehead. Her tooth on the tray beside the bed. I square my shoulders and tie my boots about my neck. I'll not indulge in tears while I forget the purpose that drives my every action! I must escape and find my sister's murderer.

Easing my way out the window, my feet dangle at first, but after a moment my frantic toes find purchase on a solid ledge. With a whispered prayer, followed by a curse when my feet slide, I edge my way gradually downward, feeling with bare fingers and toes for anything to hold on to, no matter how small. My progress is achingly slow. Perched here like an awkward bird, any false move could mean injury. Perhaps even death.

Wind plucks with icy fingers at my skirts. I gasp for air; hardly able to draw breath for the trembling that seizes me. I hug the building's pitted walls and inch ever lower. Once I nearly lose my balance but grasp at the cracks and indentations on the wall to right myself.

Och, my poor toes ache with the cold, and my legs shake. I'll not make it! Despair springs within. What a fool I was. Then my stretching foot touches solid ground.

I did it! I could scream aloud for joy. I shove my feet into my boots and rearrange my knotted skirts. Now, to the vaults. And Rob. My swift flight to the kirk goes unnoticed by watchman or bailey. My clomping boots announce my arrival on the winding stairs that descend below the chapel, and I regret not removing the damnable shoes once more.

I find Rob sitting on a barrel with a book in his hands. I nearly drop my light.

"You can read?"

Rob's face hardens, and he tosses the book aside. "So surprised, are ye?"

Curse my careless words! I study my hands. "I'm sorry, Rob. It's only..." I shrug. "Not everyone here in the city can read." Why must I always speak with such imprudence? I have no wish to hurt Rob's feelings, especially now.

"Of course, the granddaughter of Lord Ramsay can read and write," Rob says with a wicked gleam in his eye. "She recites holy word like a man of the kirk. She even speaks French, I suppose."

"Indeed. Oh, and I speak Latin, so I may talk to our house cats. That is their native tongue, you know."

Rob laughs. Then he folds his arms and regards me with a serious expression. "Makes me wonder what you're doing here, Kenna. Most fine ladies have nothing to do with lads like us. Yet here you've come to spend time with a thief."

My stomach dances within me. "I'm here because I *want* to be here, Rob. With you."

Rob's face relaxes, and he takes up the book again and hands it to me with a low laugh. "I know my letters, but Ma died before she taught me to read," he says. "I'll admit to that. Da never learned his letters, nor did he want to, so my schooling was done when Ma got sick. I was only looking at the pictures." He ducks his head and smiles in a rueful way that calls to mind a wee, playful lad, not the tall youth before me.

I open the book, a smile playing on my lips. It is a guide to herbal cures, with drawings of various medicinal plants. A similar one resides in Grandfather's library. It must have belonged to his wife, the woman who tended the garden filled with medicinal plants.

"Donny would like this."

"Aye. There's money to be had in that book, there is."

"Money? How so?" A wide grin is slashed across Rob's face, and I drop my eyes to the book in my hands, finding myself unable to return his gaze.

"One who knows how to grow these plants or how to find them can earn a fair living, ye see. The apothecaries here in town are always looking for supplies of herbs and plants for their medicines."

Smiling, I trace my finger along the drawing of a plant with large, fuzzy leaves. Lamb's ear. Donny used a few of them to help bandage the cuts on my hands.

"I spoke in jest earlier today when I hinted ye might come to the vaults to keep me company."

I glance up. "Did you?"

Rob regards me for a moment with a smile playing upon his lips. "Aye. But I'm glad ye came. Perhaps ye're not so high and mighty as Una said."

Glad the lantern's dim light hides the flush on my cheeks, I search my mind for the right thing to say. I *do* wish to spend time with Rob, but I have other reasons for being here as well. Of a truth, this is maddening. At a loss for words, I brush at my skirts, pleased to be wearing clean, though threadbare clothing.

"Ye look well in that color." Rob tosses me an apple. I catch it midair, and he smiles in approval.

"Thank you. The gown is quite plain, but it will do. 'Tis all I have aside from my ruined silks."

"A pretty face suits the dishcloth." Rob seizes a basket and loads it with potatoes.

"What?" I stammer. Does he honestly think I am pretty enough so that it does not matter if I wear fine clothing or not? Mrs. Harris would not agree. She was too practical to understand that every lass wants to be told she possesses at least a hint of beauty, be that a fair distance from the truth or no. And she made certain to remind me whenever she could that my storm cloud eyes, my square jaw, and my long nose would never call forth sweet words from anyone. Ever the realist, Mrs. Harris used to say, 'Sure, ye be plain, Kenna, but a kingly dowry ye'll have. And what man would turn up his nose at the granddaughter of an Earl?' 'Tis no wonder I do not miss her.

Rob laughs as he adds a small sack of oatmeal to the basket. "I cannae be the first who's ever said so."

"But you are."

Grinning, I take care to tuck the apple into my purse while Rob places the basket on the platform. If I fail to convince him to help me, I shall have to sneak food from under his nose. And I'll be doing so after he offered his friendship and paid me my first real compliment. My heart sinks to my scuffed boots.

Finished with his task, Rob approaches me and brushes a strand of hair from my face. He tucks it behind my ear. I cannot breathe. He inches forward until he is so near, I smell the tang of wood smoke in his hair. I shiver. This was just as I'd pictured, but now that it's real, I lose my nerve and step back. Rob's face falls.

"I feared as much." His mouth droops into a frown. "I'm no match for Lady Kenna. No' in her eyes."

"No, Rob." I take his arm before he can back away. "It's just that I was... I've never..." My voice trails off in embarrassment. How can I explain my awkwardness? Of course, I've never kissed a lad! Who would I have kissed? Grandfather's old valet, Tom? The stable hands who Oliver told to keep their eyes on the ground when I approached?

A smile spreads on Rob's face.

"You're a long time dead, Poisoner. Live your life now while ye can."

I smile at his words. He speaks the truth. I am alone in the company of a thief, but this thief thinks I'm pretty. And I like him in return. I step forward.

"Hoy there, Rob! Where are ye?" Steenie screeches from somewhere in the vaults. "I'm here for my watch." His voice echoes through the tunnels and rats squeal and scramble to hide.

Rob scowls. "Quick! Go." He points to the platform, where the loaded basket awaits.

God's great mercy! Why couldn't that awful lad Steenie have waited only a moment or two longer before heading to the vaults for his watch? I huff in frustration as I clamber onto the creaking wooden planks.

Rob leans close and murmurs in my ear. "Take this food to your friend. We're not all the heartless fiends ye think we are, Kenna. I know many are hungry and I want to help. But we must take care. Donny and Callum most of all must never hear a word of this."

With his face in shadow, his hair is outlined in fire, thanks to the glowing lantern on the wall behind him. He is like a dark-clad fallen angel and at this moment, I would follow him gladly to the deepest depths of hell. I seize Rob's shoulders and place my lips on his. He gasps in surprise. And he kisses me back. His lips are soft, and they smile as they touch mine.

"Rob?" Steenie's shouted voice is far too close at hand. Rob steps away from me and works the pulleys. The feel of his lips on mine remains with me all the way to the street as I sway on the creaking platform, the basket of stolen food clutched tight in my arms. A new, tantalizing yet confusing thought fills my head. Though I must escape this place, I might now have a reason to return to Stewart's Close. Once I am back in Grandfather's home, who could argue if I say the best shops are found on this very lane? I smile to myself and touch my mouth as though I may somehow seal the kiss there.

Then, another thought seizes me, and I gasp and laugh for the sheer joy of the idea. I will most certainly come back to the city once I am free, and Oliver pays for his crime; I must return for my wee Annie! I no longer need to worry over the lassie, for Grandfather will allow her to stay with us. The sight of Annie's sweet face would sway anyone.

Back at street level, I shiver in the chill as I knock on the door of the young wife, Bess. The hour is late, and she must be abed, as she does not answer right away. Glad of the covering darkness, I wait. When the woman eases the door open an inch and peers out at me, holding her cruise lamp aloft, her whispered voice quivers with fear.

"Who is it?"

"A friend." The woman opens the door a wee bit wider, and gasps at the sight of food. Her eyes fill with tears as she takes the packages from my hands.

"God bless ye, lass."

"If you hear of others who need food, get word to me. I live with the herbwife, Sheona, and her husband, Donny. But please do not tell anyone who gave this to you." I hand her the apple Rob had tossed to me. She thanks me once more and eases her door closed.

Before I reach Donny's doorstep, I search for a hiding place for my basket. I'd kept back some of the food, for 'twill not always be as easy as it was tonight to steal from the guild. Besides, there is no room beneath the ashes in Donny's cold grate to hide anything else. After tucking the basket beneath the wooden steps that lead to a nearby weaver's shop, I pause at Donny's door. I'd not known it would take me so little time to obtain the food. Annie slumbers, safely tucked in bed inside a nice, warm house. I have more time to explore and seek an exit from this place, do I not?

I take my knife from my pouch and turn toward the direction of the gate, far distant at the head of the rising lane. Shaw or no, watchman or no, I will make my way to the head of Stewart's Close. The guard placed there must be tired. Perhaps I can creep past him and climb over the gate. If the man awakens, I have my purse filled with coins and the promise of even greater wealth to offer. Will the man not listen if offered a kingly sum?

With resolve in my heart, I turn my steps to the head of the lane. I creep among shadows, avoiding pools of moonlight on the cobbles. Soon, I approach the gate, and my heartbeat picks up speed at the sound of murmuring voices and the flickering light of a fire. What is this? I edge forward. Beyond the closed gate, dark shapes wander, far more than one man. Someone bellows out a laugh and others join in. For a brief moment, flames flare up and brighten the surrounding area. I catch a glimpse of the vivid red coat and tall hat of a soldier.

My heart quickens painfully as I back away. Soldiers now guard the gate. Did Oliver hire them to make doubly certain he could maintain the false quarantine?

I tuck myself inside a doorway to catch my breath, puffing from my climb up the rising lane. Thanks to the soldiers, my only escape from here will be from the rooftops. I *must* find one that will allow me to leap outside the close! Surely there is a way out of here!

Once more determined, I creep away from the gate until the voices fade and search for an entry into one of the tall houses here, but no door yields to my touch. My hands grow cold and ache something fierce, but I shall not give in. I continue to creep along, moving from one house to another with no success. I pass Donny's home and descend lower and lower, passing the kirk and moving toward the abandoned house at the very end of the close. Soon, a great stench rises and causes my eyes to water. Why is the smell here always so much worse? And why does it appear that a thick fog floats from the black windows of that house, wafting toward me in the moonlight?

I foolishly allow my gaze to stay upon that wretched dwelling while I turn to retrace my steps. My fumbling feet slip, and I go down hard upon one knee. Stifling a cry of pain, I regain my footing and stagger onward. I limp past a shuttered shop and stop to lean against an iron post, my chest heaving. My knee stings and throbs. The lane is silent and the creeping mist that surrounds the empty house lends it the air of a tall burial chamber in a lonely graveyard.

Tears pool in my eyes and every inch of my body fills with a sharp ache of longing. A sob breaks from me as Cinaed's wasted face appears in my mind. Her pale skin, her withered body, and her agonizing death were all part of the price she paid for loving a man who did not love her back.

I rub my arms for warmth and allow the tears to flow freely. To see my sister die in such a manner, inflicted a wound within me that will never be mended. A muffled thump from somewhere nearby shakes me from my stupor, and I wipe my wet cheeks with my sleeve. Drawing a shuddering breath, I clench my fists, grit my teeth, and resume my exploration.

Darting again from house to house, I continue my desperate search for any open door. I even shove against the warped door of the apothecary's shop, where the toothless Mrs. Kennison lives. The solid wood defies my feeble attempts.

Dejected and increasingly shaky, I start at every slight noise or shadow. After an hour, I am chilled through and ready to give up, but decide to make one more attempt. I tug at a window shutter that appears loose, but a muffled shout within warns me away and I flee, wedging myself between two houses mere inches from one another. Squeezing my way through, I emerge into a tiny courtyard of sorts, where steps lead downward. Tiptoeing down them, I try the door at the bottom. It opens. Thanks be to God, it opens!

Not daring to breathe, I edge inside. The darkness before me is complete. Easing the door closed, I wait for my eyes to adjust. Complete blackness soon lightens to a thick, heavy gray where I can almost discern some darker shapes. There is no sound. No, there is something. Breathing? Chilly fingers of dread tickle my spine. The room is not empty. I must leave now! A rustling noise comes from somewhere nearby and something brushes against my leg. A squeak of surprise falls from my lips.

"Ma?" a child's voice cries out.

My hands fumble with the latch. I cannot work it!

Someone lights a taper. "Who's this?" a man asks. I whirl around, with my right hand feeling for my knife. Why did I not hold it at the ready as I entered a stranger's house, uninvited, in the middle of the night?

A grizzled man holds his tiny, flickering light aloft and squints at me. His thick, gray eyebrows shoot up and his eyes grow so wide the reflected flame of the candle flickers inside them.

"The *Poisoner*." To my horror, the room comes alive. Forms squirm and moan, voices grunt and whisper, and three, four, no, five people arise from the floor where they were sleeping. In a far corner, a child cries. Someone hushes it.

Fingers clutch at me, my arms, my clothes, my hair. I seize my knife, ready to slash. Hands shrink back. Then the babe cries once more. Startled, I glance toward the sound, and that's when someone knocks the knife from my grasp. I groan aloud. Donny would be so disappointed.

Despite my screams and protestations, my captors pull and push me through the chamber and drag me across another one, where there are others asleep on the floor. I trod on one or two of them, and they leap to their feet with angry cries and are more than happy to form part of my welcoming party. The crowd forces me into a tiny, musty room. Rough hands shove me inside and close the door. Scraping sounds draw close and the door shakes as my captors settle something heavy in place, sealing me inside. Hoots and cheers erupt.

"We'll be rich!" someone crows. One of my captors pounds thrice on the door that seals me in.

"Sleep well, lassie! We'll let ye out when we get our payment from the watchman!"

"No!" Kicking and pounding, I scream at my captors to let me out. I offer food, then offer money. At last, I vow to kill each one of them. These threats are met with jeers and shouts of laughter. My voice soon grows raw, and I can only croak out my weary pleadings.

"Well done, man," a deep voice growls. Several men grunt as they shove the heavy object aside and jerk the door open. I stand on trembling limbs, blinking at the light from a candle guttering near my face. When my eyes adjust, I meet the gaze of someone I've no wish to encounter. 'Tis Shaw, the baker.

"Well done! Ye've found the Poisoner!" He slams the door, and the men block it once more. I cover my face with my hands.

My sister used to warn me oft of rushing headlong into trouble. 'Tis a great shame I never listened to her.

CHAPTER 28

Noises outside my makeshift prison keep me well-informed of the goings on. The baker-turned-brewer has brought whiskey along for the celebration. Loud songs turn to drunken brawls. My captors laugh, howl, and scream. It goes on for hours. At last, the noise fades until a thick silence reigns, broken by an occasional snore.

Day must be near. Cursing my weak-minded lack of judgment, I plant my feet against the door and push as hard as I can. It is as unyielding as ever. Feeling the walls, I discover I am enclosed in a tiny storage closet, perhaps an empty larder, with bare shelves and a ceiling so low I can touch it when I raise my arms above my head. I find a few small onions hanging in a corner, snatch the dry roots and stuff them into my purse. These people have imprisoned me, so I shall steal from them. 'Tis only just.

I slump to the floor to rest my weary body. Here on Stewart's Close, how many other homes have bare shelves? Far too many. Outside the door, my captors rejoice, certain to earn what must seem a kingly sum. They will not yet perish for lack of food if they know what is available from the vaults.

Yet even that food will run out sooner or later. I shiver at the damp chill of this place. Even the guild cannot easily replenish their supplies, as they cannot leave the close. Soon there will be naught to steal. Eventually, all will starve so long as the false quarantine remains in force.

Then, I laugh a harsh, mirthless sound. Once my captors turn me over to the bailey, he'll take me to jail and the residents of Stewart's Close will be rid of the Poisoner. The white cloth will come down from the gate. Shaw and my other captors will enjoy their gold. And I will be forgotten.

I lick dry lips and squeeze my eyes shut. No, not everyone will forget about me. Donny will remember. And Annie. Tears spring to my eyes. Annie shall awaken soon, and I'll not be there. A painful ache throbs inside me. Once I am gone, what will happen to her? I've not forgotten what Donny said. She's far too old to care for the child. I close my eyes and cover my mouth with my hand to suppress the sobs that threaten to burst forth. Why was I such a fool?

A loud bang on the larder door startles me. My hands search for my knife before I remember 'tis no longer in my possession. My fingers find the small bulge formed by the coins within my leather pouch. Can I pay my way out of this place? My pulse beats within me at the thought. It may be my only chance to escape.

After several loud scraping sounds, the door swings open. Blinking, I clutch the purse hidden within my skirts and squint at my captors.

"Now then, lassie, come out nice and slow." The grizzled man who'd first recognized me takes my arm and pulls me into the kitchen, past the heavy cupboard my captors had used to block my escape. A bright fire blazes, and the room stinks of drink and too many warm bodies. I press my lips together and they curve downward as I catch a sour whiff of vomit.

Fewer people than I'd expected wait for me, but their aspect is fierce, nonetheless. Besides the old gray man, there are two younger men, thin with hard-lined faces. They remain at the ready, arms raised as though they await a fight. And there is Shaw, florid with drink. A triumphant smirk twists his ugly visage. Beside him is a woman, tall and fair, whose pock-marked face is a mask of cold contempt. She holds my knife, turning it this way and that, so it gleams in the firelight.

"Give us no trouble and we'll no' cut ye." Her voice is calm and matter of fact, as though she's speaking of the weather or the price of turnips at market.

"Aye." Shaw gurgles out a throaty chuckle. "My Elspet here'll slice ye up like a roast."

My fingers tighten around my money, and my hopes rise by a small degree.

"Please." I lick dry lips. "I can pay."

Elspet snorts. "So can the watchman, lassie. And he'll pay us more, I'll wager." She steps closer to me, her eyes never leaving mine. I shiver and she smiles.

"I don't think ye truly intend to pay us, do ye, murderess?" Elspet whispers when she is mere inches away from me, and the fetid smell of her unwashed body wafts to me. I recoil and her face contorts with hatred. "Off with her!"

"But I do have money." I wince as one of the younger men drags me by my arm. "In my purse. I have it with me!"

Elspet holds the knife to my neck with one hand, and with the other finds my leather pouch. She cuts the ties and lifts the purse from my waist. Elspet backs away from me and the two men hold my arms in a painful grip.

The woman's eyes flash as she opens the pouch and pours the contents into Shaw's waiting palm. The others shuffle near, their faces greedy, their eyes full of longing, all drawn to the lure of the gleaming metal.

Something tiny falls onto the floor and I gasp as my gaze lands upon it and swiftly tear my eyes away.

I'd missed a single peppercorn when returning the spice to Donny's cupboard. It must have fallen from within the twist of parchment and remained inside my purse.

Did Shaw notice? If he does, he will know 'twas I who took them from his house. I hold my breath as he counts the coins with a pleased smirk. All eyes are on the wealth Shaw holds in his hands. The small seed has gone unnoticed. My heart slows, but Elspet stoops to snatch it from the floor.

"What's this? It fell from the purse." She hands the black seed to her husband. His face contorts with fury and his eyes find mine.

"I..." My words are cut off as Shaw slaps me across the face. My head snaps back, my eyes blinded by tears and pain.

"She's a poisoner *and* a thief," he growls. "She's taken something o' mine."

"What?" Deep lines form between Elspet's eyebrows.

Shaw explains, breathing hard, while his bloodshot eyes glare at me, and he raises his fist high to strike me again. Were it not for the men holding me by the arms, I would have swayed on my feet and fallen to the floor. The spot on my cheek where he first struck me stings and throbs.

"The spice was *not* yours," I blurt. "You took it from Donny."

Shaw's face grows dark, and I steel myself for another blow. But then the man lowers his arm and turns his back to me.

"Let the watchman take her. We'll get our money and she'll get the noose. Come."

Shaw shoves the fistful of coins back into the purse and hands it to Elspet, who stuffs it inside her bodice.

With my confiscated knife pointed at my back, I walk. The chamber I'd entered last night is empty. When we emerge outside, a cold mist chills me. Dawn has not yet removed the blanket of darkness from the city.

"Where are you taking me?" I'm rewarded by a sharp poke from the knife, and I bite my lip to keep from crying out as a stinging cut opens in my skin. Of course, no one answers my query. The grim group marches me through the small courtyard and rough hands shove me through the narrow space that leads to the lane. We head directly uphill toward the gate. My knees grow weak. I can attempt to fight against five of the toughest residents of the city or an entire encampment of trained soldiers.

Either way, the odds are not with me.

We attain the narrow flight of crumbling and crooked stairs that leads directly to the gate. At the top, a few hammocks containing slumbering men stretch between the buildings on each side. A small number of red-coated soldiers loll on the steps, and more are clearly visible on the other side of the gate.

"Who's this?"

We stop. Elspet clears her throat. The point of my knife digs again into my back. Her message is clear. I freeze, every muscle in my body taut. Why did I try to buy my freedom from these brutish souls? Perhaps I should have waited until I was in the custody of the soldiers. Perhaps they would have taken a bribe.

"What do ye want?" a soldier calls out. He hurries to us, his musket held in his arms. He does not raise the firearm, but his stiff posture and the tight grip on his weapon betray his wariness.

When the soldier draws near the bottom step, he pauses and appraises us all. His impossibly young face is familiar. My eyes fly wide. He is Bess's husband! His wife and child live on Stewart's Close. I gave them stolen food only last night.

"We have the Poisoner," Shaw says. "The lass with a price on her head. We want the watchman or the bailey. We'll turn her over when we get our pay."

"Aye!" The others speak in chorus. Elspeth shouts the word with glee.

"The watchman is no' here." The soldier eyes us warily. "Nor the bailey." His wary gaze darts from me to the others and back again. He adjusts his grip on the musket he carries. He is now so near I could touch him. His eyes are weary; heavy-lidded and rimmed with red. They meet mine.

Please, I mouth. *Help me.*

A moment passes. Two. I do not know if he has understood. Then he glances away and addresses Shaw.

"Leave the lass here," he orders.

Within a feral howl, Elspet seizes me by my hair and yanks my head back with one hand. With the other, she places the blade at my throat. Time ceases. In this moment, the only thing that exists in the world is the cold, sharp metal placed against my neck.

"No!" Her grip on my hair tightens. "Call the bailey or that watchman, now. If ye say we must leave her here, we shall leave her with her throat cut."

The young soldier holds his musket at the ready, aimed directly at me and my knife-wielding captor.

"Drop that knife." His voice trembles. The edge of the blade digs into my skin. A trickle of blood drips down my neck.

"Stand down Ellie," Shaw says in a tight voice.

"No!" Elspet shouts. The blade digs deeper. Perhaps it is the pain that spurs me, or the terror of immediate capture, but I raise my hands and push at the knife, not caring if the blade slices my fingers. I only want the cutting edge away from my neck.

The musket fires like a crack of thunder. My ears ring, and my hands reach the sharp edge of the knife. Though it cuts my fingers, I shove it away from my neck.

Elspet cries out and releases her hold on my hair, and I drop to my knees with the blade of the knife clenched in my bloody hand. Shouts and screams erupt all around, and heavy boots pound in my direction.

Cradling my injured hand as well as the blade, now slippery with blood, I search for a way out. Someone seizes my arm, heaves me to my feet and pulls me away. Shaw wails and shouts, crouched over the crumpled form now lying at the foot of the stairs. A backward glance reveals yellow hair soaked in dark liquid.

My ears ring and my head whirls.

"In here," my new captor says, shoving me into the entrance of a shop. The heavy door thuds closed behind us. The single oval window is covered with a film of dirt, yet there is a fire blazing in a hearth at the rear of the room, lending enough light to reveal a rectangular chamber and tables scattered with bits of leather and an array of metal tools. I wield my knife in my bloody hands and whirl to face whoever it is who now has me in his clutches.

Before me is a young lass with rough hair the color of hay.

"Una?"

Though my hand smarts from its many cuts, I grow light as air at the sight of the lass before me with a gap-toothed grin. She swiftly embraces me, and I breathe out in relief.

"How did you..." Una shushes me by raising a finger to her lips.

"We must fly." She motions for me to follow. I do at once, for many voices shout outside. Someone pounds on a door nearby, calling: "Open in the name of the king!"

We flee to the back of the shop and hurry up seven flights of stairs. On occasion, we pass one of the building's residents. They only glance at us and continue on their way. Panting, we make it to the top floor. Una guides me into a low attic where we climb out through a gaping hole in the roof. My hopes leap inside me. My escape? Not only from the searching soldiers, but from the close?

Out on the roof, I once again taste the clear, crisp air that is so much cleaner up here. Una guides me to the edge, where we have only to leap across a gap of two or three paces to land on the roof of the next building, where we must take care, for this roof is angled, though not as steeply pitched as many of the others around us.

"Does this house lie outside the close?" I ask once my feet are safely under me on the solid rooftop. I study the smoking chimneys and rooftops surrounding us. Una shushes me again, and this time pulls me low to crouch beside her.

"Careful, or they'll see us," she whispers.

"Who?" I raise my head again, and Una rewards me with a cuff to the shoulder. I duck with a scowl.

"The soldiers, Kenna," she hisses, clearly exasperated. "They spy on the close from the rooftops of every house where there's room for a man to stand. There's a fair lot of them on the Martin house. That one has a flat roof and lies within leaping distance from other houses that face away from the close. 'Twould be an easy way out of here if there weren't so many redcoats encamped there."

My hopes turn to lead and sink to the toes of my boots. "That cannot be."

"Hush!" Una holds a finger to her lips. "Lower your voice!" She crawls over to a trapdoor and opens it, and I follow. "Da says we were fools to not think of making that leap the moment they locked our gate, but no one thought the quarantine would last this long." She throws me a rueful grin. "By the time we thought of it, the soldiers had already set up their tents on the rooftop."

We creep our way through several houses, climb to a new rooftop, and leap to yet another house, bit by bit wending our way back to Donny's home. I do not speak. It is as though I have been cut through with my reclaimed knife. I was on a fool's errand, risking life and capture for nothing. And now my coins are gone. There truly is no escape from this place. This labyrinth of houses along a narrow lane may indeed be my prison for the remainder of my days.

And the cobbles are watered with blood spilled because of me.

CHAPTER
29

Una bids me farewell near Donny's house. There is now light enough to see well. Should I climb the brick wall or walk through the front door? Then, Donny appears at the window.

I shrink back at the sight of the woman's troubled face. She is angry with me. Annie must be awake and wailing. Poor creature. At least I can return to her. Such a seeming impossibility only minutes earlier!

Donny ducks back inside her house and closes the casements. Trying to swallow my guilt, I make haste to retrieve my basket from its hiding place but cannot find it. My bleeding hands clench at my sides. Curse this place! Of course, I can't blame anyone here for taking any food they might stumble across. At any rate, the basket is gone and there is nothing to do about it.

I touch the handle of the door and pause for a moment to collect myself. There would be no coming back here had it not been for that soldier, the one whose wife and child live nearby. Did he mean to pull the trigger? He did not seem to wish it. No matter. The woman who'd wanted to hand me over to the soldiers lies still and cold with a splintered skull. I hang my head and fight against bile that rises in my throat.

She died because of me.

Tremors shake me head to foot. Closing my eyes, I lean my head against the door. Shaw is now bereft of his wife. True, the horrid baker has never been my ally, but I know the pain of losing someone I love. And what of Elspet? From the moment we met, she showed nothing but hatred for me. Nevertheless, she was a living woman. Now, she is a corpse. Perhaps her specter watches me at this very moment. I swallow hard and raise my head, blinking back tears while I creep into Donny's house.

Guilt hollows me inside, but I cannot forget that Elspet held a knife to my neck. I raise a finger to touch the drying crust on my skin. If the soldier had not fired, my own blood would have been spilled. But the woman's death has left its mark upon my soul.

The house is silent. Annie sleeps. At least fate has spared the child any fear. Relieved, I leave my bloody knife in the kitchen, hurriedly splash a bit of water on my neck and cut fingers and wrap my hand in a bit of cloth. With relief, I ascend the creaking stairs.

Donny meets me halfway. She pauses for a moment, studying my face. Hers is drawn and pinched, lending her the look of a dried apple left to shrivel on the tree. After a moment, she heaves a great sigh and rushes past me.

"Stay with the child. I'll be back in a trice."

A fire burns in the grate within the bedchamber. Annie lies on the bed, her eyes closed, her chest rising and falling. I kick off my boots and stumble over to the bed, grateful for at least a few moments of rest. Last night's sojourn in that moldering larder was not conducive to a peaceful night's sleep.

Annie stirs and then she coughs. A harsh, barking sound fills the room, and I sit up in alarm. The child struggles to breathe, and her rattling cough goes on and on.

"Annie!" I hold her in a sitting position so she can catch her breath. Her eyes are wide and streaming, her face red. After many agonizing moments, she ceases coughing and collapses against me. Her wee body is on fire. I brush damp hair from her forehead.

Donny bustles into the chamber. "Help me with this." She sets a cloth-bound bundle on the bed.

"What happened?" Donny does not answer. We remove the child's shift and expose her bare chest. *Och*, her ribs are like a row of sticks covered with skin. "Why are we uncovering her so?" I am peeved the old woman has not yet answered my first question.

"For the poultice," Donny answers. "Stoke the fire."

After this, Donny does not speak except to give me curt orders. I add a few bits of precious coal, likely purloined from some dead man's house to the crackling fire. We then spread a pungent yellow paste onto a cloth and lay the hot, stinking mass on the poor child's heaving chest. The fumes sting my eyes.

"Stay with her," Donny orders. "Keep a cool cloth on her forehead." She leaves. I do as I'm told, wiping the sweat from Annie's wee face, smoothing her tangled, damp hair, placing and replacing a cloth dipped in water onto her head. She does not open her eyes. Her coughing fits come more and more frequently. My body trembles without ceasing.

When I arise to stoke the fire once more, I stumble over something and bend to retrieve Annie's doll. The doll's face is more defined than before. Donny must have spent more time carving its tiny features. What's more, the doll now has arms and legs, and the wood, obviously rubbed and polished with care, is smooth and gleaming.

So much effort to create a toy for a child who has not even spent a fortnight under Donny's roof. Who is she, this old soldier who took us in? I close my eyes for a moment and let the crackle of the flames soothe my troubled mind.

Donny is a strange soul, often rude and short-tempered. She speaks in riddles and hardly ever answers my questions. Preferring to wear breeches, Donny only wears skirts when she must go out in disguise as the herbwife. I've never met a soul like her.

And yet... I glance at the odd little doll in my lap and breathe out a sigh. The hardened old woman who took me in has far more love in her heart than I ever did. She does not speak of it, for she does not need to. She shows her love in every deed.

Rising, I place the toy in Annie's arms. She stirs and coughs once more, in violent, shuddering hacks. The doll falls again to the floor.

Twenty, perhaps thirty minutes creep by. Once, Donny replaces the cooling poultice with a new one, steaming and smellier than before. Annie moans.

"What will that horrid stuff do to her?" I hop from the bed and hurry to block the threshold before the old woman can leave the chamber. "It burns my eyes so that I can hardly keep them open. And that horrible smell makes my nose drip as though I'm ill myself. What good will it do for Annie?"

"That poultice may well save her life." Donny's voice is low but with an edge sharper than the blade that sliced my skin this morning. "If it works, 'twill draw that phlegm from her chest so she may breathe."

The woman peers into my face, her eyes accusing. "If ye'd no' gone out and left that window open, Poisoner, our wee Annie would no' have lain all night exposed to the chill and damp air."

My mouth gapes. The open window. I'd not thought to close it behind me. What a fool I was! My knees buckle under me. I sink to the floor, tears streaming down my face.

"That won't help the child, now, will it?" Donny says in a gruff voice. Nevertheless, her hands are gentle as she lifts me to my feet and helps me sit on the stool she's placed beside the bed.

"Stay with her and keep damp cloths on her head. I'll prepare another poultice." She places a small bowl of water into my hands and leaves the bedchamber.

Annie continues to breathe, the sound wet and ragged, like the gurgling of water in a brooklet. My guilt punishes me thoroughly. Images fly through my head, tormenting me unceasingly. I envision Annie, her face pale and still and cold. And last night's horrifying events repeat in my mind, over and over again. I see Elspet lying on the ground with blood darkening her hair. That image will dwell within my thoughts forever. And if Annie does not get well, yet another death will haunt me all my days.

As the day passes, Donny rushes in and out, bringing fresh

poultices and hot broth, which we cannot get Annie to sip. Donny tells me to take some of the broth myself, but I cannot swallow it.

Hours crawl by. At one point, I sleep sitting beside the bed with my head resting on the pillow and my arms cradling the child. All along, she coughs, shivers, and struggles to breathe.

The bell sounds in the kirk tower. It wakes me, and I sit up, groggy and filled with dread. Annie jerks upright and coughs, harder and louder than before, her face scarlet, her eyes round.

"Donny! We need you!" I place one arm behind Annie to support her thin frame, which shudders with that horrid, hacking cough. At that moment, streams of thick, yellowish fluids spurt from Annie's mouth. She gags and continues to cough, and ropes of the stuff, tinged with red, speckle the blankets.

The old woman rushes inside.

"Good." Donny nods approvingly as Annie continues to spit great gobs onto the bed. "Get it all out." She puts a gentle hand on the child's head.

"This is good?"

"Aye." Donny squeezes my arm. Spent and weak, Annie lies back down, and Donny whisks the filthy coverings from the bed. "Now she may get some rest." Indeed, Annie's breathing is less harsh, less wet sounding. She sighs when I place a new cool cloth on her forehead.

"Mamma," she says, not opening her eyes.

I lean down until my forehead touches hers. "I'm here," I whisper. My tears bathe her face.

Donny shuffles out. I lie beside Annie and hold her in my arms. And as I begin to fall asleep, a scene floats before my eyes. I'm in my own bed, bundled in wool blankets, the warming pan at my toes, my small body shaking with chills. Cinaed never leaves my side. She tells me faery stories and places cool cloths on my forehead, feeds me porridge and hot broth.

No one else would have cared for me so. Mrs. Harris was kind, but never motherly. If my sister had not taken on the role of a parent, I'd have truly been an orphan. I raise myself on one elbow to gaze on the child who sleeps beside me and stroke her warm cheek, more determined than ever to escape the city. Though my former plan has come to naught, I shall find a different way. I no longer have only myself to care for.

I place a gentle kiss on Annie's damp forehead. When my sister died, I thought my family was gone. That I was alone. 'Tis no longer so. My family is right here. And we will find our way out of this place.

CHAPTER 30

By the following morning, Annie is awake and hungry, though so weak she cannot rise from the bed. I feed her oatmeal porridge and bites of mashed turnips Donny has prepared. When she sleeps again, I head to the kitchen, my stomach growling like a pack of Grandfather's hounds ready for the hunt.

At the table, Donny passes me hot, fragrant bread and ale. I devour my food with a complete lack of propriety and explain where I'd gone the night before when seeking an escape from the close. She nods as I speak and frowns a few times, especially when hearing how cruel hands captured me and locked me inside a stranger's house. Her eyes narrow when she learns soldiers now guard the locked gate.

"Fool of a lass." She takes a large bite of bread. "I hope ye learn from this. It seems ye did, for ye didnae run off again last night," she mumbles through her mouthful of food.

"No. I promised Annie that I'll not leave her again."

"Hmph."

My eyes sting with tears. "I'm speaking the truth." What would have happened to poor Annie if the soldiers or Elspet had killed me? Tremors shake me and I can barely raise my cup to my lips.

"What is it?" Donny asks.

"I have not told you all of my story." With a voice thick with tears, I tell Donny what happened to Elspet. The herbwife's brows draw low. She shakes her head and her eyes flash.

She rises and swiftly prepares a tisane, adding bits of this and that from her cupboard and pouring boiling water from her great kettle over the herbs inside a bowl. After a minute, she strains dark liquid into a cup and hands it to me.

The potion is slightly bitter but not unpleasant. Its warmth spreads through me. "What is this?" I take another sip.

"Valerian root, fennel, and a few other herbs. Helps clear the head and keep ye calm."

"Thank you."

Donny leaves my side and paces the length of her kitchen.

"Foolish woman, Elspet." She takes her pipe and holds it between her teeth, speaking around the stem as she continues. "She wasn't a bad sort. But we all feel the lack of what we need. That price on your head puts ye in more danger than ever, Poisoner, as well as that nonsense with the soldiers. Perhaps 'tis a sign from God. Ye best remain indoors from now on."

The room is of a sudden filled with a winter's chill, despite the crackling fire. I shiver. "Am I to remain in the city for the rest of my life, trapped within a single, narrow lane, until..." My words cut off as my throat swells.

Until we all starve to death? For how long can everyone survive? When I visited Rob, my swift glance at the storerooms within the vaults told me a sad tale. There is not as much as Donny might like to think. When the guild must resort to stealing only from the poorest of the poor, soon, there will be nothing.

"What else are ye gonna do?" Donny peers at me. "Sprout wings and fly away from this place?" Her low cackle infuriates me. "Sure, there be some here who may see old Sheona as a witch, but I can tell ye, Poisoner, she has no power to grow ye a pair o' wings." She places her feet on a low stool and stretches her legs, chuckling.

I leap to my feet, blinking away tears of rage and desperation.

"I'll not stay here and wait while the bailey's watchman hunts for me and all within the close march toward starvation!" My voice trembles with fervor. "I'll tell you what I shall do, Donny. I'll find enough people to help me overpower the soldiers. There weren't all that many of them, and there are enough of us inside the close, do you not think? We could break through the gate! Then I shall leave, along with anyone else who wishes it. The white cloth must come down and that gate must stay open."

Donny's gaze is unblinking, and I quiver beneath her steady glare but remain where I am, standing tall before the wizened old woman.

She purses her crinkled lips. "Overpower a group of soldiers?" She shakes her head. "They have muskets, lass. And they be on higher ground. They have the advantage. They'll see us coming from afar and fire on us. We'll drop, one by one."

My body freezes as the horrid realization settles upon me. She is right. This will not work. The woman's azure eyes glitter as she regards me. "What do ye say to that, lass?"

I turn my back on her, and my heart turns to a lump of lead. I was so certain. Unless...

"Wait! Una said there's a group camped on the roof of the Martin house. That house is one of the few places where one could escape from Stewart's Close. One could leap from there to the roof of another house that faces away from this lane. We could creep to the roof and take the soldiers by surprise, could we not?"

I fidget like a wee child awaiting a sweet as the old woman considers my words.

"They're *soldiers*, lass. Men trained to fight. To kill."

A painful lump rises in my throat. The memory of the red-coated men laughing and jesting as they camped outside the gate sinks into me. Their muskets shone in the light of their fire. Some bore bayonets.

My knees tremble, and I sink onto the floor and drop my head into my hands. I am such a fool. Those harsh men, with their loud voices, coarse words, and bawdy songs, were ordered to keep us locked inside the close. Like as not, those orders included firing upon anyone who might accost them.

"Finish your drink, Kenna. You'll feel better."

My drink? Lifting my head, I blink up at Donny. When I'd

discovered the soldiers encamped outside the gate, one man's voice had risen above the others, and his grating plea for more ale had followed me as I'd crept away. Soldiers are often tipplers, or so I've been told. After all, one must have something to keep him warm when on guard duty in the cold.

I leap to my feet. "Soldiers like their drink, do they not?"

"Aye. Who doesn't?" Donny smirks up at me as she lights her pipe.

"What if we bring them a gift? A bottle of fine wine, perhaps. One that happens to contain a sleeping draught."

The woman blinks up at me and her jaw works as though she is chewing on the very idea. And then a bright gleam shoots into Donny's eyes.

"Aye." She grins as she puffs at her pipe. "That might just be possible, lass. Especially if I brew my draught nice and strong. But who's going to offer the wine? If a man or a crone like me offered them a bottle or two, they'd know we had ill intentions. Which we would indeed have."

"*I* will offer it."

The woman barks out a shout of laughter and I cross my arms and huff.

"I realize I may not be considered a great beauty, but your humor is rather discourteous, don't you think, Donny?" I scowl.

Wiping her eyes, Donny rises and tweaks me on the nose. "You're as bonnie a lass any other your age, Kenna. I dinnae ken why ye see yourself as such a plain hen. I hear talk of a lad who fancies ye."

My cheeks fairly flame at this.

"Then why should I *not* be the one to...oh."

Donny chuckles to herself as she stokes the fire. "She sees now, eh?"

I grimace. I am well known by now. Everyone still trapped here knows the Poisoner, if not by sight, then by reputation. And surely my likeness, at least a description of it, has been given to the soldiers so they'd recognize me.

"I do not want to put my friends in danger, but perhaps Una would do it."

"Aye. She might. Ye must ask her that yourself. But I still have my musket from my soldiering days. I could protect her."

"What do you think?"

The old woman squints at me. "I say we make the attempt."

I clap my hands and jump up and down, caring not that I behave like a silly, wee lass.

Donny takes a puff from her pipe. "Say we make our way beyond that gate. What is your plan after that?"

"I shall go home to Grandfather and seek his aid. He'll speak to the bailey and end this false quarantine. He will save all of us. I am sure of it."

Am I? I try to deny it, but a tiny doubt continues to pester me. Rob believes Grandfather has forgotten about me. At least if I escape the city, I shall know for certain if it be the truth. I'll know if Grandfather believes Oliver's lies. The idea brings on a sudden sadness that weighs me down, then a new thought lights a spark of hope. Grandfather would never believe such a thing! Oliver must have told his father that I am dead. That I ran to the city and met with a dismal end. 'Twould explain so much.

Donny's eyes study my face. "Perhaps he will save us, lass." She takes another puff of her pipe. "Perhaps."

"Who will save us?" a voice calls out from the front chamber. My breath catches in my throat at the sound of Rob's voice.

"Come in, lad," Donny calls. "Though I believe ye already have."

When he enters, Rob's usual grin is missing. "I heard wee Annie was ill. That's why I didnae knock at the door. I had no wish to disturb her. And I wanted to know how ye fared after what happened, Kenna." His dark eyes seek mine. A sudden rush of wounded dismay strikes me. Una came to my aid when I needed it. Rob did not.

I hold my smarting hands to the fire as though to warm them, shocked at the extent of my anger. Where *was* Rob when Una helped me flee the soldiers? Why did he not come? Especially if he fancies me, as Donny implied?

When I speak, my voice trembles.

"Are you truly that concerned about me, Rob? I spent a wretched night locked away while my captors howled like dogs and boasted of selling me to the watchman." I turn around. "Una came to my aid. She is a true friend."

I cannot miss the wounded expression that washes over his face, nor the sharp intake of breath at my words. Despite this, I cannot stop.

"Where were you? Surely you heard what happened?" I step closer to him and show him the scab upon my neck where Elspet had pressed the sharp blade. "I nearly lost my life, Rob. But perhaps you were too occupied with more weighty matters. You did not bother to come to my aid when you heard I was in peril."

The moment the words leave my lips I regret them. I turn to the fire again, chiding myself for such childish weakness. Rob and I are hardly acquainted. We've known each other barely a week. But he kissed me. And when he kissed me, I had thought perhaps it meant something.

"Kenna." Rob puts a hand on my shoulder. "I only heard from Una afterwards what happened. Her Da awoke her, telling her he'd heard talk someone had found the Poisoner and locked her inside their house. He found out where they kept ye, and they waited outside. When they saw ye come out, surrounded by those fools, they followed ye to the gate. Una kept watch, waiting for a chance to help, while Callum went to find the others. By the time I learned what had happened, it was over."

My face stings with a sudden blush. I am ashamed as though I'd been caught out of bed wearing only my linen shift.

"If I'd known what was happening, Kenna, ye can be sure I'd have done anything I could to help."

Why did I have to babble so? I swipe at my wet face. A smile trembles on my lips. Blinking away tears, I lift my gaze to Rob, not wanting him to think that my anger will remain forever. He is close; so close I feel the warmth of his breath on my face. And he does not back away. He merely grins at me and bends his head. The heat from the fire grows unaccountably warmer. I stop breathing. Then he pauses and turns to the side, and I follow his gaze.

Donny is only a few paces away. She stares at us with frank amusement on her crinkled face. "Well, go on, then." She chews on her pipe. "Ye gonna give her a nip or what?"

Rob does so. His kiss is so swift I might have imagined it. He chuckles and steps away and I am suddenly colder. When we are once more alone, I will apologize for my anger and lack of trust. And I will kiss him again. The thought warms me.

Clearing his throat, Rob pulls something from within his jacket. "I almost forgot. Here."

I gasp at the item he proffers me. My leather purse!

"How?" I take it from him, my heart sinking. Elspet had it on her person when she died.

Rob frowns. "Mrs. Kennison washed Elspet's body for burial. She found it and knew it was yours."

My eyebrows raise. "That old woman at the apothecary?"

My friend smiles softly. "Everyone knows that the Poisoner carries a knife in a purse she keeps hidden in her skirts."

"Oh." I finger the leather ties that Elspet severed when she took the pouch from me and swallow, hard. "Where are they burying her?"

Rob shrugs. My eyes sting and I turn away.

Donny tuts. "Enough of such things." She regards me with a stern, though kind gaze. "There is nothing to be done about it now, lass. Now, then. We've much to do. If we are to escape, we'd best call for the guild and make our plans, eh, Poisoner?"

"Plans?" Rob lifts a single dark eyebrow. Forcing away any thoughts of Elspet, I explain my idea to my friend.

When I finish, he nods. "This may work, Poisoner."

"It will work!"

Rob grins at me. "The moment I clapped eyes on ye I knew ye were someone unusual, Kenna. A lass I wished to know better."

"*Och*," Donny growls. "Begone with ye, lad! Call the guild. Tell them the plan and have them here by sundown. Off!"

His eyes gleaming, Rob winks at me and is gone. I resume the duties Donny assigns me, grateful for the bandages she affixed to my stinging hands. As I work, my wandering mind returns again and again to the expression on Rob's face as we stood before the fire. To the brief kiss.

Foolish and uncaring lass! I chide myself quite fiercely while I vigorously sweep the hearth. My wee Annie was near death and yet lies abed, quite ill. After my escape attempt, a woman is dead. I am trapped in the city with a price on my head. But at this moment, the foremost thought on my mind is whether one of Donny's thieves will give me another kiss. I place my fingers to my lips. 'Tis true. I want Rob to kiss me again. And again.

And if we escape the close, my wish may well come true. My hands grow still. Unless Grandfather does not want me to associate with a lad like Rob. Shaking my head, I sweep again with renewed vigor. I will find a way. I will come to the city to visit my new friend as often as I choose. I hope.

CHAPTER
31

My Annie sleeps throughout the day. Each time I place a gentle hand upon her chest, I am grateful that her breathing is not labored. At the old woman's bidding, I add drops of one of her special tinctures to sips of water, which the child takes without opening her eyes.

The hours creep by as though they've drunk their fill of Shaw's whiskey and can hardly move. Blessedly, the time approaches for the return of the guild. And Rob. I leap to my feet when someone pounds at the door.

Una marches inside with a broad smile on her face. Her hair, for once, is neatly plaited. Her father, Callum, follows close behind. Though his face is hard-set as usual, his eyes appraise me with what I interpret as silent approval.

Behind him is Rob, and I find I do not know what to do with my hands. I clasp them behind my back. My injured palms are slick. Rob comes to stand beside me, smelling of leather and spices. I lean closer to him.

"Hello, Poisoner," he whispers. For the first time, I do not mind the name the people of Stewart's Close have bestowed upon me. Not when it is spoken by Rob, in soft tones, teasing tones. I smile at him, and he grins back.

The small room fills with people. I recognize Steenie and another of the sour-faced men I'd met in the vaults. Munro arrives and hobbles over to the fire, his face a mask of pain. Donny settles him in her chair and clucks like an old hen as she examines his greatly swollen foot. She shakes her head and scowls, then runs to fetch bandages and herbs.

Three men, muscular and lean, and two more women join us. One woman is slight, with hair the color of a fieldmouse and dark, deep-set eyes that gleam with malice. I tear my gaze from her. I've no desire to make more enemies than I already have. Her companion is Mrs. Kennison from the apothecary shop, who grins at me. Her empty gums give her the appearance of an overgrown infant. I smile back, grateful for the kindness.

Donny returns with bundles of leaves and pots of ointment and orders me to fetch ale for everyone while she administers to Munro's injured foot. Una assists me, and soon we have everyone settled with a drink in hand, though we must strive to ignore Munro's pitiful groaning while Donny lances his foot to relieve the swelling.

"Now." Donny frowns in concentration as she wraps linen tightly around the moaning man's foot. "We must decide upon a plan. Kenna, tell us what ye said to me earlier."

Holding tight to my cup of ale, I clear my throat and begin.

"Donny explained to me that we dare not try to break through the gate. 'Twould be an impossible task and far too dangerous, thanks to the soldiers who now guard it. That leaves only one option: leaping from the Martin house to a house that leads outside the close. Which means we must find a way to get past the soldiers encamped there."

"Soldiers?" The woman scoffs. "What d'ye mean? There's but one fellow there by the gate. And we've all seen that watchman set on us by the bailey."

Una responds before I can. "There's a group of at least ten soldiers encamped on both sides of the gate at the head of our close," she says. She takes another gulp of ale. "Since day before yesterday. And many on the rooftops as well."

"Aye." Callum glances at me. "Someone's set on keeping us, or at least one of us, from escaping."

"We all know who that 'someone' is." The angry woman spits out her words.

"Iona, hold your tongue." Donny glares at her. "She's part of the guild now."

"Don't make me laugh!" Iona's cheeks grow pink; her face contorts with anger. She lifts a bony finger and jabs it in my direction.

"This lofty lass thinks she's so grand. She's the granddaughter of an Earl, mind ye! She was mighty proud to tell us all that. But 'tis thanks to our own 'Lady Poisoner' that the bailey set the quarantine. We're locked inside our own lane like criminals. We all know there's a price on her head. Why don't we turn her over to them soldiers? God knows we could use the coin!" Her voice shakes with rage. "What if it's the only way to open our gate?"

"Silence." Donny scowls at her. "Enough, ye fool of a woman."

"She's a murderess!" Iona shouts. Flecks of spittle glisten on her lips.

"That's a lie!" Rob places a hand on my shoulder.

"Whether 'tis true or no' true, Kenna has shown her mettle." Donny glares at Iona from beneath her bushy white eyebrows, her pale blue eyes gleaming. "She's no' killed any of us in our beds, nor has she stolen from us. What food she took she paid for."

At those words, I exchange glances with Rob. Did someone see me leave food for the soldier's wife, Bess?

"She's no' stolen from us? Is that so?" Iona's face grows smug, and a cold trickle of fear slides down my throat.

"Here!" Iona reaches behind her and fetches my missing basket. She holds it high. My shoulders slump at the sight. The woman laughs in triumph, shaking the basket. Its contents, a few remaining potatoes, a parcel of oatmeal, and some shriveled turnips, roll about within.

Rob seizes my hand in his. "I took that while guarding the vaults the other night. 'Twas my payment and my due."

"Then how did it come to be here?" Callum demands. He glares at me with clear dislike in his hooded eyes.

"I saw her," Iona screeches. "Creeping out o' the kirk, late when we're all meant to stay abed. She handed food to someone and took no payment for it." Glowering at me, her thin lips pull back from yellowed teeth as she snarls like a feral cat. "She's a thief, she is. A thief who steals food from those who gave her a home!"

With that, Iona hurls the basket in my direction. It strikes my stomach and falls to the floor. Oatmeal scatters while turnips thump across the flagstones.

Several within the room exchange glances. A few lower their faces, not meeting my gaze. Callum glares, and Una stares with her mouth open.

"What I take as payment after my watch is rightfully mine, and I may share it with anyone I choose," Rob repeats. His brows lower. "I gave it to Kenna. 'Tis her right to give it to others if she wishes."

No one speaks for a moment until Una marches to my side. She links her arm in mine.

"He's right. And *I* gave her some of that myself, Da. Punish me if ye wish, but she did nothing wrong." She winks at me, an obvious gesture not lost on her father, whose eyes narrow.

Despite my predicament, my heart warms and lightens. Were it not for the lack of food, freedom, and my desperate need to seek justice for my sister, I could remain here in the city forever with such friends at my side.

"Ye see, Iona, 'tis but a trifling thing." Donny's glares at the woman. "I've had enough o' this. Hold your peace or leave. Now."

"Aye." Rob and Una speak in unison. Una giggles and Rob squeezes my hand.

"You're all mad." Iona sneers at Donny. "I'll no' remain here with anyone who chooses to shelter that, that…"

Donny sweeps over to her, seizes her by her ear, and marches her out of the room. "Away, and bile your head!" she shouts.

Iona howls. "Ma! Come!"

Mrs. Kennison aims her wet, pink grin at me one more time

before hurrying after her daughter. The others bend their heads to their drinks, murmuring to one another. The door slams.

I study my torn fingernails. Donny leapt to my defense, bless the old woman, but I *did* take food from the guild. Only to share with others, but still, I am guilty of what Iona accused me of.

Callum clears his throat once Donny returns. "Let us begin. I dinnae trust this lass, but we need her. She may be our only ally once we escape the close."

"How so?" one of the unfamiliar guild members asks. He glowers in my direction. *Och*, but I am weary of so much mistrust and anger! I keep my spine stiff and my shoulders back and meet his gaze.

"Well, once we leave Stewart's Close, 'tis not certain anything will change. The bailey will continue that quarantine unless we have help from one powerful enough to force its end. I shall find Lord Ramsay and seek his aid." My voice only trembles a little.

Munro grunts. "Why would a man like that care about any of us?"

"He's Kenna's grandfather, Da. Do ye no' remember?" Rob shoots me a glance and I cannot miss the worry betrayed by his crinkled brow. I busy myself gathering the fallen turnips so he will not read the disappointment writ across my face. Rob does not trust that Grandfather will help us. He spoke of his doubt the night we buried Master Lindsay.

"He'll have our gates open before ye can blink twice. And likely will have the heads of whoever did this to us." Una raises her ale as though making a toast and tosses back her drink. Guffaws and a few cheers follow her words.

Seizing a broom to sweep the spilled oats, I feel Donny's eyes upon me. She wears an expression that is both wary and a trifle sad. She must read my doubts, writ upon my features. Of course, she does, she sees all.

Callum clears his throat. "'T'will be a great danger to all who try to escape, but if *she* has enough pluck to join us, I say we do this." He jerks his head in my direction. "We cannot tarry much longer. The price on that lass's head has tripled."

My broom clatters to the floor.

"I heard of it." Rob squeezes my arm. "What he offers amounts to a lifetime of ease, Kenna. There be many more on the lookout for ye now. The first is Shaw, especially after what happened to his Elspet. Ye can be certain that if anyone finds ye, they won't let ye escape this time."

CHAPTER
32

"Una, wait. There's something I must ask. Of course, you can refuse me if you wish."

The lass smiles at me and turns back from the open door. Rob waits for her outside. His eyes find mine, and he rewards me with a grin but raises his eyebrows in curiosity.

"For our plan to work, the soldiers must drink the wine we offer before they see how many of us are waiting to confront them. I cannot do it as they are looking for me, and Donny cannot do it, nor Callum, nor any of the other men, so, well..." My voice trails off and my hands hang at my sides. How can I ask this of her?

But my new friend's green eyes flash with humor. "I'll do it. They'll suspect nothing if a lass comes to share a drink with them. If Donny adds her sleeping brew to the wine, they'll be nodding and bobbing their heads before they've finished a single cup."

Rob frowns at the two of us. "You're sure of this, Una?" He steps back inside Donny's home. "I hate to see ye do such a foolhardy thing, but I ken very well why a lass must be the one to offer the wine."

"I'd do it if I could," I take one of Una's hands. "But you must not if you don't want to."

"I told ye already, I'll do it." Una beams at me. "'Twill be a lark."

"Donny's promised to be close by with her musket." I give her a swift hug. "We'll all be waiting to offer help should you need it. Thank you."

Rob and Una take their leave and fly to spread word of our plan for escape, hoping to swell our numbers. The older guild members hover around the table with Donny, having moved on from ale to imbibing stolen wine as they discuss our plans. I take some broth and gruel Donny prepared and return upstairs to see how wee Annie fares.

Smoothing my skirts, I sit on the bed next to her and stroke her hair. Now awake, she has gained strength enough to eat, sit up, and amuse herself with her doll. I am glad of it, for she must be strong enough to flee the city with me. We'll make haste to return to my home by the sea, where Grandfather will be grateful to find me alive and well.

At least, this is what I tell myself. A thorn of doubt continues to pierce its way through my heart. Far too many days have passed since Oliver's men took me to the city and locked me inside this narrow lane. And I've found not a hint of anyone searching for me, save the watchman and the bailey, a man who only just tripled the price on my head. I bite my lip so hard it makes me wince.

After Annie finishes her meal, I cuddle beside the lassie, and her mouth stretches wide in a yawn. I soon follow suit. There is so much for me to worry over, but weariness wins the battle with my dread, and I fall asleep. Some time later, murmured voices below wake me.

Stretching, I rise to peer from my chamber's small window. The scene below is already familiar to me. The tall houses, jumbled together like stones cast by a giant hand, a lane so narrow one can only drive a cart through it with great difficulty, and the murmured rushing of men and woman hurrying about their business, whether it be honest or no. This place is almost like home. And I marvel it could be so.

Movement catches my eye. A man is striding along the cobbles toward Donny's house. He is tall and dressed in a ragged, torn shirt beneath a filthy doublet and wears rather ill-fitting breeches. Something about him strikes me as strange. The man is garbed in clothing that mark him as one living a life of poverty, yet his bearing and the confident gait of a gentleman would say otherwise. He does not step aside nor slacken his pace for others in his path. This is a man fully accustomed to having others make way for him.

I keep my eyes fixed on the figure as he draws ever closer, edging forward until my nose presses against the cold glass. The stranger slows his steps and speaks to a passing child, who shrugs and scampers away. He moves ahead but pauses again to speak with a woman. She gestures down the lane, making vague motions with her hands. The man nods and his steps draw ever closer to Donny's house. Unease grows within, and I back away from the window.

Why does this man make me so wary? With quickened breath, I count to twenty in my head and approach the window once more, gradually moving into place until I have a clear view of the lane outside. 'Tis empty, save for a woman splashing slops onto the cobbles and two ragged boys chasing each other. Blinking, I lean closer to the window. Where could the man be? He must have ducked inside one of the nearby houses. Curious, I open my casements.

When I ease my head out, I glance down and gasp. The top of the man's worn cap is directly below me, facing Donny's door. He raises his head, and our eyes meet.

'Tis Oliver. My sister's murderer.

For a mere, horror-filled moment, I read the changes that flit across his features. Disbelief. Astonishment that melts and hardens into anger. I slam the casements. I am burning and cold at the same time.

"I'll be back soon, Annie." My voice shakes. "Stay here." The child's blue eyes fly wide open, and she nods.

I stumble downstairs and hurtle into the kitchen.

"Oliver!" I shout. The guild members whirl in surprise. I gasp at the feel of my knife in my hand. I have no memory of removing it from my leather purse. My heart climbs to my throat and chokes me.

Donny's pipe emits faint wisps of cinnamon-scented smoke that drift lazily to the ceiling. Her eyes pierce me. I freeze in indecision. My words, my threat, my vow to kill this man return to me, and the memory burns through me as though fire is now sweeping through my body. Would I do it? Would I truly kill Oliver?

A fierce pounding on the door commences, and I drop my blade. And as I bend to retrieve it, the memory of that tiny bottle of poison torments me. With a howl of rage, I grab the knife and fly for the door, but do not get that far. Callum seizes my arms and holds them tight against my sides. I am powerless to raise the knife still in my grasp. Powerless to get to the man who murdered my sister.

"Steady on, lass."

"Let me go!" I struggle in vain. "The man who killed my sister is at the door! Release me!"

The room erupts in a flurry of voices and scuffles, and Oliver continues to pound on the door. No matter how I struggle against his strong hands, Callum does not release my arms.

"Let me kill him!" Blackness blurs my sight and clouds my mind. Oliver is here, and I must do what I vowed.

"Mamma?" a tiny voice peeps from the passageway. I swivel my head and spy Annie in the kitchen doorway, clutching her doll. Her eyes gleam with tears.

"Lass." Donny's voice fills with steel. "Think of what you're doing before the eyes of the child."

My body sags as though invisible hands have placed great chains of iron on my shoulders, and I cannot bear their weight.

"He killed her." I sob and struggle to speak past the great lump in my throat. "He killed my sister!" The pounding from outside increases in intensity.

"Take the child upstairs, Kenna. I'll send the man away." As my arms are pinned to my sides, Donny has no trouble plucking the knife from my helpless hand. "Believe me, lass. I know your pain." She takes my face in her gnarled hands and forces me to meet her gaze. "Yet killing this man will not take it away." This time, her voice is soft. Her eyes bore into mine.

I struggle to control my tormented breathing. 'Tis an impossible task while this dark desire rages within my soul. A part of me clings to the memory of Cinaed's wasted face and pleading eyes. That part of me yearns to march to the doorway and fling it wide open, so I may plunge my knife into Oliver's chest. But Donny is right. I cannot do it here. I hang my head. And Callum loosens his grip.

"Go." Donny brushes a strand of hair from my eyes in a maternal gesture that surprises me. Her gaze is gentle. "I'll not allow that man inside my house."

Annie flies to me with a sob, and I lift her into my arms and bury my face in her hair. Donny was right. I shall someday have my revenge. Somehow. But not today. Not yet. How could I do such a thing in front of Annie, who has already seen too much in her brief life?

Holding the child close to me, I feign a return to our chamber, stomping with loud steps to the foot of the stairway. Then I creep back to the now empty kitchen, whispering to my Annie that she must remain quiet. I listen to the sounds coming from Donny's front chamber, panting as though I have run a great distance. The old woman's front door creaks open.

"What d'ye want?"

"I am a friend." Oliver's voice is harsh. "Friend and protector of the lass within your house. She is Kenna Somerled, my ward. My *daughter*," he adds with careful emphasis on the final word.

I hold a hand to my mouth to keep from screaming out at him to deny those hateful words. Lies! Oliver wore the title of "Father" when it suited him, though he shed the role of parent most of the time, removing it from his person as one flicks a bit of dust from his sleeve.

Annie fidgets. Fearing she will speak and betray our presence, I put her down beside the kitchen fire and kneel to whisper in her ear.

"Wait for me here, sweet, and take care of your wee babe. She's sleeping. We must be very quiet."

Annie smiles, hugging the doll to her chest and pretending to rock her child. Clinging to the wall, I inch my way toward Donny's tiny front chamber. Callum left my knife on the table and I retrieve my weapon and tuck it back inside its hiding place. I must swat away the brief, foolish idea that I can break through the knot of men in the next room to get close enough to stick Oliver with the blade.

"Ye've got the wrong house. There be no young lass here." Donny's words are swift and certain. "Only me and a lad who works for his keep. I'm an old woman but I in't all that daft. I ken very well who lives in my house." I close my eyes for a moment. God bless that old woman!

"I saw her!" Oliver's voice booms. "She is here; you must let me in! I must speak to her!"

Donny, Callum, and the other guild members all shout at once. Oliver's tenor responds and interrupts, and the cacophony of angry voices rises and falls for several moments, until the unmistakable *click* of a musket brings all to silence.

"I see I have failed here." Oliver is breathing hard. "Please, do me this one kindness. I beg you to tell the lass I am here to help her. Please, tell her!"

"I'd tell the lass if a lass were here."

"Then please, give her this. Do me this one favor."

The door closes with a thud. Callum says something and chuckles softly. The group clatters back in my direction, so I swiftly take Annie in my arms and we flee as quietly as we can to our bedchamber.

First, I settle my wee one in bed. Then I pat my ratted hair one more time. And I take out my knife, shocked at the wild plan that has taken form in my mind. Donny's words have bored inside my head and will not leave. She claimed to have a lad working for her. A lad she shall have.

I take in a deep breath. Donny did it, and so can I. For Cinaed. For Annie. For myself. I, Kenna, meant to be a lady, am about to enter a man's world. How Donny would laugh! But Oliver's arrival has forced me to take this step.

With harried movements, I plait my hair and raise my knife. Holding my braid taut, I slice through it in one swift motion. The blade severs the plaited strands with a faint tearing sound. My shorn locks fall to my feet, while Annie gasps in surprise.

"There." I run a shaking hand through my remaining locks. Hair falls just below my ears, tickling the skin of my neck. I am frightened and exhilarated at the same time. And oddly free, as though I removed shackles I was not aware of.

Annie hops from the bed and picks up my fallen braid. "Kenna?" Her eyes are round.

I kneel beside her. "Do not be afraid." I smile. "I'm not hurt. I simply needed to make my hair shorter." After regarding me for a moment with her eyes so like pools of rainwater, the child nods as though she understands. For a mere second, a prickle of regret discomforts me as I take the shorn braid from the child's hand. I hide the braid inside the chest, tucking it beneath the folded linens there. And dismiss any thought of regret. If this helps me escape the city and avenge my sister, 'tis worth any price.

"Now I must borrow some clothing from Donny." I wink at Annie as though we are conspiring in a game. She nods again, a solemn bobbing of her wee head, and trots after me.

Donny's door is closed, but I pray she has not locked it. I seize the latch, and the door swings wide with a soft creak. Shock steals my breath.

The chamber is quite large, more than twice the size of the one Donny assigned to Annie and me. Rich furnishings gleam: a tall wardrobe, a lovely carved chest of wood so dark it's almost black, a writing desk with scattered papers and a quill in the ink well. A great carved chair that matches the one downstairs. Lush tapestries hanging on wainscoted walls.

All this wealth of fine furniture shocks me, given the plainness of the other areas of Donny's house. Another odd detail strikes me. There is no bed in Donny's bedchamber. I spot a small, neatly folded pile of blankets beside the hearth. Could it be the woman sleeps there, on the floor?

This is no time for my musings! But I cannot control my curiosity.

I settle Annie close to the glowing embers of the grate and wrap her poor thin frame in a thick woolen shawl of "Sheona's" that was draped over a nearby chair. Then I explore the chamber.

A scattering of papers covers Donny's writing desk. My eyes fall on something strange. I pick it up and gasp. 'Tis a letter-opener in the shape of a small sword. The insignia on the hilt is as familiar to me as my own name. The carved castle surrounded by a wall; why, 'tis the crest of the Earl of Chessington! Of Grandfather. How came Donny to possess such a thing?

I pace the length of the room. This letter opener was stolen! How, and when? Donny herself told me how the guild got their start by robbing from the wealthy during the plague outbreak back in '45. Did they steal from Grandfather, years before I was born? I'd never heard talk of it, but it must be, for as sure as I live and breathe, the insignia on the hilt of the letter opener is that of the Earl.

My stomach turns over. Every object in this room must be stolen property, taken by a member of Donny's wretched guild. The strange old soldier has been kind to shelter me, but she *is* a thief. I groan aloud. She is a thief. And so am I.

Something clatters on the stairs. I fly to Donny's doorway and place my ear on the worn wood. Raised voices rise from below.

I've been foolishly wasting my time spying on Donny when there are more pressing matters at hand. Donny's wardrobe provides me with a long linen shirt and a pair of breeches, worn but clean. They will do.

Disrobing and swiftly donning my man's garb, I take up my leather pouch and fasten it about my waist, grateful to still have it. The straps are now shorter as Donny clumsily stitched and patched them together, but they hold the pouch in place. I tuck Grandfather's letter opener inside it and vow to ask the elderly thief how she came into possession of something that belongs to Grandfather. Her secrets cannot remain hidden forever.

Now clad in a man's clothing, I make another hasty search through Donny's belongings and find a blue doublet to don. It has such an odd feel. The shirt is comfortable beneath it, though. I grimace, curving my lips into a frown. The breeches make my legs itch. I pull my stockings tighter and scratch at my knees, then replace my worn boots.

"Ugh." I stick out my tongue and Annie giggles. I stand, sit, walk, and sit once more. This will take some getting used to, dressing like a man.

Donny's door rattles while I hear the soft rumble of a deep voice, as though a man is clearing his throat. Is it Oliver? How did he get past Donny and the others? My vision darkens as though a cloud of blackness has engulfed me. With a gasp, I whirl, plunge my hand into my leather pouch and seize my knife.

My breath catches in my throat as I fly to the door and raise my knife. Seizing the handle, I swing the door wide and raise my knife to strike.

CHAPTER 33

With a shout, the figure before me leaps backward and my knife swishes through empty air. I freeze, blinking at the sight that greets me. Rob, eyes wide and face pallid, blinks back at me with his back planted against the wall of the corridor. He holds his hands out in a defensive position.

"I—I'm sorry!" A sickening sensation spreads through me. My own face must be as pale as oatmeal porridge. "I thought you were..." My voice trails off. Dear Lord above, I was a hair's breadth away from stabbing the only lad I've ever kissed!

Rob eases the knife from my grasp. "I certainly hope ye thought I was someone else." He draws in a shaking breath and glances at the knife cradled in his palm. "'Tis a good thing I'm faster than you. I've no wish to be carved up like a haunch of pork." He proffers me the blade and I take it with a trembling hand. Annie joins us in the corridor.

"Rob." My voice is weak. "I thought you'd left." I cringe at my words. Cinaed always chided me for stating the obvious.

"I came back." Rob also appears to have the gift of putting into words what is plain to see. He draws closer with slow footsteps.

"I am truly sorry. It's just that Oliver was here. *Here,* at Donny's door!" My pulse beats fast.

"Aye." Rob's voice is curt. "They told me. He's here no longer, Kenna."

My shoulders droop in relief. Rob's eyebrows draw together as he studies my appearance. A jolt of nerves hits the pit of my stomach as his gaze travels up and down my person. 'Tis as though I am a plump pig that has caught his eye at market. A spark of anger ignites within me.

"Perhaps you could commission a portrait." I lift my chin. "That way, you'll not forget the sight of me like this."

Rob's brows fly to his hairline. Then he chuckles.

"Forgive me. 'Twas a surprise to find a young lad instead of our Poisoner. What shall I call ye now, my lady?" His brief smile fades, and his face grows thoughtful again.

"Just call me Kenneth." Why does Rob regard me so? His expression is so serious.

"Kenneth." Rob takes hold of one of my short locks and gives it a gentle tug. "As good a name as any, that is. I like your hair shorn. It suits ye."

His words bring a tiny smile to my lips, but Rob's face remains serious, his eyes troubled.

"Donny sent me upstairs to tell ye that Oliver has left the close. His presence worries everyone. He now knows where to find ye." Rob paces the length of the corridor.

"Do you know where he went?" I clench my fists and fold my arms tightly.

"Donny sent someone after him. She feared he'd return with soldiers and demand we hand ye over. She was ready to have ye flee to Una's house. But all the man did was climb the lane to the gate. He passed right through to the High Street. He's gone for now."

I kneel beside Annie and hold her to me. She places her thin arms around my shoulders, and I seek comfort in her warmth.

"I should have run after him the moment he appeared." Fury, confusion, and fear bubble and simmer together within my soul, a poisonous concoction. Ah, my emotions are in such a state!

Rob comes closer and leans against the wall.

"Are ye certain Lord Ramsay will help?" He kicks against the wall, knocking mud from his boots. "After all, you're the only link we have to the world of men with wealth and influence, Kenna, and the Earl is our best hope. I cannae think of anyone else with the power to change the bailey's mind, nor with the power to have the Town Council send the soldiers away and get our lane open again."

"He *will* help." As I speak, a weight like a blacksmith's anvil settles over me. Will Grandfather really help? He must.

"He has not sought for ye, Kenna, though he has a grand house not far from here, right in the city." His words stun me like a blow to the face.

"I've told you, Rob, he does not have a house here!" My voice shakes.

The lad's eyes glitter. "Oh, but he does. After we spoke the night we buried old Master Lindsay, I sought out some old friends. I thought of lads I knew who might have had dealings of any sort with the Earl, ye see. I wanted to know if I was mistaken."

My body freezes.

"And what did you learn?"

"Nothing, until tonight. I learned the Earl does indeed have a grand house on Leith Wynd, filled with wine and song. Least that's how my friend Jamie tells it. His da's done work for the Earl at his house in town, delivering ale and spirits. Many there be who scheme and simper and make double asses of themselves simply to earn an invitation to dine with the Earl. His favor grants a man great advantage."

My hands clench into fists, but a sliver of icy fear pricks my heart. "I do not believe you." *I cannot. For if this is true...*

Rob shrugs.

"Even if he didnae have a home so near us, he wields great power. Power enough to find a lass lost in the city. And he hasn't sought for ye. Why?"

The words I would speak stick in my throat. If Grandfather does indeed have a house in the city, how did I never hear of it? But then, Grandfather and Oliver never spoke of business in front of me or Cinaed. It was not a subject to be discussed as we dined, nor even when we passed pleasant times together, reading or jesting before the fire, or going on walks through the fragrant summer gardens. For, as Grandfather always said, business is of no concern to women. But a house, here in the city?

Rob studies me, his jaw tense. His dark eyes regard me mournfully, piercing me as though they are reading my soul. And I am forced to admit to myself the doubts I carry with me, wound about me like a rope bound too tight. My shoulders slump.

"What else have you learned from your friends?"

Rob's eyes never leave mine. "My friend, Iain Harris, told me much. His mother works for the Earl, ye see."

"What?" I run a shaking hand through my shorn locks. Harris? *My* Mrs. Harris?

"Iain is apprenticed at Chesney's blacksmith shop. He's been trying to get word to his mother, and Chesney has connections with some of the soldiers. Thanks to that, my friend got a letter to his mother, and he received an answer today."

I swallow. "And what exactly was that answer?"

Rob hesitates before he speaks. "His mother swears ye did kill your sister. She's vexed awfully about it. Crying' every day, she says. She's known ye from birth and didnae believe such a sweet lass was capable of such treachery."

"And what of Grandfather? Hang Mrs. Harris, that old cow of a woman! Of course, she believes I gave poison to my own sister! It must be what Oliver told her, and she adores him, the mindless biddy!"

It must *be what Oliver told her, for who else would have done so?*

Rob does not speak.

"What does Grandfather say, Rob?" I repeat. "What has he said about me?"

"Nothing." The lad's eyes hold mine.

"Not one word?"

Instead of answering, Rob turns his back for a moment. When he circles around, his troubled face curves with sadness.

"I want to hear ye say it, Kenna." The lad's voice is a barely audible whisper. "The Earl is no' your grandfather, is he?"

I gape. "How can you say such a thing, Rob? I *am* the granddaughter of Lord Ramsay." My shrill voice echoes in the corridor and Annie shivers at the noise.

"Not by blood, Kenna." Rob's voice is soft but piercing. His hands hang at his sides. His eyes regard me warily. "Ye were no' born to the Ramsay family."

His words bring a chill to the marrow of my bones.

"You cannot understand." I lower my voice. "I was never treated as though I was not family by blood."

"Is that so?"

"Yes!"

The lad's face grows accusing. "Those with grand titles take care of their own, and you're not truly one of them. Perhaps that's why the Earl has not sought for ye. Or perhaps..."

Whatever he is about to add, I cannot bear to hear it. "Please, Rob, listen!" With trembling lips, I speak my story, telling how Oliver first came to us on our tiny farm, he the only son of the Earl, overseeing his father's properties. Cinaed, a comely lass, doing her best to care for her wee sister after their parents had died. Oliver was smitten with Cinaed, and she with him, and so they were wed.

"And no, I admit, Rob, I am no blood relation to Lord Ramsay. I am the younger sister of his son's wife. And she was not of noble birth."

Rob's eyes spark and he glares at me with a brow furrowed in anger. "I fear, Kenna, that what we've planned is a foolish hope. We could lose our lives for nothing."

"No, Rob! Listen. Grandfather loved me. He loves me still! I never lacked for anything, and from the moment he met us, Cinaed was his daughter, and I his granddaughter. We were part of the family, Rob. I had tutors and fine clothing! A carriage and horses!"

Rob says nothing, so I forge ahead, desperate for him to

understand. "I read to Grandfather in the evenings; he told me stories. He kissed my forehead every night."

My hands hang uselessly at my sides. How can I explain Grandfather's affection for me? I never doubted it, for I read it in his face. How to explain the way his eyes would light with mirth when I made him laugh? Or how much his fatherly attention meant to me, a child with no memory of her own departed father? For Oliver never fulfilled that role. He was mostly kind, always stern, and above all, he kept his distance. It grieved my sister.

But a dull weight now bears down upon me, as though the very air has grown heavy and would press me to the floor. Grandfather has a house in the city. And he has not sought for me.

"Rob, please."

My face flushes at Rob's expression. His lips press together in a look of disdain.

"His wee pet." He scowls at me. "One he thought to make into a great lady, with her silk skirts and her fancy speech. But in the end, he could no' do it, for he saw ye only as a farm lass. In his mind, ye cannae turn a goose into a swan."

I flinch as though he has struck me across the face. Rob walks to the stairway.

"We leave at midnight." He does not face me as he speaks. "At least some of us may make it outside the close."

"You still want to follow through with our plan?"

The lad shrugs without turning around.

"If we succeed, at least we'll be free. We'll fend for ourselves until the bailey opens the gate."

"What of the others? Will they still wish to attack soldiers if they do not believe that my...?" My throat closes. "That the Earl will help them?"

Rob glances back at me. "I told no one else, except Una."

Una. What does my new friend think of me now, when I've just asked her to do something dangerous in my place? I bow my head in shame.

"What did she say of this, Rob?" I lift my gaze to his face. It is an unreadable mask.

"We both decided it was up to you to tell the others the truth. Once they know, they can decide what they want to do."

"I will." My hands quake, and my stomach roils within me. Surely, the others will not wish to go along with such a dangerous plan without the hope of a swift end to the quarantine! But Rob is right. I must tell the others what they risk.

"Rob? Do me one kindness, if you can find it in you. I'll never ask anything of you again."

He does not turn around.

"What is it?"

"Take a note from me to your friend, Iain. Beg him to send it to the Earl's home." I swallow hard. "His home here in the city."

The lad turns to face me. "Why? What good will that do? We're leaving within a few hours. And who knows if he'll even receive it?"

"I must try." My voice shakes. "I must know what he will do when he finds out I was here. If I do not survive tonight, 'tis no matter. But if I do, and Grandfather reads the note, he will show his hand. He will seek for me and bring me home, or..." I clear my throat. "Or he will not. And I will discover the truth."

Regarding me in silence, Rob nods his head. "Be quick."

Flying back inside Donny's bedchamber with Annie at my heels, I make use of a scrap of parchment and a quill. We have precious little time, but a mere five words will suffice.

Oliver knows where I am.

Kenna

There. I fold the parchment and seal it with a bit of wax. Back in the corridor, Rob takes the missive silently. My pulse quickens at his expression. His eyes are softer. But his demeanor is still guarded.

"Ye've faced the truth, at last. The Earl's forgotten ye. 'Tis why I cannae rest my hopes on our Poisoner's plan to get his help. That's no' likely to work." His words inflict more pain.

I pick Annie up and hold her tight. Her tiny arms wrap around my neck and provide a small measure of comfort.

"No matter what the others decide tonight, Una and I still want to escape. We've no great desire to wait around here until we run out of food."

He marches down the stairs and disappears. I kick at the wall. My eyes sting. I press my hands against my closed eyelids, willing the tears away. I shall not allow myself to weep. After all, I am a farm lass. Born from hardworking, sturdy stock. After taking in a deep breath, I hold Annie's wee hand in my own and lead her to our own chamber.

I help Annie undress, kiss the top of her head, and settle her in bed. She prattles and plays for a few minutes while I sit beside her and stroke her hair, in vain willing my thoughts away from the dark place where they fly.

In the ten years since my sister's wedding, I'd never doubted my place as a member of Grandfather's family. Not until the past few months, when the house filled with confusion. There was the strange visit from the arrogant father of the even more arrogant Cecelia. Soon after, there were parties I was not allowed to attend, even though Oliver had finally yielded to his wife's arguments and promised me this privilege. There was the expected visit from the king, never fulfilled. Oliver and Cinaed began to speak less to one another. Their words grew strained. Servants exchanged concerned glances in their presence, as if wishing to help, but not knowing how. Whispered conversations ceased the moment I walked into the room.

Leaning my head against the wall, I rub my weary eyes. All was not well at the grand house in the country, and I knew it. Even before Cinaed grew ill, Oliver's marriage to my sister had begun to fray about the edges like an old garment whose beauty has faded with time. Nothing was ever the same after the death of their child, gone after only living for a year. Had that loss been the cause of all their trouble?

The tears I try so hard to hold back sting my eyes and trail down my face. Oliver must have allowed his attentions and affections to wander. The moment was perfect for the pretty Cecelia, with her ringlets and ruby lips and simpering manner. Though young and unacquainted with the world, I could read the story of betrayal as it unfolded before me. Bewildered and frightened, I had not known what to do. And then Cinaed grew ill.

And Grandfather? During these past strained months, he'd remained so kind to me. He sought out the best apothecaries in town, then found the best physicians he could to cure my sister. Ever he remained my compatriot in snatching bits of this and that behind Mrs. Harris's back. Always glad of my company, he never sent me away with curt words, as Oliver did. 'Tis why I still cannot fully bring myself to believe that he is convinced of Oliver's lies that I killed Cinaed. Or that he has forgotten me.

"Grandfather," I whisper. "What has happened?"

All these wretched days past, I prayed he would find me. That he would come and make things right. I trusted to his power and his name. Trusted his love for me. I'd refused to believe Rob's insistence that Lord Ramsay was not the man I thought him to be. But now?

Annie sighs as her eyes droop and she finally falls asleep. That one simple act, a wee child breathing out a puff of air, brings with it the memory of my sister's final breath and strikes a pang in my heart. Cinaed's final words whisper inside me:

Courage, Poppet. All will be well.

"But how?" I hang my head. "I cannot see it." Not if Grandfather will not help us, after all. What will I find if I return home? A warm welcome or disdain? The belief that I am a murderess? What will I do then? Flee back to the city? But Oliver knows I've been living with Donny. And I've sent that note to Grandfather, telling him as much.

I curl up beside Annie. At the thought of what I might find if I escape the close tonight, my pulse quickens. My hand automatically moves to check that my blade is still tucked inside my pouch. Cinaed's words sound again within me. *Courage.*

My sister believed in me. No matter how much Oliver tried to keep me under his boot, Cinaed always went to battle for me. She insisted I learn to ride, though her husband said *no*. Fought to give me the privilege of dining with the rest of the family, instead of upstairs, hidden away with the various women hired to care for me. Even when my sister lost some of her arguments, which she often did, I knew she heard me and wanted me to *be* heard. She valued me. And loved me.

A tiny smile plays on my lips, and I blink moisture from my eyes. I do not know how, but I feel as though a thread of courage is weaving itself through me. 'Tis a weak thread, easily snapped, but it is there, nonetheless.

Cinaed went to battle for me. Now, I shall go to battle for her. What will happen when I finally reach freedom, I do not know. But whatever happens, I will face it. I will make things right, whether Grandfather will help me or not.

I close my eyes and rest my cheek against Annie's warm, wee head. Tonight, we shall leave this place.

Or die trying.

Never will I forget the sight of Elspet's head, painted crimson. Once again, I am about to face a group of armed soldiers. Likely, with considerably less help than I'd hoped for.

I snuggle closer to Annie and strive to hold tight to that wee measure of strength within me.

CHAPTER
34

Donny makes no remark on my appearance when I return below stairs. She notices, of course. My shorn locks and borrowed clothing earn me a snort of laughter. After she wipes her eyes, she says nothing, but her expression is one of approval. The old woman merely grunts when I offer to pay her for the clothing.

The others have gone. At midnight, when the clock sounds in the bell tower of the kirk, we shall meet the guild in the vaults below. Swallowing hard, I plan what to say to them. Rob asked me to tell the truth about my parentage. And I shall. 'Tis only right that all understand the odds against us.

Starting with Donny.

Together, the crone and I prepare a meal of bread and cheese. But fear and guilt glue my lips together. Rob is so angry. What will Donny say? Managing to swallow a bit of bread, washed down with much ale, I struggle through the meal in silence. We are scrubbing the table clean with salt and rosemary before anything comes to me. As Donny settles herself beside the fire and takes up her pipe, I square my shoulders. Where is my courage of only an hour past?

But as I wring out a cloth and hang it from a peg on the wall, my pouch bumps against my leg and the letter opener within brings a prickle of curiosity. And I speak without thought.

"Did you ever steal from Grandfather?" My face floods with heat. Curse my unbridled tongue! Cinaed chided me so for my rushed, thoughtless words.

"No. Did ye ever steal from me?"

The woman's answer robs me of breath. I gape at her. Her eyes narrow to slits.

"No!" I duck my head. I should have known Donny was testing me by allowing me to see where she kept the key to her cupboard. She's too cunning to be so careless.

"Yes. I took some of the peppercorn. But I put it back."

"I know. I saw ye."

I fly across the room to kneel before the woman. "I am sorry I even thought of taking it, Donny! You've been so kind to me. I mean it."

The woman waves me away. "Ye thought to buy your way through the gate. Ye should've come to me first, snippet." Her eyes hold mine.

I leap to my feet. "But you're a thief yourself, Donny. You and all the guild." I tile my head to the side. "Forgive me, but did you not steal that spice in the first place?"

The woman's eyes spark. She stands and plants her hands on her hips. "I am a businesswoman, ye spiteful lass. I bought that spice with my own money. And ye must not speak so hatefully of the guild. We're no cutpurses out to rifle through a man's pockets. We only take from the dead. And we dinnae steal from our own, lass. Did ye learn nothing from Callum?"

A flash of anger sparks within me. "Grandfather is not dead, and yet you have this!" I wrest the letter opener from my pouch and hold it out to the old woman. "This is his insignia. I found it among all the rich furnishings that you also likely stole from him."

Donny's lurid cheeks grow pale. "So certain, are ye now?" Settling once more in her chair, she taps her pipe on her leg while glaring at me from beneath her white brows.

"I am. Please tell me the truth. The guild steals from the living as well as the dead. You robbed my Grandfather."

The old soldier pauses to light her pipe, using a bit of glowing wood from the fire. She puffs several times, her shrunken cheeks moving in and out, lending her the look of a bellows made of worn and cracked leather.

"We never took a thing from him, foolish lass." Smoke trickles from her mouth as she speaks.

"How can that be?" I toss the letter opener at the woman. With one hand she deftly catches it in midair and places it upon the mantel. And then, to my astonishment, the woman laughs.

"Whether ye believe it or no, 'tis no matter to me."

"But do you not fear he'll find out we belong to the band of thieves that robbed his home? And be less likely to grant aid in lifting the quarantine?"

The moment the words leave me, my cheeks sting with shame. What am I saying? I'd just vowed to tell the truth! First to Donny and then to the guild members. Instead, I maintain my story that Grandfather will make everything right. I am a double fool. I have no idea what will truly happen. Scowling at the floor, I measure my next words and search for the best way to tell Donny the truth, but she speaks before I can.

"Answer me this, Poisoner." She peers at me with a solemn face. "What makes ye so certain the mighty Lord Ramsay will welcome ye with open arms?"

The hated doubt gnaws at me. And after meeting her gaze, which proves difficult, understanding dawns.

"You know something. You know we cannot foresee what will happen. Not for certain," I whisper.

"Aye. I knew who ye were long before I set eyes on ye." She points to me with the stem of her pipe.

"How?"

"I've been on this earth many a year." Donny's lips curve in a slight smile. "Long before ye were birthed, I knew old Lord Ramsay. And his son."

"You knew of Oliver's marriage?" I stammer. "How he married a woman beneath his station?" The words are like needles that prick. I swallow and add: "A woman who had a young sister?"

"Aye." The herbwife regards me with a gaze that holds me in place. "I know of your sister's husband, though he does no' know of me. I must say that when he sought ye this day, Kenna, he insisted that we allow him to speak with ye. Only speak. He did not ask us to turn ye over to him, nor to the watchman, the bailey, or to them soldiers. I feared he'd return, but he did not."

"I heard." I huff and fold my arms.

Donny continues to stick me with her shrewd gaze. She pauses draw from her pipe and blows several smoke rings upward, where they float lazily in the air. "And he said to give ye this."

She takes a crumpled bit of parchment from the mantel. She hands it to me, all the while regarding me with her steady, sharp eyes.

"What is it?" I take the paper from her gnarled fingers and unfold it. The air leaves my lungs as though someone has plunged a knife into my chest.

Oliver has returned the drawing of Cinaed to me, the one I'd sketched minutes before her death. The image, clumsily executed as it is, calls to mind in clarity my sister's dear face. The rough portrait blurs and dissolves as my eyes fill with tears. My fingers tremble, and I fear I shall drop the precious scrap of parchment into the fire. I sink to the floor and fold in upon myself, clutching the drawing to my chest.

Why did he bring this to me?

I cannot stop the stinging tears from coursing down my cheeks, for with the return of this portrait, time ceases to exist. I whirl through time and to another chamber, another house. Rooted in place on the thick carpets beside Cinaed's bed, I relive the moment my sister breathes her last in the arms of her husband. I feel her death on me. I taste it in the air. It is in my very skin; it's a part of my being that will never leave me. My sister's murder tore a great gash in my soul. I will never be whole again.

And Oliver is the man who killed her. He is the man who destroyed my life.

Donny takes my arm and leads me to her chair. "Breathe, lass. I'll fetch ye a drink."

"I do not understand why." My hands tremble as I smooth the parchment out and trace the outline of my sister's face with my finger. "Why did Oliver leave this with you? Is it a message? A warning?"

"A warning? That's what he wrote to ye, then?" She proffers me a cup of ale, but I ignore it.

"What do you mean, 'wrote?'"

"Turn it over, lass."

Gulping, I turn the drawing over. A few words are scrawled on the back in an untidy, harried hand.

Send me word and I'll bring you home.

My thoughts are in turmoil. What does this mean? Rising, I pace while I hold my hands over my heart and the portrait. Oliver offers to help me escape the quarantined close. Is it a trick? A trap to make me believe he cares? Is he truly trying to help me?

"Kenna?" Donny squints at me. "What are ye thinking, lass?"

"I hardly know." Oliver offers his aid, but he knows I saw the bottle he'd hidden on his person! The bottle of poison that marks him as the killer.

My legs grow weak, and I must sit again. Oliver was the one who came to seek me in the city. He found me. Not Grandfather. But surely that only means he heard I was still alive. His plan did not work, so he came to take matters into his own hands and rid himself of the one who witnessed his deed. There is no other answer, is there?

"Kenna?"

Shaking my head, I hold a hand over my eyes. Donny's kitchen presses in on me. Can the tiny room have grown even smaller? The place reeks of cabbage and Donny's infernal concoctions. Oh, how I need to be free of this malodorous place! I place my head in my hands and picture the faces of the two men who have been a great part of my world for more than twelve years. First, Oliver, with his weary sighs, his brow that crinkled with annoyance each time he beheld me.

His admonishments. His impatience. He never wished to be in my presence. Then I picture Grandfather, his eyes shining with mirth. How he allowed me privileges Oliver denied. Stole sweets for me behind Mrs. Harris's back. Showed me far greater affection than Oliver ever did. For really, Oliver never showed me any affection. Never.

Rising, I fold the drawing and tuck it inside my shirt, close to my heart. I do not have all the pieces to this great puzzle. Therefore, I am not yet ready to believe that Oliver is my friend, and Grandfather my enemy. Perhaps Grandfather is simply ignorant of what has transpired. Perhaps his son has kept him blind to the truth.

I wipe my face with the back of my hand. Soon enough, I will know. I sent the note to Grandfather. He will seek me out if he's received it. If not, I will seek *him* out, if our plan to escape the soldiers works. And I will discover his heart. I will discover if he has chosen to forget about me, the farm lass he could not turn into a lady. But I cannot trust Oliver.

Donny studies me with eyes narrowed to slits. She has drunk the ale she offered me but pours me another cup. This time, I down it in one great gulp.

"I do not trust Oliver's motives for this message. The moment I saw the bottle of poison that fell from his clothing, I knew why my sister was dying. Her own husband poisoned her, Donny. He must have!"

Donny's eyes grow sad, and she rubs her hands over her shorn head.

"*Och*, but his face." Her voice is so soft; I can hardly hear her words. "So like his father's when he was young."

Like his father's?

"You said you knew the Earl." I sniffle. "How?" I do not give voice to my next thought; that this shriveled woman, so battered and diminished with age, had at one time been Grandfather's mistress. No! Yet, as Donny herself said, she was once young and rather comely. A full thousand years ago.

"'Tis of no importance now, lass."

"But—"

She holds up her hand. "What ye do need to know is this." Donny lifts my chin with one finger. "I forgive ye for thinking of stealing that spice from me. Ye changed your mind, after all. And for taking food from the vaults, as ye did it to feed hungry mouths. You're part of the guild, now. We take care of our own. Now, then. Do ye still wish to go through with your plan?"

"Yes."

"Then we shall do all we can to escape this close, so ye may find Lord Ramsay."

I sniff and blink back tears. "Even if he may not help us lift the quarantine?"

"If he will no' help us, Kenna," Donny adds in an even voice, "ye'll know for certain what is in his heart."

Though I'd come to the same conclusion, I despise the sound of the words spoken aloud. I wrap my arms about my middle and shiver.

"There is something else, Donny. Rob and Una know about my parentage as well. He wants me to tell the others so they can decide if they'll still risk the attack on the soldiers, knowing it may not help us lift the quarantine. And I plan to do so."

"Aye." Donny heaves a great sigh and pops her pipe into her mouth. A lazy puff of white smoke floats to the ceiling. "'Tis only fair. They should know."

"And what if they all leave and refuse to help me escape?"

The kirk bell tolls. Donny snuffs out her pipe and places it on the mantel.

"*I'll* still help ye, Kenna. So will Rob and Una, and Callum, and at least a few of the others, I wager." She regards me with a level gaze, her pale eyes piercing. "We all have need to escape. And if we succeed, we'll make it to the other side of that gate. We'll fend well enough for ourselves until it's open again."

She dons a thick jacket and winds a woolen scarf about her neck.

"Fetch our wee Annie."

I obey. Back beside the warm fire, we wrap the yawning lassie in "Sheona's" great blue shawl and creep outside.

My limbs shake so much I can barely walk. Annie's wee form seems heavier than usual.

"This is a dangerous path we take," I whisper.

"Second thoughts, Poisoner?"

The sound of our creeping footsteps grows painfully loud to my ears as I ponder Donny's words.

"No. I cannot simply wait here to starve."

And I must finally know the truth about Grandfather.

"Good." Donny slows her steps until she is beside me. "Then the moment you've gotten outside the close, fly to Lord Ramsay's home, and ask him to help us. I'll go with ye if I can."

"I will." The thought of the old woman accompanying me is encouraging. "But Donny, what if he does not help? I cannot think of what I shall do if that happens."

"Stop dithering, lass. Ye've got a good head. Use it. It'll come to ye."

"But..."

"There is something I must discover." Donny holds up her hand to cut me off. "If we make it to that grand house of Lord Ramsay's, Kenna, seek him out first by yourself and tell your tale before he knows I am nearby. Understood?"

I can only nod as confusion binds my tongue.

"Good."

Within minutes, Annie, Donny, and I creep unaccosted into the small chapel. The silence of the kirk unnerves me. Every tiny sound we make echoes in the empty swirl of black that surrounds us. Donny carries her musket, and every so often, I reach for my leather pouch to feel for the reassuring presence of my knife. More than once, I also place my hand over my heart to ascertain that my sister's portrait is yet in place. It reassures me somehow, almost as much as the presence of my knife. 'Tis as though Cinaed's soul watches over me.

Beside me, clinging to my hand, Annie toddles along, holding tight to her doll. We hurry below to the vaults. This time, they are not well lit. The lanterns on the wall are dark, and we have but the light of a single taper that Donny carries. Donny whistles, and the sudden, loud note pierces the silence. A pinprick of light appears ahead, and someone whistles back.

"Come." The old herbwife leads the way along the tunnel toward the moving platform. We are nearly there when someone grabs my arm.

"Who's this?" a man asks.

I wrench my arm away. "Keep your hands off me!"

At this moment, lights emerge from storerooms on every side, as many hands hold aloft flickering tapers. I blink against the sudden glow.

"It's me." I squint at the forms that surround us. Familiar faces come into focus, along with several unknown to me.

"Told ye." Rob's voice comes from the darkness. "'Tis the Poisoner. Meet Kenneth, everyone."

Snorts of muted laughter bounce about the tunnel walls. I search for Rob's face in the small crowd. He disappears the moment my eyes find him.

"Enough." Donny says. "Let's go over the plan one more time."

"No. Wait." I clear my throat. "I have something to say."

"Be quick, lass. We must hurry." Callum's voice is hard, as it always is.

My palms grow moist and my voice quivers. I wish for this moment of revelation to be over fast, so my words tumble from me in a most unladylike manner. Which suits my new appearance, I suppose.

"You must know the truth before you join in this endeavor. Lord Ramsay is my family by marriage only. I am but the younger sister of his son's wife."

Murmurs and whispers fill the darkness around me.

"What does she mean by that, then?" a woman's voice calls. Her words echo in the tunnels.

"It means that our Poisoner is not who she claimed to be." Una's voice is hard, and she spits out the words through clenched teeth. "Kenna, with her fancy gowns and her fine lady airs is just like us."

"That's why the Earl ain't bothered with ye," another man shouts. He's obviously drinking, for he takes several loud gulps before dropping a bottle at his feet, where it smashes upon impacting the hard stone floor. "You're no' his kin."

He shoves past others and shuffles back down the tunnel, towards the kirk. "I'll not risk my neck for *her*."

Wincing, I sink down onto a crate with Annie in my arms as voices rise and fall about me.

Two others follow the first deserter, dark shapes that do not spare a glance as they pass me. Then another. And three more after that.

Then the silence grows as thick as the darkness until Callum speaks. "I'll lose my head if I dinnae get out of here. I'm still going through with the plan, even if the Poisoner's of no use to us."

The man's eyes find mine, and I must look away. His mouth twists in disgust.

Una adds: "I should've seen what a fool plan it was to ask the Earl for help. If he'd wanted to help his 'granddaughter,' he'd have done so by now. But all I wish for now is to be free until they end this quarantine. I'm going along too."

My squinting eyes search in the dimness about me until I find Rob, but he will not meet my gaze. He and Una turn their backs to me. My shoulders slump in shame. My two former comrades are right to be angry with me. I never let on that I was not who I claimed to be, though they were kind and offered their friendship. Truth be told, I *did* believe myself to be above them in station, thanks to my new family's name and wealth. At first.

Shaking my head, I close my eyes. There is an icy void where my heart used to be. All I can hope for now is to escape this place. I rest my head on Annie's. Freedom is not truly all I desire. I long for the friends I've lost. Most of all, I wish to feel Rob's lips on mine once more and my hand in his. But that will never be.

Other doubts continue to creep into me. If I find I no longer have Grandfather's home to return to, I must find *somewhere* to rest my head. To start over. To be free. But how? Oliver will ever remain my enemy and a threat to my safety. And to Annie's, as she shall remain with me. Where shall I go?

"Anyone else want to leave?" Donny's voice is brisk. "No? Good. Now, let's speak of our plan."

Straining to see, I count the heads that remain. Donny, Una, Rob, Callum. Two other men I do not know. A ruddy woman with a square frame and calm demeanor, who regards me with open curiosity. A chubby youth with a shock of ginger hair, one I'd seen mending shoes inside a cobbler's shop before. No one else? My heart sinks.

And then we are off. A few at a time, we shall take the platform into the tanner's shop above and from there, creep along the lane to the tall Martin house, where we shall climb the treacherous iron stairway to the roof. There, we shall accost our rooftop quarry: the small group of soldiers who camp there.

Annie and I are the last to clamber onto the platform. I gape at Munro, whose presence had remained unknown to me until this moment. Of course. The platform is controlled by a handle on the wall of the vaults. Someone must stay behind to operate it. He glares at me.

"I didnae want my son to go along with this rotting plan, but there was no stopping him." He leans closer to me. "The fault is yours if Rob comes to harm. And I'll never forget that."

Having spoken, he turns the heavy handle and Annie and I ascend. I hold her close and try to forget Munro's words. But I cannot. What if Rob *does* come to harm? Or anyone else, for that matter? I swallow, thinking of the soldier whose wife and son live in the close. Are the others not like him; men who are merely doing as they are told? I do not wish to see any more blood spilled, even that of a soldier who enforces this quarantine.

Once inside the reeking tanner's shop, I wait against the wall as

Donny takes stock of the few weapons in our possession. She is the only one with a firearm. Most of the others, like me, have knives. Callum has his meaty fists wrapped about a heavy club; the stocky woman wields a sharpened stick. The cobbler's apprentice has a hammer. I cannot believe we are going to do this! I shiver.

"Let's go."

The others creep silently onto the lane. I step forward, ready to follow, but Donny holds me back.

"Wait, Kenna. We've one more load."

The pulleys creak and sway as the ropes fly. The platform swiftly rises to our level, bearing a wooden box. Nestled inside are coils of rope and a few bottles of whiskey.

"Your secret weapon." Donny hands me a bottle. "Here. Open it."

"Why did you not bring wine?"

Donny pulls a vial from her jacket. "My sleeping medicine is bitter and added a foul flavor to the wine. This stuff is like swallowing fire. It covers the flavor of the herbs much better."

Without another word, we add her sleeping draught to the whiskey. I cannot help but picture Oliver slipping drops of a vile liquid into his wife's wine. How did she not taste it? Wincing, I recork the bottles and we finally emerge into the open where the others await in the dark of night.

I make a mental list. There are ten of us. One is a small child. Four of us are youths and one is an old woman. We are armed with knives, clubs, sticks, a hammer, and a single musket. And three bottles of whiskey. I sigh. A fine lot of rebels we make.

As though fate has chosen to make things more difficult, large snowflakes pelt us, coming thick and fast.

"Could you not have waited a wee bit longer to send the storm, Lord?"

No one laughs at my words.

CHAPTER
35

We steal from shadow to shadow, shivering and blinking snow from our eyes. Murmuring in hushed tones, Donny instructs me as we hurry to the Martin house.

"I'll be in the lead, with Una right after me. Keep well behind. Allow the rest of us to confront the soldiers. When all is clear, ye'll make your escape."

"There are so few of us now. Why not allow me to assist in the fighting? Should I not take my chances with everyone else?"

"Even if no one else succeeds, our Poisoner must flee and find Lord Ramsay. He may yet help us." Donny squints at me through the falling snowflakes. "Nothing is certain. And we've no wish for harm to come on that child, there, do we?"

My stomach roils in protest. How will I feel if something happens to Rob or Una, despite the fact they are no longer my friends? Or to Donny, who gave me shelter and forgave me for my pettiness and lack of gratitude? Drawing in a shuddering breath, I try to force the thoughts away. The others know the danger, as well as the truth about Lord Ramsay. And they still made their decision to come. They wish to escape as much as I do.

"Quiet," someone hisses when Annie coughs. I squeeze her shoulder and try to reassure her. The poor child trembles from head to toe. She is terrified. So am I. So much could go wrong.

We reach the Martin house and creep to the side of the tall building. I stop short, bewildered. Our group huddles together in front of a solid wooden gate set between two tall houses. It bars us from reaching the iron staircase that climbs to the roof, stories above our heads. Was all this for nothing? Did the others know of this?

They must have, for Una pulls sharp metal tools from somewhere on her person and commences to work the lock on the gate. She apparently possesses a gift, for no one expresses surprise when she defeats the lock with ease. A wild thought strikes me. Perhaps when this is all over, I shall ask her to teach me such a skill. Barred doors are a hateful sight to me now and picking locks would be useful. A heartbeat later, I chide myself. The lass and I are no longer friends.

Within moments, we all creep onto the slippery iron staircase that spirals its way up the side of the building. The snow flurries about us and makes the treads beneath our feet even more treacherous than they usually are.

In the darkness and the whirling snow that bites at our hands and faces, we feel our way up the stairs with Callum in the lead. As we climb, drawing ever nearer to the rooftop, my palms grow sweaty and Annie's hand slips from my grasp. She whimpers and clings to my legs. I stop on the next landing to kneel so she may climb on my back. She twists her arms tight about my neck, and I take hold of her doll.

"Courage, my poppet," I whisper. My use of Cinaed's endearment for me when I was Annie's age brings both comfort and pain in equal measure. "All shall be well." I pray my words will be true.

Each square landing has a narrow door that leads inside the tall house, with a small oval window beside it. Though it is past midnight, there is evidence of life within the building. Every so often, a muffled voice or a child's cry comes to my ears. Yet not a soul approaches us. Perhaps they are used to the tread of soldiers on the stair and do not wish to encounter one of them.

We arrive at the final flight that ends at the rooftop. I strive to quiet my breathing. By now, we have already climbed six flights, straining to keep our footsteps and ragged breaths silent, and I can hardly draw enough air. Near the top, blinded by snow, I bump into someone and stop short. The others, all crowded ahead of me in this tight space, have ceased to move.

Rob turns around. "Pass me that bottle," he whispers.

As I do so, his fingers brush against mine. Is it my imagination, or does his touch linger for a moment? Rob swiftly turns his back to me, and I sigh. I was making something from nothing, clinging to a wish. Bottles softly clink together as the others hand over their whiskey.

Straining to see through the darkness and whirling crystals of ice that fly about my head, I can hardly make out the form of Una at the very top step. A ringing, loud *clink* emanates from above as she taps her bottle against the railing of the great iron staircase.

"'Tis only me, lads," Una calls in a high and tittering voice so unlike the throaty tones that usually fall from her lips. "A lonely lass who wishes to share her drink."

She ascends the final few steps, holding a bottle high. "Here. I've a gift for ye."

A man's voice responds. The glow of a lantern shines from above. Una laughs and steps up onto the roof and disappears. Fear seizes me straightaway. Though she no longer considers herself my friend, I am the one who asked her to put herself in harm's way. And I cannot bear the thought of her being hurt.

"Should we not go now?" I whisper.

"We must wait, but not long. We won't allow Una to tarry more than a few minutes all alone with those men." Rob remains where he is, facing away from me as he speaks.

Icy snowflakes coat my hair, and I shiver. Annie grows heavy, and I shift her weight on my back. Though the lad said it would not be long, the wait is interminable. While counting the minutes that stretch on and on, I fear we shall all grow old, die here, and remain a motley group of skeletons huddled in eternity upon the stairs. And what peril may Una be facing in this very moment!

I cannot abide the inaction, nor the sight of Rob's back turned to me for another moment.

"Rob?" He does not respond. It may be that the storm is tearing the words from me to carry them away on the wind, but I dare not raise my voice. I put my hand on his arm. He stiffens but does not pull away.

"I am sorry. I did not tell you Lord Ramsay is not my grandfather by blood because..." I must pause to gather my thoughts. How can I make this lad understand? "Rob, I cannot remember a time when Grandfather was not my family. He became and acted as such from the moment he welcomed me into his home. I never doubted his love for me. But I do not think myself any better than you."

Rob does not move. His silence grates at my soul. "I mean it. When I first came to the city, 'tis true I thought myself to be of a higher station than those of you who live here on the close." I wince at my words and rush on. "But no longer. You are as much a gentleman as any I've ever met."

He turns around to face me. Before he can speak, a shout of laughter peals out from above. The voices grow louder and louder.

"We go now!" Callum says in a harsh whisper.

"Kenna, wait just below the roof with Annie until we tell ye to come up," Rob whispers. Before he ascends to the roof above, he squeezes my shoulder. And the night is no longer so dark.

One by one, the others step off the staircase and onto the roof. Their forms fade away into the cold, snowy air. Annie and I wait alone near the top of the staircase, and I stretch my neck to glance over the edge of the roof but see nothing. So far, there is much laughter, many chattering voices, but nothing like the sound of a struggle. In a moment, though, something changes. The laughter dies away.

"Tie them up!" Donny shouts. My heart leaps with hope. They are succeeding!

But as I lean forward, straining to hear, a sound reaches me from below and I freeze in terror.

Someone approaches! Footsteps pound rapidly in my direction! The metal stair vibrates with the weight of whoever is coming. The mysterious stranger will be here soon. The child and I must take our chances on the roof.

"Hold tight, Annie." I dart up the final few steps. My knife is at the ready in my hand.

A few lanterns placed here and there on the rooftop light the scene before me. Pure snow is piling up and covering the scattered chimneys, the tiles of the roof, and the soldier's tents. The snow glitters in the flickering light of the lanterns. 'Twould be a fairyland of sorts, were it not for the hellish tableau before me.

Donny stands with her back to me, a few paces away. She points her musket at the face of a soldier who has trouble remaining upright. Bobbling as though he floats on choppy waters, he holds his hands in the air, his face a mask of shock.

Two other soldiers sit with backs against the low wall that encircles the roof with their mouths gagged, while the stout woman and two of the others tie their hands. Another soldier lies at their feet, his eyes closed. White flakes fall on his face. He does not notice. Is he dead? Bile rises to my throat; my stomach sours, and I must look away. Then the soldier emits a loud snore, and relief soothes me for a moment.

From somewhere beyond the circular glow of light shining from the nearest lantern comes the sound of muffled cries. Una appears from behind a chimney. One eye is swollen, though she remains composed. She carries two muskets in her arms.

"Got another one back there." She grins. "He's ready for trussing."

The young cobbler bolts to do her bidding. Then Callum emerges, also carrying a musket. When his eyes fall on me, his face contorts with anger.

"We've no' yet called for ye, foolish lass!" Behind me, footsteps pound ever upward, far too close at hand. I rush over to Donny.

"Someone's coming!" What a simpleton I was, gawping about, instead of instantly warning the others! Why did I remain silent?

And now, 'tis too late, for a tall, cloaked form emerges onto the roof. His hood is low over his eyes, leaving his face in shadow.

'Tis the watchman.

"Take care o' this one," Donny shouts. Callum seizes the soldier she'd held at gunpoint while Donny whirls and aims her musket at the watchman's chest.

"Stay where ye are." She plants her feet firmly on the tiles below with her musket steady.

The watchman does not raise his hands in alarm.

"Drop your weapon, old man," he growls out in his harsh, monstrous voice.

Donny does not flinch, nor does she lower her musket. "Old *woman,* ye mean."

The watchman freezes.

"Over here!" Behind me, the apprentice motions for me to follow. "Help me make a bridge." He disappears into blackness.

"Go now, fool!" Donny shouts, not taking her eyes off the cloaked figure.

"Where?" I whirl. Rob emerges from the darkness, a trickle of blood dripping from his forehead.

"Here, Kenna." He waves me closer. "This way!"

My feet slide on the snow-covered tiles as I hurry toward Rob, sidestepping the fallen soldier and almost dropping Annie, who whimpers. The lad is a mere few paces away in the shadows beyond the weak light, his hand outstretched. I break into a run.

I have only taken a few steps when an impossibly loud sound hurts my ears, and I am blinded by a flash of light. I slip and fall, dropping Annie on the tiles. Was that a crack of thunder? No, the sound of a musket! Not only am I momentarily blinded by the strange light, but the whirling snow also makes it impossible to see anything clearly. Annie screams; I scramble on hands and knees groping for her, and I find the tip of her cloth-bound foot. Thanks be to God, she is unharmed! I gather the wailing lass into my arms and crouch low, blinking and squinting at the surrounding scene. The air smells bitter.

"Rob?" I blink snow from my eyes. "Rob, where are you?"

A low moan and a gasp of pain come from nearby. I follow the sound to find Rob on the tiles, curled up tight, his hands to his side. Dark liquid seeps from between his fingers. "No!" I drop to my knees beside him. Who fired upon him? One of the soldiers? A wild glance behind me reveals naught but whirling ice and snow, but someone aimed their weapon at Rob. The tide is turning against us.

"Go, Kenna." Rob gasps in pain and jerks his head in quick, sharp motions, indicating a spot at the edge of the roof. A few paces away, the ginger-haired lad is struggling to lay a long board on the low wall to form a bridge that will cross the gap between two houses. On the far side of that makeshift bridge is the neighboring building, only a stone's throw away.

The lad glances our way, and his eyes widen.

"Quick! Help me!" he shouts. "This is too heavy for me!"

But Rob lies injured at my feet.

"No." I sob.

"Do it." Rob groans in pain. "Or all this was for nothing."

"I'll come back for you." Tears stream down my face. The moment I rise to my feet, holding Annie on my back once more, I freeze. Before me is a soldier with a raised musket. I know his face. 'Tis the soldier whose wife and child remain trapped in the close! The one who killed Elspet!

"Stay where ye are." His voice trembles. "I dinnae wish to fire at ye, but I will if I must."

My heart thunders within.

"Please. You do not know me, but I know who you are. I know your family is trapped here."

The man's face is in shadow.

"If I allow ye to leave, I'll hang." Desperation fills his words.

"Please! I'm the one who brought food to your wife. And I can make this all end if you let me leave. I'm begging you!" Hot tears drip from my chin and chill in the freezing air. "Please, help me for the sake of your son."

The soldier does not move. I do not breathe. Large snowflakes fall on and around us with whispers of sound.

"Go." He breathes the word out into the frigid air.

Slipping on the snowy tiles, I make my way toward the cobbler's apprentice. I have no choice but to settle Annie onto the cold rooftop, where she wails and reaches for me.

"I'll be back, Annie!" I shout. Together, the stout lad and I lift the long, heavy board and allow it to fall across the gap between houses, where it just reaches the edge of the neighboring roof. We glance at one another, but before either can say a word, the square woman who'd chosen to join us in our dangerous endeavor pushes us aside and balances on the makeshift bridge. She eases her way across, teetering and swaying, but makes it safely to the other side. She disappears into the night. Into freedom.

"You go now," I tell the lad. As he begins his crossing, I fly to Annie and pick her up. Settling her again on my back, she wraps her wee arms about my neck, near to choking me. And then, I step onto the rough wooden bridge just as the lad reaches the other side and disappears in his turn. "Shut your eyes, Annie," I whisper.

The board wobbles slightly as I plant my feet upon it. Gulping back my terror, I totter forward and edge my way across while icy flakes fly into my eyes. Voices shout from behind me. Another shot from a musket rings out like a great *crack* of metal hitting stone.

I stop, only halfway across, feeling the board shift slightly beneath me. I scream in terror.

"Hurry!" Rob shouts. His voice is ragged with pain. Seizing all my courage, I teeter across the narrow board. One, two, three steps. As I draw near the other building, the world tilts. The makeshift bridge is shifting beneath my feet.

"Stop, lass!" The voice roaring behind me is that of the watchman. He must have seized the other end of the bridge.

Gathering all my courage, I make a giant leap. I am so close! I must make it!

As my feet contact the edge of the neighboring roof, I lose my balance and fling my arms wide, desperate to right myself. Annie slips from my back. She screams once; a high-pitched, terrified sound. Then nothing more.

I collapse onto the snow-covered tiles of the neighboring roof. My burning face rests on the cool snow, which melts with my tears.

I have escaped, but Annie has fallen. She is gone!

What have I done?

CHAPTER 36

I scream. And scream again. The cacophony of shouts and scuffles coming from the rooftop I've left behind drown my voice. Someone fires a musket again.

"Kenna!" The sound of my name barely penetrates the surrounding din. "Get up!"

I cannot. I cannot. She's gone! Annie lies on the cobbles, seven stories below. This was my fault. I am mute and frozen with horror.

"Kenna!" The voice is louder. Desperate. "Look, for God's sake!"

'Tis Rob. He yet lives. But Annie! I wail aloud. My poor wee child.

She deserves at least a proper burial. This thought alone rouses me. I shall not leave her poor broken body behind. My eyes swim with tears, and thick snow continues to swirl around me, but I raise myself onto my hands and knees. Confused and clumsy, I crawl with limbs that feel weighted with iron through the icy drifts, turning toward the edge of the roof.

"Yes!" Rob cries. "Look below, Kenna!"

Why must I? I dread what my eyes may witness. Perhaps it's the desperation in Rob's voice, for despite my misgivings, I obey. Below me, a mere five vertical paces away, is a narrow wooden platform of sorts, perhaps what was once a balcony. A small figure lies face down with one arm dangling off the edge.

I have one thought alone. If there is any chance my Annie is not dead, I must know. Now.

"Fly, Kenna! We will help her!" Rob shouts. I lift my gaze to the rooftop of the Martin house. Though the past few moments felt frozen in eternity, not much time has passed.

More soldiers approach the edge of the nearby roof, armed with muskets. Through the swirling fog of thick snowflakes, I can make out vague images of people on the opposite rooftop engaged in a struggle. The ranks have swelled, for I now count far more people there than before. It does not bode well for the guild members who remain.

A puff of frigid wind clears my view for a moment, revealing the watchman, now engaged in a tussle with Donny. She no longer has her musket. 'Tis like seeing a great boarhound attack a tiny lapdog. Donny is swift and hard as an iron bit through and through, but she is also of great age.

"Someone shoot him!" I point at the two struggling figures. "Help Donny!"

"We can't!" Una calls out from the edge of the roof. A soldier holds her arms behind her back.

"Stay where ye are, lad!" he shouts at me.

I duck from sight. I cannot do anything to help my friends. I must get to Annie. That is all that matters now.

Whirling, I search for escape and spy a doorway set within a square-shaped shack on the tiles behind me. At that moment, the watchman once again settles the board across the gap between buildings. He places one boot on it, testing his balance, preparing to head across.

I fly to the edge of the building and seize the makeshift bridge in my hands, pulling it toward me with all my might.

The watchman roars: "Fire!"

Thunder cracks and something burns the side of my head. I cry out in pain and drop the board. I fall to my knees, ducking for protection behind the low wall that surrounds this rooftop. Muskets continue to fire. I touch the stinging spot on my head and my hand comes away coated in red. Footsteps approach. The monstrous cloaked man is on the board once more.

I risk a peek over the edge of the roof. The cloaked beast is closing the space between us. He looms in front of me like an approaching demon or Death itself, carrying a long dagger. His cloak flies out behind him in the winter wind, and his hood falls away from his face. A scream tears from my throat.

The watchman laughs. The low, mocking voice fills me with fury, for he is close enough for me to see his face. 'Tis Shaw, not the watchman. Only Shaw, that ugly, red-faced baker who has been a curse to me from the moment I arrived in the close. Why do I cower? This time, I do not pull the board toward me. Instead, I place both hands on it and shove. It grates forward and slips from the edge of the wall.

With the man's screams in my ears, I whirl and flee to the shack. The door is unlocked. I sob in relief as it swings open. Musket balls whir past me, several thunking into the doorway, sending sharp splinters into the air as I hurl myself inside and descend narrow steps. I lose my balance and tumble down the last few treads.

Rising to my feet, I gasp for air. Voices in the corridor echo from somewhere ahead. I seize my knife and hold it at the ready. The corridor is dank and reeking. Before I can gather my wits, a young woman appears from the gloom to accost me while I hesitate, trembling and bleeding.

"Who are ye?" She clutches a babe to her breast. Her hair is hidden under a white cap, her black clothing the mark of a Puritan. She holds a taper high and inches forward, squinting at me.

"I need help." I wipe more blood from my cheek.

The woman's face grows pale. "You're from Stewart's Close." She clutched the babe to her chest. "Ye'll kill us all, bringing that plague with ye!"

"No! Please, listen to me!"

"Don't touch me!" The babe in her arms stretches its wee mouth wide in a mewling wail. "Leave us!" The Puritan backs away. "He's brought the plague!" She flees from me. A door slams.

Growling like a wild dog, I run after her, for she heads toward the balcony where Annie fell. Muffled shouts tell me to go away.

"I'll split your head in with my ax," a man threatens from behind his door.

The blood grows cold on my face and my head whirls. Near the corridor's end and another stairwell, I pause. Which way? Up or down? Annie's balcony is not so very far from the roof, so I climb.

At the top of the stairs is a door with rough boards nailed across it. The latch is missing. I howl as my fingers tear uselessly at the splintery wood. This way is shut to me.

Blinded by tears, I nearly miss the narrow opening tucked in a tiny alcove as I retrace my steps. Blessedly, my feet lose their purchase and I fall to the side. My shoulder strikes wood. I'd not seen this before as the dark-painted door melts into the shadows of the stairwell and blends in with the surrounding stone.

The door is locked, but not boarded shut. My desperate kick causes it to shudder. I ram my booted foot against the latch again and again as the voices draw nearer. With one final kick, wood splinters and frigid air rushes at me as the latch shatters. I hurl myself onto the balcony outside and seize splintered wood to close the door behind me. A fool's errand, of course. My pursuers will be here any moment, and the soldiers will likely fire on me as soon as they see me.

The old wood of the balcony protests as I step onto it, but it holds my weight. I breathe in and steel myself for what I may find. With a pounding heart, I crawl to Annie.

Her body is covered with a thick dusting of snow. I brush away the powdery flakes and lift her onto my lap. Her face is pale as a beam of moonlight. Lovely as a faery from the tales my sister used to tell me. And still. She does not move.

My head drops. I open my mouth to wail but no sound comes out. I hold her to me and close my eyes. And then she stirs.

"Annie?" I gasp. The child's chest rises and falls. She yet lives! Spurred to action, I heave myself to my feet, holding my precious child, and use my boot to shove open the narrow door.

Several twisted faces glare out at us. "Ye dinnae belong, here, lad."

"Please, let me pass, she's hurt! We only want to flee this place. Let us through, and we'll leave your house. I give you my word!"

They slam the door; an instant later, the door shudders as a hammer strikes it again and again. They are sealing us outside! I sink to my knees. They only wish to protect themselves from us, and from the plague they believe we will bring. But in trying to protect themselves, they will kill us.

Loud cries no longer echo from the nearby rooftop. It hardly matters now. Something strikes me on the cheek with a stinging blow, and I cry out in surprise. A woven rope dangles from the rooftop, which lies so tantalizingly close, perhaps only an arm's length beyond my head were I to stand at my full height.

I shout. No one responds. No red-coated forms are visible on the roof, though this does not mean that none lie in wait, hidden. 'Twas most likely a soldier who let the rope down to us, and he'll be waiting. Going to him would be such folly! Besides, how can I climb with an unconscious child in my arms? All around us is naught but swirling snow. We will die out here. What choice do I have?

The wind howls and ruffles my shorn hair, and I shiver. God's beard, if I must climb, I shall do it now! I remove my doublet. Shivering, I settle Annie over my shoulder, holding her rather like one would a sack of grain, and attempt to use the doublet to tether her to me, my fingers clumsy with the cold.

The loud hammering continues as my unwelcoming neighbors work to seal me outside. The sound is maddening. Clenching my teeth, I seize the rope, place one foot on a rough bit of stone that juts out from the wall before me and heave on the rope with all my might, crying out with pain as the rough fibers tear at my already torn skin. At first, nothing seems to happen, but soon, I am a few inches above the level of the balcony. And I repeat the process and we creep, inch by agonizing inch, upwards. There is no sound save the wind and my own breathing, ragged and harsh.

My limbs tremble. I shall not be able to hold on much longer. My hands burn; blood seeps from my wounded palms, making the rope slick. Wind howls in my ears, blocking all other sound. There is nothing but the wildness of the storm and an interminable, exhausting climb, until my groping hands find only frigid air above my head. We have attained the top of the roof! All that remains is to heave myself and Annie up and over the low surrounding wall.

Somehow, mercifully, I push my way over and we collapse on the tiles. My trembling hand discovers that Annie's chest still rises and falls. I wish to sink into oblivion myself but must continue to flee or all shall be for naught. The thick rope that saved us trails away from the roof's edge and encircles a tall chimney, black with soot. Who left this here, and why?

"This way," a voice hisses.

I cry out in shock and scrabble painfully to my feet, with Annie in my arms. "Who's there?" I struggle to untangle myself from the doublet I'd used to tie the child to me.

"It's me! Hurry!"

Squinting into the swirling snow, I can just make out a form peering out from behind the chimney. 'Tis the sturdy woman I'd first seen in the vaults. Relief pours through me. We shuffle through the snow as the woman leads me through a jumble of charred chimneys.

"How do we get down from here?" The woman does not reply, but only motions for me to follow. She keeps her back to us, her shoulders hunched against the cold.

As we creep along the tiles near one edge of the building, another iron staircase appears. But the woman passes it without a glance.

"The stairs!" I cry.

The woman turns to me with a finger held to her lips. "No, lass." She shakes her head, and her eyes are wide with fear. "Not that way! The soldiers wait below. Follow me."

We move on and creep past a dark window set in an angled wall. We climb over another low wall and must leap a few feet onto a balcony. Before us is another staircase that leads into the darkness below.

"Follow me!" The woman's footsteps clatter on the stairs.

My legs tremble with fatigue as I descend. My fellow rebel moves rapidly. Burdened with my poor Annie, my progress is slow. Soon, I can no longer hear any footfalls other than my own. But 'tis no matter. As soon as I reach the street below, I'll be free of Stewart's Close. I'll search for Grandfather's house in the city, at least after I find temporary shelter for myself and Annie.

A flash of relief hits me as we reach the bottom of the stairs.

"Thank you." There is no answer but the whistling of the wind. The woman has disappeared.

Where are we? Blinking snow from my eyes, a great rush of exhilaration courses through me. I did it! I escaped from the locked close!

Yet my victory is not complete, and my task is not finished. I must find shelter. I take stock of my surroundings. We are in a small courtyard of sorts filled with rubbish. There is an arched passageway that leads to who knows where, a doorway to the building I've just escaped, and the staircase we recently descended. The passageway, it is.

The moment we emerge on the other side, I freeze. Before me is a lane filled with redcoats. The swirling snow cannot hide the crimson jackets and the raised muskets.

It cannot be!

The woman who'd led me directly to the soldiers gazes mournfully at us. "I'm sorry. But they promised to let me go if I led ye to them." With that, she throws her shawl over her head, whirls and fades away into the night.

Shutting my eyes, I hold my Annie more tightly. During my time trapped in the city, I thought I knew what despair felt like.

I was wrong.

CHAPTER
37

One of the soldiers covers my head with a stinking cloth and ties it around my neck while someone else tears Annie from my arms.

"No, please!" I cough and gag at the stench flooding my nose and choke on my words. The cloth smells like a man's shirt never once introduced to a washboard. As I struggle, the arms that hold me squeeze ever tighter.

"Take him to the bailey," a soldier says. "Toss him in there with the other lad."

Someone lifts me into the air and throws me onto a hard surface. Hands lift me into a sitting position upon the cushioned seat. Two soldiers sit on each side of me and keep hold of my arms. Someone roughly lays Annie's warm body across my lap. I sob in relief and try to wrench my arms free to hold her, but my captors do not yield.

Thus bound, our conveyance moves, and I am reminded of my ride to the city. This time, I am far, far more helpless than before. And not alone. *Och*, the poor wee one! What will become of her, all because of me? Annie murmurs at the jostling of our coach and I speak lying words to her in a trembling voice.

"Hush. Do not fret. We've nothing to fear."

The soldier to my left barks out a harsh laugh.

We drive for many minutes while I struggle to breathe with that horrible stinking cloth bound about my head. I pray that somehow, some kind soul will take care of the child lying unconscious across my lap. I fear 'tis not to be so. After all, Annie was tossed aside and abandoned in the city, much as I was.

As our carriage comes to a shuddering halt, the movement throws the poor lass from my lap. She moans. Another cry of distress joins hers, and I recognize the voice of the ginger-haired lad. Apparently, the soldiers only allowed the woman to escape them.

The driver shouts at his horses and they buck and whinny and squeal. The soldiers release my arms as someone pounds upon the carriage windows and yanks the doors open. The lad cries out as he's pulled from within the conveyance.

"Who's this?" a deep voice booms. "Uncover his face." My heart stutters at the familiar tones. Can it be?

"I'm Thomas, sir," the lad says in a trembling voice. "Please, I only wanted to go home to my da. I dinnae live on Stewart's Close."

"I'm searching for a lass," the man's voice responds. "You may go, lad."

Fleeing footsteps crunch away in the snow.

And then, my turn comes. Rough hands pull me from the carriage, and I stand on trembling legs. My fumbling fingers pluck uselessly at the knots at my neck. My body freezes at the sound of the deep, resonant voice, even closer now.

"Another lad? Let me see his face. Hold still," the man orders me.

My heart pounds out a great rhythm in my chest as large hands slash at the knots and lift the horrid cloth from my head. And t'was as I'd thought. Here before me stands Grandfather! I cannot believe it. Am I dreaming? The man's large, kind eyes are wide with fear, though his brow crinkles in confusion as he studies me. All I wish is to throw myself into his strong arms, but I do not. Not yet.

"Grandfather?" I can barely speak. "Why haven't you come for me? I was so afraid I'd never see you again."

"Kenna?" He touches my cheek. His mouth drops open in shock and he splutters for a moment until he gathers himself and snaps his jaw closed.

"I feared the same, sweet lass, but here you are. I did not

recognize you with your hair shorn! What happened? Wait, not yet. We have time to speak later. You must get warm. Come." His voice trembles.

"Wait. I've a child with me, and she needs help."

Grandfather helps me lift Annie from the carriage. He blinks at the wee bundle in my arms and his face is a mask of conflicting emotions. He'll have many questions once we are safely away from here. I smile despite my tears. Rob was wrong about Grandfather, and so was I.

Before us is a stable house. Several red-coated soldiers mill about, jesting with one another and sparing us nary a glance. One counts out coins in his hand while another watches him with greedy eyes.

"Take your leave, men," Grandfather barks at them.

"What happened? How did you find me?" Many more questions clamor to fall from my lips, but Grandfather takes me by the arm and leads me past the stable to the side entrance of a house built of dark stone. Snow continues to swirl in violent gusts, cocooning us in a whirl of white that blurs our view in all directions.

"I received your missive, Kenna. My son was not here so that I could question him, but I sent soldiers to seek for you. The lad who delivered the note said it came from within the quarantined close."

"But the soldiers were taking me to the bailey. I heard as much." My teeth chatter.

"You must get warm, first. And your head is bleeding. Let us go inside."

When we enter a large kitchen, my mouth waters at the lingering scents of roasted lamb and spices. A low fire crackles in the wide hearth, and a portly woman whose dark hair is streaked with gray sits beside it, poking at the coals and nursing a cup of ale. Her head jerks upward, and she jumps to her feet with a gasp of surprise.

"My Lord." She drops into a curtsy.

Grandfather cuts her off with one of his imperious waves and commanding words. "Tend to this lass's wound, Mrs. Landy. Then bring us some cold meats."

Mrs. Landy complies without a word, flying to gather soft cloths and pouring steaming water from a kettle hung over the fire into a bowl. She swiftly cleans and bandages the stinging wound on my head. Once the task is done, she prepares food, glancing every so often at my breeches and shorn hair with a perplexed crinkle on her brow.

Grandfather smiles at her, a twinkle lighting his tired eyes. "Yes, indeed, Mrs. Landy. 'Tis a lass you see before you. I have found my granddaughter."

Granddaughter. My heart swells and grows warm at the word.

As the woman bustles, the weight of what just happened presses on me, and I collapse upon a bench beside the scrubbed table. A large cloth-covered bowl sits at my elbow, and the yeasty scent of bread dough left to prove fills my nose. I breathe it in with a greedy hunger. Such a lovely smell. But first, my Annie needs help.

"Who is this, Kenna?" Still standing, Grandfather studies me with an expression of kind bewilderment. "I seem to have found not one lost soul, but two."

"This is Annie. And I will explain all soon, but she is hurt. Please help her! Please." I blink back tears. "She fell and struck her head and has not awakened since then."

Grandfather's great white eyebrows raise at this statement. He gestures once more, and the capable Mrs. Landy puts a silver tray laden with food upon the table and asks if she may take the child from me.

"I'll do whatever I can to put her to rights. Trust me." The woman murmurs soothingly as she takes the child from my arms.

"*Och,* what a great lump she has, this wee lady." Mrs. Landy gently places Annie upon a bench beside the fire and rummages inside a cupboard. She removes bundles and boxes, herbs, and a mortar and pestle. My mind flies back to Stewart's Close and Donny. What has happened to her? To Una? And to Rob? I close my eyes at the memory of the crimson stain upon the white snow. God in heaven, please let him be alive! Let all of them be safe!

"Grandfather, there were others who helped me escape the close, and they need help as well! The soldiers..."

The man holds a finger to my lips. "I am certain you have much to tell me. We will sort all this out, but your face is hollowed as though you have not eaten in many a day. Sit. Eat. Your friends are well enough, for now."

"One was struck by a musket ball! He needs a physician. And we were locked away under a false quarantine. Please, you must get the Town Council to lift it!"

My grandfather shakes his head. "I can do nothing in the dark of night. We must wait until morning."

"Can you not send word and command the men guarding Stewart's Close to stand down? To open the gate? T'will be an easy thing with soldiers still outside. Send one of them!"

"I do not have command of the soldiers, Kenna." Grandfather shakes his head, and his gesture for me to sit is a commanding, imperious one, not the gentle motions he'd been making until now.

A sour taste rises to my tongue. Why will he not help my friends? And how can he say he cannot command soldiers? Minutes before, he told me he'd ordered men to search the city for me, and I heard him giving the men permission to take their leave.

On shaking legs, I move to sit at Grandfather's side. He hands me a cup of warm ale. I sip gratefully but am unable to eat, despite the tempting scents of cold lamb, sliced apples, and bread. My mind is too filled with a strange unease. Grandfather is pleased and relieved to see me. But he does indeed have a grand house in the city. And he speaks as though he is powerless to help those living on the close. I know 'tis not so.

"Now, then." Grandfather smiles at me, though the way he taps a rapid rhythm on the table with his fingers belies the fact that he is troubled. "As you do not wish to eat, perhaps you can explain how you ended up quarantined in the city? I sought for you every day without cease, Kenna!" He snatches a goblet of wine and swallows most of the liquid in one great gulp.

"I will tell you, but first, where is Oliver? What happened after you learned he poisoned his..." I clear my throat and blink away tears. "After you learned he poisoned my sister?" I rise to my feet and pace. I glance at Mrs. Landy, who is now wrapping a cloth around the bump on Annie's head. She catches my eye and smiles reassuringly.

"Oliver fled," Grandfather says in a rough voice. The pain in his eyes brings me to his side, and I lay a gentle hand upon one of his broad shoulders, chiding myself for my hosting so many doubts. Not once have I remembered that Grandfather is hurting as much as I am. After all, he has lost his daughter-in-law and recently discovered that his only son is a murderer. And 'tis the middle of the night. The dark and the storm outside would hamper any efforts to send orders at this time. We should, indeed, wait until the morning. Some of my unease dissipates.

"I have not seen my son since your sister's death." Grandfather places one of his large hands over mine and speaks in a gentle voice. "She lies in our family vault at St. Andrew's. We honored her as best as we could, given our worry over what had happened to you."

A great lump forms in my throat. "Thank you." Overwhelmed by sobs, I collapse at the table and rest my head on my arms. Grandfather strokes my hair until I am spent. With a wan smile, I wipe my damp cheeks and sip more ale. "I do not understand something. The bailey accused me of my sister's murder. Only yesterday I received word that Mrs. Harris said as much herself."

Grandfather's blue eyes spark lightning. "Did she? She shall lose her place, that fool woman! I believe we have much to tell each other. Please, Kenna. I must hear your tale. I am sure we'll both have answers once we share what has happened with one another."

Using as few words as possible, I describe the terrifying events from the time the man in the black coach sped me to the city to my recent rooftop escape. I explain how the bailey locked me inside Stewart's Close, ordered a quarantine, and later spread word that I was a murderess. I tell how I met wee Annie and found shelter with an old woman and describe my escape plan and the help proffered by my new friends. I do not, however, speak of the guild's business, nor of the vaults below ground. After all, I am a guild member myself. And we take care of our own.

Grandfather rises to his feet and seizes another bottle of wine from a shelf nearby. He seats himself heavily once more and refills his goblet. "I am indeed sorry for what you have suffered, child. This was surely all my son's doing. He must have paid the bailey to do what he did. I never wanted—" He pauses and clears his throat. "I would never have wished this upon you."

I place my hand over one of his. "I was so afraid I'd never see you again, but we are together once more. I am home." I pause and foolishly glance about. "Although I do not know exactly where I am. Why have I never seen this house?"

Grandfather smiles tiredly at me. "This is Oliver's house."

"Oliver's house?" My voice is faint, but a rush of relief pours through me. The Earl did not have a grand house in the city, after all! Oliver did. One he kept hidden from his wife. Cinaed would have spoken of it had she known.

"You did not know of his home in the city?" Grandfather's eyebrows draw together as he leans toward me. In a moment, his brow clears, and he sits back in his chair. "He came here often to oversee some of my business endeavors. He must have never spoken of it. After all, business is of no concern for women."

His familiar words bring to mind a brief memory of Una's tirade, when she regaled me with tales of all the women who ran successful trades in the city. The thought ignites a tiny flame inside. Of late, I have become acquainted with more than one woman thriving in the man's world of business. Starting with Donny. But this is not the time to discuss such matters with my grandfather.

"I had no idea Oliver had another house. I do not believe my sister ever came here. She rarely left our home by the sea."

Grandfather sips his wine and closes his eyes as though savoring the flavor. "I do believe she preferred the country to the city's crowded streets."

With a sigh, I pick up my cup of ale. "Since Oliver spends time in the city, he knows it well and has friends here. 'Tis likely he heard talk and realized that I was alive, not lying dead somewhere in Stewart's Close, thanks to chill or starvation. That must be how he found me when he attempted to see me yesterday."

"He what?" Grandfather slams his goblet onto the table, and I blink at him.

"Oliver asked to see me. I would not come out, of course. He soon left."

Grandfather turns his tempestuous visage away from me. Without a word, he strides to a wine cabinet. He pauses there with his back to me, leaning heavily against the wood. "There is much to do," he says with a sigh. "You must rest, Kenna. You need it. You certainly need a bath, as well. And find lady's clothing for her," he orders Mrs. Landy.

"Aye, my Lord." She gathers Annie into in her arms and glances at me. "Come. The lass is only sleeping. There's color upon her cheek. She'll soon be well. I am certain of it."

Before I follow her, I give Grandfather a swift hug. "I'm relieved you found us." Tears sting my eyes once more. "But please, do not forget that my new friends need help. We must go to them in the morning."

"In the morning." Grandfather places a hand on my shoulder. "Yes, dear lass. Here." He hands me a goblet filled with a dark, red wine. "Drink this tonight so you may sleep. You must rest. We shall talk in the morning."

"Thank you." I rise on tiptoe and plant a swift kiss on the old man's cheek. "Good night."

"Good night, child." Grandfather strokes my cheek. He plants a gentle kiss on my forehead. When he straightens, he gazes at me with eyes that droop with sadness and glitter with unshed tears.

Mrs. Landy hands me a candle, and with Annie in her arms, leads us up a curving staircase to a corridor lined with doors. She opens the first one we come to.

"This chamber is at the ready and 'twill suit ye well, I'm sure, miss." She settles Annie upon the bed and brushes the lass's soft hair away from her forehead. "Shall I bring ye hot water for a bath now?" She bustles to the grate and lights a fire.

"No, thank you. I will bathe tomorrow. But I would like a nightdress."

"Easily done, miss." She adds wood to the fire and bustles from the room. The woman returns before I have taken more than a few sips of wine.

"I've plenty to choose from." She carries a bundle of clothing in her arms. "Here's a linen nightdress, a clean shift, and a lovely gown for the morning. I believe they will suit you. They look to be your size."

The woman hands me a bundle of beribboned white cloth, and I duck behind a screen to disrobe. The flowing nightdress is edged with white ribbons and delicate lace. 'Twill be such a relief to remove these itchy breeches! As I pull the nightdress over my head, I catch the faint whiff of a floral scent. Rose. Or jasmine? My brow furrows. Why is there a supply of fine lady's clothing in Oliver's house in the city if my sister never came here? This clothing does not belong to a servant!

As I finger the fine lace of the nightdress, my thoughts return to Donny. She wanted to come with me so she could discover something. What was it?

When I emerge, Mrs. Landy has arranged a fashionable gown of blue silk over a chair. I must swallow hard before I can speak.

"Where did this clothing come from?"

"The viscount's wife, of course. D'ye be needing anything else, miss?" She drapes a pair of silk stockings over the arm of the chair.

Mutely, I shake my head and the woman leaves.

I am cold. Bile rises in my throat. Could this clothing belong to Cecelia?

My skin crawls. I fly to the screen, remove the night dress and once more garb myself in Donny's borrowed clothing. Then I march to the bed and settle myself, breeches and all, beside the slumbering Annie. I'll not sleep in a nightdress that belongs to Oliver's mistress! That must be the owner of the silk gown and the perfumed night dress! For Cinaed never knew of this house in the city.

Scowling, I blow out the candle and tuck myself next to Annie's warm body. I close my eyes, but anger pricks at me with hot needles, and I cannot relax. After several minutes of wild tossing and turning, I remember the wine Grandfather gave me. I sit up and grope for the goblet I'd left on the little bedside table. And, of course, knock it over as I reach for it in the dark.

"Devil take me!" I plop onto my pillow with a huff. Perhaps if I lie still, sleep will creep upon me. As soon as I awaken, I shall seek justice. First, we will open the gate and lift the quarantine. And then I will make certain my friends are safe. Starting with Rob.

Please, let him be well.

Forcing myself to ignore the wee undercurrent of unease that yet flows within me, I say a quick prayer for the safety of my friends. Surely, even if the redcoats arrested Rob, someone would have tended to his wound.

My eyelids droop. I found Grandfather, and I must have faith that this will end well. Sooner or later, Grandfather will locate Oliver, who will finally pay for what he has done. My disquiet surely stems from exhaustion and the confusion of my fright-filled days within the city. I smile grimly up at the ceiling in the dark and listen to the hiss of snowflakes that continue to tap against the windowpanes. And a blessed sleep overtakes me at last.

CHAPTER
38

A noise startles me, and I sit up. I stretch and scratch at my side and gaze in confusion at a strange bedchamber filled with the wan, gray light of a snowy day. What just awakened me, and where am I? Then Annie coughs beside me, and a jolt of terror shoots through my body. Her illness has returned. We need Donny!

My head is so stuffed with wool it takes my clumsy fingers several tries to fling aside the coverlet. When I hop from the bed, my feet land upon the sticky spot where I spilled the wine Grandfather gave me last night, and yesterday's events come back in a rush. After drawing a deep breath, 'tis now my turn to cough. The room is filled with a thick haze. What devilry is this? As I make my way across the chamber to investigate, bitter-tasting smoke threatens to choke me.

Fear jolts me fully awake. Something is wrong! Is our chamber on fire? But I find no evidence of flames within the room as I dart a wild gaze about me.

With Annie in my arms, I rush to the door and seize the knob. 'Tis locked. I shake the latch, bewildered. I had not heard the scrape of a key in the lock when Mrs. Landy left us last night. And should not the key be on my side?

My knife! Perhaps I can use it to pick the lock. Coughing, I dart to the small table beside the bed where I'd left the leather purse holding my blade. 'Tis gone.

There is no time to search for it. Coughing, I gaze about the room and spy a small dressing table. Will I find a key? I fly to the table and rifle through the drawers. Nothing. The only thing that might help is a nail file. I grab it and fly back to the door. I plunge it into the keyhole. 'Tis too large. In vain I struggle, marring the polished wood of the door with scratches. We are trapped.

I pound on the door and scream for help. And then cough so hard I double over. The smoke grows ever thicker, stinging my eyes and burning my throat. The chimney must be blocked. Setting Annie down beside the door, I make my way to the fireplace. Coals smolder as bitter fumes pour forth from them into the room instead of wafting upwards. The smell chokes me. A quick search of the chamber reveals the washbasin is empty. So is the pitcher that was filled with water when I went to bed. My head whirls, and my movements grow shaky. Stumbling my way back to the door, I pound upon it again.

Annie coughs and wails at my feet as I yell. "Please! We shall die in here! Open the door!" I twist the latch in vain and kick at the solid and unyielding wood. The smoke grows so thick 'tis almost impossible to draw breath. Annie wails once and resumes her choking cough.

My last hope shrivels and disappears like a scrap of paper thrown into a devouring fire. We shall die here. Slumping to the floor, I cradle the child and try to remember the words to Cinaed's lullaby. They do not come. I hold Annie close and squeeze my eyes shut.

Please, God above, just let it be over, quick. And please forgive me for lying and for stealing. You know I did it to survive, don't you?

The smoke fills my mouth and nose. 'Tis near to unbearable and I squeeze my eyes closed. Then I open them an instant later. I will not allow Annie to die this way!

Leaping to my feet, I fly to the wee dressing table. I dash it against the wall until it splinters and breaks into pieces. Seizing the largest bit, I bring it down upon the lock again and again. At first, nothing happens. Then the knob loosens and wobbles, and I redouble my efforts, smashing my makeshift tool again and again against the lock. And finally, it falls away from the splintered wood and I kick the door open.

A sudden rush of clean air engulfs me. I seize Annie and drag her away from the smoking bedchamber, coughing and gasping. Then my strength leaves me, and I collapse to my knees.

"Quick, lad! Get away from there!" someone yells.

Summoning all my energy, I rise on trembling legs and barely keep my feet beneath me as I struggle to carry Annie. A stranger takes my arm and leads us away from the acrid smoke. I am blinded, coughing, and struggling to draw air into my burning lungs as we go.

We stumble down the corridor and a curving stairway, while others sweep past us heading back to the upper floor, shouting and carrying buckets. With great relief, we arrive at a dim salon filled with scattered chaises. I collapse in a heap with Annie on my lap. I cradle her and draw great gulps of clear air into my lungs.

"What happened?" My voice is a croak, my eyes are streaming. "Where is Grandfather?"

"Kenna?" Someone touches my hair, and then fingers lift my chin. "Is it you? How are you here?"

A renewed fit of coughing seizes me, along with a jolt of pure fear. Before me is a man whose pale cheeks have sunken, with hazel eyes that droop with exhaustion. His tawny hair hangs lank over a tall brow, which seems far more lined than I remember. Despite his haggard appearance, I know the man. Oliver! How is he here, now? Grandfather said he fled!

I shout and strike his hand away from me.

"Grandfather! Where are you?" After placing Annie on the floor, I leap to my feet, brandishing the only pitiful weapon I have left: the nail file. "Murderer!" My entire body trembles as I face the man. "Murderer! She loved you! She loved you and you killed her!" My voice ends in a high-pitched wail.

"Kenna." Oliver's voice is rough with emotion. "Please, let me speak!"

"How could you?" I barely get the words out. My chest aches from coughing and from the pain in my heart. No, the pain comes from a wound in my very soul.

"I did not kill Cinaed." Oliver's eyes fill with tears. "How could you ever think such a thing!"

"Liar!" I scream. I leap forward and jab the file at Oliver, aiming for his neck. It strikes his cheek. He cries out and backs away, holding his hand to his face. Crimson droplets ooze from between his fingers.

"Listen to me, Kenna." His eyes hold raw anguish, and I admit to a thrill that rushes through me at the pain I have caused him. "I beg you, listen to me!"

I do not answer but remain as I am, holding the file at the ready, relishing the grim satisfaction that the bit of metal in my hand tore Oliver's flesh. Blood pounds in my ears. Alarmed shouts reverberate inside the house as servants deal with the blocked chimney. I pay them no mind. This is the moment I longed for when I shivered, barefoot, betrayed, so terribly alone my first night in the city. The moment I prayed for each evening as I lay upon the hard floor beside Donny's fire. 'Tis what I have wished from the moment I discovered the reason for my sister's death. I shall have my revenge at last.

Oliver will die.

"Kenna." Oliver breathes out in a ragged voice. Blood trickles down his cheek. "You fled after you found that bottle. I was so torn inside, I did not follow you as I should have. I was shocked, wretched with grief, and could not leave Cinaed. When I came to myself and sought you, Father told me you had run away. The servants and I went out to search for you in vain. When you did not return after that first long night, I began to fear the worst."

I am hardly able to speak. "You did not fear for my safety, you feared I would tell everyone how you poisoned your wife!" A fit of coughing seizes me.

"That bottle was not mine, Kenna! It must have fallen from the pocket of the one who administered the poison, but it was not I."

"Who else would have had reason to kill Cinaed?" I say in a ragged voice. "Grandfather obviously suspected you because he sent me away to keep me out of danger! *You* had me captured and taken to that stinking alley. *You* had the bailey declare quarantine so he could lock me within Stewart's Close! I'm sure you thought I'd not find a soul to help me." My voice grows louder. "You enjoyed the company of your mistress in this grand house while you waited for me to die!"

I raise the file in my hand, ready to strike again.

Olive backs away. His face twists with confusion. "Mistress? What do you mean? I have no mistress!"

I shake my head in disbelief. "You liar! I saw how you looked at Cecelia! You rid yourself of your wife for her. And when I discovered your treachery, you wanted me to die like the wife you poisoned!" I tear my sister's portrait from within my shirt and hold it out with a trembling hand. "Look at her!" I throw the parchment at him, and it strikes him in the chest. "Look at the face of the woman you killed. The woman you abandoned for that black-hearted witch!"

"No!" Oliver's face twists with an expression of horror. "Kenna, you do not know what you are saying." Keeping an eye on me, he snatches the parchment from the floor. And when he unfolds it and gazes upon my sister's portrait, the color drains from his gaunt cheeks. "Oh, my darling Cinaed," he whispers.

"'Tis far too late for regret." I spit out the words.

Oliver studies the portrait with a fierce longing in his eyes. Suddenly, his pain-filled demeanor grows calm, and all expression drains away. His lips tremble and another drop of blood seeps from the wound in his cheek.

"Go on," he whispers. "If it will make things right by you, take my life. I read it in your eyes. You do not believe me. You never will."

I take one step closer. And another. Oliver is so near now. So near. Licking dry lips, I raise my hand to strike. I take in one ragged breath. And another. My heart thunders. My hand shakes. 'Tis time! I must act!

"Go on. I have nothing left." Oliver loosens his collar and lays it open his to expose his bare neck. He closes his eyes. My heart leaps in a painful, twisting way. Before me is not the defiant, villainous man I expected to find. Why is he so broken?

"Mamma!" Annie sobs.

Her voice pierces me. I hesitate, unsure, and in that moment, the battle is over. I cannot do what I have planned. Oliver is a wicked man who deserves to die, but I cannot be the one who takes his life. I cannot spill his blood before the child's eyes. I could not do so even if we were alone with naught but God at the watch, for I cannot become what Oliver is.

I back away, keeping my eyes locked on my brother-in-law.

"Stay where you are. I'll call Grandfather if you move from that spot."

Annie screams and I whirl. A man garbed in a dark cloak has appeared, hood pulled low over his face. A wild thought that Shaw somehow survived falling from the towering Martin house strikes me. But how? The monster has seized Annie and holds her by the hair with one hand. In the other hand, he brandishes a gleaming dagger.

"Drop that blade, lass, or I will kill the child." His voice is a demon's whisper. And as familiar to me as my own. 'Tis a voice that became dear to me almost from the moment I first heard it. This is not Shaw. Of course not.

This is Grandfather.

My world draws in on itself. It cannot be. My body folds and I sink to my knees. The pain is too great. I cannot bear it. And what a fool I was!

The file falls from my fingers. I show my empty hands.

"Please." I sob. "Don't hurt her."

"It cannot be." Oliver's breathes out the words as his face drains of color. He certainly wishes to cling to his faith in the one who is the axis of his world, as would I. But now, we both see clearly. We can no longer trust in the benevolence of the man we so admired.

"Silence!" Grandfather roars.

Shuffled footsteps draw closer to us. One wild glance reveals the bailey, creeping forward with a wolfish smile upon his face. His beady eyes regard me with a gleam of triumph. He raises a pistol and points it directly at me.

"No!" Oliver flies to stand in front of me and the bailey falters and lowers his pistol. "Drop that weapon and stay where I can see you, man!"

"Don't listen to him. Do what I pay you to do, fool!" Grandfather hisses.

The bailey's features harden as he raises the firearm once more. With an enraged roar, Oliver launches himself at the man, striking at the arm that holds the pistol. It fires but the shot goes wild. A crack of thunder rends the air, and a round table holding a vase shatters. From elsewhere in the house, servants cry out in alarm.

Both men fall, and the bailey's head strikes against the wall as he plummets downward. Oliver leaps to his feet, but the treacherous bailey lies in a crumpled heap on the floor.

My brother-in-law's lips twist in disgust as he turns back to his cloaked father. "Show yourself," he spits. "We know who you are."

Grandfather does not move, nor does he make a sound. Annie weeps and squirms in his grasp, and he gives her a shake, hissing like a snake for her to remain still.

"Please, just let her go. Take me." I rise on unsteady legs.

Grandfather raises his knife higher in the air. "Stop! I'll strike if you come any closer."

Oliver holds out his hands. "Father, stop! Why are you doing this?" His face remains pale, but his eyes burn like coals.

"I am doing this for *you*, you fool!" Grandfather roars. With a single motion he sweeps the hood back to reveal his face. His great blue eyes with their great, puffy pouches widen with outrage and his lips tremble.

"I will establish your name and your place in history! Do you not understand, lad? I am doing this to help you!"

Oliver's body grows rigid. He draws in a single, shaking breath.

"*Help* me?" His voice fills with the same pain I bear. He presses a hand over his mouth and his eyes gleam with tears. "It was you, wasn't it?" Oliver's voice catches in a sob. "You who poisoned my dear wife."

Grandfather stands before us, defiant and deadly. His is not the face of the kindly man who used to laugh with me as we stole sweets or shared stories. Nor is this the face of the man who gazed at me with such sweetness mere hours ago.

My heart crumples inside me, a bit of old parchment crushed in a strong fist. 'Tis no wonder that a hint of unease threaded itself through my body last night, even after I chose to ignore my doubts. Rob was right. I did not know my grandfather as well as I thought I did.

"Grandfather." I sob. "How could you?"

"Silence!" the man bellows. And he raises his knife.

CHAPTER 39

With a howl, I dive to seize the nail file at my feet and fling myself at Grandfather.

The man releases his hold upon Annie and simultaneously raises his dagger, swinging it toward me. A searing pain spreads from my shoulder down my arm. Annie screams and Oliver curses. He lunges at his father and wrests the dagger from the man's grasp. It falls to the floor with a clatter.

"No more of this, old man! You will not hurt anyone else!"

I crumple to my knees, holding my shoulder as hot fluid flows from my wound. Annie flies to me and huddles against my chest. Holding her with my uninjured arm, I scoot away from Grandfather. His eyes widen at the sight of the blood soaking my shirt. Of a sudden, his shoulders stoop and he appears so much older than before. He gazes mournfully at me as I strive in vain to comfort the wee, wailing Annie, who buries her face in my neck.

"I never wanted any of this," he says in a hollow voice. Wearily, he sinks into a chair. We gaze at one another, mute, both breathing heavily.

Oliver hurries to me. With trembling hands, he offers me a handkerchief and I press it over my wound.

Then Oliver rises to face his father. His jaw is set, and his eyes burn with rage.

"Explain yourself," he hisses. "Now. Tell me everything."

Grandfather obeys, meek as a mewling babe. "'Twas I. I gave

your wife the elixir. I never imagined her passing would take so long. Nor cause such pain." He speaks so softly; I hardly hear him over my ragged breathing.

"Why?" Oliver squeezes his eyes shut. "Dear God, Father, why?"

"I'll tell ye why." We all start at the sound of a voice by now familiar to me. Donny marches through the doorway. Clad in her man's garb, she stands as tall as her wee frame can stretch and walks with swiftness, though one eye is swollen closed.

"Sir, who are you?" Oliver says, while Grandfather bolts upright and stumbles toward Donny. He collapses at her feet.

"Mother!"

Oliver and I gasp while the old woman with short-cropped, white hair gazes down with great sadness. She places one of her tiny hands upon Grandfather's head.

"What have ye done, Reginald?" Rays of pale sunshine stream from the tall window and betray trails of tears that streak down her crinkled cheek. "Such a good lad, ye used to be," the woman whispers. "But the gold poisoned your soul."

Grandfather raises his head and seizes Donny's hand. "I could not be discovered! I couldn't bear it!"

"Who would have found out, lad? I kept to myself and never said a word."

"Lord Helmsley, Mother!" Grandfather rises clumsily to his feet and towers above the diminutive form of his aged parent. "He knew Lord Ramsay as a lad. He knew we were not one and the same."

Oliver strides to his father's side. "What do you mean?" His gaze darts wildly between Donny and his father.

The old woman appraises him with her ice-blue eyes. "I'll be quick about it, for my words will cause pain. Your father is no' Lord Ramsay, because my husband was no' the true Lord Ramsay. That one's dead. Dead and gone, with all his family and their servants."

"How?" Oliver's face grows pale. "You killed them all?"

"Don't be a fool!" Donny scowls at him and plants her hands on her hips. "They all died of the plague, ye daft man. Thousands of souls died, and with none left to mourn them. We only did what so many others did, for none were left to know the truth. We took the Ramsay's house. We took their land and their titles. Their wealth."

She stole from the dead. Donny has been at her thievery for a very long time. But who could blame her for what she did? For the chance to take another's wealth when none there were to claim it? A mirthless laugh escapes me.

At that moment, Donny's eyes fall upon me, She gasps and rushes to my side, tutting and shaking her head. "*Och,* Reginald. What have ye done?" She kneels beside me and examines my wound.

Oliver backs away several paces, shaking his head in disbelief. "Father, tell me this isn't true. Tell me you didn't poison my wife so no one would learn who you really are."

"I didn't merely do it to hide the truth, 'twas done for you, lad!" Grandfather says, holding his hands out in a pleading gesture. "I saw the glances Helmsley's daughter gave you and thought you'd already made her your mistress. We all saw how unhappy your wife was after she lost that babe and had no other. I knew you'd wish for better company and thought you'd found it."

Oliver buries his face in his hands.

Fresh tears spill from my eyes. "Monster!" I can barely speak past the thick lump in my throat. "How could you do it?"

Grandfather pulls his silver timepiece from his waistcoat and fiddles with the chain, gazing at the crystal as though seeking for the right words inside the sphere. His face is pallid as a bowl of porridge and his eyes gleam with tears.

"I did not mean to hurt you, Kenna. Nor did I wish to cause you pain, Oliver." Grandfather's brows draw together. "Helmsley was growing more suspicious of me. I could see it in his face. I knew a marriage had to take place. Cecelia clearly wished for it and Helmsley never denies her anything. With such a connection between our families, he would remain silent to protect his daughter. And thus, I would have secured your future forever."

"My future?" Oliver seizes a small chair, which he hurls at the wall with a roar. The chair strikes a looking glass, knocking it from its spot beside the mantel. It falls with a tinkling crash. The dancing shards gleam in the firelight, and the flames lend a reddish tinge to the jagged bits of glass. My chest pains me as though 'tis my own heart fallen and shivered apart on the floor.

Breathing hard, Oliver faces his father. "What future do I have without my beloved wife? Cecelia was never my mistress, nor did I ever wish for her to become such!"

The men remain standing, eyes locked upon one another, both shaking with emotion. One defiant, enraged, ready to strike. The other cowed, subdued, beaten. Defeated. Neither the man I thought him to be. Glancing at Oliver's contorted face, I muse at how easily I thought him possessed of a murderous heart. Granted, I'd seen the bottle of poison beside his doublet. But it was *beside* the torn jacket, not hidden within it. Had Grandfather been in his place, I most likely would have allowed him to give an explanation. And I would have believed him. But not Oliver.

Wincing in pain, I rise to my feet and take Annie's hand. I'd allowed Oliver's distance and lack of parental affection to color my perceptions of him. Just as I'd taken Grandfather's loving attentions as sincere. Perhaps they were, once. Until he needed to be rid of me. Just as he found the need to rid himself of his daughter-in-law.

Despite the searing pain of my shoulder, I tug gently on Annie's hand, and we edge toward the door. A few tears flow from my stinging eyes and drip from my chin. The rich furnishings throughout the room seem to crowd in on me. Polished wood, satin wall coverings. Thick Persian carpets. Gleaming candlesticks. Polished brass shields upon the wall. Evidence of wealth, a mountain of it. None of it belonging to anyone here. Not to Grandfather. Not to Oliver.

"We don't belong here," I whisper. "Do we, Annie?"

Another room comes to mind. A small kitchen with a warm fire and a gleaming table, freshly scrubbed. Fragrant herbs hanging from the ceiling. A pot steaming over the coals, filling the air with the promise of a simple, though filling meal. More than enough. And an old woman smoking a pipe that emits a spicy scent while she puffs away and teases me, or chides me, or praises me. Who offered me a home.

We reach the doorway. Donny glances in my direction. Does she understand what I am about to do? She does. Ever has she read the thoughts writ upon my features. The lines on her face soften. *Go.* She mouths the word. She knows I will not stay here.

"Son—"

"Stop!" Oliver's trembling lips are pale as he interrupts his father. He strides to stand directly in front of Grandfather, forcing the man to look him in the eye. "From this day forward, I am no longer your son. You are no longer my father."

My eyes fly open wide.

Grandfather's shoulders hunch, and he takes on the appearance of a wounded, hunted fox. His lips tremble before they form words. "You cannot mean that."

Oliver's voice is clear. "I do. You will never see me again."

"All I ever did was for you!" Grandfather roars. His eyes burn and his mouth contorts with rage and pain. He bares his teeth like a cornered hound. "For you! I allowed your marriage to that penniless lass with a child in tow, did I not? I allowed you to give them a grand home they did not deserve. I gave you all I had, and when your wife did not give you a son, I..."

Another memory strikes me in the heart. The dawning realization sickens me so that I hold a hand to my stomach. There is something else I've been too daft to see. Because I did not want to see it. I glance down at the wee golden head beside me. The golden head of a lass with a tiny scar, with eyes that are so familiar. Eyes like Oliver's.

Grandfather snaps his mouth shut, whirls and strides toward the door, crunching through the shards of broken glass.

"What?" Oliver's voice is a deadly growl. "What else have you done to me, old man?" He flies after his father and seizes the man's arm.

"Speak, Reginald." Donny's eyes are hard as flint. "This matter is of concern to all of us."

Grandfather's head bows. He is somehow smaller. A once great mountain of a man diminished before my eyes.

"'Twas for my son," he whispers. "I did it for my son's benefit. I found someone to care for her. I did. I paid for her keep."

My stomach twists inside me. I was right. Oliver and Cinaed's child did not die. The confirmation forces me to my knees. Two months after the wee Isla had received her scar thanks to my carelessness, only days after we had celebrated Michaelmas, she'd grown ill with the croup. And died. At least, Lord Ramsay's trusted surgeon from London, Doctor Ogilvie, had said as much. And insisted Isla's grieving parents not see their poor, dead child, for 'twould have been too much to bear. Broken with despair, they'd agreed. We'd buried a wee coffin the next day, never catching a glimpse of what was inside.

Isla had disappeared from our lives, but she had not died. I know this because I found her in the city. And refused to see the truth when I first glimpsed it. How adept I have become at ignoring what is before my eyes, of lying to myself.

Before anyone can reply, Grandfather wrenches his arm from Oliver's grasp and shoves him to the floor. He stumbles to a rack on the wall displaying several firearms. He seizes a pistol and points it at his own chest.

"No!" Donny shouts. But as the words leave her lips, the air is rent with a sharp crack that makes me jump and Annie scream. Grandfather crumples to the floor. Oliver gapes at him, his hands outstretched in a helpless gesture.

Donny stands frozen. Then, as if shaking herself from a dream, she walks to Grandfather. Silently, she kneels upon the floor and places her hand on the man's broad chest. It does not rise and fall, and a red stain spreads over his silk shirt. The old woman smooths a stray hair from Grandfather's forehead and leans down to kiss her son. She remains bent over her child, their foreheads touching.

"*Och*, Reginald. What have ye done?" She whispers. Tears drip onto Grandfather's motionless face.

Oliver collapses on a chaise and buries his face in his hands once more.

My throat closes. I have my revenge, but 'tis a hollow one. I am free from my confinement in that narrow close. I discovered my sister's true killer, and the man shall trouble me nevermore. But the shock of everything I have just learned encircles my being like a cold, winding shroud. I pull Annie, the child I have grown to love so desperately, closer to me. She is not Annie, but Isla. The wee lass that is not mine to keep. I cannot. I must not, though it will tear me in two.

Sometimes the truth we seek so desperately is a hard thing once we find it.

CHAPTER 40

In a ragged voice, Oliver calls for servants. I huddle upon the floor with Isla while men come to carry Grandfather's body to his chamber. Outside the salon, Mrs. Landy bursts into loud wails at the sight of her master. The bailey sits up, groggy and groaning, and after a swift, horrified glance at the crimson stain on the carpet, the man lumbers to his feet.

"I'll be going, then," he mutters as he slithers out the door.

Someone places gentle fingers on my head, causing me to start at the touch.

"I'll not hurt you, Kenna." Oliver's voice is a strained whisper. "Nor that child. Who is she?"

I wince as Oliver touches the cloth that binds my wound. 'Tis searing agony. Yet this is nothing compared to the pain within me, for the moment of truth has come. I cannot deny Oliver this revelation, for he has already lost so much. And as I have learned of late, denying the truths I discover, lying to myself and to everyone else, has done me no favors.

"You'll want to sit down," I tell him. With a slight frown of confusion, he draws a chair close to me and settles himself upon it, his face a mask of weariness laced with deep sadness.

"I found her in the city." I pause to gather my words. "Without a home, like me. At first, I took her to be a lost child or one of the many waifs that roam the streets. An orphan."

Donny kneels beside me and checks the bandage on my shoulder.

She sniffles as she gently has me move my arm. "So, ye've discovered this as well, have ye?" she murmurs. Her voice is thick with tears. "Ye ken very well what will happen, do ye not? The lassie needs a mother, and ye'll do quite well. Ye've proven that to me."

My lips quiver. "Her mother is gone. But she has her father. A father who loves her."

Oliver darts to his feet. His arms dangle at his sides as he gapes down at us. "What do you mean, Kenna?"

I hesitate. The words tremble on my tongue. Donny's azure eyes find mine. Her gaze no longer reminds me of chips of blue ice, for I now see the warmth that shines from her soul.

"He is not the man I thought him to be, is he?"

The wee woman smiles softly as her face crinkles into a thousand crisscrossing lines. "No."

I rise clumsily to my feet. And lead Isla to Oliver. With shaking fingers, I brush aside the golden wisps that hang over the lass's forehead.

"Do you see that scar? And the color of her eyes?"

Oliver blinks several times. His face is ashen. He sinks to his knees and gently touches the lass's cheek. Then he lifts her chin with gentle fingers to gaze into her wide eyes. He brushes a strand of hair from her forehead and his fingers graze against the tiny scar there. He remains there, frozen, not breathing. Then he draws in a ragged breath, and something alters in his eyes. His face crumples, and he holds his hands out to Isla in mute supplication.

She first edges away from the man who is a stranger to her, but soon Isla responds to the simple gesture and reaches out to Oliver. Mutely, I release her.

Sobbing, Oliver sits cross-legged on the floor and cradles my Annie, his Isla, in his arms, holding her to him as though she is a priceless treasure.

"Isla," he sobs. "My wee Isla."

He looks up at me with streaming eyes. "How?"

"It happened two years ago on Twelfth Night. Isn't that right,

Donny?" I hold my clasped hands to my chest to keep from reaching to snatch Annie away from Oliver. Her father.

The old woman nods. "I spied Reginald in the lane near my house. Nearly swallowed my own pipe at the sight." She chuckles, though the sound is without a ring of mirth. "I'd no' seen the man in many a year. Thought he'd come to visit his old mother at last, so I poured wine and warmed oat cakes by the fire. But he never crossed my threshold. The next day I heard a tale that gave me reason to believe my son had come to the city with a secret to hide."

Oliver rises, holding Isla close. She does not struggle against him, but her eyes seek mine with a questioning look.

"It's all right, Poppet," I tell her. She snuggles against his chest.

Holding his wee daughter, Oliver paces rapidly back and forth in front of a carved cabinet. "Dear God," he mutters to himself. "Dear God."

"After Donny saw her son in the city, she heard word of a babe left with a family who lived on the close. The Lindsay's. Is that right?" I whisper.

The woman nods. "Old Lindsay swore they must take it in though his wife didnae want it. Caused a great row, it did. Mrs. Lindsay thought the child was one of her husband's brats from his carrying on. But from that day hence he had a heavy purse and plenty to spend on his drink." Donny's weathered face is grim, and her jaw is set as she tightens the binding over my wound. "I knew Reginald was paying him to keep the child. I thought she was *his*. The result of a dalliance." Donny shakes her head and huffs. "My son used the close as a place to hide his secrets, but I didnae make it known to a soul. I thought the lass was well cared for. Until Kenna brought her to me, and I saw for myself she was not." She closes her eyes. "I should have made certain of it. I'll carry this shame with me the rest of my life."

Oliver sinks down into a chair, still clinging to his daughter, as though he's afraid she'll disappear if he lets her out of sight for a mere moment.

The two of them look so *right* together. Despite my loss, some of the tears that sting my eyes arise not out of grief, but of gladness. And relief. I am happy for the lass, for she is returned to her father and I know she is loved.

The dull ache of my wounded shoulder grows stronger. The hurt Grandfather inflicted on my body pales in comparison to what he has done to my soul. For what is to become of me, now? I cannot return to the man's house. Once again, I picture a poor but peaceful, comfortable room in the city. But this time, the vision is cold. Bereft of any real comfort. For the child I knew as Annie will not be there. Besides, do I truly want to return to the city and live among many who cursed my name? But where else can I go?

Shivering, I glance at Donny as my heart quickens. I do not yet know what happened to everyone after I left them last night.

"How did you escape the soldiers, Donny? And Rob? Is he all right?" I steel myself for what I am afraid I shall hear.

"He lives, child. He's well enough for now."

I sob and clap a hand over my mouth. Donny puts one of her wee, rough hands upon my cheek in an unaccustomed gesture of kindness. "I removed the ball from his side and bound his wounds. He'll be laid low for a bit, but he lives. His father and I will look after him."

For a moment, I cannot speak. When I can draw breath, I wipe my face with the handkerchief Oliver gives me.

"Who is...*och*, never mind," he says. "My head is swimming. I need a drink. Let us go to the kitchen."

Back inside the warm room, I slump at the table; the very table where I'd told Grandfather my tale last night. Oliver speaks softly to a weeping Mrs. Landy, who soon puts a hot drink in front of me. I sip it without tasting it.

"The blame for all this is mine," Donny murmurs in her gruff voice.

"How?"

The woman pats my hand. "I convinced my husband to take over the Ramsay's house. The grand old place was empty, after all. We could give our son a life that had always been out of reach before then. My husband never liked when others called him 'Lord Ramsay,' but after he died, my Reginald took the title and bore it with pride. And within a twelvemonth, Reginald's bearing, his manner, and his words suddenly sounded so different, so, *ach*. Never mind." She shrugs and gulps her ale.

"So English." I say with a sour smile. "London-bred."

Oliver settles Isla into my lap and heads to a sideboard lined with many bottles.

"Good God," he mutters to himself as he pours a glass of whiskey, which he gulps in a trice. Keeping both glass and bottle in his grasp, he sits across from me.

Shame forces me to look down at my steaming ale. What a monster I took him to be! Simply because he was stern with me, I refused to see his decency. How he truly loved my sister. And adored his child. And the man who indulged my whims, who encouraged my fancies? How I refused to believe he was capable of treachery!

"You know, Donny, I cannot count how many times Mrs. Harris accused me of speaking like 'an English lass who thinks herself a wee bit better than her northern cousins.'" I put my chin in my hand. "I've never really liked that woman."

As Donny chuckles, I place my cup on the table and examine my rough, unladylike fingernails. Thanks to Grandfather's London-bred tutors, I did learn to speak as Grandfather wanted me to, like a high-born lass from England, polished and refined. I scowl down at my drink.

"All those tutors I had. Grandfather did not hire them for my benefit. He hired them for his. I was part of his act. I needed to play my role well."

Oliver finishes his second glass of whiskey and reaches for the bottle. "London-bred tutors," he mutters. "How I hated mine."

Donny heaves out a great sigh. "Reginald was no longer the lad I'd once known. Many years ago, I left him and came to the city." She blinks away tears and squares her shoulders. "I left when I realized the life my husband and I took for our own had poisoned our son's soul. I left behind what was never meant for me. Reginald was glad to be rid of me. He never once sought for me."

"Mamma?" Isla's voice plucks me from my pain-filled reverie.

"What is it?"

"Mamma, I want my doll."

The memory of the child's dreadful fall from the rooftop rushes back, and I shudder. "I will find it, my sweet." Mollified, she settles herself against me and my heart aches at what is now lost to me.

"Donny, how *did* you all escape from the soldiers?"

The old woman chuckles and her eyes light with mirth. 'Tis a blessed sight, easing away some of the pain painted upon her features after the death of her son and the discovery of what he'd done.

"After ye yanked that board from under Shaw's feet, some of the soldiers thought better of what they were doing."

"But they fired upon me." I tilt my head at her to show where a ball grazed me.

"By the heavens," Oliver mutters. He gestures to the still sniffling Mrs. Landy, who sets bread and apples on the table. Oliver takes a single bite of a russet apple and returns to his whiskey.

"Some did." Donny shrugs. "But most fled, and we soon overpowered the fools who remained. I took Rob home and tended to his wound, leaving Callum and others from our guild to take the redcoats' muskets and force the gate open."

"Good." I breathe out a sigh, but another thought strikes my soul with dread. I gasp. "I made Shaw fall from the roof of a tall house. Is he dead?" I clap a hand over my mouth.

"*Och*, aye. He's dead, lass."

My eyes open wide with horror. "That means I'm—"

"A lass who narrowly escaped murder. He was coming to stick ye with that dagger, Kenna."

Oliver groans and rubs his eyes.

"Ye did no wrong." Donny covers my hand with hers. "Shaw

tried to kill ye. He was certainly filling his purse with my son's gold. So was that bailey. And where's the vermin crawled off to?"

"I shall find him," Oliver says grimly. Mrs. Landy puts a bottle of wine on the table and Oliver pours himself a full goblet. "He was friends with Father. He visited oft after you fled, to help us look for you. Or so I thought." He drains his goblet and refills it. "And he claimed to be searching for the mysterious person who dropped that bottle in Cinaed's bedchamber. Believe it or not, Kenna, I never suspected you of poisoning your own sister."

I study my hands. This man gave me the benefit of the doubt without question. Whereas I suspected him the moment I saw the bottle.

My brother-in-law drains his goblet and refills it. "What a double fool I've been. How did I not see what was right before my face?" He slams the wine bottle onto the table with such force 'tis a wonder the glass does not break.

"I've been asking myself that very question." I manage a tiny smile. "What did Grandfather tell you about me?" 'Tis still hard to raise my eyes to meet Oliver's.

"Simply that you'd fled, for we could not find you anywhere. I began to search for you as soon as we buried Cinaed." His voice breaks. "I soon heard rumors of a lane quarantined within the city. Not long after that, I heard tales of a lass within the close who claimed to be the granddaughter of an Earl, and I knew it had to be you. I dressed in poor cloth to escape notice and went to look for you. You know the rest."

At last, I raise my eyes to his. "I am sorry I did not trust you."

Oliver huffs and pours himself another glass of wine. "Why should you have trusted me? I was never much of a father, was I?"

He does not wait for me to speak, and I do not attempt words. We both know the answer.

Isla snuggles in my arms and closes her eyes. She yawns, and so do I.

"I must go. The bairn needs to rest and I am an old woman. My bones are weary." Donny gets to her feet. Her eyes find mine.

"My door remains open to ye, Kenna. 'Tis your home now as well."

A heaviness settles within my chest. What shall I do? I glance between the old woman and Oliver. Donny continues before I can speak.

"I'll trust my grandson to take care of matters here. I would like to attend the service for my son. Will you send word when it is time?"

Oliver's face falls. "I do not believe we may have a service," he tells her. "He cannot be buried in sacred ground."

Donny's eyes droop with sadness as she places a gentle hand on Oliver's arm. "We must say he died of an accident. 'Tis better that way, lad. Do ye no' think so?"

My brother-in-law nods, and Donny pats his arm. "I'll take my leave. Kenna?"

Shaking, I get to my feet and gently place Isla in Oliver's arms.

"I'm ready." I follow the old woman to the doorway. I cannot help taking a final glance at my sweet Isla. She reaches for me; my heart twists.

"But where are you going?" Oliver raises his eyebrows. "When you said 'home' I thought you meant *our* home. You cannot mean to leave with Donny?"

"I do." My voice breaks.

"You have a fine place to live, Kenna." He runs a hand through his disheveled hair. His face is covered with confusion. "With servants. And your own carriage. Do you not wish to return to your home in the country?"

The great yellow toad of a house at the end of a long lane floats like a hellish vision before my eyes. How I've wished to return to it so many times over these long days trapped in the close! But a sickening dread now fills me at the thought of seeing it again.

"I do not belong to it, Oliver. I never did." Like the close when locked and guarded, Grandfather's house was a prison. Granted, 'twas a fine prison filled with rich furnishings, fine clothing, and servants to do my bidding, but the only real happiness I found there was when I was alone under the sun. Or with my sister. And she is gone.

My brother-in-law studies me in mute amazement. Then his brows lower and his mouth twists into a frown. "I supposed I never belonged to it, either. But what do you expect me to do, Kenna? Live here in the city, instead? In this horrible place where Father spent time with his mistress?'

Mrs. Landy gasps from her spot beside the fire. I recall her telling me the clothing she'd lent me belonged to the viscount's wife. Grandfather was adept at spinning tales to suit his needs. I suppose 'twas an easy thing to claim the mysterious owner of the clothing was married to his son.

Blinking, I frown in return. "Of course, I would not wish to live here!"

"Where else then, Kenna? Though Father and I are not of the Ramsay bloodline, the true Ramsay's are all gone. Should *I* walk away, then? Leave all the servants to fend for themselves? Allow the land to lie fallow and the houses and cottages to fall into ruin? I have responsibilities to many, whether earned or not."

"I do not expect you to do anything except care for Isla. I simply cannot stay with you."

My throat closes, so I turn my back and join Donny in the doorway. She puts a gentle hand on my back. "I'm sure he'll allow ye to visit the lass all ye want."

A black storm cloud fills me from head to foot. *Visit.* 'Tis all I can hope for. But the house in the country is a long day's carriage ride from the city. Visits will not occur that often, I'm afraid, for Oliver will forever be burdened with his many responsibilities as an Earl.

Shaking, I follow Donny through the door. But behind me, a whimpering cry tears into me, and I turn back.

Isla's eyes gleam with tears, and her wee hands reach out for me. I hesitate, and in that moment my resolve is lost. Returning to her, I bury my face in the child's golden hair. I cannot leave her. The separation would be unbearable.

With the lass's wee hand in my own, I face Donny. Her eyes are soft.

"Go. As I've said, my door is always open to ye. And to that lassie. After all, you're family."

As usual, Donny seems to read my thoughts. But she has not read all of them. I step closer and whisper in her ear. Her eyes light up.

"Aye. That I will do."

She chuckles as I plant a swift kiss on her cheek. "I shall wait for word."

The old woman leaves, closing the door softly behind her, and I turn back to my brother-in-law. "Oliver? I'm ready. Shall we go?"

The man's face clears. "I'm glad you've seen reason. You'll not regret it, Kenna." After he issues curt orders to Mrs. Landy, promising swift action to take care of the "problem" in the house, we leave.

Outside, the city is uncharacteristically quiet, blanketed in thick snow. The castle stands upon the hill in majesty, clad in a white cloak as she surveys her realm. Somewhere, not too far away, my new friends are back home, no longer prisoners inside their narrow lane. They are free. But I am not. Not as free as I wish to be.

Isla falls asleep in Oliver's lap as he gazes down at her in mute wonder, stroking her soft hair. The light of adoration in his countenance warms me. Isla is where she belongs.

Scratching at my itching stockings, ignoring the aghast glance Oliver bestows upon me, I draw in a deep breath and close my eyes. I do not fully belong anywhere. Therefore, I must find my own place.

And so I shall.

CHAPTER
41

Two days after the death of Lord Ramsay, a small group attended while an elderly priest performed the funeral rites and the Earl was entombed at the kirk near his grand house. Donny, clad in Sheona's black skirts, attended, sitting next to Oliver. His lips remained pressed into a thin line. No doubt he did not wish to be there. Nor did I, but the expected ceremony had to occur, as was proper. The Earl could not leave this earth without at least the appearance of a grieving family seeing him off into eternity.

Both Mrs. Landy and Mrs. Harris attended, sniffling and dabbing at their eyes. Though stern, Grandfather had always been generous to his loyal staff. A handful of other servants, including old Tom, Grandfather's valet, joined us as well. I barely tolerated the sight of him. 'Twas he who'd led me through the tunnel and bade me farewell as I unknowingly embarked on a most dangerous journey. My rancor cooled somewhat after noticing how his rheumy eyes glistened with tears. He'd merely been following the orders of a man he admired. Perhaps he'd even loved Grandfather as much as I had.

My bodice is laced too tightly. I strain against the confines of my new and quite fashionable soot-black gown. The finely stitched silk calls to mind the gown of the woman who was Grandfather's mistress at his house in town. I do not know her name, nor do I wish to. After the funeral, Oliver had quietly taken Mrs. Landy aside and inquired after the woman. Mrs. Landy informed him the mysterious woman had taken her possessions from the house the moment she learned of Grandfather's death. No one has seen her since.

Oliver promptly bequeathed the keys of the house in the city to the housekeeper, as neither he nor I wished to have anything to do with the place. Forever will I recall the wide-eyed expression of shock on the old housekeeper's face. May it bring the woman and her family prosperity. And may the bloodstains come out of the floor in the salon.

I squirm again. Frowning at my fine clothing, I am also uncomfortably reminded of the gown I'd destroyed the day my sister died. It appears I shall have to accidentally ruin another set of clothes. But there's no need for such wastefulness. Perhaps I can simply leave this gown here when I go to my new home. When that will be, I do not know. Donny had not yet received an answer to my inquiries when I last spoke with her.

"Be still, Kenna," Oliver says. I comply with a small sigh. Ten days have passed since the funeral. Once more, I am seated to dine at Grandfather's gleaming table. Mrs. Harris bustles in and pours me more of her detestable, poorly prepared tea. I gaze down the line of empty chairs at the table. Isla does not dine with us. 'Tis not befitting for such a young child to eat with the adults of the house. Her new nursemaid will feed her in her nursery, a grand, ugly room filled with toys.

"Where were you this morning?" Oliver sips his wine and eyes me warily. And wearily.

My cheeks flush only a little. I do understand his chagrin. No longer do I pay any mind to the strict tutors Oliver sent for, or the great ticking clock on the mantel in the drawing room. I burn a candle down reading through the night. I sleep until I wish to arise, play with Isla when I want to, or run outside on a whim to visit the horses in the stable or climb the trees. After all, my living here is only temporary, though Oliver does not know this. Yet. For now, I escape this house whenever I can. Like I shall today, after I complete my midday meal. And change out of this ridiculous gown.

STREETS OF SHADOW | 349

"I went for a walk."

Oliver gazes at me tiredly. "I surmised as much."

I had indeed spent the morning out in the brisk wind beneath an overcast winter sky, poking through the remains of Lady Ramsay's physick garden. A few scraggly remnants of the medicinal plants she used to grow for her household yet remain. And Mrs. Harris sometimes still gathers mint leaves from the old garden when one of us has an upset stomach.

"Kenna, please attend to your studies this afternoon." Oliver pins me with a narrow gaze. "And please return the books you left on the library floor to their proper places. You left quite a pile of them beside the fire, and I've ordered that no one else return them to the shelves. That is your task, as you were the one who left the room in such a disordered state."

"Yes, Oliver." I had, in fact, left the library in disarray, but I'd finally found the book I'd been looking for since returning to Grandfather's house. 'Tis a book with drawings of plants and roots, much like the one I'd seen in the vaults beneath the close. If the plans I am forming are to succeed, having this book will be a great help to me. Along with the abandoned physick garden.

And we continue our meal, devoid of any meaningful conversation. At least the food is plentiful and delicious. I sigh in pleasure as I savor my roast pheasant.

"*Och*, Kenna, your hair," Mrs. Harris says as she serves us fruit. "I see Lorna could no' make much of it, shorn as it is. Here, I've made ye something. Put it on, lass." With that she hands me a lace cap that calls to mind the drooping, bedraggled thing old "Sheona" wears. I giggle and comply.

Mrs. Harris surveys the result. She shakes her head sadly. "Your hair was your only grace," she says in a mournful tone. "Thankfully, it will grow back."

I shrug and resume my meal. I now know that in Mrs. Harris' eyes, I do possess at least one sliver of beauty. And I also know that to the plump woman, I remain the incorrigible, unladylike lass who will never be tamed. The thought makes a smile spring to my lips.

"Thank you, Mrs. Harris," Oliver says, glancing at me in reproof for my lack of manners. "And Kenna, slow down. You're gulping your food as though you've never seen a poached pear."

I smile at him. I'll never again be one to scorn food. *Och, aye,* this must be why my gown feels too tight!

"Will that young lady be visiting again any time soon?" Mrs. Harris asks. "The one who tramped mud on the carpets in the salon?"

"Una?" I gulp my tea and wink at the gray-haired woman over the rim of my cup. "I've invited her back for luncheon this Sunday." After all, I still have use of the coach Grandfather gave me, so 'tis an easy thing to send it and fetch my friend. I'll miss having use of the coach, as Oliver likely will not allow me to keep it once he learns of my plans.

Mrs. Harris tuts and throws her hands in the air while I giggle at the memory of Una's visit. She'd brought word that Rob was on the mend. And shared her expert lock-picking skills at my request. I'd shown her how to curtsy, and she insisted I curtsy to her each time she waved her hand at me. How we'd laughed!

"And there's that old, er..." Mrs. Harris gulps and casts Oliver a guilty glance. He kindly chooses to ignore it, finishes the last drop of his wine and strides from the room.

"You mean Donny?" I lean back in my chair, satisfied after another tasty meal and enjoying our housekeeper's discomfort.

The scowl deepens on Mrs. Harris's round face. She snatches a cloth and brandishes it, as though trying to scour the very air that was somehow soiled by the old soldier's presence. "She was as bad as that lass, with muck all over her boots. And she wears breeches like a man. Nothing good can come of that."

I slurp the dregs from my cup. "I cannot wait until they both come back. I want to show Una how well I can pick locks now. She's a good teacher."

"Lock picking." Mrs. Harris scoffs and takes our plates to stack them on the sideboard. "A fine occupation for a lady."

Laughing, I leap from my seat and plant a loud kiss on Mrs. Harris's wrinkled cheek. "Indeed, it is. A true gentlewoman should never find herself trapped behind locked doors." I give her a hug and whisper in her ear: "Or without means of defense." My words are meant to taunt, since our old housekeeper throws fits each time she spies my knife.

I take my leave and dash to my chamber to rid myself of the stifling gown. In its place, I don a plain old blue gown that Cinaed used to wear. Though it brings a pang of sadness, it also comforts me. Lorna grins as she helps me lace my bodice.

"When I first saw ye, miss, I was certain ye'd turned into a lad. Mrs. Harris says she's surprised you're no' still donning a man's garb, the way ye like to climb in the trees."

I laugh. "I'd considered it. But breeches are itchy and I like my skirts. 'Tis easier to hide my knife in the folds."

Lorna glances at my new leather pouch with a wary eye. I grin at her as I tuck it away inside the skirts of my much more comfortable gown, then study her with a thoughtful air. I shall have to provide her with her own blade. And teach her how to use it. At least as soon as I finally master wielding my own.

"Ye look well, with color upon your cheek. So does Isla," Lorna tells me, dipping into a curtsy. "I'm glad of it."

I give my maid, no, my *friend,* an embrace. "I never really wanted to eat before, but now I cannot wait for the next meal."

Lorna's gray eyes fill with tears. "When I think of what almost happened to ye, miss, I can hardly bear it." She sniffs as she gathers my abandoned black skirts.

"It's Kenna, remember?" I give her arm a squeeze as I pass by, take my leave, and hurry to the library. Reshelving the books takes little time. And then I hurry to the second floor, managing to escape my scheduled lessons by darting through a side door just as Master

Williams, my most hated tutor, enters the library through the main entrance.

Isla's newly hired nursemaid flushes with happiness when she spies me on the threshold. Maggie has a soft spot for old Tom and the man returns her sentiments. I never would have guessed the shriveled man even had a heart. He does not seem to have eyes, for Maggie is a round woman, all pale skin and faded eyes and colorless hair, with a great mole on the end of her nose. Leastways, Maggie and Tom enjoy the free time I give the woman. Maggie leaves to find her fellow, and Isla giggles as she runs to my arms.

The sight of Isla's wee face growing plump and pink with returning health warms me. Her nursery is filled with lovely playthings, but no toy shall ever take the place of her wooden doll. Donny retrieved it from the cobbles where it had fallen on the night I took my fateful leap. Isla prefers her precious doll to any other toy.

Once Isla is wrapped in her thick cloak, we crunch across fields covered with a scattering of December snow, turning to slush under a freezing rain. Humming, I ignore the weather. Though iron clouds hang low in the sky, and I am soaked and chilled within minutes, I love being outside. The fields that spread out before me undulate like frozen waves of the sea. I can hardly get enough of this world of freedom and space. Were I to make a running start and lift my arms, I am positive I would grow wings and soar into the sky. I want this feeling to last as long as it can. And Isla and I will be warm again soon enough.

Within a few minutes, we arrive at the old cottage with its gray, crumbling walls and leaking roof. I open the door of my wee former dwelling. This home, the one I shared with my sister and our parents years ago, still causes a rush of pleasure each time I behold it. There remains a warm feeling of comfortable familiarity. We were all happy, here. And I have great hopes that once more, I shall soon be happy here again.

"Kenna!"

Isla giggles and waves at the sight of Lorna trotting as fast as she can across the sodden field. She holds a letter in her hand. My pulse quickens. Have I received my answer?

While Isla squeezes through a break in the wintry hedgerow and skips off to meet Lorna, I draw water from the well, if only to give my hands an occupation while I wait. A battered wooden bucket is still attached to a frayed rope. After testing the fibers, which seem to have held their strength, I lower the bucket to the water far below. When it returns, filled to the brim with clear liquid, I take a sip. The cold, pure taste is a delight. The water is as sweet as ever it was before.

With Isla in tow, Lorna skirts the gooseberry bushes that border this side of the old dwelling and rushes to me. Her face is alight. She knows how important the contents of this message are to me.

"Here." She takes Isla in her arms, and we duck inside the cottage to escape the rain.

For a moment, I press the parchment to my heart. *Please let this be the answer I wish it to be.*

My name is printed in wobbly letters, like the script of a child learning to hold a quill for the first time. This missive did not come from Donny. Who sent it? I break the seal with haste.

Thursday, 10th December
> *Dear Kenna,*
> *Donny did as you asked. She found a man in the city who will pay you to keep his animals in the country. You will need a lad to feed and tend them, but as you are now a businesswoman, I leave that to you. I was given the task of bringing the animals to you. We arrive the day after next.*
> *Rob*

The hand is childish, with many words fashioned of misshapen letters and misspelled as well, but this matters not. Gasping out loud, I throw the square of parchment into the air and shout, a most unladylike action. Grinning, I retrieve the letter and tuck it into my pouch. I have not set eyes upon my friend since he received a ball to his ribs that awful night on the rooftops of the city. His father did not allow visitors aside from Donny, so Rob used the time confined in bed learning to read and write. Or so Lorna had told me, hearing this from a cousin who shared the news after visiting Donny to obtain a soothing poultice for chilblains. And this letter confirms it.

"He's coming, Lorna!"

My friend raises one eyebrow. "Who, miss?"

I take Isla into my arms and dance about, ignoring the twinge of pain in my healing shoulder. The lassie squeals in delight.

"Rob is coming! He said, 'day after next,' and this letter was written two days ago! He's coming today!"

Laughing, Lorna watches us twirl around the room. "Would this be the lad you told me about?"

"Yes."

Her eyebrows raise. "Shall I tell Mrs. Harris to plan for a dinner guest?"

I pause mid step. "Perhaps not yet."

With a perplexed crinkle on her brow, Lorna takes her leave.

"Come, Isla. We've work to do."

I retrieve the bucket of water and take the child's hand. Together, we circle behind the cottage, passing the gooseberry bushes glistening with freezing droplets and head to the square barn built of stone. It looms lifeless before us, with an air of lonely neglect, but the place is beautiful to my eyes. I am now a businesswoman, one who is about to earn her own money for the very first time. I pat the barn door. The place will not be silent for long.

CHAPTER 42

We ease the heavy door open and Isla skips to the far corner to play on a pile of straw. Though dusty and empty, the stalls inside the barn are in good shape, the wood having been protected from the elements. A leather tack yet hangs from a peg on the wall and a curry comb lies upon a shelf. I pour the water into the stone trough and take up a twig broom that waits against the wall. As I work, I listen for sounds of approaching footsteps, a voice calling out, or the clopping of hooves. Rob had not said the exact hour he would arrive with the animals. I must hurry to ready the barn.

Before long, the floor is clean. But when will they come? At that moment, the soft sound of distant hoofbeats drums a steady rhythm. I fly to open the door, and the smell of rain rushes inside.

And there, in the distance, hazy beneath the drizzling weather, someone approaches on horseback. Behind the horse and rider, several sheep meander. Beyond them are distant fuzzy shapes, but as they draw closer, the form of a red pony appears, as well as the shape of a lad who drives a fat sow before him, prodding her forward with a willow branch.

My heart skips within me. The horse and its rider draw closer, and Rob's cheerful face comes into view. Despite the wintry weather, my cheeks grow warm.

Rob grins at me as he reaches the barn. He dismounts, wincing and holding a hand to his side.

"*Och,* my poor ribs! What a ride that was!"

I take the reins of the black horse and lead it inside a stall, while Rob drives the sheep into the barn and closes them within the large pen at the back. The young lad who came with him takes the curry comb from a shelf to groom the red pony. I watch all with my tongue frozen in place, and silently curse myself. I am never at a loss for words! Closing the stall door, I stroke the velvety nose of the black horse, who snorts and bobs his head. Finally, I turn to face Rob.

"You've arrived." Inside, I cringe. That is all I can think of to say? An obvious, silly statement?

Rob's grin slashes across his lean face. He saunters closer and pats the horse. "Do ye have nothing else to say to me?"

His lips twitch with merriment. He gazes down at me, so close I see the flecks of gold in his brown eyes.

No other words come to mind. So, instead, I reach up to wrap my arms about his neck and raise my lips to his. He does not pull away. His kiss is warm and sweet. And when I back away, he encircles me with his arms and draws me close, and I rest my head against his chest.

"I'm so glad you're here," I murmur against his jacket. "And that you are getting better." His frame trembles as he laughs and his voice rumbles against my cheek.

"I had that impression."

I join in his merriment, but when I would lift my lips to his once more, someone clears his throat. We step apart, Rob with another grin, I with heat flooding my face.

The lad stares at us. "Where do I put that sow?"

"I'll tell ye where to stick that sow, Liam," Rob mutters at the lad. Laughing, I open another stall and drive the large pig inside. Together, we unload the bags tied to the black horse, containing oats for the pony. We lift the sacks together, for Rob's ribs are still healing and my shoulder will pain me a good long while.

"These creatures belong to old Will Ross. He tells me he's met ye already. Says he gave ye shelter one night in exchange for work."

"He did!" My heart swells within me. "Mr. Ross saved my life. But I saw soldiers take his animals away!"

"He got payment from the Town Council. The young Earl's been busy, making certain those of us in the city who were locked away received due payment for our troubles. Old Will is back in business now and expanding his wee herd. In the city, there's little room for animals. He was pleased to hear of a place in the country to keep them."

Finished with our work, we sit on a bench against the wall, while Liam whistles and feeds the pony a bit of carrot from his pocket.

"Where do you live, Liam?"

The sturdy lad turns to me. "In the village, miss. I work in Lord Ramsay's stables."

"You do?" I blink. "I've never seen you before."

He ducks his dark-haired head shyly. "I've only just started, miss."

"Well, Liam, would you like to earn an extra coin or two by feeding the animals here? After you've finished with your work at the Earl's stables, of course. I'll pay you each week. Only, I do not quite know how much I should pay you." My face flushes as Rob chuckles. "But I shall find out. I'll pay you well. As much as the Earl pays."

"Yes, miss. Thank you!"

Flushed with the success in my first business dealings, I inspect the latches on the stalls. After all, they must be solid. I cannot have animals escaping after promising a safe place for their keep.

Rob takes Isla's hand and joins us. The lass giggles as the sheep come to the edge of their enclosure, bleating in their quavering voices. She talks to them by making her own bleating noises, and Rob and I laugh. He places a hand on my back; I move closer and press myself to his side. He winces and rubs his ribs.

"Careful, Kenna. My bones still feel as though the ball is stuck fast in my ribs, especially when the clouds are heavy."

"I am sorry! You must visit Donny. She'll have something to ease the pain."

"Aye. But there's something else I'd like better. 'T'would make me forget all about my aching ribs." His warm brown eyes find mine. I step closer and wrap my arms about his neck, ignoring the twinge in my aching shoulder.

"Kenna!"

Rob and I break apart and whirl to face Oliver. His eyes narrow to slits as he strides inside the barn.

"I've been looking everywhere for you! I thought you were in the library attending to your lessons. And here I find you attending to something entirely different. And highly *unseemly*, I might add." His nostrils flare, and his jaw is set.

Though my cheeks flush scarlet, I raise my chin. I have naught to be ashamed of. "Oliver, this is Rob Munro. He is one of the friends who helped me when I was trapped in the city."

"A friend, is he?" Oliver purses his lips as he regards Rob with clear dislike. "A rather close friend, it appears. We shall speak of this later. Just where did these animals come from?"

Swiftly, I plant a final kiss on Rob's lips, partly in defiance, but mostly because I want to. He gives me a wink and a devilish grin. I wink back before turning to Oliver.

"I've something to tell you, Oliver. Something I must explain." I brush straw from my skirts and compose my features. If I wish to sway Oliver and convince him of the viability of my plan, 'tis vital for me to behave as a lady ought. At least, as much as possible, for Oliver has already seen me kissing a lad. Inside a barn, unaccompanied by anyone other than Isla.

Oliver sighs. Light streaks of gray have appeared at his temples and in his beard. This change, coupled with the weariness I read so clearly on his face of late, makes him seem many a year older.

"I can see that. Isla, come to Papa." He holds his arms out, and the lass flies to him, giggling as he sweeps her into his arms. He settles upon a bench against the wall. "Well?" His eyes find mine. They are bloodshot, rimmed in red. I swallow my sudden doubts and stand tall.

"As I have told you, I cannot live in Grandfather's house. I returned here because of Isla, but I have been working out a plan of sorts. 'Twas at first a mere idea, but today's events have proven my plan will succeed." *I think.*

Shaking his head, Oliver closes his eyes and rubs his temples. "And I suppose this plan of yours involves a barn full of animals?"

"Yes. I'm renting it to someone in the city who needs more room to keep his animals."

My brother-in-law's expression is incredulous. *"You* are renting the barn? *My* barn? Kenna, do you not understand that this land, this house, and this barn belong to me?"

Whistling softly, Rob gestures to Liam and the two head out into the blustery day. I will my limbs to stop shaking and remind myself to speak with a dignified and steady voice.

"Of course, I understand! But what if one day I earn enough money to buy it from you? To buy the land my parents once farmed. Would you not consider it?"

Isla leaps down from her father's lap and returns to her sheep, squealing and bleating at them. Oliver rises and paces. His hair has come loose from its ribbon and the tawny waves fall in disarray about his face.

"I fear, Kenna, that you do not understand how much money you speak of. How long it would take you to earn it. You are a mere child! You know nothing about business. Renting this barn for the remainder of your life will not earn you what you need to buy this land."

He scowls at the floor and kicks at a bit of straw beneath his boots, while inside, my hard-won courage shrinks back. How much money *will* I need?

Oliver faces me. "Am I correct in assuming that you plan to live in your family's old cottage? A cottage that happens to have a leaking roof?"

His lips curl in contempt as he speaks. My insides boil and my determination to succeed returns to me in a rush.

"I shall fix the roof."

Oliver gapes. "Once again, Kenna, how shall you pay for it?"

"Renting this barn is not the only business I have in mind, Oliver! I also—"

"Enough! Nothing you do will earn you the money you require!"

"Then I'll fix the roof myself if I must!" I shout, no longer striving to behave as a lady.

The man's face darkens with outrage. "Soften your voice, Kenna. Shame on you for speaking thus to me!"

Gulping air, I force myself to speak in even tones and ignore how Oliver scolds me as though I am nothing more than a bad-tempered child. "How can I make you understand that I can succeed in my endeavors? I survived abandonment in the city, Oliver! Surely, I can find a way to earn more money. Do you not wish to hear what else I have in mind?"

The man shakes his head. "It does not matter, Kenna. What if you somehow manage to repair the roof? What then? You know 'tis not proper for you to live here, alone and unescorted." Oliver narrows his eyes as he gazes at me. "Especially after seeing your behavior with that lad."

I lift my chin. "Mrs. Harris could come. Or perhaps Lorna. Of course, I won't stay here alone. Please, Oliver!" My voice shakes. "If you do not wish to do this for me, do it for the memory of your wife. Do it for Cinaed." I can barely breathe as I wait a response. He must see reason!

Oliver's face darkens. "I will not tolerate this. Come, Isla." He holds out his hand and beckons me with sharp, impatient gestures. "We shall speak of this when we get home."

But the chains that once bound me are broken. "No."

"What?"

"I will not go back to that house. If you'll not allow me to stay here, I'll return to Donny's house. She has offered me a home." I kneel and take Isla's tiny face in my hands, studying her as though to memorize every detail, hardly believing what I've just said. 'Twill tear me in two to live so far from her!

"Don't be such a fool," Oliver snaps.

After a final caress of Isla's sweet face, I rise to my feet. "I will not stay in Grandfather's house."

"Then you'll not see Isla again!" Oliver storms to my side, takes the child in his arms and stalks toward the door.

"Mamma!" Isla cries. Wriggling wildly, she frees herself from her father's arms and flies back to me, burying her face in my skirts.

Oliver's face drains of color. He sinks down upon the bench and gazes at me in silent, desperate supplication. "What am I saying?" He rubs his hand over his face. "God's beard. Forgive me, Kenna. I am so sorry. I didn't mean that."

I cling to the child. "Didn't you?"

"No." Oliver lets his hands fall limply to his sides. "But, Kenna, you cannot live here in this cottage. And Isla belongs with me. She is my daughter."

"I know." My words are a whisper. "But I can no longer bear to live in Grandfather's house."

Oliver's eyes hold mine. His gaze is filled with pain. "What, then? What shall we do?" A sudden shrill whistle makes us jump.

"Kenna? Where are ye hiding, lass?"

Donny's graveled voice reaches us from outside. With slow steps, I move past Oliver and outside into the wind. Isla joins me and puts her hand in mine. Oliver does not stop her.

A small, horse-drawn cart is parked beside the wicket gate. And a white-haired woman, wee as a pixie and clad in breeches and a worn doublet, waits for us. Isla tugs her hand from mine. "Donny," she calls, bouncing joyfully as she runs to her. The old woman stoops to greet her with a hug.

Oliver joins us and nods stiffly at the old woman.

"Aren't ye going to invite me inside?" Donny nods toward the cottage. "My old bones are chilled through. I need a fire to warm me."

With wooden movements, I open the creaking door and we troop inside. I take our old tinder box from the mantel and kneel before the grate, where a few half-burned logs remain inside. And then I sigh. I do not know how to use the flint and striker to create a spark. Who was I to think I could buy this old place and repair the roof? Let alone run a business? I cannot even light a fire.

"Here."

Oliver takes the fire-starting implements from me. "Like this." He shows me how to strike steel and stone together until a spark appears. "You try it."

Blinking at the man, I attempt to create a spark. It takes me many tries, but finally, I create the tiniest of sparks that catches in the tinder. It begins to smoke.

"Well done," Oliver says in a soft voice. My brother-in-law rises and sits at the scrubbed table with a weary sigh, holding his chin in one hand.

Soon, we have a warm fire. Donny seats herself on a rickety chair and puts her feet up as though sitting before her own grate. After she fishes her ever-present pipe from inside her doublet and lights it, she draws deeply and regards me with her usual calculating gaze as she blows smoke rings toward the ceiling.

A soft knock at the door brings me to my feet and I answer it. Rob is outside, his hair tousled by the wind, and his lean face reddened with the cold. His warm eyes make me feel as though I am melting on the inside. I'd revel in the feeling were I not so disheartened by Oliver's decision to thwart my plans.

"May I come in?"

"Of course."

The lad squeezes my arm as he passes, but keeps a wary eye on Oliver, who does the same in return. Rob leans against the far wall, folds his arms and watches the flickering flames. Isla skips to the corner beside the grate and reaches for Donny, who settles the lassie on her lap.

The woman's azure gaze finds mine. "So, I hear ye wish to become partners." I blink, momentarily at a loss for words. Donny was never one to stand on ceremony.

"I did." I study my hands. The chance to discuss my proposal should please me, but at this moment it does not. Not now, when Oliver has so thoroughly quashed my hopes of living here in this cottage. "I did wish it, Donny. But 'tis no longer of any importance. It appears I must return to the city."

The woman's eyebrows fly up. "That so?" She fixes Oliver with a narrowed glance.

He pinches the bridge of his nose and closes his eyes. "She cannot live here alone. Even if I were to agree to that, Kenna does not seem to understand that she has no money to pay for this cottage, or the land her father used to farm. Even if I were to agree to sell it to her."

A prickle of hot anger ignites inside. He did not even allow me to explain the extent of my plans. Well, now I shall make him listen! I plop down on the worn bench across from Oliver, so he is forced to look upon me.

"I do not have the wealth I need *now*, Oliver! Of course, I do not! But one day, I shall! Look at this!"

With swift, sure movements, I untie my leather purse and open it. After removing my knife, I spill the purse's remaining contents onto the table.

"Look! Do you know what any of this is?"

With a crinkled brow, Oliver gazes down at a pile of waxy, dark green leaves, and at several pouches of cloth bound with twine.

"The leaves from a box myrtle tree can be made into a tisane." I pick up one of the leaves and inhale its sweet, aromatic fragrance. "The drink is a fine remedy for fever." I open one of the cloth pouches and display the tangle of dark roots inside. "This is the root of a meadow sweet plant. The crushed flowers help to treat pain."

Donny grunts as she chews the stem of her pipe. "Use that in my healing ointment." She grins at me.

Then I untie a bundle of twigs with dried, purple flowers still clinging to them.

"That's heather, is it not? The branches are for roof thatching," Oliver says.

"Heather makes a liniment for rheumatism," I tell him.

"And an infusion to treat a cough." Donny calls. "Dinnae forget about that come winter."

I untie more bundles and show Oliver the other things I've collected. "I found these on my walks around Grandfather's estate and in Lady Ramsay's old physick garden. St. John's wort, foxglove, and fern leaves all have their uses. Apothecaries need them for their remedies. And so does Donny."

Lifting my eyes to meet Oliver's, I take a deep breath. "I can sell herbs and roots to the apothecaries in town." The man regards me with an inscrutable gaze and does not respond. The fire crackles and Isla sings to herself as she cradles her doll.

Donny gently sets the lass upon the floor and comes to the table to inspect my collection of medicinal plants. "Well done, Kenna. I'm glad to see ye make use of that mind of yours. How did ye learn about all these plants? Ye weren't with me for long."

The fragrance of the herbs tickles my nose while I tie my cloth bundles back together. "I remembered seeing a book about herbs and plants in the library. It took me some time to locate it, but I did. I needed it to identify the plants I found. The book must have belonged to Lady Ramsay."

Donny sighs. "Mary was a kind soul. If Reginald had called me to deliver his child instead of that fool of a physician, she wouldn't have died. At least my grandson lived."

Oliver clears his throat. "How much can you earn selling herbs? Pennies? A few shillings? Kenna, you'd need a lifetime to buy this land!"

Tying my leather pouch about my waist, I rise. "I'll not only sell herbs and roots. I'll sell the tinctures and poultices and draughts Donny promised to teach me to make. We can sell Donny's medicines all over the city, and in the country as well."

My brother-in-law says nothing. Instead, he rises and walks about the tidy room. He regards coals that glow in the grate, thanks to the fire I managed to start. He studies the clean floor covered with scattered, fragrant rushes and the rosy curtains at the window, which I'd clumsily made from an old, torn skirt. He peeks inside the old bucket I'd placed beneath the biggest leak in the roof, now half-full of rainwater. He shakes his head.

"I simply cannot see it," he says softly. "I'm sorry, Kenna."

My stomach sours. "I plan to pursue this business, whether you wish it or not. If I cannot live here, I'll return to the city. I suppose you do not think it proper to lend space in the barn. If not, I'll arrange for the animals to be returned to their owner. But if you decide to allow for it, I'll leave that business to you. You can have the payment. It's rightfully yours, anyway."

Donny regards us with pursed lips. "I see I've brought my pots and kettles for nothing." She fixed Oliver with a decidedly unfriendly stare. "So be it. At least we have our conveyance back to the city."

My disappointment fills me with a heavy sluggishness. Mine *was* a good business plan. I'd already written to several apothecaries in town, and they were keen to have whatever supplies I could procure for them. Medicinal plants are harder to come by in the city. But now that I cannot live in the country, where I'll have easy access to the old garden and the open fields, glens, and woods, the plan will have to change. But I will not give up. Somehow, I will earn my own way. And make a place for myself in this world on my own terms.

"I am ready to go, Donny."

Rob clears his throat. "Mind if I come along?"

Isla comes to me with shining eyes and takes my hand, as though we are about to tramp back across the fields again, returning to the toad house together. My heart twists inside me.

Oliver puts a hand over his eyes. "I must say something."

"What?" I whisper. My eyes fill with tears. I detach Isla's fingers from mine and lead her to her father. Oliver places her in his lap, and I turn away from him, gazing out the window. Before my eyes, the rain becomes a heavy, wet snow. Cold seeps deep into my bones, as though the snow is falling inside my heart.

Oliver puts a hand on my shoulder and turns me to face him.

"'Tis thanks to you my child is once more with her father. I'll forever be grateful for the way you cared for her when you found her in town with no one to look after her."

A great lump forms in my throat.

"She is your niece, Kenna," he says with a falter. He swallows once before continuing. "You are the nearest thing to a mother she has left. And Kenna, you are my ward. You should have been treated as my daughter. It grieved Cinaed that I could not see how much you needed a father. So, now, I will finally do what I should have done all along."

I do not breathe. Donny leans forward in her chair and removes the pipe from between her lips.

"I promised to provide a life for you, and I'll not go back on my word. If you will not stay with us in Father's house, then you may stay here. You may pursue your business endeavors. But I have two conditions."

My lips tremble and I can barely speak around the lump in my throat. "What are they?"

"First of all, Mrs. Harris will stay here with you. Not Lorna. If Mrs. Harris does not wish to live out here, I will hire someone else. And she'll be under strict orders that no gentlemen are to call on you without permission. Nor are they to be left alone with you. At any time."

His gaze darts to Rob, whose face flushes dark. The lad wisely remains silent.

"And the other condition?"

"You will indeed buy this land from me. We'll work out the terms of your payment."

Donny huffs. "Ye've got more land than ye need, lad. And gold that never belonged to our family in the first place."

Oliver's face flushes. "But the true members of the Ramsay family are all gone. Must I give up all I've ever known now that I know the truth? Leave everything so another can take my place? It would be chaos."

I fly to him and wrap my arms around his neck. "No, Oliver! I never wanted you to give up anything. I only want to live in a place where I feel I belong. I was never going to become what Grandfather wanted me to be." With slow, hesitant movements, Oliver raises his arms and folds them around me, patting my back with awkward movements. 'Tis the first time we have ever embraced one another.

Isla runs over to us, giggling. Oliver laughs and picks her up and the three of us embrace.

Stepping away, I return to Donny and kiss her cheek. "Donny, I *want* to pay Oliver." I beam down at her. "One day I want to remember that I earned this land. I'll always know that no one gave it to me."

Donny marches to Oliver and peers up at him. "Ye'll offer her a fair price?"

He grins. "Of course."

The old woman pops her pipe into her mouth. "Well, now. I'm happy to learn my grandson has a bit of good sense after all."

Rob catches my eye, and I run to him. He takes me in his arms and spins me around, laughing. I plant a swift kiss on his lips before Oliver clears his throat and regards us with a look of thunder. Rob's eyes twinkle. "I'll visit as oft as I can," he whispers into my ear before he steps away.

"I'll visit you in the city as well," I promise him. Mrs. Harris, or whatever peevish old woman Oliver hires, cannot keep an eye trained on me all the time. Besides, I'll have deliveries to make in town.

Oliver releases Isla and paces the room, casting sharp glances at Rob every so often.

"This house is small, but sturdy. You must fix the leaking roof, though, before I'll consent to you living here. I have a man in mind who does sound work. Shall I send him?"

"Yes!" I gulp and swallow my tears. "Thank you."

Rob takes my hand in his, and I smile at him through my tears. Then Oliver steps between us, separating our hands. I stifle a giggle.

"I'll be going," Rob tells us. He bows to Oliver, plants a kiss on Donny's cheek, and winks at me. I beam as he ducks out of sight.

The world is often a cruel, cold place when one is alone. My experience in the city taught me that. But if one has even a single friend by her side, cruelty can be faced and fought. One can survive. Not only survive, but truly live. Donny taught me that. And though Oliver may be the son of the man all knew as Lord Ramsay, he is not like him at all. No one is doomed to become what their parents were.

Isla hands me her doll, shushing me with a wee finger over her lips. "Sh! Sleeping."

Nodding, I cradle the toy in my arms. Isla skips away and I turn the doll over in my hands, marveling. What was once a chunk of wood I'd plucked from a pile of rubble is now a lovely toy. Donny has carved and polished it so that it has the appearance of a real babe, wrapped in a bit of linen. It somehow calls to mind the way I feel now. Like a creature once trapped in an unyielding prison that had to be carved away, bit by bit, until the being within was revealed.

Oliver resumes his wanderings and examines the sagging shelves on the wall. "This house needs many repairs." He fingers a crack in the wall and tugs on the latch of a small door that leads to the larder, but finds it locked. "Do you have a key, Kenna?"

"No. But I shall get that door open." I withdraw the tools Una had fashioned for me from my leather purse. Oliver's eyebrows raise.

Donny chuckles. "Let's see it, then."

My jaw sets with determination as I focus on my task. After working a bit, I jiggle the lock and find the mechanism within has loosened. The door swings open. With a satisfied sigh, I return my tools to their pouch and rise, smoothing my skirts and short hair.

"Well done." Donny grins at me.

"Come, Isla. Let me show you how to pick a lock." The child skips to me and we kneel in front of the door. I demonstrate how to insert the thin iron tool into the keyhole, then place my hands over hers, guiding her through the task. Her pink tongue pokes out of her mouth as we work together.

"What on God's earth are you teaching my child, Kenna?" Oliver laughs as he speaks.

"I am teaching her a useful skill." The smile I direct at him is filled with true affection. He is far kinder and more open-minded than I ever believed him to be.

Dropping my gaze, I concentrate on helping Isla's wee hands complete their task. Despite the man's change of heart, I'll not tell Oliver I plan to have Donny teach Isla how to fight. Raised as he was, propriety would not allow for it.

The old herbwife seems to read my mind, for her eyes gleam at me, and she chuckles. Puffs of white smoke rise from her pipe. The lock clicks open, and Isla squeals with delight. My heart glows. I pull her to me, hugging her tight, and make a vow.

Never again will I allow anyone to trap me behind a locked door, or a barred gate. Neither will my Isla. Nor will she find herself without means of defense or some way to make a living. 'Tis certain that Oliver believes his daughter will be well cared for by whichever gentleman she marries. Perhaps he is right. But 'tis no matter. Isla shall be prepared to face anything life may bring her.

After all, a true lady can fend for herself.

AUTHOR'S NOTE

Streets of Shadow was inspired by a real place in Scotland. Mary King's Close is a time capsule—a section of old and narrow alleyways lying hidden beneath the modern-day streets of the city of Edinburgh. In the historic Old Town area, these alleyways ran perpendicular to the High Street and the Royal Mile, forming a tangled web of narrow side streets. Some of these passageways were known as "wynds," while others were called "closes." The wynds were public passageways, but the closes were private streets that were locked up at night with iron gates at the entrances to keep out thieves and other less desirable visitors.

Overcrowding in the city of Edinburgh had long been a problem by the time of my story, the year 1665. The town had been built on top of Castle Rock and had a wall surrounding it to protect its residents. This meant that the town could only expand so far if people wished to remain within the wall's safe boundaries. Enterprising residents dealt with the problem by building up, instead of out. Towering tenements soared up to eight stories high.

The tenements of the closes housed many residents of various social classes. The poorest of the city mingled with successful merchants and tradespeople, including one Mary King, an affluent burgess, or merchant, who owned property and lived in the area starting in 1635. The cluster of passageways where she lived and worked was named after her.

The city's many winding, narrow lanes were rumored to host all kinds of illegal activities. They were also overcrowded and filthy. In 1750, the Edinburgh city council decided renovations were in order. They wished to build what became known as the Royal Exchange, a safe place for merchants and traders to work, away from the crowded and crime-ridden streets. And so, some residents of Old Town's closes were evacuated. The top few stories of decidedly dilapidated buildings were knocked down, filling the area below and causing the level of the street to rise. Partial buildings, including shops and houses, remained but were sealed off, and the rubble formed the foundations of the Royal Exchange, which was built in 1753.

I found it interesting that some of the closes were not completely sealed off, and resident merchants continued to do business in their now partially buried neighborhoods. When the Royal Exchange was expanded in the early 1900s, the Chesney family's saw-making business, the city's final "underground" business, was forced to close its doors.

Mary King's Close lay abandoned for decades, buried out of sight and inaccessible to the public. The city's underground realm became fodder for stories about hauntings and murders. However, in the early 2000s, interest grew in the buried closes, as they preserved a vivid slice of Edinburgh's history. Archeologists and historians began to study the place and its former residents, learning all they could about the winding closes. In 2003, Mary King's Close was opened to the public as a visitor's attraction. Tourists are led underground and through passageways and various buildings, where a costumed guide takes on the persona of one of the actual residents of the place and shares that individual's history.

I first learned about Mary King's Close by chance after watching a travel video on YouTube. I was enthralled to learn that such a place existed and could give us so much information about the past. I wanted to find out as much as I could about the people who once lived in these narrow alleyways. What would it have been like? Intrigued, I hit the books, visited libraries, and scoured the internet.

The stories I learned fascinated me. I learned about successful businesswomen, and how wealthy residents rubbed shoulders with the poorest of the poor. I learned about filth, crowding, and want, and outbreaks of bubonic plague. I found the story of a mysterious, dangerous man who walked the closes at night. I came across many tales of thievery and murder, including the account of a woman who killed her husband in a fit of rage. Some of the details I discovered became an integral part of "Streets of Shadow."

My favorite story from Mary King's Close turned out to be a ghost story. "Wee Annie" is rumored to be the spirit of a child who was either abandoned or whose mother died of the plague, leaving her alone and uncared-for. Those who claim psychic or spiritual abilities say they have felt her presence in a specific room, and inside that very room you will find a shrine for the little girl. Visitors leave her gifts of toys. Whether she truly existed or not, my heart broke thinking about a lost and abandoned child, so Annie became an important part of my story. I did, however, decide that she deserved a happy ending. Instead of a toy, this story is my offering to her.

BIBLIOGRAPHY

Writing historical fiction is challenging. Much research went into the creation of this book, but I acknowledge that my interpretation of daily life in the city of Edinburgh in 1665 may not be completely accurate. I did my best to faithfully recreate the time period, especially in portraying the foods people might have eaten as well as their clothing and customs. It's also difficult to recreate the speech patterns and slang terms of a bygone era, while making the story easy to understand for the modern reader. I have included a few slang terms that I thought added depth to the characters, but tried not to use too many, as I worried this might bog down the story if the reader had to spend too much time interpreting unfamiliar words. The close in Streets of Shadow is obviously based on Mary King's Close, but I altered numerous details to tell the story I wanted to tell, including the overall layout and size of the area. Here are some of the resources I used in researching historic details for this story:

Books:

Albee, Sarah. "Why'd They Wear That? Fashion as the Mirror of History," 77-91. Washington, D. C.: National Geographic, 2015.

Cook, M. "Rebus's Edinburgh Palimpsest: The Spirits of the Place." In: Detective Fiction and the Ghost Story. Crime Files Series. Palgrave Macmillan, London, 2014.

Doyle, D. "Edinburgh Doctors and Their Physic Gardens." Journal of the Royal College of Physicians of Edinburgh. Issue 38, 361 – 367, 2008.

Foyster, Elizabeth and Watley, Christopher A. "A History of Everyday Life in Scotland, 1600 to 1800." Edinburgh, Scotland: Edinburgh University Press, 2011.

Gerard, John. "The Herbal or General History of Plants." Facsimile Edition of 1633 edition. New York: Dover Publications, Inc. 1975.

Henderson, Jan-Andrew. "The Town Below the Ground: Edinburgh's Legendary Underground City." Edinburgh and London: Mainstream Publishing, 1999.

Hanson, Liz. "Lost Edinburgh." Amberley Publishing, Gloucestershire, UK, 2019.

Henessey, Kathryn, editor. "Fashion: The Definitive History of Costume and Style." London, New York, Munich, Melbourne and Dehli: Dorling Kindersley Ltd., 2012.

Tabraham, Chris, with photographs by Baxter, Collin. "The Illustrated History of Scotland." Anacortes, WA: Oyster Press, 2004.

Yarwood, Dorren. "Illustrated Encyclopedia of World Costume." Mineola, New York: Dover Publications, Inc. 1978.

"Traditions of the Plague in Edinburgh." The Edinburgh Literary Journal, or Weekly Register of Criticism and Belles Lettres; Edinburgh. Issue 29, (May 30, 1829); 415 – 416.

Online Resources:

Czerkawska, Cathrine. "When the Gorse is in Bloom." The Scottish Home blog, 2012.
http://thescottishhome.blogspot.com/2006/06/when-gorse-is-in-bloom.html

"Old Scottish Sayings, Scottish Words And Slang Your Granny May Have Used!"
ScotlandWelcomesYou.Com
http://scotlandwelcomesyou.com/scottish-sayings/

The BS Historian: Commentary on Pseudohistory and the Paranormal. "Wee Annie at Mary King's Close," May 30, 2009.
https://bshistorian.wordpress.com/2009/05/30/wee-annie-at-mary-kings-close/

The official website for Mary King's Close:
www.realmarykingsclose.com

ACKNOWLEDGMENTS

As always, a good novel is created by a team, and I owe thanks to numerous people. First of all, I'm grateful to my husband, David, and my children, who have been incredibly patient and willing to allow me the time to write. Beta readers helped me in the formation of my story, including Spring Paul, Terri Swensen, Lucy Banks, and my late mother, Evelyn Israel. Their willingness to read sometimes multiple drafts and to provide feedback, as well as their enthusiasm for Kenna's story helped me shape and improve the novel. I'm also very grateful to John M. Olsen, a thorough editor whose patience I likely tried more than once, as well as the other team members at Immortal Works. Their guidance and expertise helped me bring the story to the next level. Finally, I acknowledge someone who may or may not have existed: Annie, one of Edinburgh, Scotland's most famous ghosts. Learning about her sparked my idea for this novel, so without her, Kenna's story would not have come to life.

ABOUT THE AUTHOR

Rebecca Bischoff is the author of three previous novels, including: *The French Impressionist,* a young adult novel, *The Grave Digger,* a historical middle grade mystery, and *Hole in the Rock,* a humorous middle grade novel. Rebecca loves to read everything from mysteries to paranormal to historical novels. She tends to research quirky and little-known facts from the past and loves anything that might make her laugh. A dedicated Anglophile, Rebecca loves watching BBC shows and reading mysteries that take place in the British Isles. Rebecca lives in Southern Idaho with her family, where she enjoys *not* visiting the outdoors. She'd rather stay inside, eat chocolate and write. Visit her website at: www.rebeccabischoffbooks.com.

This has been an
Immortal Production